Touched by Fortune's Shadow

a triptych

زیر سایهٔ هما : سه‌تایی [1]

Quinn Tyler Jackson

Foreword by Dania Sheldon, DPhil

☙•❧

Knight Terra Press
littera manet sed lector oraculum

est. 1995

---

[1] *Zir-e-Sâyeh-ye-Homâ: seh-tâi* ("Under the Shadow of the *Huma*: a triple")

Touched by Fortune's Shadow: a triptych

Copyright ©2024 by Quinn Tyler Jackson

Content Advisory: This novel features discussions describing fatal violence and the narrative explores the impact of this in both thematic and concrete human terms. Domestic violence against property and a very brief controlled physical altercation is depicted. There are highly stylized and contextual references to off-stage consensual sexuality, including frank discussions of open relationships and polyamory. Some characters consume alcohol socially and occasionally smoke tobacco socially, and alcohol addiction and its impact are explored in the narrative as it directly impacts the family and friends of those surrounding the substance addiction dynamic. Reader discretion is advised due to mature themes.

MA-LSV (alcohol addiction, tobacco, mild language)

Typesetting: This novel was typeset by the author using a font size of 10.5 points in Times New Roman. Inset citations have been set at 10 points and footnotes at 8.5 points. To maximize the utility of accessibility tools, care has been taken to avoid breaking sentences between pages, without altering font size or layout schemas to achieve this end. Further to this same end, pages have been numbered exclusively in Arabic numerals.

Stylesheet: Knight Terra Press uses its own in-house stylesheet. Although a Canadian press, the spelling and Oxford comma conventions followed are American rather than Canadian, unless in citations or guest editorial content.

```
ISBN:      978-1-896188-08-9 (Paperback)
           978-1-896188-09-6 (Digital)
Title:     Touched by Fortune's Shadow: a triptych
Genre:     Postmodern novel
Format:    Novel (101,000 words)
Author:    Quinn Tyler Jackson
Imprint:   Knight Terra Press, Burnaby, BC
Size:      347 pages (14 cm x 21.6 cm)
LCC:       PR888.L68 (Postmodern novel)
Notes:     Historical metafiction, 1990s Western Canada
```

Quinn Tyler Jackson

Front-matter

پندار نیک، گفتار نیک، کردار نیک [2]

---

[2] "Good thoughts; good words; good deeds."

Touched by Fortune's Shadow: a triptych

About the Author

Quinn Tyler Jackson has been a silkscreen printer's apprentice, a bookseller's assistant, a gas pumpist, a freelance editor, a literary agent, a researcher, a Chief Architect, and is currently a Chief Scientist (Mathematics). Jackson is a Fellow of the Royal Society of Arts, a Chartered Scientist, a Fellow of the Institute of Science & Technology (UK), a Senior Member of both the Association for Computing Machinery, and the Institute of Electrical and Electronics Engineers, and a Member of the London Mathematical Society, the American Mathematical Society, and the Writers' Union of Canada. His publication history spans three decades, and he has had novels, short stories, and poetry published, in addition to scholarly research papers and a research monograph.

Quinn Tyler Jackson

Acknowledgments

The content in this novel is depicted in and was created and composed on the traditional, ancestral, and unceded territory of the Nations of the xʷməθkʷəy̓əm (Musqueam), **Sḵwx̱wú7mesh** (Squamish), kʷikʷəƛ̓əm (Kwikwetlem), and səlilwətaɬ (Tsleil-Waututh) Peoples. The Editor's Foreword was composed on the traditional and unceded territory of the **Snuneymuxw** First Nation, who have lived on and cared for those lands and waters since time immemorial. We thank the Peoples of these Nations who continue to live on these lands and care for them, along with the waters and all that is above and below.

Dania Sheldon, DPhil, was commissioned to provide peer review and assessment, and her comprehensive and insightful analysis resulted in impactful revision and polishing of the final manuscript, as well as during all prior phases of composition and revision of this work.

Front and back cover art generated by OpenAI's DALL-E 3 with the author's artistic direction.

Finally, the author wishes to acknowledge you, the reader, for it is the reader who completes such a poststructuralist text as this.

Touched by Fortune's Shadow: a triptych

Table of Contents

Front-matter 3
About the Author 4
Acknowledgments 5
Editor's Foreword 7
The Novel 11
Part One: *Audere* 13
Vancouver, mid-April 1998 15
Vancouver, September 1981 27
Vancouver, mid-April 1998 31
Vancouver, mid-October 1981 47
Vancouver, mid-April 1998 53
Vancouver, late October 1981 71
Vancouver, May 1998 79
Part Two: *Scire* 111
Vancouver, June 1998 113
Vancouver, mid-July 1998 173
Vancouver, mid-December 1984 187
Part Three: *Tacere* 193
San Francisco, late September 1998 195
Vancouver, mid-October 1998 205
Vancouver, 31 October 1984 247
Vancouver, mid-November 1998 253
Port Coquitlam, mid-April 1993 275
Vancouver, December 1998 281
Coda 305
Epilog: Paris, late April 1999 307
An Unsent Declaration of Love 315
Manijeh's Reply to Brett's Love Letter 319
Back-matter 323
On Writing Brett as Autistic 325
On Writing a Novel *Tabula Rasa* 329
The Epiphanies 347

Quinn Tyler Jackson

Editor's Foreword

I began working with Quinn Jackson in late September of 2023, when he approached me about providing editorial input on *Midnight at the Arcanum*. At the time of writing, we have exchanged over 1,400 emails about his writing and life—which, like Philemon and Baucis, are inextricably entwined within each volume of the Epiphanies trilogy.

This has been an intense collaboration in which, as reader and editor, I have been traversing the fascinating interior landscape of someone just a few months older than I who, by sheer serendipity, happens to have grown up in the same locale as I did as a teen. Indeed, our paths intersected, although we did not know of each other at the time. Intriguing as this synchronicity was, it would not necessarily have sustained a productive author–editor relationship. But the sheer brilliance and *sprezzatura* of Quinn's ideas, and his ability to articulate these in fluid, gorgeous, and startlingly original prose and poetry, swiftly caught and held my attention. And I believe readers will have the same response.

When you enter the world of *Touched by Fortune's Shadow*, set aside expectations of being carried along by dramatic twists and turns, or gasp-worthy revelations. This is not a novel that launches itself at the reader with the violence of an assault. Instead, the narrator will gently take your hand and invite you in, asking you to remove your outer footwear and slide into a pair of finely embroidered slippers. You will travel between the 1980s and 1990s in Vancouver, with a few detours, alongside a trio and then quartet of friends whose decisions taken and not taken frame their growth into self-aware, independent, but mutually empowering individuals unafraid to decide, "Enough is okay."

Touched by Fortune's Shadow: a triptych

As much as that message was fairly radical in the 1990s, it may be even more so now, with the unparalleled ways that the Internet, large-scale globalization, and an epically frenetic level of consumerism have permanently changed the interior and exterior landscapes of most human lives. As the author explains in his note "On Writing a Novel *Tabula Rasa*," his starting point for *Fortune's Shadow* was "an ethical unit of friends and family, in 1998 Vancouver," who "would show *absolute* loyalty to the group" and engage in no "betrayal from within this circle." (You'll find his note in the Back-Matter section, which I highly recommend reading, whether before, during, or after you've completed the main text.) The primary character, Brett Lloyd-Ronan, is not from a rich, posh background, as his double-barreled surname might suggest, although we first meet him in the affluent surroundings of his well-appointed penthouse overlooking Vancouver's Coal Harbour. Rather, Brett grew up a blue-collar boy with a brilliant mind but lacking the means to pursue formal higher education. But this is not your standard working-class-lad-makes-good story.

Several thematic nebulae overlap and swirl around one another in the book, one being the long-term impacts of family trauma, and the choices we make about how we do or do not prevent the resulting ripples from continuing within us and thence outward. Another is what Quinn in one of our exchanges dubbed "the acceptance of blunders past"—an aspect of healing that today receives considerable lip service but much less in the way of genuine social support (unless one happens to be a wealthy demagogue with a gold-plated broom for sweeping things under the carpet). The other side of the accepting-one's-blunders coin is accepting responsibility for the fallout that may have resulted, and both are key materials in the building of any redemption arc. Each of the works in the Epiphanies trilogy contains these arcs, all of them at once unique and also universal. You will find, trace, and perhaps celebrate those in the stories of Brett and his circle.

Without being anything like exhaustive, I would invite readers' attention to two other themes in this narrative constellation, both of them perhaps more overt in *Fortune's Shadow* than in the other two volumes (although perhaps not— that is for you to decide). One is that there is great strength to be found in authenticity.

Quinn Tyler Jackson

Living authentically begins with oneself, although numerous external factors and forces can delay, suppress, or even crush an individual's desire and need to realize their authenticity. It is a complex topic, and this foreword is not the place for me to indulge in my own speculations on the matter. I do, though, encourage readers to keep it on their radar, consciously or otherwise, as they meet and get to know the various characters in this narrative, and to pause for reflection when something particularly resonates. Secondly, readers will find a strong current of gender equity coursing through this book. We are presented with beliefs and practices that rationally reject the noxiousness of patriarchal hierarchies, paradigms, and behaviours, in the process unfolding a vista of greater potential well-being and happiness not only for those whose shackles have been hewn away, but for everyone.

These are some of my thoughts, at this moment, about the book in front of you. Ultimately, though, it is a post-structuralist novel, which means that you, the reader, will always play a vital role in its (re)creation as you read it. So take or leave the foregoing words, as you wish. But be assured that in any case, the time you devote to reading *Fortune's Shadow* will be exceedingly well spent.

Dania Sheldon
Gabriola Island
24 April 2024

Touched by Fortune's Shadow: a triptych

Quinn Tyler Jackson

The Novel

This is a work of *fiction*, and therefore *all* of the characters, dialogues, situations, technologies, methodologies presented as innovations, and settings surrounding its characters are the products of artistic invention, interpretation, and presentation for narrational esthetics and effect. No claims, implicit or explicit, or representations are made of the technologies and methodologies presented and any resemblance to actual people, either living or dead, or non-public places is coincidental.

یکی بود، یکی نبود ....[3]

---

[3] *Yeki bud, yeki na bud* (lit. "Was one, wasn't one...."), "Once upon a time...."

Touched by Fortune's Shadow: a triptych

Part One: *Audere*

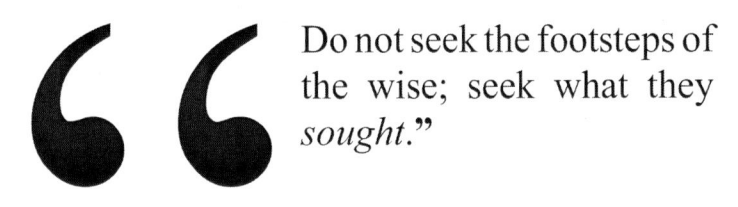

"Do not seek the footsteps of the wise; seek what they *sought*."

—**Matsuo Basho (1644-1694)**

Touched by Fortune's Shadow: a triptych

Quinn Tyler Jackson

Vancouver, mid-April 1998

Touched by Fortune's Shadow: a triptych

1

In the crisp dawn of mid-April, Vancouver's Coal Harbor awoke under a vanishing cover of silvery mist, its waters an emerging mirror to the seven-thirty sky. At the zenith of a sleek tower, perched like an impenetrable aerie on the northwest corner, Brett Lloyd-Ronan's penthouse surveyed the twin vistas of both the North Shore's verdant expanse and Stanley Park's curated, but nonetheless untamed beauty. It was a sanctuary not just of height, but of perspective, where the city's pulse fused with nature's calm, his home at the chosen fulcrum.

At twenty-eight, Brett chose and cherished his solitude. His life as a successful quantitative analyst and cofounder in a financial modeling firm was a blend of numeric precision and the always unpredictable human element that constantly sought to contradict probability distributions in order to extract some profit from them. That morning, like every morning, began with a ritual that bridged these dual worlds. Clad in a loose house robe that swayed as he walked, he approached his La Marzocco espresso machine—a testament to Italian craftsmanship and a herald of his day's start.

The machine whirred to life with a familiarity that spoke of many such mornings. Brett measured the ground coffee with an exactness that mirrored his professional accuracy, tamping the grounds with a practiced press. The rich aroma of espresso had begun to fill the suite, mingling with the early air drifting in from the moderately ajar balcony door.

As the city stirred below, Brett's calm gaze wandered over the water, the park, and the distant mountains shrouded in the morning's embrace. This moment, suspended between night's shadow and day's illumination, reflected his equilibrium. Here, in the stillness, he found a clarity that eluded many—a moment of peace before the day's demands encroached.

Touched by Fortune's Shadow: a triptych

The espresso dripped into his cup, a dark elixir against the porcelain white. He took his first sip, the sharp, robust flavors contrasting the serene view before him. This was his harbinger of the day ahead, a day of data and decisions, but grounded in this moment of reflection and the panoramic sweep of nature and city intertwined.

Brett Lloyd-Ronan was more than an observer of the dawn; he had been a participant in the day's unfurling story, his morning ritual a prologue to the narrative of his life and work in the heart of Vancouver's trading community. On any other morning but this mid-April dawn, the prelude to what was to come would end there and the story of his unfolding day would only continue after his twenty-minute walk to the office, where he'd begin his day as Chief Analyst at Vector Affinity Insights.

This exact morning, however, found him on a tall stool in his kitchen, at the Lemurian blue granite counter, sipping an espresso as his business partner's sister, Manijeh, continued to sleep comfortably in the other room on the pillow beside his own in his bed. Allen Saunders' words from *Readers Digest*, turned to lyrics in John Lennon's "Beautiful Boy" came to his mind: "Life is what happens to you while you're busy making other plans."

2

"Are you sure? I *could* take—"
"I'm sure," Brett interrupted Manijeh. "I'll be there in about three-quarters of an hour. No problem at all."
"Thank you so much, Brett," she said. "See you then."
He let her hang up first and then hung up at his end. He was quickly changed into more casual clothes and a light windbreaker, and soon on his way in his Lexus SC300 to the Vancouver Airport to pick up Manijeh Yazdpour. Her call had caught him completely off guard; she had never called him after having headed to Boston. The last he had heard of her news from Rostam, she had recently finished her MBA at Harvard and had taken a position at an extremely prestigious Toronto firm.

As he caught sight of *La Preziosità*, he pulled over and parked. Quickly, he was in and out of the store with a small box. Just over half an hour later, he was at the airport picking up Manijeh. He jumped out of the car, threw her bags into the trunk, and then gave her a polite hug. Once both were in their sets and buckled up, he handed the box he had gotten from *La Preziosità* across to her.

"Really? For me?" she said, her eyes lighting up. She looked as one might expect someone who'd just flown nonstop from Toronto might look.

"A small gift for your Harvard achievement," he replied.

She opened the box and pulled out the Omega Constellation lady's watch. She took off her watch, put his gift on, and displayed it proudly. "It's lovely, Brett! Thank you so much!"

"It's the least I could do with all the help you've given me." Brett turned the ignition and switched to drive. A quick glance later, he was in the loop on the way out of the messy airport traffic. "You hungry at all?" he asked.

"Not right now," she replied.

Touched by Fortune's Shadow: a triptych

He was silent for several lights, until finally, he asked the question that he had until then been putting off. "So, please explain what's up if you can. I'm quite confused. Pleased to help… but confused." They were waiting at a red, so he turned his head as far as needed to be able to see her reaction. She seemed pained.

"You *must* swear an oath of secrecy," she said. Her words were anachronistic to the ear given the tone she said them in, but Brett could tell without any doubt that she was serious about what she was asking of him.

"You have my word. Absolute secrecy."

"Including from my *entire* family."

"I really don't want to get right in the middle of—" Manijeh's expression was sufficient for him to then say, "Even from your entire family."

Manijeh inhaled very deeply, held it in for five seconds as they drove, and then let out half a breath before saying, "My boss at the firm started harassing me and when it was clear what I felt about that, started making my life there utter hell."

Brett turned his head to face the open driver's side front window and coughed. Rather than speak, he waited for Manijeh to continue, which she eventually did. "To make a long, dramatic story very short: I resigned and here I am."

Brett's mind flashed over a few hundred patterns deep within his memory. Everything told him that if Manijeh Yazdpour had walked away from a position of the magnitude she had, she was *entirely* justified in doing so.

"Whatever I can do, at any level, personal or professional, you have my full support in this, Manijeh."

Manijeh smiled brightly. "Let's just go to your place," she said. "We'll figure out what you just said *means*."

"I'm on it," Brett replied as he accelerated just enough to punctuate his eagerness to get his distraught passenger under a steady roof overlooking a peaceful view.

3

With attention to not drag the needle across the vinyl, Brett lowered the diamond-tipped interpreter of plastic memories onto Lennon's *Double Fantasy* and, as it proceeded at low volume, began reading Cohen Benjamin's latest novella, *No Hero over New York*, until "Beautiful Boy" came through the speakers, when he put the book on down so he could go to the turntable to turn the volume up to better hear the lyrics.

Three-quarters through the song, Manijeh wandered in the half-daze of the morning, draped only in Brett's oversized tank top. Brett removed the record from the turntable and put on instead Bowie's *Young Americans*, turned the volume down and walked over to her as she leaned gingerly against the frame of the bedroom door. He quickly kissed her forehead and said, "Good morning. Hope you slept well."

Manijeh quickly kissed him back. "I did, thank you," she said. She made a slight smacking sound with her mouth like she needed mouthwash at the very least and said, "Do you have anything I can banish my dreadful morning breath with?" She smiled through her grogginess and brightened the room to do so.

"There's a guest kit behind the right mirror in the ensuite," he informed her. "And there's a guest robe in the closet."

"New toothbrush still in packaging—for *guests*?" she called out after going into the ensuite. "You weren't kidding!"

As Manijeh freshened up for the morning, Brett quickly dressed in his indoor clothes and began making breakfast for the two of them, which he placed on the kitchen counter with a full glass of pulp-free orange juice and a cup of black coffee, as he knew she preferred hers.

When she sat with him at the counter and began to eat, he said to her, in as calm and nonchalant a voice as he could muster this early, "I wasn't expecting last night."

Manijeh smiled. "I can't say I was *expecting* last night, either, but I won't say that I wasn't *hoping* for it if I'm being honest. I'm quite *pleased* about it all, personally."

"It complicates life somewhat, don't you think?" He sipped his coffee and enjoyed the sparkle of the daylight behind her against the north-facing window, glorious and gorgeous at once in an instant. He was speaking of complications, but in the very moment he inhabited, with the two of them in his sanctuary, there was only gentle simplicity, which he by far preferred. But his mouth moved on about complications.

"No, it doesn't." Her face gave all the stoic seriousness of a recent graduate. "I am accountable to no one else but myself in matters of my body, mind, and soul. I neither need to apologize nor explain these matters to the family. And that includes Rostam. That's pretty simple."

"But what about when they figure out you're not in Toronto anymore? Like the first time they call your phone number over there and it comes back as out of service, for instance." In need of sugar to think more clearly, he switched from the black coffee to the orange juice and took two solid sips. "That's just about not alarming them with such things if they needn't be."

"They'll find out I moved back to Vancouver eventually," she said. "From *me*. When I can deal with all that."

As the album had played through the first side, Brett flipped over the record and started it on the second side. "How about you and I go for a walk around the Seawall, and then cross over at Lost Lagoon and come back?"

"I thought you'd *never* ask!" Manijeh said.

ം•ി

After about an hour of walking and talking, they arrived at Prospect Point Lookout, near the Lions Gate Bridge, and as they quietly stood there, looking into Burrard Inlet, Brett decided to risk returning to the subject of Manijeh informing her family that she was back in Vancouver. He reminded her that, while he offered her a roof for as long as she felt she needed a place to figure things out, Rostam did occasionally expect to be able to come over for a beer and brainstorm, as they often would do in their day-to-day planning of their various strategies at numerous tiers, some of which they did not yet wish others in the office to become aware of due to the sensitive nature of what they were discussing or speculating on.

"I figure I have two weeks to figure out all the details," she assured him with a delicate and convincing smile that reassured him of her acknowledgment of the seriousness of the situation her being under Brett's roof presented if discovered by accident rather than design.

He decided to actively change the subject. "When you look westward," he said, "you'll see what I call the Face of God." He pointed out the watery horizon. "It is calm. It is balanced. It is fluid, and yet it is also set. It just is."

"Are we standing in the presence of your god?" she asked, her tone of calm solemnity betraying no sense of irony in her question, given his longstanding status as a secular humanist.

Brett cleared his throat and said, as sincerely as he had been asked, "If this here Face of God is only *my* god, then it is no god at all. This is where mathematics meets metal. From out of the Face, functions come, and spin upon manifolds, to keys, to characters, to code, to electron movements not unlike the mist just right there, against a soundscape perhaps not too unlike water crashing on rocks. I think that would make this place be… just what it is. It's the closest thing to a Higher Power that you'll find for *this* here stardust traveler."

Rather than complete an entire circuit of the Seawall, they returned the way they came, and within an hour's walk were back at Brett's suite. They put on sweaters and had a beer on his balcony as they talked more.

"I truly don't want to sound like a 1950s movie," Manijeh said, "but would you like to go steady, Brett? You're kind of my crush."

Brett nearly choked on his beer. "Goodness. I'm *more* than flattered, Manijeh. I'm *chuffed*, as Dad might say. But I must disclose, now that you've opened the door to the conversation, that I have always lived my adult life as a free agent," he replied. He sat on the balcony seat beside hers and got to her eye level so they could both feel more at ease in the moment. He had endured undisclosed feelings for Manijeh for several years and had never stepped into the confidence to admit them to her. Because of open relationship history with women, he also knew it was only fair that she should understand his views on relationships, but suddenly did not know how to speak.

"Do you mean you don't date exclusively? I knew that from keeping tabs over the years from afar," she said. "You never *hid* the fact from anyone."

Touched by Fortune's Shadow: a triptych

"I just wanted to make sure it wasn't simply *implied*," he explained. "To avoid hurtful mishaps."

"It doesn't bother me in the *slightest*, and I think we'd get along astoundingly well," she said.

"I don't doubt we would, Manijeh. You're a fantastic person, all around. We found out last night that we have enough chemistry to set the place on fire." He brushed her hair aside slightly, smiled, and then added, "I have no fear of commitment, but I don't *own* anyone, and no one owns me." He was surprised at his own words. With all he felt for her, to say what he was saying stung his ears; it both did and did not seem necessary to clarify. He took a breath to catch his thoughts in a silent lasso. Still, it felt fair to warn her here and now.

Manijeh took a sip and put what he'd said through analysis if the expression in her eyes told of what she was thinking. "I'm fine with whatever parameters you want to put on how you conduct yourself on your own time," she finally said. "I'd just like to start dating. As I said, you're kind of my crush. More since I've been gone. I picked up the phone and called *you*, not a taxi to a hotel, which I could afford for more than a few months. I called *you*, Mr. Crush. You, Brett." She pointed at him and grinned mischievously. "So, thank you for the full disclosure, it helps avoid any surprises, which I appreciate not having to find out some other way, but don't overthink things here."

"Given the whole issue with your brother? You sure?"

"You have *your* notions of not being property, and so do I. I'm not the property of the eldest male Yazdpour to monitor and approve. But what's the use of having the finest MBA that blood, sweat, and tears can buy if I can't do basic Ethics 101 and deal with the fact that you have legal duties to my brother that require disclosure if you and I start dating? As much as I hate how that makes me feel as a cog in the patriarchal hegemony. You answer my question: can we go steady? If you say yes, I'll deal with my family. Rostam needs to hear it from me, not you."

Brett leaned over to her and kissed her upper lip. "Now you're cooking with gas. Sure, let's date, or 'go steady' or 'hang around' or whatever the kids are calling it these days. And I will leave all of the family communication to you. We have always made a great team, and things are just going to get better from here."

"Can we…" she began but stopped herself.

"Can we what?" he asked.

"Oh, I was just going to ask if we could shack up for the rest of the week, and *then* surface to tell the rest of the world where we're hanging our panties to dry." She put both her feet over the side of her seat and started to stand, bringing Brett up with her by the hand as she did. Brett and she entered the suite, closed the balcony door, and proceeded toward his bedroom.

Touched by Fortune's Shadow: a triptych

Vancouver, September 1981

Touched by Fortune's Shadow: a triptych

4

No more than twenty feet down the creek, down amongst the soggy rock moss and entrapped twigs, stood a boy the same age as Brett Lloyd-Ronan. "You stuck?" he called out when his gut told him something didn't quite look right about the boy's situation. The boy folded his arms across his chest in defeat and nodded a strong *yes* in reply. "Caught my boot in the muck!" he called out. "I could pull my foot out, but I don't want to get my sock all wet and rot the inside by getting it soaked."

Brett ran along the creek, which was in a stonework duct about three feet deep in total at most places. He got alongside the boy before offering his hand to shake. "Hi. I'm Brett."

"I'm Rostam," the other boy replied as he shook Brett's hand. When Brett clasped harder, Rostam understood that he was meant to get better leverage and purchase on the rocks with his free foot, and with that extra pull from Brett and the best angle from Rostam, the boot was out of the mud. Rostam shook his boot about in the water to rid it of excess clinging mud, and when he was satisfied, he climbed out of the duct and onto the grass above. "I feel so completely stupid."

"Nah," Brett replied. "I've done that a *few* times myself. And you're right, it rots right out if it gets wet. And that mud is thick, so it's not easy. Say, your name is new to me."

"Rostam. It's a Persian name. I'm from Iran," Rostam said. "We moved to Canada a few years ago, but then we just moved from Halifax to Vancouver this school year."

"Iran?"

"A town called Khorramshahr," he replied. "But it's a long story and also sad. Right now it's all occupied by Iraqis and has almost been destroyed."

"Okay, I understand. That's horrible. We can avoid talking about that. I understand. My full name is Brett Lloyd-Ronan."

Touched by Fortune's Shadow: a triptych

"That's a really neat last name, Brett. My full name is Rostam Yazdpour," Rostam offered.

"Yeah, my surname *sounds* fancy and even has a hyphen, but honestly, my parents just joined their last names into one when they got married."

"Are you Canadian?" Rostam asked. "I hear Canada has a lot of immigration, so I'm just checking to be sure."

"Well, I was *born* in Canada, but, like you, my parents are not from Canada originally. My father was born in Aberystwyth, Wales and my mother was born in Cork, Ireland. That explains the surname. I'm a citizen of all three countries. But I've never even traveled outside Canada, and certainly not for the reasons you had to leave Iran. It's nice to meet you."

"Wow. Three citizenships!"

"May I ask if you're Muslim? It will help me not be rude or something by accident."

"I am Zardoshti," Rostam replied quickly to Brett's query. "My family was originally from Yazd but went to Khorramshahr for business. That's probably why our last name is *Yazd*pour since we're talking about last names. That means 'from Yazd.'"

"Zardoshti? You're a Zoroastrian?"

"Yes. My family isn't practicing, though. We celebrate key days with the community, and we respect our heritage, but Mom and Dad call us *secular humanists* when people ask. You know about the Zardoshti?"

"I have studied the major religions, yes," Brett replied. "Good thoughts; good words; good deeds. I've never met a Zoroastrian before, though. I'm also pretty much a secular humanist. I'd say atheist, but I prefer to say what I believe in, rather than what I do not believe in."

"I've never met a Canadian who knew about us before. Until you," Rostam replied. "Are you ready for the school year?" he asked as they reemerged on the trail before the elementary school they both now attended in the same grade and division.

"Never am," Brett admitted. "How *could* we be ready? We're here to learn what we don't *already* know, right? We can't be ready for what we don't know yet."

Vancouver, mid-April 1998

Touched by Fortune's Shadow: a triptych

5

Having learned earlier that week from his sister that she was now dating his best friend and deeply interconnected business partner, Rostam Yazdpour sat at Brett's desk, across from him, with a brooding stare that ultimately, even after so many years of having known him and having played poker with him across scores of hands that provoked more reactive emotion, Brett could not read.

"First I'm going to say something plain and simple, so you don't get all wrapped up in your overactive mind," Rostam began, articulating very slowly and precisely.

"Fair enough," Brett replied.

"I'm very *happy* that you and Manijeh are dating," he said. "You're both adults and I love and trust you both. So you needn't stress yourself out over *that* if you have been."

Brett's chest dropped to the floor and returned by his next breath to the place it belonged. He had *not* been expecting that from Rostam. "That means a lot to me," Brett finally replied.

"It was *fated*. When I found out the news, I asked myself: why would this in any way bother me at all? I trust you with my fortune, and I trust you with my sister." He stood, leaned over to shake his friend's hand, shook it, and then sat down again. "You know my parents feel the same way. Especially Mom. She absolutely *loves* you, man."

Brett felt as if he were blushing for the first time in longer than he could remember. "I appreciate the vote of confidence."

Rostam then reached over to his briefcase, pulled out a thick folder, and handed it across to his business partner. "And now, of course, we have other things to go over." His face was scrunched up into the face he used when he was about to get business-serious with Brett.

Touched by Fortune's Shadow: a triptych

"What other things?" He, too, scrunched up his face as he flipped open the folder he'd just been given to peruse.

"Since Manijeh is back in Vancouver to *trade*, and since we serve that community across multiple competitors, we have to be proactive about compliance. Thus this pile of paper. She's my sister, so I have signed my version of these documents already. Conflict of interest declaration. Some NDA amendments with new provisions. A few brief memos of understanding, to preempt any potential future issues, foreseen or unforeseen, *ad nauseam*. I hate to even have to put this in front of you, but I must."

Brett pulled the small folder of paperwork closer to himself and flipped through the colorfully tabbed and annotated pages quickly. "This all went by Margaret?" He read the headings, audited the text under each, and gained a general sense of what he was in for if he was going to be in any kind of relationship with Manijeh, well above and beyond what any family blessings might grant him informally. But this was the financial services industry, in the competitive and secretive niche of quantitative finance, and he was, since launching Vector Affinity Insights five years earlier with Rostam, amongst the three recognizably most successful practitioners of this Dark Art on the North American Pacific Rim, according to the industry brag rags, with working model and code to back up his reputation in increased returns, and the only blessings that mattered to anyone with any real skin in this game came from Kafka's ink tattooed on the prisoner's left shoulder blade.

"Of course. This looks pretty benign. And since Margaret has vetted it." Brett called in his assistant Winston Rampersad to witness, removed his Montblanc from its case, and started signing and initialing where noted. Once done with the signing, he asked Winston to leave and close the door. Once his assistant was done, he said, "There we go with *that* out of the way."

"You see, Brett? That wasn't too bad, now, was it?" Rostam asked as if he were holding out an olive branch.

"Can I ask you a favor? Can we put this legal and compliance crap in a box and never mention it again, especially to Manijeh? It's boilerplate, sure, but it's egregious at best. I find it extremely distasteful, as necessary as it may be."

"Consider it already done, Brett!" Rostam said as he took the signed paperwork and put it in his briefcase. "Now, how about a cold beer to celebrate?"

Brett stood, walked over to the coat rack, and grabbed his windbreaker. "Sure. I'll buy."

"Oh, you better *believe* you'll buy!" Rostam returned with a sudden poke to Brett's ribs.

As they were getting into the elevator to leave the building, Brett said as an aside, "So, your mother loves me, eh?"

"She's your biggest fan, man. Speaking of mothers, how's *your* mother doing?"

Rostam's question caught him completely off guard and had him feeling his right leg buckle as if the planet's gravity had shifted or Vancouver had finally been hit by the Big One. But it was neither: it was the memory of his mother, Siobhan, in her hospital bed six months earlier, after her stroke. This often was the first thing to come to his mind when he heard mention of her.

"She's *almost* one hundred percent overall," Brett replied. "Dad's as fit as can be and is taking care of any shortcomings the stroke put on her. She's ready for the rest of her life."

"At least you paid off their house, so there's none of that for them to worry about going forward."

Brett tried mightily to find Rostam's optimism somewhere inside himself, and when he felt he had the feeling in his grasp, he replied, "We've had a good run. Let's keep it going."

A few blocks from the tower their office suite was in, they arrived at Taf's Cafe, and in no time they were having a sandwich and beer. "This is where I bought my first real cup of coffee, back in 1988," Brett said.

"Seriously? That late in the game?" Rostam contested. "Surely you must have had coffee before then. I remember—"

"Your parents only ever served me *tea*," Brett explained. "I'd chugged a few cups of my mother's percolated campfire coffee before that. They only ever offered me coffee when we were out in the Interior camping, for some reason. Otherwise, with them, it was *always* tea. But Taf's is the place where I first bought and paid for a cup. With money I'd earned."

Rostam leaned back in his chair and carefully sipped his beer. "It's cool that you remember that. How was it?"

"It was a *great* feeling. I felt like an adult for the first time in my *life*."

"Was I even there? I don't have your memory for distant things like this." He put his bottle down and took a big bite from his pastrami sandwich.

Touched by Fortune's Shadow: a triptych

Brett wasn't sure if he should bring up past relationships, but when this doubt encroached upon him, rather than hold his tongue, he recalled how he had felt signing the stack of legal memoranda he'd just gone through to be able to get the legal and regulatory blessing for dating his business partner's sister, and he decided to disregard the usual rule about not making others uncomfortable about their past poor judgment. "Oh yeah. You were there. You were dating Tracie at the time. The two of you were there. I was on a date with Lori Kildare."

Rostam's composure shifted somewhat as his face paled and he pushed his plate neatly away. "Come to think of it, I *do* remember that night. I didn't realize it was your first coffee."

"Well, I had a *date* to impress back then," Brett admitted. "It's not like I was going to put a big neon sign above my head, flashing how utterly *naïve* I was."

As if to return the poke of the rapier he'd unsheathed upon him over Tracie, Rostam replied, "And that you were."

Brett started to laugh at his friend. "*Touché.*" When the check came, he clipped his card to the check tray and sent it to be processed. He tipped and signed when it returned and started back toward the office northward down Granville. When they reached their tower, he turned to Rostam and explained that he wanted to go home for the rest of the day and that he would be emailing Rostam later in the evening on their secure account once he had the new models he'd been working through in a more stable state.

Rostam leaned into a warm hug and again assured him in as few words as he could muster that he was happy that Brett and Manijeh were now an item, and that all of his money was on them. Just as Brett was about to leave earshot distance, he called out a final proclamation: "Literally! All my money... *all* of it! No pressure!"

6

The scope and scape of Brett Lloyd-Ronan's sanctuary atop his downtown perch had shifted like the sands of Ambleside Beach across and just behind the view. Though he could not see it from his vantage point, he imagined driftwood, footprints in the sand, and the slight perturbations on the manifold of his usually well-curated and manicured living room brought these natural features to mind, affording him peace. A slight ruffling of a lambskin covering. A cushion marginally out of place on the B&B Italia Cerulean blue "Charles" sofa. Even the glasses in the cupboards were *almost* amiss. Each of these variances, her standard deviations from his mentally constructed norm, arose from Manijeh's presence in his day-to-day life.

It had been a week that she had slept in his bed, shared breakfasts with him, and headed into the world of Vancouver's financial services community to find prospects for a position. Each of those days had left a small artifact, if only in the alignment of a plant that needed rotation to be properly watered and wasn't rotated back into its original position.

His inner vision could see each of these Moiré patterns, each an artifact of his limerence; for if it were not electric limerence he was negotiating with her presence in his life, he would have instinctively reached over and turned a cup aright or smoothed a pillow. Instead, he leaned back, not forward, and tried to increase his vista rather than limit it based on the past and how past human engagement in his most private of places made him feel. This was *not* the ripples of those from his past—this was uniquely and completely because of Manijeh Yazdpour—and he was not going to permit himself to brush away the imaginary dust bunnies from under his ever so slightly crooked sofa just to keep it as it always had been before.

It was fine as it was. Imaginary dust and all.

Touched by Fortune's Shadow: a triptych

To his left was the sizable open kitchen, with its expressive Lemurian granite. Before him was the North Shore out the main full-length window, and to his right was the art wall with its recessed niches, one of which esthetically ensconced a rippled blue Robert Held vase that matched the kitchen in spirit, and his large abstract silkscreened poster with pride-of-place beside several smaller pieces.

He readily accepted that anything of his that Manijeh could perturb, move, turn, or adjust, was made all the better for it. Each such site was a possible nucleation point toward a vast future lattice of golden and gossamer scaffolding on decisions as yet unanticipated or even considered. He had not ever expected to feel this way about disorder of any kind, but to his mind came inept Polonius' sometimes unexpectedly apt words: "Though this be madness, yet there is method in't."[4]

He hadn't admitted it to her during her own full disclosure about her feelings for him, but he, too, had crushed on her over the years. He remembered having debated, more than a few times, whether or not he would do anything about it. Her life became about her education, and then about her career, and although they had always mostly kept in touch, his life became about the shared onus of the business and then she went on to Harvard. Those years were far too foundational for all of them, it seemed to Brett at the time, to introduce a variable of such human magnitude as how exactly he felt about her.

He could not have been with her then.

And then, hardly a week ago, like a lightning strike down the center of his solid oak path from sky to earth, she called from Vancouver Airport and asked, having returned from years of absence, to come intimately into his life and into his third and fourth dimensions: space and time. As he reviewed the models he needed to get back to Rostam on soon, his perspective and projection were adjusted to this adapted free functor.

Now Brett must commit his space and his time to another human being and find the optimal Pareto frontier that satisfied two, rather than simply one soul. As he had said to her when they first discussed his views on open relationships, he was not afraid to make commitments.

---

[4] William Shakespeare, *Hamlet* (2.2).

Time and space. These were amongst the resources he most coveted. They were sewn into his décor. Selected in the bubbles and whorls when he purchased blown glass. Present when he authorized the final and total vista out his windows at purchase. These were his agency and autonomy; he was also committed to these constant principles.

The slight ruffling of a pillow translated into the model he stared at before him. They presented latent variables of impact, occult origins with only minor artifacts: but a local effect nonetheless, and important to the whole manifold. And it was in the midst of this liminal space that Brett Lloyd-Ronan found himself over work and life's practiced intersection: no matter what the magnitude of any relationship, when one *commits* to that, one truly commits to another human being. He had known Manijeh for many years, and although his primary relationship in the Yazdpour family was through Rostam, their lives were plaited beyond any undoing by human hands.

He had Rostam's blessing, which, while not needed, was not something any rational person with a beating heart would push away as redundant, in his understanding. Even the delicate ropes that he now ran his mental hand along to feel any as yet missed fray, frustration, or betrayal—these ropes of relationship that he had modeled after his many interactions with Rostam's family, as they were more robust and established than his own family over the many years since he'd met them. These were the ropes that bound his affection for Manijeh tightly to his heart, to a degree the present situation had brought beautiful but almost agonizing authenticity.

Now that Brett had time to more completely grasp where he stood, tested against his sense of consistency and ambition, he eagerly awaited Manijeh's return from her day's merciless search for career success.

Touched by Fortune's Shadow: a triptych

7

When Manijeh's keys started to rattle on the other side of the door to Brett's suite, Brett stood and walked down the hallway to the foyer. As the door swung open, he smiled and greeted her. She returned his smile with one of her own that seemed to speak of good news when accompanied by the shine in her mesmerizingly clear slate-gray gaze. As she'd been to an interview that afternoon, she was dressed in her finest cream blouse, tailored blazer and skirt, all accompanied by a canary yellow Yves Saint Laurent bag and her finest pointed-nose nude black patent Choos. She was wearing the watch he'd given her.

"*Ziba hastid*!"[5] he said as she closed the door and locked it behind her.

"*Merci*! You learned some more Farsi!" she said with a huge smile. She leaned in and gave him an enthusiastic hug.

As they walked the hallway into the main area, he said, "I made you some decaf so you can tell me about your day." Once at the counter, he took both their cups, and they went to the couch and sat beside one another.

She sipped her coffee, nodded her approval, thanked him for it, and began with the news of her day. "I interviewed with Klein, Holdum, and French today." She stared straight at him as she said this, most likely trying to gauge his response, given the prestige of the house.

Brett first sipped his coffee, and then swirled the cup abound by swaying his hand in an elliptical path. He watched the patterns of the many reflections on the surface of the black decaffeinated liquid as if he were Jamshid himself trying to read the mysteries of all the universe, but he saw only her smile over the lip of the mug he was holding.

---

[5] "You're gorgeous!"

Finally, he found words that fit both what she had to say and also what he eventually wanted to discuss with her that evening if the conversation could be made to drift there comfortably. "That's a truly wonderful opportunity, even just to interview there and get on their scope. I've known many top traders who didn't even land interviews with them. I assume by your bright demeanor that it went well?"

Her smile grew in intense joy as she said, "They offered me a position, full role conditional upon my registration."

"Right on the spot without follow-up interviews? That's *glorious*!" Brett instinctively reached out and touched her left hand as she sipped her coffee with her right. He stroked it by way of gentle congratulations. "What exactly did Klein *et al.* say you'd be responsible for?" he asked.

"I'll be tackling portfolio hedging and diversification, with special attention to buffering with the European Market, most of that after the euro kicks in next year," she replied. "So there will be some European travel, for certain, as well as a series of necessary certifications once I get general registration. But at the end of the path, it's all *very* promising. Once I'm licensed, I'll be the Director of European Portfolio Diversification."

After putting his cup on the coffee table, he reached over and offered to do likewise with hers, after which he leaned over and hugged her, kissed her warm cheek, and said, "Promising is an *understatement*. That's absolutely *amazing*. *Mobarak*!"[6]

"I know, right?" she replied, clearly very proud of her day's achievement. "It might take a few months to get the registration out of the way, but they've offered me general office work at a baseline salary that doesn't involve any trading until then, so I can at least get to know my eventual portfolios and the playing field I'm going to be running around on."

For a very brief moment, Brett's mind drifted into business as his pattern-searching psyche began to dissect what it could mean for Vector Affinity Insights for him to travel to Europe now and again with Manijeh when she went there for her work, as it was a market that he had considered entering for the last few years but felt he couldn't justify traveling over until it was likely to promise returns. This intrusion of business into his mind reminded him of the stack of paperwork that Rostam had gotten him to sign in front of Winston as a witness.

---

[6] *Mobarak!* (lit. "Congratulations!")

He put aside such matters and refocused his thinking onto the moment he currently inhabited, on the sofa, with Manijeh in her clear bliss about her career coup. "What do you say we celebrate at the Sitar?" he asked.

"Sounds lovely!" she agreed.

∽•∾

"So did they ask you why you returned from Toronto after so little time at you-know-where?" Brett asked as he bit into the tender, medium-spicy piece of lamb. Over the candle that lit their table, still in her cream blouse, with her subtle eyeliner and shadow, Manijeh almost made his chest shake from his excitement just to be there with her. The more time he spent with her, the more he heard her voice, the more he searched for words in his mind and breath from his solar plexus, the more she shook him about, perturbing his mental curves beyond a simple arc or multivariate regression. Discovering who she was, after so many years of being at arm's length from her but always just around life's corner, held him rapt.

"I told them I came back for family and community," she said. "Which wasn't a lie, after two years in Boston with no visits and then six months in Toronto straight on. They nodded and accepted a variation of the truth and that closes that book." She spooned sauce from the curry bowl onto her rice, and then added, "Now I have to find a place my reduced salary will let me afford. Vancouver prices sure aren't what they were when I was last looking in this rental market."

Upon hearing this, Brett put his utensils down and looked directly across the set table, over the candle flame, and into the cool recesses of her passionate gaze, and said, "About looking for a place...." He waited, almost as if he expected her to prompt him to continue, but when she did not, but instead smiled and stared intently back into his regard, he finally continued on his own. "How are you enjoying living with me?"

At this, her face jumped for what could have been described as baseline happiness for a day well spent to utter delight. "You won't think me too feckless if I'm honest?" she asked, almost cautiously but without breaking the tone of her clear contentment with her evening.

"The feckless most certainly do *not* land positions at Klein, Holdum, and French, in one sitting," he replied. "Be honest."

Touched by Fortune's Shadow: a triptych

"I've been walking on sunshine this last week we've been together. I don't regret a second of it."

Hearing this, Brett crossed his utensils, pushed aside his plate, and lifted the napkin from his lap. He then folded his hands in front of him, took a slow, deep breath, held for five seconds, and then exhaled. Finally ready to continue, he asked her, in as confident a voice as he could put forth to her without sounding *too* theatrical, "Would you like to move in with me, Manijeh?"

Manijeh Yazdpour's eyes lit from their usual cool gray to an almost blue simplicity at the exact moment his lips and mouth voiced her name at the end of his question. The apertures of her pupils grew like animate *camera obscura* trying to take in more of what they saw before her. The corners of her mouth folded softly at first and then almost exaggeratedly into an almost perfectly appointed smile. She brushed her shoulder-length black hair, with its light wave, behind her ears, tipped her head back, touched her lip to stop the first words out of her mouth as if she could barely contain herself, and said, "Brett… I was *not* expecting to hear you *ever* ask me such a thing." A tear formed in the corner of her right eye, and when he said it, Brett handed her his napkin so that she could wipe it without getting any makeup on herself. She wiped delicately and with precise decision.

"It's a sincere question," Brett replied, to assure her that he had given it thought before letting it leave his lips to her ears.

"I know you, Brett Lloyd-Ronan. I've known you for a *long time*. You don't kid around. No need to explain."

She put her utensils on her plate, pushed it aside, and put her napkin on the table from her lap. Then, she reached around the candle, one hand on either side, motioning for Brett to hold her hands in his own, and she gave her answer, "I would be overjoyed to move in with you, Brett. *Overjoyed.*"

A powerful rush of adrenaline bolted through Brett at that moment. He had not been expecting it but did not mind, and let it course through him. She was slowly stroking his hand with her right thumb. "Since you were so vulnerable with me, I am going to admit it: I have crushed on you for years, as well," he confessed.

After a moment, she asked, "What about all your views on ownership and openness in relationships? I'm quite curious as to what parameters you propose once we move in together officially, given that means we've a shared address."

He laughed lightly at her query and admitted, "I have had some time to consider that."

"And?"

"Let's talk about all that as we walk home," he suggested. "I'm all for having the *rasmalai* and then heading back."

"Home…," Manijeh said as she nodded her agreement. "Suddenly the reality of that word jumps right out of your mouth. Home. Yes, I like that. *Home*."

✥ • ✥

"To answer your question from earlier. I don't feel a need to put barriers around people by telling them how to conduct their autonomy as if I'm their keeper or something," he explained when they had turned onto West Cordova from Water Street on their way back home. "That doesn't change one *iota* due to an address change. Relationship openness centers on consideration, safety, and discretion."

"I've no interest or intention at all of dating anyone else," she said. "If *you* want to, just stick to those three guidelines and we're fine." She squeezed his hand in hers.

"Limerence," he then said.

"Pardon?"

"It means obsessive crushing or something like that," he replied. "Here I am, after years of limerence. I'm not in the least bit interested in diluting my attention from you now that we're together. You're one-of-a-kind. My vision is singular."

She laughed and smiled quickly at him under the lights of the street, and when she did this, he leaned to kiss her lower lip and squeezed her hand tightly when he did. "I have pretty much had a crush on you since you beat up Willard in the Still Creek ravine," she then admitted before adding, "So what you're saying is that the rules you *normally* conduct your intimate life by magically don't apply as far as I'm concerned? Is this how you tell a woman she's *special*?" Her eyes sparkled at this. "This is the same you who always keeps a 'guest' toothbrush and tampons behind the ensuite bathroom mirror, just on the off chance of an unexpected overnight stay by some lady caller?"

"Limerence," Brett admitted simply. "I've never felt it for anyone but you," he admitted after stopping and turning to face her to say it. "It changes all my calculations. I don't know what any of it means yet, and a suave reply wouldn't serve justice."

Touched by Fortune's Shadow: a triptych

After a few moments, he insisted, "And I most certainly did not 'beat up Willard.'"

"Oh, really, are you forgetting that I was there, too?" she asked, her eyes alight with a blend of nostalgia, mischief, and perhaps no small amount of limerence of her own.

"I set him right straight, is all," he at last clarified.

"Don't you go clouding up my misty recollection with your infamous *clarity*," Manijeh teased. She locked her wrists behind his neck as she put her arms over his shoulder and pulled herself into him as they stood near Canada Place and embraced against the chill of the cool evening air. "Limerence. I agree that it's a nice word," she said. "It's going to be fun to figure out what it truly means in *practice*, given history and providence. Are you ready for this?"

At this, Brett laughed, and they resumed on the path home. "I'm never ready for what I don't know yet," he said, holding her hand in his as they marched on. "But I'm okay with that."

"Me, too," Manijeh agreed.

Quinn Tyler Jackson

Vancouver, mid-October 1981

Touched by Fortune's Shadow: a triptych

8

The three of them aligned to an isosceles triangle as they walked the grassy knoll above the engineered creek at the bottom of the ravine. They had spent the greater part of their lunch hour engaged in stick swordplay without falling from the stone wall section they'd chosen to be their *piste*. Rostam had won by far, Manijeh, one year his junior, had scored second-most, and Brett was soundly defeated. As they drew to the end of the creek, where it went into a tunnel that nobody knew the other end to, they encountered Willard and his crew of two henchmen.

The stories of what transpired ten minutes before the end of lunch break that day differed until they went away altogether with the coming winter break a few months later, but even only two months left a lot of time for speculation and variation. Willard and his crew had told their accounts, but Brett, Rostam, and Manijeh refused to grouse on even the bullies who had tried to push them down. Their joint silence, however, spoke to the truth of their mutually shared account of that afternoon.

As they stood in a triangular formation, with Brett on point, his stick still ready at hand, they were confronted with being on the Low Ground. Brett knew from the swing of Harry's arms at his side that his chest was pressed out under his jacket, and he was physically postured and mentally prepared to support Willard in something unpleasant. He recalled to mind Sun Tzu's strong caution to not fight uphill. Sun Tzu also advised, however, that one *must* fight when on desperate ground, which the Low Ground almost *always* was. While Brett searched for *anything* to make the ground less desperate, Willard spoke.

"Where are you idiots going?" Willard challenged with his right nostril intentionally poised from his contempt.

"To school!" Manijeh called out.

Touched by Fortune's Shadow: a triptych

"To—*school*!" Willard parroted her, intensifying the whine of his tone. "Do you play with *girls* now Brett? Are you a *girl* now?" The boy to his left and the other to his right guffawed loudly at his taunt.

Willard took a step downward toward Brett, putting six feet between them. Brett went through wireframe scenarios in his head, carefully tracking his two friends and their positions. The golden mental threads of the netting flickered yellow and orange with the autumn leaves of the ravine's many deciduous trees. In his mind, he could see the shining letters of Sun Tzu again: "Appear at points which the enemy must hasten to defend; march swiftly to places where you are not expected."

"Who wants to beat up the sand n—"

Before the next word came fully out of Willard's mouth, Brett lunged with practiced intent and precision, and the tip of his stick, sharp and sure, pressed against Willard's Adam's apple and Brett had transited from the *en garde* to the completion of a lunge, with his left arm bent and his legs in position. He put some of his weight into his lean, compensating for this with the counterweight of his free arm. His opponent's eyes were wide and startled, as were those of his two companions.

Willard started to erratically move his right hand up to his throat, presumably in an attempt to grab the tip of the stick Brett held there so precisely, and with a movement that blurred to all but the quickest eyes, Brett's stick struck Willard's knuckles, producing a loud crack not unlike one might hear from a whip, and then jumped directly back up to his Adam's apple. Willard's eyes were even wider than they had been earlier as he reached over to rub his knuckles.

Though enough time for anyone to catch their breath had not passed, Brett was on top of Willard, on the ground, with his stick across his chest so he could get leverage to hold his arms down and out of the way better. Perhaps Willard could see behind Brett's eyes, perhaps he was in no mood to fight after all, but at this moment, as he faced down his once imagined prey, Willard called out to his cohort to leave everyone alone, and at this, Brett stood, offered his hand to pull Willard up off the ground, a gesture which Willard refused to accept, and the three boys from Grade Seven sulked amongst themselves as they walked off. Brett brushed the dust from his pant legs as they vanished over the top of the ravine and out of sight.

When the boys were out of earshot, Rostam said to his friend, "You were being *easy* on us. You *could* have beaten us wooden swords *dozens* of times down here." Rostam started to laugh, and Manijeh joined him, and hearing them both, Brett could not help but laugh as well.

"It's not sporting to get the better of someone who has less experience," Brett said to Rostam. "Just not good cricket."

"But *you* got the better of *them!*" Rostam pointed out.

"'You must understand that there is more than one path to the top of the mountain,'" Brett quoted from *The Book of Five Rings*. "When defending, you indeed *may* use necessary advantage, but always taking due care to avoid needless injury."

"I'm confused. What does this have to do with paths and mountains?" Manijeh asked. "Or crickets, for that matter? And thanks for that gross image of *locusts*, by the way!"

"Not good cricket? That's just something my dad says," Brett explained to her.

"It's not about bugs; it means *adâlat nist*[7] or something like that," Rostam explained. "Brett means cricket the *sport*, not the bugs. It's like baseball where his dad grew up."

"Anyway, all this has a *lot* to do with paths up mountains, I think," Brett explained. "When we *must* fight, even if we find we are fighting an uphill battle, we must *adapt* and *act* if we're going to even have a *chance* to make it to the top. Graveyards are *full* of Hamlets on the many paths on the way there. If we are going to make it to the top, we must act against each barrier that arises to try to stop us from doing that, and there will be many."

"Speaking of paths, let's get up this one and get to school before we're late!" Manijeh called out. "I'm not even going to *ask* what the heck 'Hamlet' means."

---

[7] *adâlat nist* (lit. "[it] is not justice/fair"), "That's not fair."

Touched by Fortune's Shadow: a triptych

Vancouver, mid-April 1998

Touched by Fortune's Shadow: a triptych

9

First, his bare left foot, and then his right, touched the smooth runner on the left side of the bed. He reached for the fresh pair of boxer briefs he'd stashed on his end table, put them over his ankles, stood carefully to not disturb Manijeh's sleep, and slid them up. His robe was on the floor, so he leaned down, picked it up, put it over him, tied the belt loosely, and gingerly made it to be bedroom door, which he carefully closed behind him as he exited the room.

He went to his refrigerator, kept stocked by his twice weekly home cleaning and supply service, and took out the pitcher of orange juice. After pouring himself a full glass and taking a sip, he approached the west-facing window near the formal dining area, at the northwest corner of the suite, just to the left of the open kitchen. The fabric of the kitchen table chair gave just enough traction to his robe that he had to adjust to avoid it bunching up under his right leg, and once he was comfortable staring out at Stanley Park in the cool, crepuscular gray of an April morning, he finished what remained of the juice in his glass in an almost continuous gulp.

He then stood, walked over the parquet walnut floor, and found the Persian grammar text in amongst his many other books. With this in hand, he refilled his glass of juice, returned to the kitchen table, put the book open before him, and began reviewing it. It had been a few years since the last time he had gone through it. As he flipped across the lessons, his inner ear began to hear disjointed words slowly connecting into short expressions such as *sobh bekheir* and *man az shomâ kheili mamnun-am*.[8]

---

[8] *sobh bekheir* (lit. "good morning"), *man az shomâ kheili mamnun-am* (lit. "I thank you very much").

Touched by Fortune's Shadow: a triptych

These were phrases he'd heard many times over the years around the Yazdpour family, but which completely transformed when written in Farsi script without most of the vowels, making it sometimes difficult to map what he heard spoken and what he saw written. He had never really had a reason to learn Persian beyond polite formulas spoken quickly before switching entirely to English, but as he sat over his orange juice and his cool morning view of the Park, he committed to putting in the study every week to improve upon the *status quo* he'd fallen into. Since the events of the week had traveled by his vision so quickly, he was uncertain how the decisions that had been made in the splendid isolation of his perch atop the world were going to stand up when he faced Manijeh's parents, embraced them in greeting, and was up against their meticulous scrutiny.

A few new, meaningful things to say to them in Farsi, at the very least, would serve as a reassuring gesture of his intentions. He understood that Rostam had represented Mrs. Yazdpour as being supportive and had even suggested that Mr. Yazdpour was not thrown off by the fact that Brett and Manijeh were now together, but he knew from hard, unfortunate experience that two things could upset even the most serene and sincere setting: blood and money.

Brett's life and the Yazdpours' from this point forward were now interwoven in both these ways, and he promised himself to tread lightly, especially given that he'd invited Manijeh to live with him. The small dam along the creek had given way to a brief flood of noisy and enjoyable delight; it was time for the stream to regain its composure and return to forming still pools alongside its shore for reflection.

As he sat at the table, sliding through the pages of Persian formulas and sentence forms, his phone on the counter started to indicate that he'd just received a text. This was unusual, especially at this time of day; it was only six in the morning. He checked and was greeted by a message from Rostam: "Fencing at 7:30?"

He played with the numbers on the phone's keypad until it read, "Sure thing!"

Rostam's reply came: "Loser closes the next deal."

10

After adjusting his plastron, Brett slid on his fencing jacket. Rostam was as far into his gear across the bench. "I've been thinking about how we can expand our operations," he said. He fumbled with a buckle before continuing. "So, I was looking through those adjusted models you sent me last night, and it came to me: if we find a way to package up subscriptions to regular automatic model updates, then—"

"—then we'll have found a way to clone me," Brett replied as he tightened his jacket's suspender straps and moved his legs around in the breeches to see if the tension was correct. "But, yes, it has proven to be our bottleneck that only I seem able to adjust models when they have been initially trained, I agree."

Rostam finally was ready to put on his mask. "That's an open problem I'm leaving for you to solve," he replied. He tapped his friend's shoulder and the two started for the *pistes*. "But when you do, then our models will be able to dynamically update as the market conditions shift, without that automatic reconfiguration costing us any future revenue, since we would be relieving that unnecessary customer pain and removing *you* as a primary and lynch-pin cost-driver."

On these words, Brett put his left arm around his friend as he readied his mind to compete. "Isn't cloning humans still on ethical moratorium?" He then bleated out his most sheep-like rendition of a single word: "Dolly."

"Always the details man," Rostam replied with a chuckle. "Find a way to update our models in the field that doesn't involve two or more of you, and we're set for life." He stood in position at the end of the *piste* and called out "*En garde, prêts, allez!*" as he seamlessly fell into épée bout position. Brett, his opponent, immediately followed, and the *piste* became their playground.

Touched by Fortune's Shadow: a triptych

As they were equally matched in every respect except for Brett's height advantage, the bout went on for approximately twenty minutes before Brett finally called out, "We're equally matched! Five double touches this far in. I propose we call a draw on our friendly assault!"

"But the loser closes the next deal!" Rostam then protested. "Sudden death on next touch?" he asked.

Brett gave Rostam a nod, and right after he did so, Rostam lunged and touched the win, leaving Brett the fair and clear loser of the match as he called out his "*Touché!*" They saluted one another and headed to the changing room to take off and store all their gear in their shared rental locker. They showered and headed to work.

Three hours in, Rostam came to Brett's office and asked if they could head to the café for lunch. Having no other plans, Brett agreed, and they were soon on their way. Rostam was quiet for the entire walk but did not seem to be in any kind of bad mood. Once at their table out front, in the enclosed window section, he tipped his beer and said, "Cheers."

Brett lifted his bottle and tapped the glass.

"So, Brett, I was on the phone for an *hour* with Manijeh this morning. She called me at ten-thirty. And then I was on the phone for half an hour with Mom. That was just as fun."

Brett took a quick sip of his beer. Though he did not smoke, he instinctively felt that had he been a smoker, this would be the exact moment he should light a stick and break the silence with a comment about how it was a nasty habit. Instead, he held up his beer and said, "I prefer mine darker. Pilsner isn't really my thing."

"We're not on the *pistes* anymore, Brett," Rostam chided his friend. "I've got to say that I'm confused. I'm not unhappy about anything, mind you, but confused."

Their food arrived and Brett took the opportunity to bite into his sandwich before the conversation became so involved that he forgot to eat. Once he had swallowed, he said firmly, "Confused about what?"

As he stirred sour cream into his tomato soup, he started to chuckle, almost to himself. "About how quickly you're moving along with Manijeh," he explained. "It's one thing to start going steady. That's a *huge* step for you, given your history as a dandy free agent, and probably for her. A *big* change!"

"You're not kidding," Brett agreed.

"But then, out of nowhere, and so soon, to be asking her to move in with you to your high tower of perfect bachelor playboy solitude?" He spooned some soup, blew on it until it was likely cool enough to eat, and then slurped it noticeably. "It feels like you've been hit on the head and aren't quite the Brett I know, I'll admit."

"I'm as right as rain," Brett insisted.

"Not in some kind of manic episode? No matter how I turn the lights and adjust the mirrors, this scene still has too many shadows. Your engine is running on nitro with this relationship. Are we heading for a hairpin turn?"

After another bite of his sandwich, Brett contested, "Aren't you the one who said you were enthusiastically behind her and my getting together a while back?" As he asked this, he remembered that Manijeh had made it clear how she felt about her brother and father's unnecessary and unwelcome blessing upon her love life.

"Please don't get me wrong. I *am* happy that you two have decided to date," he assured Brett. "And so is Mom, as I said." Rostam then looked across the table straight at his friend of many years and calmly said, "But I worry you're going to rush this, Brett. I worry that if you do, you'll hurt Manijeh for no reason other than you woke up to realize one day that you rushed it and regret being in such a *hurry*." He wiped the corner of his lip with his napkin. "Friend to friend. No bull. That's just not good cricket. So tell me: what's with the hurry? Who lit the house on fire?" He put the napkin down and started on his sandwich.

Without saying a word, Brett Lloyd-Ronan took a long sip from his beer, and turned his head left and right to watch the pedestrians pass the café in front of him. Rostam's back was to the street, so when he saw him tracking the people outside, he turned his chair slightly to see what was so interesting to his friend. "I'm not in any particular hurry," he finally said.

"It's been a matter of all of what—*one* week?—since she came back from Toronto," Rostam offered in disagreement. "What the heck would *you* call fast if *that* is not being in any particular hurry, my friend?"

Brett hemmed and asked, "Do you remember when Manijeh got accepted into her program at UBC?"

"The proudest day of everyone's life!" Rostam replied.

"She opted for campus dorms, right?"

"Yes, but honestly, I'm not following."

Touched by Fortune's Shadow: a triptych

After a long pause, Brett continued to explain. "I was living over in Port Coquitlam, working that crappy job pushing broom and plunging commodes for the thespians at that old theater." He took another sip from his beer and waited for his last words to register in Rostam's eyes.

"Oh, let's just wait a second here. Are you suggesting what I think you're suggesting?"

"If you think I'm suggesting that I had been planning to ask her to start dating back *then*," he admitted to his friend, "then you're smashing sixes." His beer done, he motioned for the waiter and then asked for a pint of Guinness. Rostam ordered another of what he'd already been drinking. "I had it all *planned*. Down to the last *syllable*. Signed and sealed. But she decided to go to UBC and live so far away—further than I could manage to travel by transit on the regular basis that a real relationship would call for, given my budget at the time, since I was helping out my family with whatever little I earned, I decided to not even *sit* at the table with Manijeh and play *Pasur*[9] unless I brought a full, fair deck with me. Exactly so I wouldn't hurt people and regret being in a hurry. So… signed, sealed, but not delivered. Not back then when it would have complicated everyone's lives."

Not another word was said between the two men until their second round of drinks arrived.

"*Carpe diem sed finem respice*," Brett finally said.

"I get the first part, but *finem*…?"

"Seize the day but consider the end. In other words, grab life by the brass ones, but be sure to have a long endgame. I can't say I was expecting things to go the way they went this last little while since Manijeh flew back to Vancouver," he admitted. "Humans aren't as predictable as ticker returns and *those* are hard enough to figure. But once she was right there in my life, I wasn't going to hurry-up-and-wait myself into my thirties, forties, fifties, and possibly beyond wondering what *might* have been between Manijeh and me."

"Wow," Rostam said. "You have it *deep*. I didn't realize. I really do *not* know how I could have missed it. You kept it well to yourself, Brett."

---

[9] *Pasur*, also known as *Basra*, is a traditional card game of Middle Eastern origin, played with a standard deck of cards, where players aim to capture cards from a central pool by matching their numerical value or utilizing strategic combinations, accumulating points based on specific cards and combinations captured.

Brett continued: "Then here we are, sitting in April these many years later, and the time came for decisive action. I finally could sit at the *Pasur* table with a full, fair deck. So I did. Then and there. It only *looks* hasty to an outsider."

Rostam nodded his understanding. "Sounds like you waited longer than many would have."

"I sure have. If it's true that patience is a virtue, then my vote is that I've been a patient *saint*. And guess what about anyone who didn't wait that long to be with Manijeh? *They* lose. This is one of the few times in my life, Rostam, brother-at-arms, my friend, that I'm prepared to make it about *me*. I've wanted to be with her for too long for a heart to keep carrying without the light of day. And everything Manijeh tells me has her right in the same frame of mind as me."

Both men chuckled the understanding. "Make haste slowly," Rostam almost whispered. "Thank you for explaining this to me. It clears up any lingering questions I may have had."

"Anyway, enough years of inaction have passed us by, so let's not worry one more *minute* about my being in a hurry with her and me. Deal?" he reached eagerly across the table to shake Rostam's hand on their understanding.

Rostam reached back, shook his hand, and replied, "Deal." As the word left his mouth, his eyes went wide with excitement and surprise. "Did you just…? Are you…?"

A hearty laugh came from the core of Brett Lloyd-Ronan as his business partner and long-time friend realized that he'd been snookered. "If I'm not mistaken, my friend, it seems that I just closed the next deal," he agreed.

Rostam slapped the side of his head, put his face down near the table in admitted defeat, and said simply, "*Touché!*" After a few moments, he sat straight up again, smiled, and said, "Now how about that Klein, Holdum, and French hattrick Manijeh pulled off, eh?"

Before replying, Brett turned his chair enough to be more at ease. "Yeah, that's truly something. Even coming straight out of HBS like she is, that's something."

"Well, not *straight* out of Harvard. She did earn her chops in Toronto." His eyes betrayed that he had not been told by Manijeh *why* she had left her position in Toronto, and Brett was committed to his oath of secrecy with Manijeh about the truth.

"Once she gets her registration, she'll be in her element," Brett finally replied.

"You know... Klein, Holdum, and French are *clients* of ours. Like literally our angel early adopter from way back when you wore Levi's bought at Value Village to boardrooms not to be different but because that was what you could afford. *That's* when they met us." He looked downward and fumbled with his spoon. "So, naturally I have to do this. I absolutely do *not* want to be *that* guy, but..."

"Rostam, VAI *pays you* to be *that* exact guy," he replied. "Do I need to sign something else? As long as Margaret—"

"No, no. She already made sure there was a clause in the case of eventual cohabitation," Rostam interjected. "The key word here is 'eventual.' Nobody was expecting things to move *this* quickly. But the paperwork's solid as it is right now, no more need for any of that. The recusal protocol stands, and nothing is amiss or a concern *per se*," he confirmed.

"Just be aware of paperwork and such, especially in any shared spaces you end up having. Using it only as an example, but her knowledge of our relationship with her employer must be that which she would have from her employer directly, and through us only in a personal context. I feel like an asshole saying this. I don't mean to be so invasive."

With his eyes closed, Brett went through the thin wireframe memories that were his suite and its various rooms and dedicated areas. His actual home office was in a locked, video-surveilled room with three weeks of digital loop time off premises, and he never put anything related to work anywhere but in that one room. He then realized that she did not have a similar room for her use, and he began to imagine how he might reconfigure his suite to accommodate her being able to carry work home with her at the end of the day.

"The trophy room," he finally declared.

"Pardon? Rostam returned as he accepted the check tray from the waiter.

"I can convert the trophy room into an office for her so she can have her own non-repudiable confidential space." He pulled out his Montblanc, pulled the customer's copy of the check from the tray Rostam was holding, and did a quick sketch of the layout of his suite. "On opposite sides of the master bedroom. They don't even share a wall."

"I think that flies," Rostam agreed.

"Okay. Anything else at all for me to sign?"

Rostam pushed the check tray over to Brett and then added, "Just sign for lunch."

"Closer always pays," Brett replied as he signed.

"And may you 'Always be closing,'" Rostam said. "And why is that?"

"Because coffee—the very best part of waking up—is for *closers*," Brett replied as he handed the signed credit card slip to the waiter. They soon both stood and started back to the office.

"And on to another matter," Rostam began when they were halfway to the main entrance of their building. "So let's talk about my *mother's* call now...."

Touched by Fortune's Shadow: a triptych

11

"She wants us to *what*?" Manijeh contested over her plate. Brett had made them both salmon, rice, and asparagus, and served it with the right authentically oaked chardonnay.

"To go over to their house for dinner. But *you* make it sound like a tooth drilling without Novocain," he noted with a wide grin. "This Saturday night."

She inhaled, closed her eyes, and a moment later, let out the air she had been holding in. "Do we *have* to?"

Brett cut off a small piece of salmon, put it to his mouth, and before beginning on it, said, "I suspect we kind of do. We've announced our cohabitation. Libations and shared cheer *must* ensue, or family will rebel." He started chewing while watching her face across the narrow of the walnut B&B Italia "Athos" table. "If you're uncomfortable because of what you mentioned before, this is not about asking for their approval or anything. This is about giving them access to our shared joy. If that makes any difference to your thinking on it."

Manijeh smiled enthusiastically. "When you put it like that, it takes off the bite, yes. I love them both to bits, and Rostam, too, but I very much enjoy my autonomy from their approval. But yes, I can share our joy, as you put it." She leaned and put her hand across the table, which he caressed before returning to his meal.

When they were done, Brett suggested they sit out on the inset balcony for a while. He turned on an electric heat lamp to keep the chill of April off them and then began to talk. "Have you thought about where you're going to work at home?"

After thirty seconds, she replied, "I was just assuming that I'd be piling it all on the kitchen table for a while," she said. "Piling all my papers on the table got me through UBC and Harvard and even Toronto."

He smiled. "It's no longer quite that simple, I'm afraid," he eventually offered. "Klein *et al.* are clients of VAI. And this won't be the first thing that will crop up. Compliance, confidentiality, guidelines, ethics firewalls between you and me, and a secure place to store paperwork offsite. It's quite a messy business if one has a messy business."

Her eyes lit up. "Oh! You mean all *that*! It will certainly get more complicated now that I think about it *that* way. Do you have any suggestions? Since you're the one who brought this up, I assume you have."

Brett leaned over and held both her hands in both his own and said, "It just so happens that I may have the room for you." He stood and led her to the walk-through closet that led to the ensuite. He pushed aside a number of his shirts that were hanging there, and behind this was a door with a numeric keypad for a door lock, into which he entered his code after signaling for Manijeh to avert her eyes.

"Now, the reason I don't want you to know *my* code to get into the trophy room is that you'll have your own, and we need a timestamped non-repudiable record of entry." Having said this, he stepped into the large room with her. On the far side was north north-facing window, and alone on the walls, were shelves holding the many years of his fencing trophies. On the walls also hung swords of some value, each labeled with its year and a brief history. Far in the corner, on a proper stand, were his *keikogi* and *hakama* with *katana* on full display.

"I never knew about this room!" she exclaimed. "Rostam never mentioned it. And he certainly described your place to the last Herringbone in the floors."

Brett put his hands in his pockets and kicked the ground, a coy expression on his face. "I've mentioned it to him, but he's never seen it. Except for the contractors who finished it, you're the only one who's seen *this* room."

"What's that?" she asked, noting the *keikogi* and *hakama*.

"Those are my formal *kenjutsu* attire," he explained. "My mother made those for me for ceremonies and demonstrations."

"*Kenjutsu?*"

"Well, in addition to fencing, which, as you've known for years, I do competitively, I am also a *kenjutsu deshi*, or student of *kenjutsu*, which is a Japanese martial art of the sword. It's not a competitive sport the way that fencing is. It's a blend of philosophy, culture, meditation, and martial discipline.

"I guess the closest thing you might think of it as is *samurai* swordsmanship, which is both a philosophical martial and non-martial discipline at the same that that has carried into our time. It's more than physicality of the sword and involves meditation and the pursuit of personal insight. It's one path to self-discipline and clarity."

Upon hearing this, Manijeh's smile shone. "All of this—all of who you have been since I've *known* you—and you want to turn this into my home office?" she asked, walking up to the north window, admiring the clear evening view it afforded her. "You're so generous, Brett, but there's no need to be self-effacing about it to the point of losing something so *meaningful* to you. I don't expect you to sacrifice so much."

"It needs some work to get all of the ergonomics of regular office-type use right," Brett replied as if it was no bother at all. "It already has a camera installed, which spares us the need to run any more cables. The closet portion at the door needs to be cleared up. I'm thinking of getting a contractor in to get this out of the way as soon as you give him the floor plan you want." He reached into his pocket and produced a small slip of paper. "And since it abuts the washroom plumbing on that wall, you can even have a self-replenishing water cooler, if you'd like. Hydration at all times."

He then directed her outside the room, closed the door, and typed a code into the lock. The light on the lock started to blink, and he turned around. "Put a seven-digit code into the keypad," he said. "Then press the number sign. I suggest you write down your number on the slip and keep it safe."

When he heard seven beeps, and then another of a different tone, followed by a final whir, he turned back around. "That's *your* code now. Don't even tell *me* what it is. The security company at the other end of the live connection, who keeps the video on loop, are the *only* people who know by whom and when this room is used."

"You've given me my very own PIN code for Easter!" she teased. "Kidding aside… I'm quite touched. I'll plan a *nice* home office to do the loss of access to your collection justice."

"What would please me most is for you to make it suit you and whatever it is *you* need to do, Manijeh," he said. "I'm not going to be going in there once it has been set up. Which is the whole point of this ethics firewall in the first place. It's for *your* eyes only."

Touched by Fortune's Shadow: a triptych

As they returned to the main living room area, she put her arms lightly around his forearm. "And what are you going to do with all those swords and trophies?" she asked. "I'm stealing your sense of pride just to turn a buck on trading."

Upon hearing this, he turned to face her, put both his arms around her waist, and gradually pulled her toward him. "I'll loan most of the blades to a museum for them to display to the public, and as for the trophies… it's time to put trophies away, don't you think? Rostam touched me out this morning after five double touches in a row," he bragged on her brother's behalf. "The torch is his to carry now. It's not about keeping a record of winning. It's about the music."

Manijeh stood on her toes and quickly kissed the tip of his nose. "Thanks for the office space, Brett. I'll do my best to not take it for granted."

"Time and space," he replied.

"Pardon?"

He turned to her and explained. "When I committed to you, I committed to sharing my time and my space with you. This is what that means in square feet." He made a gesture toward what would be her new workspace. "So… no kitchen table for you. Except for meals. The ones we don't eat at the counter or on the sofa, I mean."

She smiled and nodded her approval. "Or cards. Tables can be used to play cards."

"What say let's do a loop around the Lost Lagoon and then return here and get lost in one another?" he suggested, pointing in the direction of the foyer hallway.

"Oh yes, I could certainly use a good walk followed by getting lost in you." Since they were already standing in their closet, she found one of Brett's sweaters, threw it on, and said, "Maybe we can do a *few* laps if the mood takes us there."

"I'm always up for walking," he replied.

༺ • ༻

In his tailored Armani and lightly patterned burgundy silk Charvet French cuff, his neck under a golden paisley cravat, and his posture shielded at his fulcrum behind the Hermès buckle, Brett was ready to take on the evening. The Lobb polished black Oxfords were made for walnut, and he glided toward the entrance foyer and the coat closet, where he found Manijeh's saffron Chanel cape.

He returned to the living room and put it over her shoulders as she adjusted the contents of her blue clutch. Her red Manolo Blahnik heels matched her ensemble and her lipstick perfectly. The sparkle of her Omega watch matched that of her eyes and the shimmer along the slow wave of her shoulder-length hair.

"You look gorgeous," he said, kissing just enough to the side to miss her perfectly applied lipstick.

"As do you. Now let's not be late!" she said.

Touched by Fortune's Shadow: a triptych

Quinn Tyler Jackson

Vancouver, late October 1981

Touched by Fortune's Shadow: a triptych

12

The door to Rostam and Manijeh Yazdpour's parents' home loomed solidly before Brett Lloyd-Ronan, almost telling him to be sure to knock soundly lest he not be heard. He curled up his hand, knocked firmly, and waited. Within a minute, he could hear shuffling feet just at the other side of the entrance. A lock clicked, and the door opened a crack, revealing Rostam's eye, and then face as he opened the door more fully.

"Hey!" Rostam greeted his friend.

"Hey, Rostam!" Brett replied. He wasn't sure what to do next. "May I come in?" he asked.

At this, Rostam waved him in and called out in Persian, "*Mâmâ, Bâba! Dust-am injâ hast!*"[10] He motioned for Brett to come in, and then added, "Please, remove your shoes." He pointed at a diverse selection of slippers. "The green ones are for guests."

Brett removed his shoes, put them neatly on the rack, and put on a pair of slippers that best fit. "Thank you," he said as he snapped on his left slipper and was ready to proceed.

Standing at an archway to the main entrance were a tall man with a graying traditional Persian mustache, a woman who was clearly Mrs. Yazdpour, and to her side stood Manijeh, smiling and holding her hand up as if waving hello at her friend, but without actually moving her hand.

"Good afternoon, Mr. and Mrs. Yazdpour," Brett greeted them. "Thank you very much for inviting me to your lovely home for lunch. I hope you are well?" He stepped toward Mrs. Yazdpour and quickly pulled a small gift box from the bag he had been carrying with him.

---

[10] "Mom, Dad! My friend is here!"

"This is for you, Mrs. Yazdpour," he said as he presented it to her. He then pulled out a smaller box and handed it to Manijeh. "And this one is for you, Manijeh. I hope you like it." Finally, he offered his hand to Mr. Yazdpour, and said, "I am very pleased to finally meet you."

Rostam's father extended his hand to accept Brett's gesture and returned it in kind. "As are we! We are all very well, thank you. And I hope you found our place easily."

Mrs. Yazdpour insisted that they advance from the foyer to the salon, which they then quickly did. As they walked side by side, Rostam poked Brett lightly in the ribs to get his attention, and when Brett looked over at him, gave a discrete thumbs up to his new friend.

Brett accepted the seat he was offered as the whole family sat together on the couch. Mr. Yazdpour then left the living room and returned with a tray of what Brett could only think of as deserts. Some of them he had never tasted or seen before, and he planned an approach that would allow him to try a few without seeming greedy about it.

"*Befarma'id*!"[11] Mrs. Yazdpour said when the tray was on the coffee table. "Help yourself!"

At this critical junction, Brett had a decision to make: to reach for a treat first or to wait for the host. He knew that each culture had *its* way when it came to this delicate matter of etiquette, and he knew that the Yazdpours had been in Canada for only a few years, which left him unsure about what would be most polite. Rather than guess and be an embarrassment to Rostam and Manijeh in front of their parents, he settled on a compromise: a polite attempt at manners was better than no manners at all, even if it didn't quite fit. "If I may," he said as he reached for what he knew was called *halvah* but which he had never tasted before.

The moment his fingers touched the small treat, the others leaned in and took one of their own. From what he could tell of their collective reaction, he had followed the correct path by being the first to partake. "May I ask what it is you both do, Mr. and Mrs. Yazdpour?" he opened the conversation.

Manijeh jumped in to answer the question for her parents. "Mom's a nurse and Dad's a chemical engineer." She was very proud of her parents' accomplishments.

---

[11] "Please [help yourself]!"

"Rostam explained to me when he and I met that you are from Khorramshahr. Originally from Yazd?" he continued, acting as if it hadn't been Manijeh, but rather they, who had answered his question.

Manijeh sat with the small gift box sitting beside her on the couch, whereas Mrs. Yazdpour had carefully placed her gift on the coffee table.

"We—my wife and I—were both born in Yazd, as were the children. But my position with the oil company brought us into Khorramshahr before the Revolution and before the current war with Iraq," he replied.

Brett could see that the faces lost their glow on this topic, and immediately set out to correct his misjudgment of the topic for discussion. "Please… open your gifts!" he insisted with a huge smile and optimistic tone.

Both Manijeh and her mother carefully opened their small gift boxes. Their eyes lit up in concert at what they saw. Each had been given what most would have called precisely painted Easter eggs, had it not been for the extremely intricate Faravahar on each. Under the winged figure, in delicate lettering, it read, in Persian script:

پندار نیک، گفتار نیک، کردار نیک [12]

The eyes of both Manijeh and her mother lit up as they carefully examined what they had been given. Mrs. Yazdpour handed her egg to her husband, and Manijeh then gave hers to Rostam, and they, too, slowly turned the gifts in circles and said nothing. Though they were all silent, they were happy.

"Both of our cultures decorate eggshells, but for different celebrations. This year, your *Nowruz* and our *Easter* are both passed, since it's October now, but I wanted to make something you could keep for more than one *Haft-sin*."[13]

---

[12] "*Pendâr-e nik, goftâr-e nik, kerdâr-e nik.*" (lit. "Good thoughts; good words; good deeds.") A central tenet of Zoroastrian living.

[13] *Haft-sin* (lit. "Seven S's"), is a Persian New Year table display of seven items all beginning with S (*sin*), and often includes decorated eggs not unlike Easter eggs.

Touched by Fortune's Shadow: a triptych

"Make?" Mr. Yazdpour replied. "You *made* this yourself?" He examined it more closely. He tipped his glasses down, leaned forward on the sofa, and stared intently at Brett. "What do your parents do?"

"My mother is a seamstress, Sir, and my father is a master machinist," Brett replied, straightening his back slowly into full position as he did so and putting his shoulders back.

Mr. Yazdpour then put his eyeglasses on properly again and continued to examine the egg. As he slowly passed it back to his wife, he said, "This is a wonderful gift that you have made, Brett."

"It really is!" Manijeh agreed enthusiastically. "Thank you so much!" She carefully placed it back in its box. "Can you put this with yours somewhere safe?" she asked her mother. "It's a real eggshell. I never want it to break."

Mrs. Yazdpour nodded at her daughter as she took the small box. "I will certainly!" she replied.

"Master machinist and seamstress," Mr. Yazdpour repeated as he mulled over something in his mind. "Were either of them artists? Did you grow up around art?" He waved his hand as if to point out the many colorful pieces that surrounded them on the walls. "Mahnaz, my wife, did many of these you see here."

Brett immediately carefully wiped his hands with the napkin at his place, stood, and approached each piece with his hands locked behind his back. When he saw a feature that he enjoyed, or found technically exceptional, he noted it to his hosts. Finally, after a walk around, he looked directly at Mahnaz Yazdpour and said, "Mrs. Yazdpour, you have an exceptionally expressive style that reminds me quite clearly of Wassily Kandinsky, while still borrowing from the Persian miniature tradition."

Mahnaz Yazdpour turned to her husband, with a confused expression, and said, "*Ardashir-azizam, in pesar bacheh kist ke kar-e man râ bâ chenin basirati tamashâ mikonad?*"[14]

Brett folded his hands on his lap while holding a straight posture. He looked at Rostam, Manijeh, and Mr. Yazdpour in turn for some notion of what Mrs. Yazdpour had just said. Finally, Mr. Yazdpour spoke.

"Mahnaz expresses astonishment at your artistic ability and insight, given your *young age*," he said.

---

[14] "Ardashir, my love, who is this boy child who looks at my work so insightfully?"

Brett blushed profusely at this. He waited a moment and then explained, "I have been told by teachers and the pediatrician that I have 'precocious reading and comprehension.' I can also read *extremely* quickly. That's all. I read a great deal. My father says I ought to have a private pew at the local library."

"Hyperlexia?" Mahnaz asked. "Is that it?"

"Yes," Brett replied. "That's what the doctor says. I read *very* quickly and he says I also understand more than I probably *should*. There are some things I *wish* I didn't understand yet."

"He can also *swordfight*!" Manijeh declared with such glee that the room was instantly saturated with her enthusiasm.

Brett could feel his ears turning red from embarrassment. While he did not in any way feel *uneasy*, he preferred to avoid direct attention, especially from adults who for the first time discovered his precocity as the Yazdpour family just had. He thought at that moment that perhaps he might have simply *bought* a gift for Manijeh and Mahnaz, but after a flash of mild regret for putting a light to his face as he sat in their home, he pushed through his discomfort and said, "When I was seven, my father gave me the goal of selecting a martial art for self-defense and the defense of others. After some exploration, I chose fencing and my family has paid for my training."

Mr. Yazdpour started to nod at Brett's fuller explanation. "I understand the benefits of having a martial art. Especially from a young age. I have a first *dan* black-belt in judo myself. But why, if I may ask, did you settle on *fencing*?"

Since he'd been asked to explain his choice, Brett stood, walked to the foyer, found a decently sized umbrella, and called out, "May I?" as he pointed to it.

Mrs. Yazdpour nodded and Brett took the umbrella, acting out walking down the street with it almost like a cane, with enough exaggeration to almost bring Chaplin to mind. "I look pretty much defenseless."

"Watch *this* though," Manijeh said, tugging at her mother's arm and pointing at Brett.

"But then, someone suddenly reaches, lunges, or whatever, and… the whole situation gets *upended*…"

Within a quick flash, he was in position with the tip of the umbrella right where he wanted it to be. "I have one full sword length between whatever the opponent has to offer and my face, neck, and groin: my three most vulnerable points in hand-to-hand defense."

Touched by Fortune's Shadow: a triptych

He pointed along the length of the umbrella. "The entire length of this can be used to control the opponent, and I can hold it with both hands, giving me leverage and a great range of motion." He held up his arm and added, "If I fight hand-to-hand only, my forearms and hands, and maybe my feet if I want to risk being set off my balance, are my primary weapons, and they, too, are vulnerable like the other three points."

He again stood in position. "But with *this* in my hand—even an umbrella—I can maintain control without aggression, and without active aggression, the fire *may* simply blow out." Feeling that he had demonstrated what he came to show, he returned the umbrella, went back to his seat, and sat again. "That and I also study regular judo in case I don't happen to be carrying anything long and pointy, but I'm only third *kyu*."

Mr. Yazdpour leaned forward, reaching out his hand to shake Brett's. "Green belt! Welcome to our home. Call me Ardashir, please, Brett."

"And please call me Mahnaz," Mrs. Yazdpour added. "Let us eat lunch now and talk more."

"Just not about *me*, please!" Brett teased. He could see that Rostam was beside himself with pride that he'd brought his new friend home to meet his parents so soon in the school year.

"I want to know how you met! Something about getting a boot stuck in a creek is all I was able to figure out. Tell us all about that," she said as she motioned them toward the dining room.

Vancouver, May 1998

Touched by Fortune's Shadow: a triptych

13

"Do you mind at all if I smoke?" Ardashir Yazdpour asked, holding out a half-full pack to Brett, who took one out of politeness. Though he didn't smoke of his own accord, he never turned down an offered cigarette. Seeing that he'd taken one, Ardashir offered his lighter flame to Brett and then finished by lighting his own as they stood on the upper patio of his south-facing West Vancouver house.

Rostam, Taraneh, his date, Manijeh, and Mahnaz Yazdpour were all in the living room, having a conversation of their own. Ardashir had specifically asked to talk with Brett alone, so those in the other room maintained their distance out of earshot as they chatted outside.

"Just how many years has it been, Brett?" Ardashir asked a rhetorical question as he stroked his gray mustache as if trying to keep it from touching his cigarette. "Your eggs still are on display in our home." He reached over and patted him on the back. "You pretty much saved Rostam from that dark bout of depression he had after graduating university and then realizing that wasn't that life for him."

"That was an extremely *rough* time for him," Brett agreed. "But *here* we are."

At first, there was a still silence between the two men after this, as they remembered that period of everyone's life and how it had rattled their ambitions as Rostam adjusted to his revelations about not wanting to become an engineer. Finally, Ardashir spoke again. "Mahnaz and I are *very* pleased about you and Manijeh. And *very* happy for you both."

Brett was content that Ardashir outright stated this so that he wouldn't have to carefully dance around the conversation for the rest of their private talk. "I'm delighted to hear that you are both happy about this all. It's nice to hear you say it aloud."

"I knew it the day we all met at our home," he continued. "Touched in the head, that kid. But the *right* kind of touched in the head. Touched by light, not darkness. Mahnaz saw the same thing. We talked about you for two solid hours that night when you left; once the children were asleep and couldn't hear us."

Brett almost choked up. "I was equal parts Oscar Wilde and Charlie Chaplin back then."

"Back *then*?" Ardashir contested. "You have not changed in all these years. Not at all, except that now you have the full Oscar Wilde *budget* to go with the *attitude*."

"The budget certainly does keep me in nice wallpaper," Brett teased in return. "And flamboyant cravats."

"I'm going to tell you something the Yazdpours don't normally *ever* talk about," he said, taking a deep drag from his cigarette. "Once we talk about this tonight, please don't ever bring it up again if you can avoid it, as it is very painful to us all. But I want you to finally get some answers about *exactly* why we left Khorramshahr and then Iran when and how we did."

This topic was one that always drew silence from the entire Yazdpour family and Brett had learned many years before to avoid it at all costs and direct others away from it when he heard them asking. He knew to avoid it, but he had never learned exactly why from any of them.

"I drove every day from Khorramshahr to Abadan for my job with the oil company. This was back in the late seventies. Do you know of the Abadan Cinema Rex fire?"

Brett searched his mind for familiarity. "I was young and wouldn't have, I'm afraid."

Ardashir turned his head. His eyes were shiny with tears. "Back in mid-August of 1978, during the screening of a movie at Cinema Rex in Abadan, the theatre doors were locked, and an accelerant was likely used as well, and the theatre was set ablaze, killing more than three hundred souls, possibly five hundred. There were other signs, but it was the beginning of the end."

On hearing about this, Brett began to choke and cough on the cigarette, as the graphic account had caused him to accidentally lose his concentration and inhale the smoke. He placed his hand on Ardashir's left shoulder and squeezed through his shirt and a light cardigan. Though he knew it was an effect of the mind, he could almost feel the load this man had been carrying across just short of twenty years.

"The children's uncle Farokh—Mahnaz' brother and only sibling—and Parisa, his wife, and their two teenage children, the children's cousins, Fariba and Darius, were amongst the souls who perished." He hung his head very low.

"I have no words," Brett replied, hanging his head down.

"There *are* no words; there are only painful memories and trauma," Ardashir replied. After a long moment of naked silence, he continued, "Mahnaz and I *immediately* pooled our resources, paid whom we had to pay whatever we had to pay them, and fled to Turkey. This was just before Shah fled Iran and was exiled in early 1979, mind you. This was *well* before the hostage crisis. But we saw the writing on the wall and got the children out of there while we could.

"And now you know the burden our hearts endure as a family. Khorramshahr, Abadan, and other cities and towns were wiped from the map later on, more or less, during the eight years of war with Iraq that followed, as you're well aware since you met us during those years. Those places are still scarred and healing even now. Khorramshahr, called 'City of Blood,' was *eighty* percent destroyed, by some estimates. Just try to fathom that, even for a moment., and what that *means* in human terms."

For half a minute only breathing could be heard between them, until finally, Ardashir found enough strength and focus to finish recounting the Yazdpour family's journey. "For me, it was when we found out about the fire and the fate of our family that I stepped into secular humanism and away from the metaphysical. Mahnaz soon followed this path as well. With all respect to the many paths to personal truth.

"And now, here we are, living by Ambleside Park, jumping over fires with new friends, new family and old, and community every year, building new bonds of love and life here and now because we have nothing to return to in that land as ancient as Cyrus the Great's freeing of the Hebrews from the Babylonians. We honor our past but have *no* desire to return to it. Its best aspects travel with us and others like us. The rest can stay where we left it, frankly. This is our hope, anyway."

Unable to speak, Brett just took in a pained breath and exhaled the grief that had been released from Ardashir's mouth to his ears and heart. Finally, he said, "I understand why you kept this a private family matter for so many years. It is not something to be brought up lightly over a polite dinner. Thank you for finally sharing it with me. I won't mention it again."

"You are right: this is a *family* burden to carry," the aging man agreed. "And *you* are now family, so I figured it was time you knew." He again turned his head slightly, the weight of his message slowly beginning to lift from his face and his old familiar sparkle returning to his slate gray eyes.

"To answer your implied question, Ardashir, there has been no talk of marriage," Brett offered.

Ardashir put his arm around Brett's back and took a drag from his cigarette. "How did you know I was going to ask that out here, Brett? Can you read my mind now?"

"I have parents, too," he replied.

"You know, one of the things I appreciate about how this all came about is how you took time—as you always seem to do—to be careful with people's feelings. So if there hasn't yet been any talk of marriage, I am happy to know that you two are moving forward at your own pace, because I know that path will be a carefully measured and considered path."

"To answer the unasked question in what you just said," Brett then began, "I'm waiting until she feels established as a person in her new life and career before I ask. Whenever that is and however that manifests."

Ardashir squeezed his shoulder a little more firmly. "*That's* what I'm talking about, Brett. Long-term *intentions*. That's enough for me, and I never doubted it. May I tell Mahnaz?"

"Do you remember that time I soundly took you out in that judo match when I was just fifteen?" Brett asked.

"Oh, do I ever!"

"And do you remember how you asked me to *never* tell a soul about it?"

"Yes."

"Well, I haven't. Not *one*. Even though it would have been *sweet*. So I'm asking you to hold onto *this* one for yourself for now, while we just let everything settle down and can take time to admire the surface of the still pond of our current lives."

Ardashir turned to face Brett, held out his hand to shake, and said, "You have my word on it." He then added, "And rest assured that you have both our support. Your happiness is *our* happiness. I give my word on something else: we may ask you questions from time to time, but we will never second-guess the two of you. Your happiness is also *your* happiness. We'll support that as we can without meddling in it. I know that is all something that Manijeh demands, and we support her in this fully."

"I appreciate that very much, Ardashir, as I'm sure Manijeh would as well. So how's business been?" Brett asked.

Ardashir lit his second cigarette, and fortunately for Brett, did not offer him another, even though his had also finished. "It's good," he said. "Your father's recent tooling adjustments reduced structural wear and tear in several places that I'm pretty sure will let us get in a good bid and make a great profit on a decent project. That's just one in a dozen such situations that are going well these days."

⋙ • ⋘

"So, what do you think, man?" Rostam asked his friend as he leaned over his parents' patio railing.

Brett glanced over his left shoulder through the patio glass at Taraneh, Rostam's date for the night. "She's a truly *wonderful* conversationalist," he said. "Quite entertaining. *Amazing* sense of humor. She's also *stunning*."

Rostam nodded enthusiastically, smiling. "Brilliant, isn't she? She used to be a concert pianist and was a regular guest soloist with the VSO and others until two years back; she moved on to being a professional classical and jazz piano instructor from all that. Her Rachmaninoff is second to none."

"That's great. I *love* Rachmaninoff. Some of my favorite," he offered. "And you *know* my thing about Oscar Peterson!"

His friend's face ignited with excitement at this news. "Wow! I never knew that! I always took you for a *Bach* type." He flipped through his pocket, pulled out a pack of cigarettes, and lit up. "I think she's the *one*, man."

Brett rested his hand on Rostam's right shoulder. "How long have you known her? I didn't hear either of you talking about how you met tonight. And you've never so much as mentioned her to me before tonight."

After a moment, Rostam admitted, "Taraneh and I met in my third year at university. We were introduced by a classmate who mingled in both our circles."

Brett searched through his memories from around that time of their life. He was in Port Coquitlam in those years, the reason he'd avoided asking Manijeh out, and that also meant that he and Rostam met up and caught up less often during those years than they had before or after that dark time in the late eighties and early nineties. "It's the first time I've ever heard of her," he replied with a pronounced chuckle.

"We dated off and on, casually," he explained their history. "Her family is also Zoroastrian. Secular, like us. But then I hit that wall once I graduated, and we just grew out of touch over the following year. Nothing unsightly or ugly ever—just distance and time. No drama at all."

"Hey! Wait a second," Brett said, holding up his hand. "You mentioned the Symphony Orchestra. *She* performed that night I took Mom to the VSO with those tickets you gave me for my twenty-third birthday. Ah yes. She played Liszt." He listened to some remembered passages of her past performance in his mind's echo chamber. "I lost track of the name, but yes. Wow! Quite a pianist, indeed! World-class!"

"That's right! She and I had broken up by the time I got you those tickets, but I knew how much you and your mother loved piano, so there you have it."

"It's about space and time," Brett then changed the tack of the conversation. "Space and time."

"Hey?" Rostam asked, taking a drag from his cigarette.

"When we get into a relationship, then we commit some of our space and time to the other person," he explained. "How'd you get back in touch? Did you just run into one another by chance? Fill me in a little here."

"No, no, it wasn't just by chance," he said. "I looked up her parents' number and called them."

"Out of the blue?"

"You and Manijeh inspired me," he said. "I was so happy for you two, and I remembered how great Taraneh made me feel. Now I was out of the dark hole that my studies put me into. I have some stability with VAI, and you, and Mom and Dad. In a good place. So I just picked up the phone and used some elbow grease and dialed the number. They put her in touch with me right away."

From where he was, staring calmly into the pleasantly cool evening, Brett squeezed the railing, inhaled then exhaled three quick bursts in a row, and emptied his mind of all but the view before him and his friend. He cleared away the business details of the week, noted the stars that were visible before them, and accounted for some whose position he knew by instinct and memory, but could not see due to the current time of day and other visibility conditions.

"So what's your take, Brett?" His eyes betrayed his eager anticipation of his friend's opinion.

"I normally don't say these kinds of things about people and their relationships," Brett began. "*Even* when asked. You know that. It leads to all kinds of regretted early enthusiasm or cynicism, and then it leads to feeling like you're second-guessing other people's hearts at arm's length and nobody's typically the happier for it. But she's wonderful as near as I can tell and I'm not being polite because that would serve nobody here. And I *do* remember very, very well how *dark* those years were for you. If she shone through all of that darkness to you, so brightly that you chose her to call in your little black book—which I'm sure is overflowing with other options you just as easily could have called instead—then perhaps she *is* the one. Time will tell."

"Thank you so much, man!" Rostam exclaimed, giving his friend a tight, secure embrace.

"And I won't even make you sign any paperwork for it."

"*Touché!*"

As the two entered the living room, Taraneh called out to Rostam from her place on the vermilion sofa, "And what have you two been on about while we non-smokers are in here?"

"Rostam was just telling me that your Rachmaninoff is flawless," Brett only partly teased. "I attended your April 1993 performance with the VSO at Rostam's behest," he admitted. "But that particular night was Liszt's *Transcendental Études*, and your performance was *superb*. I hear you now teach?"

Taraneh smiled her gracious appreciation. "I have both my ARCT in Pedagogy and my Performance LRCM," she replied. "The VSO was an experience, but I prefer to pass it on than carry it on my shoulders under the concert performance lights. Have you studied piano formally at all?"

Brett replied, "My mom has Royal Irish Academy of Music, Grade 8, which she tested up to Royal Conservatory Grade 10 once arriving in Canada, and she taught me up to Grade 9. But since her stroke, of course she hasn't been able to help me advance to Grade 10."

"Oh, I'm so sorry to hear about her health," Taraneh said.

"Thank you. She's recovered now for the most part and isn't in any grief. Just a few changes. In any case, I haven't been at the piano with any seriousness for a while.."

She leaned forward toward him. "How long has it been since you last played, Brett?"

"Some time," he replied. "About a year."

Touched by Fortune's Shadow: a triptych

"Would you mind?" she asked, pointing at the Yazdpours' black baby grand Yamaha.

Brett looked quickly at his hosts' faces to judge their response, and when he saw they were both smiling at Taraneh's invitation for him to play, he walked to the piano, lifted the cover, and sat down. He closed his eyes, cast the golden netting of the sheet music before himself, and let his hands continue for him, without interpretation, playing Bach's "Prelude and Fugue No. 2 in C-Minor" to completion.

After Brett's performance, Taraneh slowly opened her eyes and smiled. "I think you are quite well enough along that you might want to consider pursuing Grade 10," she announced after about half a minute of silence had been allowed to pass.

"I appreciate your opinion," he replied. "I may do that yet. I could feel about five finger slips in my performance," he then said. "I have a lot of piano-specific mechanical strength and dexterity to catch up on in my hands."

"To be precise, you executed seven notable inaccuracies in finger placement, with only two resulting in significant deviations from the intended notes. After a year of not practicing at all, that is *completely* to be expected. On the remainder of the piece, your articulation was *impeccable*. You really might enjoy Grade 10."

Brett wiped down the keys, closed the cover, and then wiped that down as well. He stood and pushed the stool back into its proper place. "Thank you all for putting up with my infernal racket *so* patiently, everyone."

From that moment on the conversation jumped from topic to topic for the rest of the evening until Rostam and Taraneh left first, followed shortly thereafter by Brett and Manijeh.

"What did you and Dad talk about on the patio tonight?" Manijeh asked as they headed in the Lexus over the Lions Gate Bridge for Coal Harbor.

"Oh, mostly just a lot of blessing-giving and receiving," Brett replied. "The usual level of fishing expedition one expects."

"How about Rostam?" she asked.

"He's all wrapped up in Taraneh," he answered. "Says they used to date back in his UBC days."

After half a minute, Manijeh said, "I *thought* I recognized the name. I never met her back then, though. I was too busy doing my own thing. I remember the name now. That's funny that they'd start dating again after so much time like that."

Brett looked over at Manijeh, smiled, and said, "He says that *we* inspired him to look Taraneh up after all these years and give it a another try now that he's finally got his head more or less screwed on right."

"How delightful! We're inspiring! I love that! That said, however," she added, "I think you may have gained an *admirer* in her tonight."

"Polite dinner party conversation," Brett mildly contested.

"A third person can sometimes tell these things with higher fidelity than those right in the midst up to their neck in the bog of enraptured admiration," she insisted. "Your circumlocution and elocution are taking hold of me!"

"I'll be mindful in future," he finally ceded with a chuckle. "For now, it does feel nice to have inspired Rostam to seek out a past healthy relationship," Brett added as they continued along the narrow lane of the bridge toward Stanley Park, and from there, Coal Harbor. "That's where we might best focus our concerns, notwithstanding your *caveat*."

"Absolutely," Manijeh agreed. "You and I have already been down the road of the conversation that says I'm fine with whatever you do on your own time. You put a temporary moratorium on the open aspects that you brought up in the first place—that is for you to decide in your way.

"That said, I'm one hundred percent on Team Rostam on this one, so let's just be careful with people's lives and feelings, should my intuition be correct. You are, after all, akin to the *Huma*."

"Pardon? I'm not familiar. *Huma*?"

At this, Manijeh laughed gently, and returned, "The *Huma* is a legendary and mythical Persian bird of great beauty, mentioned by the Sufi poets, that is noble, alluring, compassionate, and lucky. A singleton; a *sui generis* like you. Sometimes it's called the Bird of Paradise. It never alights, always flying, and to see the *Huma* is *extremely* rare, but if its shadow falls on you, or it touches you, great fortune, even kingship or immortality, or at least a very long life, will fall upon you.

"It is said to land on the heads of those who then become kings. Or CEOs like Rostam, for instance. There you are, always flying, circling above your penthouse, watching over the North Shore and the Face of God. Bird of Paradise. Bringing others' wealth."

"Please do not flatter me, Manijeh. I am honestly really just a blue-collar bloke with great friends and exceptionally good luck."

Touched by Fortune's Shadow: a triptych

"The *Huma* is depicted ambiguously in terms of its gender, like the *sâqi* of Persian poetry, who pours the metaphysical wine of sheer ecstasy for the poet and is depicted as male, female, or genderless as suits the poet. The role they play transcends these things. And thus, you're my *Huma*," she returned simply, her gentle smile lingering as she turned back to the road. "Which means you're an attractive nuisance for others as well. They want the fortune you bring to hearts and coffers alike. Remember Hafiz' warning to only cast your shadow on those who know that a parrot transcends a sparrow. She was coveting you, or I can't read at middle-school level, let alone read people. You just don't *know* that. Stay gold, Ponyboy. Stay gold."

"Ah, from Persian lore to S. E. Hinton all in the tail end of a conversation. That is why I love you so," he said wistfully. As the words left his mouth from his heart for the first time in their relationship, they did so without his usual caution and care about his emotions getting the better of his tongue, and he quickly looked over to see how his indirect declaration of his love had fallen on Manijeh's ears and attention.

Her head was half turned in his direction, her eyes wide-a-shining, her smile extremely satisfied. She remained silent, but smiling, for the rest of the drive home.

On turning left into the parking gate, Brett looked over at her beside him in the front seat of the Lexus and he was completely at ease. Even in the dim light of the parking lanes as they descended underground, she was more beautiful to his eye than she had been the day before, her delicately curated and applied makeup as subtle as her confidence in herself and her form and frame, and in this all, he was content. He backed the coupe into his parking stall and turned off the engine. It was time to be two and together again in uninterrupted intimacy for the rest of the night.

14

Less than a month earlier, Manijeh Yazdpour had swiftly and intimately entered into Brett Lloyd-Ronan's previously cyclical, predictable life atop his harbor view, and in doing so, she had adjusted a number of his dials, habits, and decision path weights. She hadn't turned any dial far enough for him to consider any realignment within himself to be a compromise or concession; he was, however, finding himself over early coffee and meditation pondering matters that normally would not have drifted across the pond of his tranquility. His legs were crossed, his arms resting on the forearms against his legs, his eyes closed. He imagined the silver silk strands of steam rising from the coffee cup that sat before him on the mat he had placed on the terrace for his meditation. Onto the black wet surface of the coffee inside the mug, he projected networked trails and cones of distraction and futile paths to untruths, and as these touched the steaming surface, he imagined those concerns vanishing as vapor into the screams of the gulls that made it through his selectively penetrable perception of the sounds about him as he drifted the waves of his converging sense of tranquil lucidity.

The previous night, he had somehow allowed himself to admit to Manijeh's father that he intended to propose marriage to her when she had settled in her career and general personal life. By admitting this of his deepest ambitions to Ardashir, he had set a mental and emotional Newton's cradle into swing, and the next ball hit was his off-the-cuff confession and admission of love to Manijeh on the drive home.

What should have been a scented moment in a fine restaurant over the best cuisine and wine, was instead a simple casual aside during a broader after-dinner session of friendly banter. He did not regret it, but he did wish it had been at a more mindful moment.

Touched by Fortune's Shadow: a triptych

To his delight, Manijeh's response was a happy one, and of matters of her heart he was certain that she was well in her serenity, but in matters of his own self-discipline and emotional self-control, he was very concerned.

Why had she called him her *Huma*? There was no wisdom on his pond, only ripples and probabilities and eventually, at the end of the fibers that now melted into the coffee's steam, imperfect uncertainties. What value had such false idols as the general human capacity for wisdom, let alone his proven track record of holding so little in his breast? No, there was no wisdom; all wisdom is hubris. What there *could* be, however, was *intent* and *benevolence*. Good thoughts; good words; good deeds. With many dozens of amendments and corrections to update the model of what was to about to justly be called damaged-goods, adjusted after new experience and insight. Not wise. Benevolent.

Like a *kintsugi* bowl, broken and then repaired with gold and lacquer along the cracks, he accepted, thanked, and then released all the broken places and the shards they produced, breathed out the momentary pain of grieving their release this morning, and admired the new and now perfect cup that took yesterday's broken vessel's place.

His meditation done, without opening his eyes, he reached down to his coffee, lifted it to his lip, and sipped. At this, his eyes shot open, and he was ready for the new day. He lifted the *katana*, which had been placed with the handle to the right, placing it on his right hip as he was standing. He entered the code for his office, went inside, placed the *katana* with its *wakizashi* partner, with the blade up and handle left, and locked his office.

When he returned to the kitchen, he noted that Manijeh was seated at the counter with a full glass of orange juice. "Good morning!" she greeted him.

He smiled and replied in kind.

"You meditate with your sword?" she asked, clearly from having seen him that morning.

"Only on Sunday mornings," he replied. "Other days I just meditate at the counter or table or sofa. I meditate with my actual *katana*, not a display weapon," he added an explanation. "So I only take it off camera as little as possible."

After a quick sip of her juice, she asked over the top of her glass, "Have you ever had to … ?"

"Fight for real?" he asked. "With steel rather than wood?"

"Other than Willard back in elementary, I mean." Her eyes sparkled as he knew only hers could.

Brett went to the fridge, grabbed the orange juice pitcher, and poured himself half a glass of juice. "The true goal of *kenjutsu* is not martial victory, but reconciliation and harmony. I have drilled many cycles of the *kata* and I have done demonstration combat with live steel that came as close as dexterity, choreography, and good sense permit, but, I've fortunately always found other ways to reconcile with others than steel outside of those controlled settings. Besides that, it is a disrespect to the *katana* to not use it properly, and so, in a world that resolves its matters peacefully and with diplomacy at all times unless provoked beyond choice, anything more than ceremonial uses of the *katana* would be considered disrespect in a modern context."

"You wove your explanation like a silk carpet," she replied.

"It's one of those topics that can't help but come up. I think of it like this. Let's say I have my *katana* on and someone breaks in. I have two choices: pull my *katana* and stand my ground or offer him one thousand dollars to leave. I would offer the money."

"It seems rational in a hypothetical scenario like this, sure," she agreed.

"But some will ask, 'Let's say the burglar wants *more* money to leave. At what point *do* you pull your sword?'"

Manijeh nodded. "That's a tough question," she agreed. "Those swords of yours, if used as they're designed to be, can *easily* take the burglar's life. The moment the sword is drawn, it is a possibility that it *will* be used. So the question is not how much you are willing to give in ransom to have him leave, but at how much value you are willing to judge a human life."

"Indeed. If *anything* else at all can be a solution, it must be, instead of drawing live steel. This applies to much of life and is not about swords. It's a necessary point of meditation once in a while." He then added, "I'd jab him with an umbrella. Or even a pointy stick. But I'd never draw steel to protect only money."

"Do you have any ideas for what we can do today?" she asked.

"Personally, I think would enjoy taking some fresh air."

Brett turned to face her, leaned in, and kissed her right cheek. "I'm a creature of habit," he finally said. "A walk around the Seawall on a Sunday after morning meditation, and breakfast out at a café along the way seems like it might make a good new *shared* Sunday morning habit. What do you say to that?"

Touched by Fortune's Shadow: a triptych

Manijeh smiled. "It's worth a shot trying to get hooked! One could get hooked on worse things," she added. "By the way—" She cut herself off and then used her right index to motion him to stand closer to her. When he was close enough to her, his face almost touching hers, she whispered....

"I love you, too, Brett." Her lips met his and their kiss caught a fire of its own, until she pulled back and said, "But thanks for saying it *first*. It meant a lot to me to hear it from you first. That put to delightful rest an ache inside me I've been carrying for some time now."

Brett put his arms around her and pulled her to himself until she was as close as a hug could comfortably put her, and he said, "*Man to râ dust daram.*"[15]

"In Persian, too? Why are you *such* a perfectionist?" Manijeh teased him. She made a fanning gesture over her heart as if nearing a faint.

"It hides my many flaws," he returned.

ଈ • ଈ

Across the table from him at the Prospect Point Restaurant, Manijeh, in her spring morning walk attire, brought a sense of heat to his core, to his bones, behind the cool surface of the face he had tamed over years to be still. Indeed, people could even now once in a while say something that made him blush with embarrassment, but these were temporary flashes. She made the smile behind whatever look happened to be displayed on his face struggle for release in his joy.

"Close your eyes for a moment," he requested. When she did so, he continued. "Now, imagine a metal ball bearing rolling along a winding track, around, down, but always on the track. Nod when you have it in your mind."

After a few moments, Manijeh nodded, smiling fully.

"Now open your eyes," he said. When she did, Brett said, "That is what it was like for me the moment you phoned me from the airport. The moment I first saw your face after so many years. The moment we danced into my bedroom that first time and made love like the world was nearing its end. The moment you asked me to go steady."

Manijeh took a sip from her glass of Perrier and said, "I'm intrigued to know how this demonstration will end."

---

[15] "I love you."

He reached his arm across the table, offering his hand to her, which she took in hers before he continued to speak. "I was a metal ball, cold and hard, rolling along metal tracks, cold and hard and *statically fixed*. They appear to wind and turn and thrust the ball about, but it is a toy. A *game*. A demonstration in a physics class pointing at gravity or inertia or momentum. But then…" He closed his eyes and reopened them with some exaggeration.

"… but then I opened my eyes to life and saw *you* there. And suddenly, things weren't so *sure*. Did the ball that had been rolling along so precisely all these *years* fall from the rails? Did it stop altogether? I couldn't know, because when I closed my eyes again this morning, I saw simply a broken coffee cup in need of repair."

Her voice seemed concerned when she replied, "Broken? Like *smashed*? I don't feel smashed."

"Not in any dramatic sense," he assured her. "We all break a little bit, every day we're breathing. Life chips us, bends us, or at least tries to bend us and we crack and split as we resist, rather than bend with the force life is putting against our journey's path."

"Yes, it does hammer away at us at times, I agree." She took another sip of her drink, her gaze intently on him. "Case in point being Toronto."

"*Kintsugi*, the Japanese art of repairing a broken bowl with gold so that it is new and better than before it broke, is how I usually begin my Sundays and is why I meditate so intently, especially then. It restores me to push through the contusions and to re-engineer what that patina means in the larger picture."

He squeezed her hand. "I'm coming to accept that the track I was running on before simply will not *do* anymore. There are new turns, new possibilities, and new concerns, now that you are part of my life, and there must be similar consequences in your concept of where you wish to be and who you see yourself as becoming, on many levels."

She nodded in the affirmative. "Yes, I've certainly thought about what these things mean to *my* plans. After fleeing Toronto, of course, I also had to be sure I wasn't just running into your arms because they—well, I'll admit it, damn it—they wrap around me and make me feel *safe* and *shielded* and *protected* from the world like the day you put that stick to Willard's throat and wouldn't let him so much as *utter* another hateful word.

"Your arms wrapped around me are like being touched by the wings of the *Huma*. I hear a Women's Studies professor in my mind rightfully chastising me for this line of feeling."

Touched by Fortune's Shadow: a triptych

Manijeh then stared directly into Brett's eyes, quietly gazing at his soul, and as she did so, she smiled as if journeying along her memories of them across the time they knew one another. She then continued to speak.

"But this need to feel safe and just whomever it is who makes us feel that way in our own life *transcends* gender roles, just as with the *Huma* and *sâqi*. So I'll stand by it *for myself* and how I feel about things. It's how I feel. It's how you make me feel."

"It's fine to want to feel safe. You know you can run your own life autonomously; you've done a great job of that to this point. You've duly earned your *Sudreh* and *Kusti*[16] and needn't prove anything more."

"I don't have any answers for deeper questions than the next month or so, and I'm okay with that for the time being," she said. "I plan to keep enjoying a good and happy life with you, without taking anything right in front of me for granted."

Hearing this, Brett reached deep into his chest with his resolve and pulled the words fighting every inch of the way from his heart to his mouth, his calculations of how long he should wait now utterly meaningless to the time kept by his thunderously crashing heartbeat. He needed to ask her.

"Manijeh-*jânam*,[17] would you consider doing me the honor of marrying me? In June of next year?"

Manijeh's fork, which she had been playing with her left hand, made a metallic sound against the plate under it as her hand contracted from surprise. Her eyes could not have shown any more delight than they now displayed for all the room to notice, as her right hand slid to sit on top of Brett's and squeezed the back of his hand firmly.

"Honestly," Brett finally continued after almost a minute of silence, "I considered waiting until you were settled more fully into your life and career before asking. That would have been the ball-bearing rolling on the tracks version of me. Shouldn't you know, as soon as I know, where my heart is with our life together, so you can make decisions for yourself about how that might impact *your* life?

---

[16] "You've earned your *Sudreh* and *Kusti*…" The *Sudreh* (sacred undershirt) and *Kusti* (sacred cord) are granted to Zoroastrians after the *Navjote* coming-of-age ritual, signifying that their arrival into adulthood.

[17] Manijeh-*jânam* (lit. "Manijeh, my dear/soul").

"Ought I go on for a whole year holding my tongue, letting you wonder about my view of our what-should-be-shared story?" He put his left hand over hers and cupped her hand in both of his. "So I decided it best to let you know where my heart rests here and now, when it may matter more immediately to how you may frame your decisions about things. Life is what happens to us while we are making other plans."

"First off, I'm so flattered and *completely* caught off guard by your proposal that it's almost embarrassing," she began to reply. "Second, I have one important question to ask." She paused for him to acknowledge this request.

"Ask."

"It's my *only* question, so think carefully before you reply."

"You've asked for my careful consideration, and I promise I'll not rush to answer you," he pledged.

"When did you *know* you love me?"

On this question, Brett softly pulled his hands away from hers at the center of the table and reached into the left inner pocket of the light jacket he had hung on the back of his seat. He pulled out a time-yellowed envelope, addressed to Manijeh Yazdpour at a UBC dorm address. His own previous Port Coquitlam address was under his name on the top left of the envelope, which was still sealed and stamped, but without the post office cancellation stamp; it had never been sent. He slowly pushed it to her hand, which was still near the middle of the between them.

Manijeh took the envelope, used a butter knife to open it, pulled out three sheets of folded, aging paper, and began to read what Brett had last seen when he'd written it years before, but still, he trusted his memory well enough to not have opened and reread it first before showing Manijeh. As she read, her face flushed and changed expressions, and she periodically looked up to watch Brett's face for a moment, only then returning to her reading. Finally done, she placed the letter from the early nineties back into its envelope, and then put the envelope into her purse. "Now that you've *finally* delivered this letter, it's *mine to keep*," she insisted.[18]

"Yours to keep," he fully agreed, trying to gauge from her expression anything at all about her inner world at that very moment. He was unable to discern what she may be feeling after having read his words.

---

[18] See "An Unsent Declaration of Love," in the Coda for the full letter.

"I have to say," she eventually began to speak, "that three more vulnerable pages of declaration of love for another soul I have only rarely read, and *never* addressed to me. And the use of a fountain pen makes me sentimental since that's what we learned to write with back in my early school days in Iran." She smiled with her entire face at this moment. "I was not expecting such a deep and *sincere* answer to my question. I shan't show a soul what you've given me today, as I understand the intimacy of your vulnerability, and I know you intended this only for my eyes."

"It presents the *best* answer to your question," he replied. "I pushed through my intense feelings back then, not by denying them to myself, but by not putting them at the center of my focus, to make progress in life as best made sense at the time." He let the weight of years be released. "I can't do that anymore and wouldn't if I could. Things have changed."

"Have they ever!" she replied.

Brett paid the check and the two headed to the Point along the Seawall. Once there, Manijeh finally spoke. "Ask *again*, here," she said, waving her hand toward the ocean. "At the place you call the Face of God. Ask *here*."

Brett Lloyd-Ronan held Manijeh Yazdpour's hands in his own, standing with his back to the wind, staring into her slate-gray eyes as they searched his face for the truth. He brushed her soft, shiny hair over her left ear and asked her in as faithful a tone to his feelings as he could muster into speech in as few words as needed: "Manijeh Yazdpour, will you marry me?"

She smiled, stood on her toes, leaned her mouth to his ear, and replied, "Yes, of course I will." She kissed his neck and put her arms around him under his jacket, which he had forgotten to zip up before leaving the restaurant. Her warm embrace brought him to himself, to the very place they were, and he held her also in his arms there on the path.

A loud clack from Newton's cradle hitting against the next ball of steel in the network of cause and effect, from his admission of intent to Ardashir, to his declaration of love to her as they drove the night before, to the proposal at the Point, to showing her the one document in all Creation that spoke of his heart, as it had been fixed upon her star during a lonely, painful time stuck at a blue-collar job that would never release its grip upon his social agency, each of these spheres had passed energy and activation on to the next, and he again finally felt centered.

"In case you ever wondered back in the day what would have happened if you *had* sent that letter you gave me today," she assured him, "I would have most definitely come running into your arms back then, too, Brett."

"Even with the state of my finances being what it was then?" he asked.

"*Eshq pul nist*,"[19] she replied simply.

For the moment, for the day, for this instant with her arms wrapped around him and his about her at the Face of God at the Seawall's Prospect Point, he had ecstatic clarity, and in this, he knew he had certainly done the right thing by not listening to longstanding habits and practical calculations before listening to his own immutable heart.

---

[19] "Love is not money."

Touched by Fortune's Shadow: a triptych

15

"So, Brett, have you considered what I asked you about yet?" *Shodai Soke* Hashimoto asked from across the table.

Brett looked down at an angle, to avoid his teacher's direct gaze, and said, "*Soke* Hashimoto. It would truly be an immense honor to accept certification as *Menkyo Kaiden*,[20] especially given my extremely young age of only twenty-eight, but my whole life will be changing permanently soon, and my lifestyle will have some new commitments that make any teaching and mentoring difficult to honor properly and respectfully. I do not wish my reach to exceed my grasp, and thus disappoint you."

His teacher was quiet for a long time, and then he laughed very lightly. "I'm not getting any younger, Brett! I suggest you accept it *now* and work out those details of your future calendar *later*. After eighteen unbroken years under my supervision, your commitment to *kenjutsu* is not in any question, even if you have this new 'lifestyle' coming up.

"This all can only be for the overall good. Come out of the dank cave and mossy grotto when you're *ready* to teach. I am not at all unreasonable or out of touch with how life works around here in Vancouver, with the high cost of living and the need to focus on careers outside of teaching martial arts on a full-time basis. All of that said, I feel that you are too accomplished to miss this chance for advancement on your path; you were ready for this long ago. Your *calendar* doesn't decide who's ready for the *Menkyo Kaiden*. I *alone* do. And I say you are ready *now*."

---

[20] *Menkyo Kaiden* (lit. "license of complete transmission") is a traditional Japanese martial arts certificate that permits one to teach and pass on the tradition and skills of the martial art, such as *kenjutsu*. It provides certification of complete mastery of both the techniques and principles within a specific school's tradition. This certificate is also used in other traditional Japanese martial arts disciplines for the same purpose.

Touched by Fortune's Shadow: a triptych

Embarrassed at being both praised and gently chided by his teacher, Brett choked to find words as his face flushed bright red around his cheeks and ears, but he finally conceded to him, realizing fully that any further protest at this point would be extremely rude given this high estimation of him. Coming from a *sensei* this would have been nice to hear, but coming from the *Shodai Soke*, the sole and final authority of matters in the school he had founded, this was an implicit endorsement with potential implications for his lifelong journey with *kenjutsu*.

"I will accept your generous offer of the *Menkyo Kaiden*," Brett returned. "I will endeavor to live up to your high estimation of my ability and knowledge and bring honor and continued respect to *Shinpo Nagare-ryu*."[21]

"Wonderful, Brett! I'll present your certificate on the second Saturday of next month," Hashimoto announced. "Now, tell me… why has your life changed so quickly that you will have no time to teach? That's just *not* like you! And I've known you since you were a ten-year-old stick!"

"I've become engaged to marry," Brett answered simply.

The *Soke* started to laugh from glee. "You? Of *all* people!" He put his hand over his heart as if feeling for a heartbeat. "I'm still alive. That's great, Brett. Who is she?"

"Do you remember Rostam, my business partner, whom I introduced to you at the recruiting demonstration?"

"Two years ago. Yes."

"His sister, Manijeh. I've known her since I was a kid, just like I've known him. I met her a *year* after I met you, *Soke*."

Soke Hashimoto stood, and immediately when he did so, Brett jumped almost straight and then gave him a *saikeirei*, or full, held bow. The *Soke* walked slowly toward him, put out his hand to shake, and said, "Congratulations on your newfound happiness, Brett. You have always had contentment; now may you have *happiness*. May I tell Mrs. Hashimoto?"

"Of course," Brett replied as he accepted his teacher's hand and shook it firmly.

"When are you thinking?"

"June next year," he replied.

---

[21] *Shinpo Nagare-ryu* (lit. "Advancing Stream Style/School"), also known as "The School of Advancing Flow," is a branch of *kenjutsu* founded by Hashimoto, who is the *Shodai Soke*. As the school's founder, Hashimoto serves as the final judge of the conduct and transmission of the tradition under his oversight.

"I'm looking forward to it," he invited himself. "If you elope before then, I expect postcards."

"Of course!"

"Second Saturday of next month. Wear only your very best, *Sensei* Lloyd-Ronan. I want to see your parents watching you accept your honor. Be *sure* to invite them. And invite your fiancée and her parents, and her brother and anyone he wishes to bring."

"I will, *Soke* Hashimoto," Brett agreed.

"And it is *very* important to be sure to bring with you the *Heiko-kai daisho*. I will have *Tenku wo Kiru* as well."[22]

"The first time *Heiko-kai* and *Tenku wo Kiru* will be in the same place together since my father presented them to us."

"Let's give them something to remember on their reunion," Hashimoto replied.

※•※

On returning home after four loops around the Lost Lagoon, Brett and Manijeh sat on the balcony, each with a steaming cup of hot chocolate. They then sat in silence for some time, until Manijeh asked a question.

"About your sword," she began. "Why is it that you don't want it off-camera?" She took a sip, clearly found it still to be too hot, and then started blowing on the drink.

"Pardon?"

"You said you don't take it out of your office more than once a week, so it won't be off camera. Is it really expensive? You got me all curious."

Following Manijeh's lead, Brett blew on his drink before even attempting to sip it. "It's one of a kind," he replied.

"How so?" she asked.

"My father made the set," he replied. "It's high-carbon steel, and specifically an alloy he owns the patent on since he's the sole inventor. It's a prototype. It's priceless to me because my father made it to commemorate his firm commitment to his and my relationship, and I therefore treat it with respect and care."

"Oh! Wow!" she smiled. "It sounds like invention runs in your family."

---

[22] *Heiko-kai daisho* (lit. "the cycle of balance sword pair") implies that Brett's personal *daisho* (sword pair) has been given a unique name. *Soke* Hashimoto's *daisho* is named *Tenku wo Kiru* (lit. "Cuts the Sky/Heavens").

Touched by Fortune's Shadow: a triptych

The drink's having finally cooled enough, he took a sip before continuing. "So I keep it on camera because it's priceless to me. Well, technically, my set is the first of two sets, since Dad made two *daisho*. Mine and *Soke* Hashimoto's. Which reminds me… I am soon to be presented with a *Menkyo Kaiden* certificate. You, your parents, Rostam, and Taraneh, have been explicitly invited to attend the ceremony. It's to be the second Saturday of June."

"Brett, I'm utterly *lost* in all the new words," she admitted. "Farsi, English, French, and now Japanese, as well? Please… have mercy on me!"

"There are no *belts* in Hashimoto's school, but rather, a traditional certificate system is used to grant rank and standing in the *kenjutsu* community at large. The *Menkyo Kaiden* is the highest certificate and denotes *complete* knowledge of all aspects of the school, both in technique and philosophy, which will make me a *sensei*. In this *Ryu*, or school, only the *Kaiden* or the *Soke* can teach without higher review. Everyone else is a student. This sounds like authoritarianism, perhaps, but is actually to protect the *ryu* in its first generation, since *Soke* Hashimoto founded this *ryu* and in its first generation wants to have more direct oversight to assure consistency. So, this allows me to pass on the tradition and gives me the full authority, backed by the *Soke*, to teach and certify others, and those certifications are in turn recognized."

"A *sensei*! Now there's a word I can get my head around." After putting her cup down, Manijeh stood, approached him, and kissed his forehead. "Congratulations! And thank you for the guided tour through the organizational stuff."

"Thank you," he replied. He, too, stood and embraced her. "I was somewhat concerned when I was told all the specifics, though," he added.

"Oh?" Her eyes betrayed her curiosity.

He sat down again and continued. "When I protested I would not have any time to teach because my life is going to changing because I'm going to be getting married, Hashimoto acted a tad *off*. The *Shodai Soke* is the head of the school—the whole modified style of *kenjutsu* that he has developed. Over the years, his *ryu* was eventually certified as his innovations gained credibility and his *kata* proved out over time."

"Ah, so he carries the responsibility to pass it on," Manijeh observed. "And must be careful who he hands the torch."

"Yes," Brett replied. "That's *exactly* it. It's ultimately a very serious matter of his *legacy* and *kenjutsu* tradition overall."

104

"That is somewhat… hesitation inspiring," Manijeh agreed.
"It's *very* important at the level he's proposing to promote me that I teach and continue to pass on not only the overall *kenjutsu* traditions—keeping with tradition in most things is expected—but also those modifications and *kata* that were developed by the *Soke*, so that they aren't a historical blip. Only his son in Ottawa and a small handful of others have *ever* been promoted to *Menkyo Kaiden* by *Soke* Hashimoto; he's been *extremely* conservative."

"I see. You're worried you won't have time to pass on that legacy, so you tried to politely refuse the honor? To avoid not doing it justice due to lack of time? Seems a fair thing to bring up to him." She placed her hand on his shoulder, as if she understood how hard that must have been to do, given how many years of his life he had given to sword mastery.

"Exactly. But he *insisted* I should accept it and just let the other matters be for now, as if it were *urgent*. Said I would get to teaching when the time came. That he didn't have forever to promote me. That's the part that got me concerned."

Manijeh immediately started nodding her head. "Oh. I see now. That's an unwelcome omen. But, you know, to be more optimistic, sometimes people just talk like that as they grow older. Kind of like how some people end everything with *ensh-Allah* in the Persian community just to cover all their bases should things go awry. Then they end up outliving everyone around them."

Brett stood back up and held her again. "I'll try to not read too much into it. It's just that I've trained under him since I was ten. Even before I met you and Rostam."

"I've known about the fencing and judo since forever. This *kenjutsu* stuff, not so much."

"Rostam only found out about it two years back."

"Why so quiet?"

"My Zen garden, I guess," he replied.

"Why are you letting me in now?" she asked.

Brett looked into her eyes and smiled. Finally, he answered her question with one of his, "Why did I keep you out in the first place?"

She put her left hand on his shoulder and her right palm on the left side of his neck and kissed his chin and then his lower lip. "You know what else you've kept a secret?" she asked while taking a break to breathe.

"What else?" he asked, his breathing and his heartbeat racing from her kiss.

"You never said just *why* you've spent your whole life turning yourself into a *samurai* warrior. You're one of the *gentlest* people I know. Your ability with maths is top tier. You don't need me to tell you that; you've made a lot of people a lot of money with your quant brain. But you just don't sing martial master—at least not until you snap into action. I guess I'm saying, what's with the alter ego you've been carrying around all these years?"

"First off," he began, with a *faux*-cocky tone, "I'm not a *samurai*; I'm a *ronin*. Robin, Ronin Hood."

"Are you avoiding the topic by trying to be insufferably cute? Because it's working…"

He straightened his back, triggering several joint cracking sounds, and then cleared his throat with a rumble in his chest. "When I was just seven years old, I was involved in something terrifying. Afterward, my father told me to take lessons in any self-defense I chose, two if need be, until I found one or two that I was willing to commit to. He encouraged me and paid for the classes, even though we were pretty tight on cash at times."

"Seven? Something *terrifying*? At that age?"

Brett walked over to the railing and looked over to the bridge to his left. "I was with a childhood friend one winter. Richard. We were walking along, kicking snow around. Richard was ten, I was seven. It was night." He motioned for her to come to stand to his right so he could put his arm around her and feel her soft warmth against him, and soon, he found the strength to continue with his account.

"Richard spotted a young girl. No older than either of us. Aggressive idiot that he was, he started throwing snowballs at her from a distance despite my very loud protestations." Brett sighed deeply. "And he hit her in the head with a very icy snowball. She fell, got up, and ran away screaming and crying. I felt like a complete jackass for being anywhere near any of this, so I kicked Richard in the leg and scolded him. But he didn't give a damn and insisted we keep marching down the lamp-lit snowy streets of Burnaby."

Manijeh put her arm around his waist very tightly and said, "Richard sounds like a complete asshole."

Without skipping a breath, Brett replied, "Yes."

"What happened? I'm assuming there's more to this nasty childhood story." Her eyes shone even in the levels of light out on the terrace, pools of soothing regard.

"The girl's older brother, and his entourage of teenage male friends, hunted us down in the streets looking to cause a world of hurt." He could feel her shudder, and the night breeze was particularly warm this night, so he assumed it was not from the temperature.

From this explanation, Manijeh asked him outright, "Did you two get beaten up?"

From his chest, Brett forced a cough as he went over the incident in his mind. He removed his sweater and then slid off his polo shirt. Along his left side, at about the height of his heart, he placed Manijeh's hand on his bare skin. "Can you feel the scar?"

Manijeh gasped, pulled her hand slowly away, leaned more closely toward him to better see, and held her breath until her delayed breathing all released in a single gust. "I assumed that was from a fencing accident. I noticed it while we were making love that very first time, of course. But I didn't think…" She leaned and kissed the scar repeatedly.

"You think just fine. It *should* be from a fencing accident. That's a reasonable thing to think. Richard, however, didn't think. They all had switchblades on them and absolutely no hesitation whatsoever about using them on us."

At this, Manijeh's eyes went even wider than they had been. "What happened to… ?"

With a solemn turn of his head, hanging, and his eyes closed, he said, "It's *quite* grotesque."

She put his sweater over his shoulders, pulled him in for a close hug, and said, "You know that the Yazdpours have been through our share of the 'quite grotesque.' What happened to Richard?"

"The crew cornered us up against the stairwell of a house where we had tried to hide. They came into the yard, a circle of them, five in all, and the girl's brother confronted us, asking if we threw the ice ball at his little sister's head. I kept my mouth shut. Richard not so much."

"And?"

"He spouted something offensive at them and then the pack of them came at us with switchblades in their hands. The next thing I knew, I woke up in the hospital."

Manijeh reaffirmed her grasp around him. "Terrifying."

"Richard didn't wake up."

Her body sagged for a moment, and then she regained her composure. "That's *so* horrible."

Touched by Fortune's Shadow: a triptych

"After I was stabbed once, which missed my heart by half an inch, the girl's brother called out for the others to leave me alone and focus on Richard. I was flashing in and out of reality from shock at this point, but I did hear him say, 'My sister told me you tried to stop your idiot friend, so I'm letting you skate free. This time.' Then I passed out."

"When I recovered, Dad committed to putting me through martial arts training, my choice of which. I chose judo and fencing."

"It all makes much more sense now that you've told me about this," she said. "*So* much more about you falls right into place now. Were they ever caught?"

Brett nodded in the negative. "It was all dealt with under the Juvenile Delinquents Act. There was lots of deeply unpleasant courtroom stuff for the adults to attend which all just ultimately resulted in short stints and sealed records. Richard's parents served more years over this than the lot who did it served. I doubt *they'll* ever get over it. I'm *still* serving time over it," he said, pointing at his left ribcage. "It *remade* me."

"Anway, a few years later, the year before I met you, *Soke* Hashimoto visited the fencing club, seeking recruits who might wish to move on to his *kenjutsu dojo*. He watched me compete, and then approached me and my father and offered me a place in his *dojo*. He *insisted* that I should continue to pursue judo and fencing. So I pursued all three. I realized years later that he insisted I continue to take these because despite his conservatism in *cultural* matters, when it comes to *technique*, he's actually quite a progressive, believing in interdisciplinary modifications to the *kata*, the choreographed forms that serve as the basis of our flow and conditioning, as well as our mental focus points."

He swept his arms from left to right over the beautiful night vista. "And here we are. You and I met in 1981, so you know much of the rest. The making of a blue-collar *ronin*."

"Why *ronin*? Why not *samurai*?"

"You mean other than the fact that it jives with my double-barreled surname?" he teased.

"Other than that," she played along. "Why did you pick the dark, tortured sword-for-hire?"

"At the end of the day, when the ceremony's done, the only title I'll have earned will be that of *sensei*. *Samurai* and *ronin* are notions *long* since put aside with respect and are symbolic."

"You earned the title 'Chief Analyst,'" she gently corrected him. "I helped you study for the CFA, remember?" She smiled.

"Indeed you did. I will always be in your debt for that, too. But I'm referring to Japanese titles. Of the two, it is the *ronin*, the 'one adrift' who is masterless."

"Aren't they considered *mercenaries* or something?" she asked. "That's the part that I'm not getting my head around."

"To be masterless, and adrift, doesn't necessarily mean one *must* be a mercenary. Miyamoto Musashi, the greatest *ronin*, who wrote *The Book of Five Rings*, has given us more wisdom than many with more worthy titles than 'one afloat.'"

"And we *all* know what you feel about ownership. How do you reconcile this with how you treat the *Soke*? How does your current relationship as a student change when you become a *sensei*, in this specific aspect?"

Brett collected his thoughts before replying, "Becoming a *sensei* changes the dynamics, but it doesn't sever the ties that were formed through years of learning and growing under the *Soke*'s guidance. I may no longer be his direct student, but there's a continuous exchange of respect and knowledge.

"As for ownership and mastery, becoming a *sensei* myself means I will assume responsibility for my students and the teachings, yet I remain a student of the art in a broader sense. The philosophy that I have fully embraced—much like the *ronin*'s independence—emphasizes freedom and the ongoing journey of learning, not the possession of title. So, while my *role* changes, my respect for the *Soke* and what he represents in my life remains unaltered. In this framework, one shows obedience out of *respect for their wisdom and mastery* not from their *masterhood*. If we wish to learn, we trust our teachers. When we wish to push away our teacher, the time has come either to learn another way or to learn why this feeling arises in us. It's about carrying forward the legacy, not holding a title. A teacher *toward* mastery is not a master *over* others."

Manijeh Yazdpour kissed Brett Lloyd-Ronan repeatedly on the lips, her affection perfuming the night air. "Thank you for explaining your long journey to healing," she said.

"I've been quiet about this side of my life," Brett replied. "There were some loose strings that needed tying. Now you know why I have dedicated so much to these three martial arts, and why these three specifically and not something else. And why from such a *young* age."

Touched by Fortune's Shadow: a triptych

"From the day you took down Willard to now, I have always admired, but *never* fully comprehended, your relationship with swordsmanship and why it was so central to your entire way of going about things. Thank you for *finally* tying that string for me. It all falls into place. Well, let's be honest—not *all* of it makes sense yet—enough falls into place for now and the foreseeable future. Which is maybe—*what*—next week? That's about how far I'm able to foresee lately."

Part Two: *Scire*

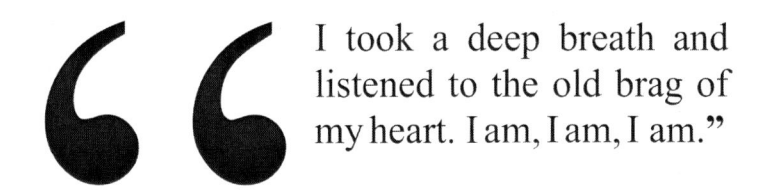

" I took a deep breath and listened to the old brag of my heart. I am, I am, I am."

—**Sylvia Plath,** *The Bell Jar*

Touched by Fortune's Shadow: a triptych

Vancouver, June 1998

Touched by Fortune's Shadow: a triptych

16

"Violence is *never* the answer. Sometimes, it is a *solution*. But it is *never, ever* the answer. *Kenjutsu* is where that lesson is learned, and its meaning uncovered.

"Rectitude, courage, benevolence, respect, honor, loyalty, and self-control. Those are the Way of the Warrior. You *will* find answers in these qualities, if you practice them, live them, meditate upon them, and seek to nurture them in your own conduct and existence. But *where* in this list is *violence*? You won't find it on this list because the Seven Virtues do not *include* violence.

"Do not be deceived by what you see in movies about who the martial artist is. *Kenjutsu* is not a sport or path to violence."

Soke Hashimoto stood on the mat of the *dojo*, attired in his best *keikogi*, emblazoned with the emblems of the *Shinpo Nagare-ryu*, the school he had founded. His *katana*, from the *daisho* pair named *Tenku wo Kiru*, hung at his left hip. To his right, stood Brett Lloyd-Ronan and another two students who were to be promoted, but to lesser certificates than Brett.

The atmosphere in the *dojo* was charged with anticipation and solemnity as the many students and other attendees quietly observed the ceremony. *Soke* Hashimoto began to speak, his voice steady and imbued with the weight of his experience.

"Today, we stand at a crossroads of tradition and progress," Hashimoto continued, his gaze sweeping over the audience, ensuring every word was absorbed. "The martial path is fraught with *contradictions*. It teaches us to fight, yet it insists—above *all* else—that we seek *peace*. It equips us with the *tools* for violence, yet it commands us to use them only as a *last* resort and asks us to meditate and find indomitable inner peace. This paradox is at the heart of our way—the way of *Shinpo Nagare-ryu*. For those who aren't familiar, our name means 'School of the *Advancing* Flow.'

"We are a school of tradition afloat in the river of our ever-advancing world. We adapt... with respect. We hold firm on immutable truths, but we do not hastily declare what those truths are, and instead let the living world we inhabit negotiate with us what they are. And so we are always willing to adjust and modify with respect and only after consideration and validation."

He paused, allowing his words to sink in, before turning his attention to Brett, who stood attentive, his posture a reflection of the discipline and respect instilled in him over many years of rigorous training.

"*Sensei* Brett Lloyd-Ronan," Soke Hashimoto addressed him directly, his tone softening with evident pride. "Your journey to this moment has been marked by dedication, resilience, and an unwavering commitment to the principles of our school for over *eighteen years* of uninterrupted, disciplined learning, as my *chokudeshi*.[23] You are here now as a testimony to that dedication, and with you are friends and family who have been beside you. Over these years, you have not only mastered the techniques and philosophical foundations, but you have also embodied the advancing spirit of *Shinpo Nagare-ryu*."

Brett, feeling the weight of Hashimoto's words, bowed deeply. The *Soke* then turned to his left, laying a hand on the hilt of *Tenku wo Kiru*. With deliberate motions, he drew the *katana*, the blade gleaming under the *dojo's* lights—a symbol of razor-sharp clarity and purpose.

"As we prepare to demonstrate the *kata*, or choreographed form, specifically tuned to *Tenku wo Kiru* and its cousin, *Heiko-kai, Sensei* Lloyd-Ronan's *katana*, of the same steel made by the same master swordsmith, Arthur Lloyd-Ronan-*san*, the *sensei's* father, let us remember that each movement, each *breath*, is an affirmation of our commitment to the path of the warrior. A path that always seeks *harmony*, even as it prepares for life's *unending* stream of conflict."

An assistant quickly drew a rope across the length of the mat and yelled, "*Shinken shobu! Kiken na tame, seiza ni ite kudasai!*" and then in English, "Real sword combat! Please remain seated for your safety!"

---

[23] *chokudeshi* (lit. "direct student"), a direct disciple who is trained and mentored directly by the master, rather than through *sens*ei who might normally take on these duties at the *dojo*.

Soke Hashimoto faced the room with a solemn gaze. Two assistants, students also slated for promotion, carried in a stand with two *tameshigiri*, tightly rolled *tatami* mats that had been soaked, designed to approximate the density and resistance of flesh and bone. He carefully slid his *katana* back into its *saya*, and then, after a glance over each shoulder to ensure the area was clear, in a seamless motion—executing *iaijutsu*—one of the *tameshigiri* was cleaved in half at an angle chosen in the moment. Hashimoto then stepped aside, allowing Brett to position himself before the stand. Mirroring his teacher's template, Brett drew his *katana* in a swift, fluid arc, and the second rolled-up mat fell in two pieces, split cleanly without any hesitation in the arc of his swing, at exactly the angle the Soke had selected at random. He had publicly shown his harmony with the *Soke's* technique and absolute precision and the ceremony could proceed.

With that, *Soke* Hashimoto then stepped back, positioning himself opposite Brett. The two other students carried away the debris from the sword test, stepped aside, and discretely removed themselves from the mat, providing them with space for the demonstration. The room fell into a hushed silence, the only sound the gentle rustling of *keikogi* as each man moved to his starting position and mentally prepared themselves to be as flawless in their next actions as the gravity of losing their concentration demanded of them. It was a requirement of *Soke* Hashimoto's *Ryu* that the candidate execute perfect *shinken shobu* before witnesses to be fully granted promotion to *Kaiden*, as it was felt by the *Soke* that no *sensei* who had not actually tasted the responsibility of the utmost expression of *kenjutsu* could truly know why such care in honoring the passage of the knowledge needed to be taken to protect life and limb.

When they were in position and ready to begin the *kata*, *Soke* Hashimoto called out in a commanding voice to all those present at the ceremony, "*Aiuchi no Ken kata—Hajime!*"[24]

---

[24] "Form of the Mutually Striking Swords—begin!" This customized *kata*, designed specifically for a pair of matching custom *katanas*, not only refers to the two equally balanced swords used in the demonstration but also underscores the extensive sword-to-sword contact characteristic of this form. Moreover, as Brett is set to be promoted to *Menkyo Kaiden* status following this *kata*, the choice of name subtly emphasizes the evolving dynamic between him and the *Soke*, marking a formalized transition from a master-student relationship to one of equivalence.

Touched by Fortune's Shadow: a triptych

The *kata* they performed was a precise and fluid series of movements, a dance of controlled power and grace that spoke to the years of practice and dedication behind each motion. It was a display of martial prowess, but also of a deeper understanding—a communication beyond words of the values and philosophies underpinning their art. It had been modified by the *Soke* to accommodate the balance point, weight, and particularities of the Lloyd-Ronan high-carbon steel alloy as manifested in these exact dueling cousins, and these parts of the bespoke *kata* had been shown in excruciating detail by Hashimoto to Brett before the demonstration, and this was the reason he had asked specifically that both sets of the blades Brett's father had made be brought to the certificate ceremony.

To a bystander, every motion had the appearance of true and potentially lethal combat, and this was accented by the fact that the custom *kata* had been designed by Hashimoto to differentiate and exhibit the particular martial values of the *katana* as much as possible, given the setting of the display.

As the demonstration ended, *Soke* Hashimoto sheathed *Tenku wo Kiru* with a single smooth, practiced motion and Brett followed suit respectfully with *Heiko-kai*. The *Soke* faced Brett once more, they turned toward one another and bowed deeply. After this, they turned in synchronized time and bowed to the audience. Brett remained in his bow with his hands upturned in front of him as he looked down, held in position to receive the scroll that would establish his *bona fides* amongst the larger world-wide *kenjutsu* community.

"This sealed *Menkyo Kaiden* certificate that we are about to present," *Soke* Hashimoto announced, gesturing to the scroll held by an assistant, "is not just a recognition of *skill*. It is a mandate to carry forward the legacy of *Shinpo Nagare-ryu*. To teach, to guide, to advance the forms as the world around us changes, and, above all, to uphold the principle that violence is *never* the answer."

Upon receiving the scroll, Brett again bowed to the *Soke*, and again to the audience, his hands still out with the scroll in them. He then said firmly enough to be heard through the room, "*Kono meiyo o mamorimasu*. I will protect this honor." An assistant then took the scroll from him, put it in a Paulownia wood box to keep the paper safe, and handed it back to him respectfully.

The ceremony continued with the presentation of certificates to the other students, each moment imbued with the traditions and values that made *Shinpo Nagare-ryu*. As the assembly applauded their achievements, the sense of community and shared purpose was palpable—a reminder that the martial path, with all its seeming contradictions, was also a path of connection and growth.

When the end of the formal portion of the event was declared and everyone was invited to stay and socialize, Brett was finally able to approach Manijeh and the others, who had been sitting in a small, dedicated set of folding chairs to one side. Manijeh walked most quickly of them and gave him a respectful hug.

"I can't believe it. I've never in my life ever imagined *that*. Pointy sticks in the ravine and umbrellas in the living room that was *not*." She held his hand and smiled. "That was *amazing*." Her eyes sparkled as much as they had the day he had Willard the bully's Adam's apple at the sharp end of a long stick. "And the sound when the swords connected and slid along one another's blades! Wow!"

"Thank you." Brett smiled at Manijeh and then turned to greet the others who were right behind her. "As beautiful as that was—and it felt wonderful—the level of true combat movements in that *kata* is rare for a very *good* reason. There's *zero* room for error when one thrusts and swings at those velocities in close quarters. And that's why we cannot teach until we can handle *that*. My adrenaline is still on high alert."

"As is mine!" she agreed, then leaning in and whispering, "We'll figure that out later."

He first hugged his mother, Siobhan, and then shook his father's hand. "I never thought I'd see the day those two sets were up against one another," Arthur commented. "Did you *hear* that? You two were *both* smashing sixes out there. Bloody good cricket, that was!"

"Oh, I heard it," Brett replied. "Just like water hissing in a kettle when those two blades dance the *tsubazeriai*."[25]

"Some ready kettle, indeed!" Siobhan agreed.

---

[25] *Tsubazeriai* (lit. "hilt touching") a moment in *kenjutsu* combat when opponents' blades lock together, often leading to a close-quarters struggle for dominance. During this exchange, blades often touch at high pressure and may slide blade-to-blade for much of the length of the *katana*.

Rostam stood forward next. "Congratulations, man! I swear you're *still* holding back on me when we fence. All these years later." He then embraced him in a hug. "But I don't care. After seeing you up there tonight, Brett, I'm glad you're holding back, believe me."

"That was quite spectacular!" Taraneh interjected. She took Brett's hand, shook it lightly, and then added, "You've managed to keep all your piano fingers after eighteen years of *that*?"

"Demonstrations of *shinken shobu* like *that* one are very, very rare," he said. "Normally for that level of complexity and momentum as seen in the *kata* you witnessed, we'd have used *bokken*, the wooden swords, rather than live steel. So my fingers are safe most days. *Soke* Hashimoto and I rehearsed extensively all last week, so I could keep my finger attached." He pointed at his ring finger and the polished silver engagement band upon it.

At this point, Ardashir and Mahnaz approached him in unison. "It's amazing what one can achieve with a *very* sharp umbrella," Ardashir said with a chuckle, causing Mahnaz also to smile. "*Mobarak!*"

Brett felt a gentle hand on his shoulder. He turned to look and saw that it was the *Soke*, who had his other hand on Arthur Lloyd-Ronan's shoulder. "Everyone, I must borrow these two gentlemen for just a moment. I will return them to you shortly." He smiled and led Brett and his father out of the other's earshot.

"Do you see those four men over there? In navy blue suits. Japanese men."

Without staring, Brett and Arthur quickly glanced over, and Brett nodded that he saw them.

"They are all *unofficially* here because of your work, Mr. Lloyd-Ronan."

"I don't understand," Arthur replied.

"They're with Cultural Affairs, and specifically, I asked them to *consider* beginning the process of possibly authorizing your alloy to be used in registered *nihonto*."[26] He smiled at some guests, to show that he wasn't ignoring the crowd. "Come with me," he then directed. They followed him as he approached the men from the Agency.

"Nakamura-*san*," the *Soke* addressed one of the gentlemen.

---

[26] *nihonto* (lit. "traditional Japanese sword")

Mr. Nakamura bowed deeply to the three men, followed almost immediately by his companions. In turn, the *Soke*, Brett, and Arthur returned the respect.

"Arthur Lloyd-Ronan-*san*!" Mr. Nakamura then began. "We watched the *kata* with your steel. We've also already examined and admired Hashimoto-*soke*'s *daisho* in some great detail. Let me say that you are *clearly* a master swordsmith. I saw it already in your work, but today, I could *hear it in the steel*," he explained, pointing at his ears, one with each hand.

"You honor me, Nakamura-*san*!" Arthur replied.

"I heard that you invented this high-grade carbon steel alloy specifically for the two *daisho* that you made? And that you were granted a patent for this alloy?"

"It was a project for my son," he replied. "I wanted him and *Soke* Hashimoto to have the best I could produce, and so there was no room to just *look* beautiful but then go and use bad steel. I patented it when I was done in order to make the matter more exclusive. I have patents in other areas of machining."

"Is there any reason you did not use *tamahagane*,[27] Lloyd-Ronan-*san*?" one of the other men asked.

Arthur smiled. "I have *great* respect for methods such as *tatara* smelting, Mr. ...."

"Suzuki *desu*," the man supplied his name.

"As I said, Suzuki-*san*, I have very much respect for *tatara* smelting, and have made prototypes using this steel, but I wanted an alloy created by a uniform, consistent, reproducible process. I am a master machinist, after all, and this is what I do. So I designed an alloy that allowed the artistic freedom inherent in *katana* making to fall into areas other than the blade composition. This leaves creative freedom for the hilts, for instance. As for the actual blade, I wanted to obtain uniform results *regardless* of *who* poured the melt."

"So you already had the idea of producing more swords in mind?" Nakamura asked. "Did you document the entire process from alloy to finished *daisho*? The number and kind of folds, and other technical matters?" Nakamura asked. When he did, his companions' eyes and ears went to obvious attention.

---

[27] *tamahagane* (lit. "jewel steel"), a traditional Japanese steel used to craft nihonto (Japanese swords), produced through the labor-intensive *tatara* smelting process. *Tatara* smelting is an ancient Japanese method of making steel by heating iron sand and charcoal in a clay furnace until the metal fuses.

"Yes, of course," Arthur said. "That's the *only* way to make two swords, let alone two sets of two. I guess it's hard to beat the training out of me: old-school master machinists such as myself tend to like to build things in ways that they can hand them over to others and have them repeated to the letter."

"Could you make two more of these *daisho*?" Nakamura asked. "I'll be as direct as I can since there are many guests here today and we shouldn't steal their time or much more of yours. We'd like to investigate allowing these exquisite works to be given special consideration. Unofficially for now, and to not set expectations beyond what can be delivered, we caution you to remember that this is a very traditional, conservative matter of cultural preservation, and thus we cannot overstate that we make no promises. But we *are* quite serious about this. Especially if there are practical benefits."

Brett knew that his father understood what a rare honor that would be, given the heavy regulation of *nihonto* in Japan. For one, it would perhaps allow him to sell them directly to the Japanese *kenjutsu* market. With *Soke* Hashimoto's specialized *kata* to accommodate the weight, balance, and swing of this sword, he would be contributing to the Advancing Flow of the *Ryu* tangibly.

"I would be absolutely *honored*. I'll start the two sets right away. I only ask that they be returned to me and the end of the whole process."

"Of course, Lloyd-Ronan-*san*! We will treat them with the utmost respect they deserve and get them safely back to you when we have done our investigation."

The four men bowed again and bid their leave. When the three men were alone, *Soke* Hashimoto said, leaning toward the other men, "From what I can tell from testing with my *daisho*, this alloy is impervious to chipping in normal use, maintains its edge superbly at full force against even a cousin blade, and … did you hear it *sing* tonight?"

Brett and Arthur both nodded. "Even though we practiced the *kata* last week, I was *not* expecting that sound. Manijeh also noticed it. With just that extra bit of force from the presentation adrenalin, the steel *chanted*."

"The esthetics of that alone might convince them once they have a few weeks with your *katana*," the *Soke* said. "Keep me up to date when you have another two sets."

"What was that about?" Manijeh asked.

"Some potentially good news for Dad," he replied.

"Really? At *your* ceremony? *Az âsemân oftâdeh!*"[28]
"They are considering his patented alloy for use in making *nihonto*, traditional Japanese swords, a *highly* regulated matter. It may not pan out, but it's an honor to even have it under unofficial consideration. Fingers crossed."
She looked confused.
"It's more or less a *he-shoots-he-scores* moment for Dad," Brett explained.
"It's busy and crowded around here," she said. "I'll be able to understand it all better later when we have some peace and quiet to talk about it later." Manijeh then smiled. "But I can figure out enough to know that it is an awesome moment for your father," she said before returning to the polite conversation she had been having with the others.

---

[28] "*Az âsemân oftâdeh!*" (lit. "That fell from the sky!"), "That came from out of nowhere!"

Touched by Fortune's Shadow: a triptych

17

Brett took the box Manijeh had passed him on their Sunday morning walk around the Seawall, which they had started this time by first crossing over to Second Beach via the Lost Lagoon. That she had waited until they were at Prospect Point to hand it to him told him something of the level of importance she had put behind the gift.

He carefully opened the box, discovering that it contained a Rolex GMT-Master II, with rose gold finishing on the signature bezel. He took off his modest Casio F-91W, put it into the box, and then put the strap of the Rolex around his wrist. He presented his arm with the watch atop his wrist to her when she gestured, and she secured the strap to fit.

"A small gift for your glorious achievement last night," she said, punctuating it with the click that came with fastening the strap. "We were *all* so impressed. I'm *still* breathless."

The watch now secure on his arm, feeling a perfect weight there, he put his arms around her and held her close in the light breeze. "Thank you so much, Manijeh. Any particular reason you chose the GMT?"

Manijeh readied herself to speak and replied, "I chose it on the assumption that you and I will be doing a lot of travel together in Europe once my registration goes through and Klein *et al.* start sending me to London and Paris. You *can* develop models on your laptop, can't you?" she asked with a smile. "By the way, after staring at your left hand there, I remembered how last night you enthusiastically pointed out to Taraneh your ring finger has an engagement ring on it."

"You noticed me do that? Something so…"

"… trivial? Yes, of course, I noticed you pointing it out to Taraneh. What was *that* about? The whole interaction seemed a bit *performative* in the moment, from my point of view."

125

"I was taking your advice," Brett admitted. "I reinforced that you and I have announced our engagement, and she might place her eyes on some other *Huma*. Like Rostam."

"Some might take it as a *challenge* rather than as a *gate*," Manijeh cautioned.

"We'll see. Was there any news at all on the progress of your registration?" he asked, motioning for them to resume their walk as he held his left arm out to see the time. "This is truly a *lovely* gift. The fact that it's a GMT is spot on."

"It pairs with the Omega Constellation nicely," she agreed. "I felt you needed something to commemorate last night, and to represent all the swords you loaned to the museum and lost sight of." She held his hand as they walked. "According to Charles Holdum, all my background checks and such have been processed favorably, but there are some administrative loose ends. I don't remember that from my Ontario registration, but maybe it was all done on the lay low, and I was just never told about any of that background administrative process."

"That's a big pain in the ass," Brett said. "It might not have been that thorough in Toronto because of several differences in the situation for you now. Perhaps because you're going to be doing international trade, in both Europe and America as well? That's Rostam's field. I'm just a quantitative analyst with a penchant for writing computer code; I mostly try to stay out of all the detailed international persnickety hoo-ha."

"International persnickety hoo-ha? I *love* that. I want it to say that on my license. 'The bearer of this document is authorized to persnick your hoo-ha.'" She squeezed his hand again and picked up the pace of their walk. "Oh my… that has quite a hearty *ring* to it, don't you agree?"

"Reality and biases being what they are," Brett then added after a strong chuckle, "there may be myriad reasons for all the time this is taking. First, you live with me. Your dad's Ardashir, a prominent businessman with business connections outside the usual beaten path, who is also a major non-voting shareholder in Mind Flame Holdings due to his extensive early-stage funding there. And your brother is Rostam, connected to all this in his own equally complex ways. The scrutiny is *high*."

"Why does it have to be so complicated?" she asked.

"It's a complex compliance web of relationships that must be vetted. I'm guessing here, of course. In practice, there may be chicken entrails involved. Or coin flipping. I don't know."

After waiting a long moment for all these variables to be considered, Brett then continued, "Margaret Kaur is the Chief Compliance Officer at VAI. You may have met her back when you did your stint with us. She came on in your second year. But I don't know if you've met her, she rarely comes into the office. She does things like look over home office floor plans to make sure VAI is always proactively in compliance and not at risk of falling out, which would sink us pretty fast in our trust-based niche. Taken as a whole, things like this may simply have put tar into your gears and slowed down the process."

Manijeh sighed deeply and said, "I can wait. Everyone's happy with me doing what I'm doing now, and I'm getting a good sense of what I'm in for once I have the license. So I can wait. They don't seem in any rush for it to arrive."

"A good idea. Hurry up and wait. It covers a multitude of other people's sloth," he agreed.

"The fridge got filled Friday. Let's put together a wicked brunch, get naked, and celebrate all afternoon," she suggested.

The two of them walked hand in hand the rest of the way home without feeling the need to say much more. While walking, Brett couldn't help but check the current time on his new watch just to feel its weight on his arm before the sensation went away with familiarity. Manijeh's hand felt good in his. The air smelled good to breathe. Hurry up and wait. *Carpe diem sed finem respice.* When maxims rang of truth, they did so spectacularly, and he was happy for it.

Touched by Fortune's Shadow: a triptych

18

Exactly at what moment in life Brett Lloyd-Ronan realized that Monday morning at a work desk was the often the same for the white-collar and blue-collar worker alike, accounting for what the definition of what a *work desk* could be for any particular person—from an actual desk to a yard in need of landscaping—he could no longer exactly recall, but as he stared at the instantiations of adjustments for the market price of risk, the responsibility squarely on his shoulders for any coefficients of adjustment he introduced, he knew absolutely that it did not matter what his percentage ownership in Mind Flame Holdings, the separate and insulated parent of the subsidiary Vector Affinity Insights was. His requirement of due diligence was at least as high, since the cost of egregious failure, also as impactful, given that the digits on the screen represented, even though sometimes in a derived or abstract sense, was other people's money. Of all the riskiest things to handle, other peoples' money was the most so.

A fool and money may soon be parted, but certainly no one enjoys playing the fool. Years growing up in blue-collar scarcity taught him keenly how those numbers made people behave at one end of the scale, and years in finance had given him a clear idea of how this changed when the stakes increased. Good friends who owed forty dollars changed sides of the street when they were less than flush, rather than have an uncomfortable greeting, and its implied IOU; how much more so when the amounts were in the six figures or greater.

The numbers themselves were abstractions; the concepts involved drove the entire machine, from the check at the café table paid Dutch, to crushing corporate debt under Commission review. It felt the cautious thing to do to be careful with something people felt they knew so exceptionally well but could only define with any clarity when they lost it.

Touched by Fortune's Shadow: a triptych

While he had heard that some enjoyed this level of internal tension, it was necessary friction in his estimation, but the true joy came from breaking through invisible walls that before his investigations, nobody had yet declared as even *existing*. Here he sat on the Monday morning following the weekend of his *kenjutsu* certificate ceremony, wearing his new watch gifted by Manijeh, and this Monday was more than just something that must be patiently endured.

As adjustments for the market price of risk vanished into the mists of validation runs, signed off and approved, he progressed to model-driven hedging at dynamically determined change-point intervals. These, too, passed tests and this left him sitting at quarter to noon, according to a glance at his wrist, ready to call Rostam into his office. With a few buttons on the phone, he'd called his line directly.

"Come look," Brett teased and hung up.

Rostam's head popped around the doorframe. "What's up?"

"Come here, come here." He made a wide inviting motion for Rostam to come and look at his monitor.

"Okay. Shoot."

Brett said, very precisely, "This hedging model was trained on de-identified portfolio K. Standard stock, yes?"

"Good old portfolio K. Okay. Your model pulls some nice confidence intervals and weighted accuracies. Looks decent, but don't we have others that do *better* on K than this?" He put his hand on Brett's shoulder as if he were consoling him, given the sound of his voice.

"But wait," Brett insisted. He clicked a button that read K+1 and within ten seconds, new run results and new metrics appeared aside from those of the prior run.

"Did you…? Is that…?"

"Automatic model retraining in near real-time when market conditions *and* measured risks fluctuate, which is exactly what K+1 denotes, a real-time market disruption moment. Dynamic model adjustment to present market conditions."

"How does it all generalize? You surely knew *that* question was coming." His face was excited, but still had the necessary skepticism that made him the CEO.

"That question is *always* coming," Brett agreed. He pushed a button marked L, and then another marked M. Their residuals displayed, and he said, "Trained on K, retooled on K+1, results against datasets L and M. *You* tell *me* how well it generalizes."

But keep this in mind: L is more like K in shape and M is more like L+1 in shape, so effectively the model that comes out after adjustment accommodates *both* market states, not just the new one, and should the new state be but a perturbance…"

"… the model can already account for a self-correction without the cost of retraining," Rostam finished the thought. "It does what you used to waste your time doing. Your *clone*, as it were." He then blurted: "Dolly!"

"Can I get an *amen*?"

Rostam walked over to Brett's liquor cabinet and pulled out the single malt. He poured a small shot into each of the two tumblers, and brought them over to Brett, who then stood, as he toasted, "To… what are we going to *call* this new shiny object we've put in our box of tricks? I'm never any good at naming this kind of thing."

"Adaptive vector attunement," Brett said.

"Sounds as dry as my throat in a meeting," he said, but then Rostam raised his tumbler again and toasted, "To adaptive vector attunement. And all that it represents. Seems we *have* figured out a way to clone you, after all." He then coughed theatrically and asked, "Is this a patent-level thing? What do you think? My mind always gets into a back-and-forth whenever it comes time to think about this topic."

"It will be soon," Brett replied. "But we may also just wish to keep it in the vault."

"Write it up for posterity in an IP memo and get me and Gerry a copy, flagged as ACP. We'll figure out the part about it being patent-worthy or trade-secret material as we move along. We have a GC for a reason. Gerry *loves* your IP memoranda."

"Sounds good!"

"Say, Taraneh is dropping by the office and she and I are going to Taf's for a light bite to eat and a bit of small talk. What say you come along?"

"Sounds good," Brett replied. "What time we aiming for?" he asked, flashing his watch to check the current time.

"The reservation's for twelve-thirty. *Yowch*! Since when do *you* wear *that* kind of metal? Wow."

"Manijeh gave it to me yesterday," Brett replied proudly. "To commemorate my *kenjutsu* promotion."

"Awesome, man! Much flashier than that plastic thing you always wore. You two get one another the best gifts. Anyway, see you at the café at half-past."

Touched by Fortune's Shadow: a triptych

When Rostam had left, he stored his working files in their secure location on the local network, and constructed a brief memo, addressed to both Rostam and Gerald Cheung, VAI's General Counsel, marked "Attorney-Client Privilege" in the subject line, being sure to note that the original idea for doing automated updates had been given by Rostam, back in mid-April, and sent the brief disclosure on its way before leaving and locking his office door.

~ • ~

"You were right," Brett said, kissing the top of Manijeh's head from behind as she sat on the sofa. He walked around with her glass of shiraz and sat beside her. "*Absolutely* right. How do you keep on being right all the time like that?"

"Indeed! As always!" she beamed. "About what, though?"

"Taraneh," he admitted.

"Oh?" she exclaimed with feigned surprise. With a Cheshire Cat grin, she added almost with a hiss, "Do, *please*, tell…" Her fingernail gently tapped on the side of the wine glass, giving off a particular tone.

Brett straightened himself, leaned over to put his wine glass down on the coffee table, and then turned to face Manijeh as they sat. "She and Rostam were set for lunch at Taf's today, so Rostam threw an invitation my way to join them. No problem, but three-quarters of the way through my sandwich, somehow the topic of her bringing me up to full speed with Royal Conservatory Grade 10 piano becomes all today's *rage*." He rotated so that his back met the back of the sofa squarely, and then leaned his weight as far back as he could. "She gave me her card, even," he added, reaching down to his Coach wallet, producing Taraneh Khoshrangi's linen business card, which Manijeh eagerly took.

"Beautiful business card!" she said. "Nice, I see she's in the Kitsilano neighborhood. She's all of just a fifteen-minute drive from us."

"Top-notch card," he agreed. "*Great* neighborhood."

"So, when are you starting lessons, then?" Manijeh asked, handing the card back and sipping her wine.

"May I ask why you *assume* I accepted her offer?"

"I mean, surely, in front of Rostam you can't turn down her teaching you piano, after all the song and dance at Mom and Dad's that night." The satisfaction on her face doubled the glow of the room in Brett's vision.

"That would cast shade on his choice of romantic partners and their competencies right in front of both of them, which is *so* not you. You have been around us all long enough to have *ta'arof*[29] in your blood by now."

"Wednesday at three," he finally conceded, putting his face in his palm.

"Told you!" she laughed. "*Huma*, you!"

"*Touché*, that you did, but we still don't know…"

Manijeh put her glass down, folded her arms in front of herself in a *faux*-scolding gesture, and then wagged her finger at him. "Brett Lloyd-Ronan, there is no reason on Heaven or Earth for this person to insist on teaching her boyfriend's well-to-do, brilliant business partner who can fight like a *samurai* on fire in a crowded room a single *thing*. What's the Maximum Likelihood Estimation on a thing like that being the only thing that's going on here?"

"That's not—"

She gave him a huge smile. "I love you, my *Huma*."

Brett reached out, put his hand on her leg, and replied, "I love you, Manijeh. I appreciate your vote of confidence and will be sure to mind my manners."

After a quick lean to kiss him, she replied wryly, "It's not your *manners* that will need minding."

Both laughed together until Brett asked, "How about *your* manic Monday?"

"I wish it was *Sunday*," she replied. "It was fine, I suppose. I just want my registration *approved* already."

"Would you like me to ask Margaret what kinds of things might make it all take this long? She could answer in generalities, at least, and she's the compliance person, so…"

"I'd appreciate that," Manijeh replied.

"I'll ask tomorrow, then," he said.

"Thanks. Supper time!" Manijeh declared.

"I'm thinking we should call for Chinese," Brett said.

"You read my mind!"

---

[29] *Ta'arof* is a Persian cultural practice, both in Iran and amongst the diaspora, of politeness and social etiquette that involves offering and sometimes refusing favors or hospitality in a dance of humility and respect, to maintain social harmony and demonstrate mutual respect.

Touched by Fortune's Shadow: a triptych

19

"So, Brett, just what is it exactly that you want to discuss?" Margaret Kaur, the Chief Compliance Officer of Vector Affinity Insights asked from the office's guest chair. She only came to the downtown site when requested, as her position did not require her presence in the office full-time.

"I only need generalities and hypotheticals," he began, "but since it pertains to VAI through me and Rostam, and also possibly Mr. Yazdpour...."

"Ah, the matter of your fiancée's registration, I will hazard a guess?" she asked with a rhetorical tone and a smile.

"Yes," he confirmed.

"What are your concerns, Brett?" Margaret asked, her stare meeting his, but in a friendly sweep of observation rather than penetrating investigation.

"Not really *concerns*. I'm just looking to better understand potential reasons for the slow progress on that," he said. "First, as all that extra paperwork you had me sign when she and I started dating demonstrates, there's the matter of conflicts of interest, information leakage, and that family of mortal sins."

"Those may be some reasons to delay registration, pending consideration of the various mitigations put in place," Margaret commented. "Which you did by giving her a separate dedicated home office." She smiled. "These little details may make a world of difference when it comes time to show due diligence, in any case, before or after it's necessary." She then shifted about as if trying to get comfortable. "But they can be a little off-putting in a personal setting like home. Business and personal must *never* blur into one, even in the most intimate of closet corners behind the shoe boxes and the pile set aside for mismatched socks. *Especially* in a case like the two of you are presenting on paper."

Touched by Fortune's Shadow: a triptych

She jotted a note to herself on the pad she was holding. "Can I make a comment? An aside, but relevant?"

"Always," Brett replied with a smile.

"You're wearing a Rolex," she replied. "Since I've *known* you, you've only ever worn a Casio. I knew that watch because my brother used to wear that exact Casio, too. Anyway, is your watch *new*?"

"It was a gift from Manijeh for a martial arts achievement," he explained, holding out his arm. "Very recent."

Margaret leaned in, looked appreciatively at the watch, and then said, "Do you have a *receipt* for it? I assume you do, since it likely had to be added with its serial number to your regular home insurance policy as a scheduled item."

"Yes."

"Does the receipt have a note on the back saying when the gift was given, and most importantly, *why*?" She asked, still jotting notes. "Home insurance doesn't care about that meta-level of detail. But here we *do* care, because as you know, the mandate I was given, and as stated in the corporate charter, VAI doesn't *just* comply, it proactively predicts and mitigates risk in its practices. We do our best to care about matters before they arise to cause harm, *whenever* and *wherever* we can reasonably anticipate such issues of this kind."

Introduced as an 'aside' or not, Brett knew not to contest the line of questioning she had been pursuing. "I'm not sure if Manijeh did that with the receipt, to be honest. I didn't ask."

She put down her pen and leaned back into her chair. "We just did a thing, you and I," she said, holding out her hands in a grand gesture. "Because of your relationship with Manijeh, an employee of a client, the sister of our CEO, and the daughter of a major shareholder of our parent holding company, each person coming with complexities, everything with a price tag that you and she do *for one another personally* could fall under an intense level of scrutiny about as annoying as people asking *who*, *why*, *when*, and *how much*. Perhaps not this Rolex example from today, but maybe a Mercedes or BMW with a ribbon around it one day in the future."

Putting his hand to his chin and massaging the tension from his jaw, he replied, "This kind of thinking through the *minutiae* is slowing things down over there, you think? Has this business really come to this level of nitpicking? And that's coming from a *professional* nitpicker such as myself."

"Honestly, to be fair, we can't be sure," Margaret admitted. "My job is to advise and direct VAI and its interests on matters of regulatory compliance, and also to flag concerns that step into that area of the mandate the charter puts on me. Your position as Chief Analyst, and this key relationship you've entered into by dating, moving in with, and then becoming engaged to marry this person at the central nexus of a complex lattice of business interests, *directly* impact how we must conduct our affairs and stay within that mandate. That's all absolutely *fine* by my books. Relationships happen to traders, and they happen to letter carriers, and to grocery clerks. Everyone is allowed to have a relationship; some just come with extra *paperwork*. Your and her relationship is one such situation."

Before continuing, she shifted about and took a few more notes. "I met Manijeh back when I started here, and she's a lovely, lovely person. And she's *your* lovely person and you hers. Nobody expects to push your relationship around and form it like a *bonsai* to look good for regulators; it's sacred. Let it grow organically.

"But remember that there's no such thing as overcaution in regulated financial market trading or consulting. So be careful about property or asset exchanges above moderation. An ounce of prevention is worth a pound of cure. Always remember that one must not only *comply*, but one must also always be *seen to comply*. That second one is a Zen *koan* for you, *Sensei*, to fully understand how it applies to your specific presentational self.

"And yes, Brett, I heard about your martial arts promotion! Rostam caught me up on it on my way through the front office. Congratulations!"

"Thank you! I *do* appreciate your advice. I gave Manijeh a watch a while ago, when she first arrived back in Vancouver, for her Harvard graduation. Not that I feel the need to fess up, but just to show that I hear you."

"And I'm sure it was lovely, too, knowing your taste and attention to brand names," she said.

"Omega Constellation," he said.

"Indeed a lovely brand, and of course, knowing you, I would expect you to buy anything less for her or yourself," she replied. "I suspect the delays, if they even are *delays*, are just a bunch of diligent regulatory evaluators doing a thorough job, which can only protect everyone's long-term interests here. Could have even fallen behind a filing cabinet; this kind of thing has been known to happen. That and the chicken entrails."

"Ah yes, the entrails. I *did* warn Manijeh about the dark art." He pushed back his chair, stood, invited her to stand with a gesture, and walked over to the liquor cabinet. "That's the close of business. We're off the clock. Single malt... if I remember?" he asked her.

"What's the occasion?" she asked. "But yes, certainly."

"To my wonderful partner in life, Manijeh Yazdpour, and to *your* health," he replied.

"Here! Here!" she said, taking the tumbler, tapping it to Brett's, and putting back the shot. "And to home offices with perpetual water coolers. I wanted one in my office the moment I read those floorplans of yours."

"That was a coup, that," Brett agreed with a second shot for them both. "And yes, I do have a thing with brand names, don't I? Rolex, Omega, Armani.... Smitten."

"You have shown yourself to be rather *particular* with brands over the years," Margaret noted.

"Just as we have to be seen to be compliant, we have to be seen to be a lot of things in life, I've learned. Seen to be *confident*. Seen to be *credible*. Seen to be *discerning*. Seen to be *successful*. Ad *nauseam*. I learned that brands help us be seen how we wish others to see us. It helps me to better navigate this strange new world," he explained more fully.

"I mean, I really *do* prefer the weight of a Montblanc pen. The actual difference between a Montblanc and some generic pen is considerable, and of course, so is the price difference. But I also tend to use brands to signal how I wish to be perceived. What it says when I pull the pen out. I admit it. It's an expensive way to 'speak' but it's a way of speaking that gets people to listen most closely."

Margaret nodded. "It's a shorthand. What seeing the Rolex on you tells me compared to the Casio happens without a *word* being exchanged. Everyone does it, I suspect; you are just more self-aware than many of it being a conscious act when you tighten a certain brand of tie."

Lifting his tumbler after a small additional pour, he said, "Exactly. It helps me tell others who I am and why they should listen to me when I need to tell them something. I think part of it is the fact that I'm a blue-collar boy living in a white-collar world. I used to buy *all* my clothing, for years, from thrift stores. Wore them to meetings meant for closing deals. I got heard less clearly, I think."

"Life is a performance. So you'd best wear your absolute *finest* to the matinée," Margaret replied after a pause. "*Whatever* your finest may be. If they hadn't heard you in Levi's, would you and I be here, having this conversation?"

"Maybe the jeans did it once or twice, but once I could afford to speak Ralph Lauren or Armani, I hired labels to do most of my speaking for me. They make for very good spokespeople, and besides that, there's nothing like a tailored fit and a silk cravat to satisfy my Oscar Wilde leanings."

With a laugh, Margaret Kaur closed with, "And the story is told so much the more smoothly with The Glenlivet. A lovely *brand*!"

"So that's enough of that introspection, then!" he suggested cheerfully. "Here's to continuing to forge *our* brand here at VAI!" he toasted on the last drop in their tumblers. "Thanks for listening to me blather on."

"My pleasure!" Margaret assured him. "We don't get many chances to just relax and chat. I spend too much time in my home office these days. It feels good to get out and catch up."

≼•≽

The evening breeze from directly over the Park to the terrace caressed Brett's face as he and she drank their Perriers in their *chaises longues*. "So, from what I was able to gather," he said, "it's most probable that your registration is taking its sweet time due to the issues you and I talked about last night."

"Oh, *bother!*" Manijeh replied, sticking out her tongue at him playfully. "In a world counted in minutes and seconds where the close of day is so important to this or that much fiscal gain and any lost time is costly, I must patiently and obediently sit on my hands for the Holy Bureaucracy."

"With things like Bre-X," he said, crossing himself like a Catholic when he said the name, "and whatever that Livent nonsense is going to become—who has any idea with that one?—trading in general in Canada is falling under the axe, and rightly so, in my opinion. So we are to expect a few extra servings of the bend-over-and-cough treatment. Especially given our..." He searched for an exact word, but it escaped him.

"Our? Especially given our what, Brett?" She waved her hand impatiently but was smiling as she did so.

"Especially given our level of *entanglement*," he said.

"Yes, we have become quite intricately woven together," he agreed, tapping his glass with hers.

"Margaret remembered you well from when your times at VAI overlapped," he then said. "Anyway, she brought up a good point today. A lesson worth having the meeting if nothing else had been said at all."

"What's this?"

"If we exchange gifts, such as the expensive watches, we should try to do so only for notable and documentable reasons of commemoration, and what have you, and when we do, we should take care to note this on the receipt."

Her expression spoke volumes of how this made her feel, and Manijeh said in a sour tone, "Now there we have a fine example of the commoditization and transactionalization of human affection expressed in gift-giving if *ever* I saw it."

"It's a proactive approach," he tried to soften the sting of what he knew sounded antiseptically awful to a lover's ear. "She put it succinctly as: 'Always remember that one must not only *comply*, but one must also always be *seen to comply*.'"

"The micromanagement of generosity of spirit. O brave new world, that has such cynicism in it! Let's walk this First-World-Problems conversation out of our systems and move on to the evening. I suggest we rent a video after a loop around the Lagoon."

At this, Brett jumped up, held out his hand to give her balance as she swung up out of her *chaise*, and headed for the open balcony door. "Race you to the door!" he said once he had a decent lead.

20

The final few notes of Rachmaninoff's "Prelude in C-Sharp Minor" rang from the black concert grand piano through Taraneh's medium-sized living room and back to his ear. She had asked Brett to play it from sight, after first verifying that he had never played it, to get a better idea of his ability after so long since obtaining his Grade 9 certificate, given that Bach's "Prelude and Fugue No. 2 in C-Minor," which he had performed for her at the Yazdpours' had been something he'd once practiced relentlessly. In amongst the echoes, he could hear the cacophonies and acoustic interference patterns in what he had just so naively performed.

"That was good for sight reading on that *very difficult* piece," Taraneh encouraged him. "You captured the overall mood quite well. Of course you need improvement; there is absolutely *no* shame in being able to play that piece as well as you did."

To release the day's heavy weight from his back, he sat at attention and listened to all his vertebrae align in his mind, to overpower the noise of what he had just produced at the piano. "I may have benefited from a metronome. I am not going to beat myself up over it, but I need work."

Taraneh approached the bench, swept her hand to point at the spot beside him, and asked, "May I?"

With a quick shuffle, Brett moved over to the bench to allow her to sit beside him. As she sat, she flipped through the pages of the sheet music and found the *Più mosso*. She then played several bars with intensity, saying as she did so, "This section requires *clear* articulation, control, and phrasing and is *crucial* for conveying the contrast in the prelude. The tempo picks up, requiring more than *just* speed. Let's break down what you need for improvement." Her melodic voice rang with a blend of encouragement and precision.

Touched by Fortune's Shadow: a triptych

"First, articulation. Each note, even in rapid passages, must speak clearly. You're not merely playing notes faster; you're expressing them with *intent*. Think of articulation as the clarity of your musical speech. Use a lighter touch on the keys, almost as if you're *dancing* on them. This dancing will help you avoid a heavy, muddled sound."

She moved her smoothly dexterous hand gracefully above the keys, demonstrating without actually touching them. "Control is your ability to maintain evenness and accuracy at a faster tempo. Practice this section slowly, focusing on even finger pressure and consistent rhythm. Gradually increase your speed, ensuring your precision remains intact. Don't sacrifice control for speed. It's about finding the *balance*."

She then softly hummed a few bars, emphasizing the dynamic changes. "Now, for phrasing. Even with the increased pace, the sentences should flow *naturally*. You might think a metronome would have helped you keep your concentration on other things, but the phrasing will stab your trust in that False Idol in the back the moment you arrive right *here*—since it has no eyes of its own to read Rachmaninoff's sheets and cannot anticipate the next shift of pulse of the section. Pay attention to the *crescendos* and *diminuendos*; they're there for a reason. Keep the future in your peripheral vision, especially when you sight read, but always when you can, and let that anticipation *agitate* your execution as the piece demands. Each phrase should have exact *direction*, leading to a particular moment or providing contrast to the surrounding measures. Think of it as telling a story—your pacing, emphasis, and how you navigate transitions *all* contribute to the narrative."

Brett nodded so that Taraneh was certain he was listening intently to her direction and advice, and then she continued.

"Lastly," Taraneh added, looking Brett directly in the eyes, "connect with the emotional core of this particular section. The metronome has no heart, it breathes without breath. Connect with the flowing breath of piece not the mechanical *tick-tock*."

Brett was certain that he saw fire flicker in her eyes, and he suddenly came to fully understand what Manijeh had been so cautious about: Taraneh was ablaze behind her regard, holding back spark and cinder. He centered himself to try to determine if this was her, him, or both, and he realized and accepted his accelerated heartbeat and rapid breathing. To calm himself, he immersed himself in the pool of her guidance.

"Performing Rachmaninoff isn't just about technical prowess, although you will need your fair share of *that*; it's about expressing *profound* emotions through music. It's the same as what you did with those swords during your certificate ceremony. Let the technical aspects serve your *expression*, not the other way around. Your goal is to bring the listener into the heart of this piece, to feel what you feel as you navigate these passages." She then leaned back, giving Brett a moment to absorb her words. "Take it one bar at a time if you need to, and remember, patience is key even at the most passionate phrases of this piece.

"You have the skills; now, let's refine them. You're really quite close. Almost to the point where you only need polish. I can tell that your mother taught you very well. Now, let's see if together we can get you past *almost there*."

At this, she placed her hands on the keys. "Place your hands on mine lightly," she said. When he did so, she began slowly playing the *Più mosso*. "Do you feel the difference in how my hands move compared to how your hands felt when you played this section?" she asked. When Taraneh stopped playing, Brett lifted his hands from hers.

"I can feel a fluidity with your technique that I am nowhere *near* having," he admitted.

When he said this, her left hand left the keys and landed on his right thigh. Given that he was only a human being, her touch on his leg shot through his instinct and he hit a windshield of arousal in what could have easily been an unbuckled driver's seat of a Porsche navigating a hairpin turn. "*Misuzam*,"[30] she whispered so quietly that he was likely not meant to have heard it. Were this not Rostam's girlfriend, or were he some other man, the chain of events following this touch would have carried itself to its conclusion. But she *was* Rostam's girlfriend, and he arrived onto this mountain highway forewarned, so he was not actually without his seatbelt in this excruciatingly visceral moment.

With gentleness, he lifted her hand from his leg, placed it back on the keys, and softly said, "No thank you, Taraneh." His gaze did not leave hers, and because he knew that she could see through his pupils in her way, he was sure to put his excruciating arousal behind a wall of years of tranquil pond and star gazing. Cold flares of his true level of desire hidden behind the peaceful obfuscation of a more constant bliss.

---

[30] "I'm on fire"

Touched by Fortune's Shadow: a triptych

She put her hands to her face to cover her embarrassment and closed her eyes tightly. "I feel *so* stupid!" she said. "You must think *horribly* of me. I'm so sorry. I'm *aghast* at my behavior." She appeared to be trembling lightly from the realization of what had just been lit aflame only moments before, but which had been smoldering in her somewhere for some weeks.

To break the mood, he started to play the *Più mosso* at half tempo, with minor improvisations and flourishes added from his playful repertoire. "There's no need to be so rough with yourself," he replied with a smile.

"But I, well…"

"What? You had an overwhelming flash of lust and acted on it in a quiet, private setting? I'm not going to read into what it means, and neither should you," he said. "A judge is a *fool*. So much more so the judge of human emotion and desire. I will not judge in *you* what I also feel; I simply make a choice to stand back from my senses and desires in the moment. As said Rumi: 'Do not be satisfied with the stories that come before you. Unfold your *own* myth.'"

After a long silence, Taraneh asked, "What now?"

"Now? Let's put this behind us like the adults we are and move forward with our lesson. You can trust my discretion. I have no intention of saying a word to Rostam. I am not on this planet to write anyone else's myth."

Taraneh inhaled deeply, closed her eyes for a moment, reopened them, put her hands back on the keys, and started to accompany Brett in his improvisation. "Do you know any Oscar Peterson?" she asked, turning to him with a calm smile that suggested that she was beginning her moment of *tabula rasa* in their relationship at the piano bench, and by extension, in Rostam and the Yazdpour family's life.

To cue, Brett slowly shifted from Rachmaninoff's Prelude and started working into Oscar Peterson's take on "C Jam Blues," at which point, once Taraneh had registered which piece he was aiming for, she adjusted in turn and the two were soon in a shared world of musical effervescence.

❧ • ☙

"You're batting two-for-two," Brett greeted Manijeh as she opened the apartment door.

"Taraneh?" she asked, with an immense grin.

"Need I even?"

"Tell me all about it," she said, "as we make that Wellington we were planning on putting together. I'm just going to jot into the shower first and freshen up. The weather's been *balmy* today."

∽•≈

"Wow," Manijeh said, putting her fork down for a moment and taking her wine glass. "I'd like to propose a toast."

Hearing this, Brett took his glass and added a quarter fill of the shiraz. "A toast to *what*?"

"To dancing through minefields without blowing off any of your limbs," she said, one hand on her forehead in feigned amazement and disbelief. "Good on you for being able to pull that off. I like your limbs."

He lifted his glass and said, "God bless dancing through minefields." He took a sip and added, "She pulled out of it on the surface, we finished the lesson, and she even gave me a polite peck when I left. So I think she's going to be fine. We'll count our limbs again in a week or two just to be sure, though, what say?" He stood, grabbed her plate and his, put the dirty dishes into the dishwasher, and invited her to the sofa.

"Can I ask you a question?" Manijeh asked once they were seated beside one another with the remainder of what was in their wine glasses.

"Of course," he said.

"How exactly does that open relationship thing work inside your psyche?" she asked. Her eyes were curious and at peace. "I don't judge it at all, but I can't say that I fully understand how that *works* for you. Now that we've had a 'close call' in the real world, it might help me better understand what we're up against in practice with this little understanding we have about things."

"I'll answer if you play a few rounds of *Pasur* with me after I do," he replied with a grin. "I mean, I will answer you anyway, but I want to play cards tonight."

"It's a deal!" she said.

"So here's my take on it. How it 'works in my psyche' as you put it…. For countless eons human beings have treated other human beings as property to be owned and part of that ownership was expressed as the patriarchal so-called right to exclusive control over the agency and autonomy of others," he began to answer her question. "History tells us that an awful lot of their time was spent consider the myriad ways to control women.

"Now, there are surely plenty of people for whom physical monogamy is a perfectly suitable choice and I do not doubt that within their frameworks there is very often a basis of mutual respect, and if that exclusivity is an informed vow, I find no issue with this. And why should I? I don't question it at all. It's not my business to question. But it's not the *only* option that works well, and it's not the path for me. Monogamy is not a universal human moral imperative," he summarized his stance.

"Are you separating physical and emotional monogamy?" she asked. "The cliché 'she meant nothing to me' is…"

"… rather objectifying, by my opinion. If she truly meant *nothing*… why share *intimacy* of *any* kind, let alone *that* level of intimacy? To satisfy a craving? Take a long walk or a cold shower. Or both, in whatever order that works. Intimacy should arise naturally from conspiracy."

"*Conspiracy*? There's a new one on me! Are we now secret agents? Quick, kiss me before our cover's blown!"

"*Conspiracy* comes from *con* and *spirare*, which means 'to breathe with,'" he explained. "So I using it in the sense that we should share intimacy, and that most intimate kiss, only with those with whom we can *breathe*. I have attempted, though not always *entirely* successfully, to avoid transactional intimacy."

"So you're saying *what* about your past relationships? That they all meant something to you?" she asked, tapping her glass to show that it was empty, at which point he leaned over for the bottle and put in a little more. "That you could 'share breath' with them all? Except for those few outliers you've already confessed to as being 'transactional' as you put it, I mean."

"Yes."

Manijeh's face lit up as if she'd just heard something from Brett that she had not expected. He tried to decide what she might be feeling, but could only guess, and so tried not to project. "That 'something' doesn't have to be *love* or even *limerence*, but there must be some common human connection, some spark beyond the purely sensual. Some shared song; some shared note; some shared breath. At least for me. Some human recognition of another agent on the manifold of existence. Something to warrant a visit to the most intimate and vulnerable place that we can visit with another person. For me, there should be something to justify sharing that most intimate kiss. So 'she meant nothing to me' is *not* my refrain. I simply refuse to own *anyone*, and by the same token, I refuse to *be* owned by anyone."

From behind her eyes, the curiosity continued to sparkle, and after a while of contemplation of his answer, she asked, "So, given what you and I have, and where we've decided to go in life, how does your past position play into your future understanding? Assume Taraneh, for instance, had not been Rostam's girlfriend today. How would things likely have gone, all else but her being his girlfriend being equal?"

Honesty in his reply to her mattered to Brett, and so he closed his eyes and sat again at the bench at the moment Taraneh's hand had touched his thigh. He remembered how it felt. From that moment he went backward to the moment he had recognized the lust in her gaze, and how that had made him react in turn. The rush returned to him and he could feel his chest constrict and his hands suddenly become slightly clammy as they touched the piano keys.

Brett carefully considered his next words, and then replied, "Absent any connection to Rostam, there is every real possibility it could have gone somewhere more intense, *very* quickly."

"You *cad*!" Manijeh jested, given her smile, as she jokingly made as if she was going to throw the contents of her wine glass into Brett's face. "Or is that *rapscallion*?" she teased him some more.

Brett smiled and then replied, "She's her own planet, not a moon around planet Rostam. I still find her quite an interesting and engaging conversationalist, with a good sense of humor. She's also stunning. She's an excellent piano player, and even is quite into Oscar Peterson and can improv in duet as fast as I can hammer that jazz. So yes, it could have ended up much more heated, absent any connection to Rostam."

"You're a fascinating bird, Brett." She put her hand over his heart. "How do you keep all of that inside yourself? How are you not exploding, with all of that in there? All that *eigen-stuff*...."

"Years of personal training, meditation, and—"

Before he could continue, she had leaned over and kissed him so deeply that he could not speak anymore. After a few minutes, they played two hands of *Pasur*, with each winning a game. Though they intended to play a tie-breaker, they instead made love on the sofa and fell asleep there afterward for a while. He awoke at two from the discomfort of a crooked arm placement and led them into the bedroom to retire for the rest of the evening.

Touched by Fortune's Shadow: a triptych

21

Melodious and cacophonous bird calls from all directions, both close and far. Engine acceleration and deceleration behind and downward. Thousands of souls all around, humming with the last Sunday morning of June. In Brett Lloyd-Ronan's inner lattice of gridlines, the only inner visualization surface he could form, even when recalling faces. Sometimes, under the right states of mind, brief almost-images would flash like photographs, but these were rare enough in his meditations that he had long since learned to satisfy himself with whatever was on offer. When the tree of his understanding of his past life, as lived until this very morning stood shining like some personal Yggdrasil before him, he lit the tree with sacred fire and watched yesterday become the yet unadorned tree, for the fire did not take down this makeshift golden chicken-wire oak but let it become its present self.

He lifted his coffee cup to his lip, eyes still closed, and the liquid touched his lips as his eyes shot open to see the new day before him. He turned his head to Manijeh, who sat only feet beside him, also in the lotus position, still in her meditation. Within a few minutes, she too, opened her own eyes.

"Hello," he greeted her.

"Hello there," she said, smiling. "I was able to fully silence my internal verbalizations and I'm feeling steady. What now?"

"Now keep in mind, what I'm about to cover is my *personal* practice and is not to be taken as canon or anything like that. If you think about it, the right-handed person will draw the sword from the left hip. This means that the sword is active and ready.

"Here we are, moving the sword *through* our home, which is not the same situation as entering the house of someone else with our sword." He looked into her sparkling eyes to see that she was still listening, as coming out of meditation sometimes left one dreamy and unable to center back into the external world.

"So put the sword in front of you onto your *right* hip. Watch me," he said as he took his *katana* and placed it in his belt on his right hip. "This is the inactive position. Because it is on the wrong hip, it's clearly not intended to be drawn, and thus we acknowledge that we are wearing it, but that we have no intention to draw it. Others can see that. We carry it through our home in this *inactive* position because our home is safe and sacred, and we do not wish to disrespect the sword by carrying it in the active position in our safe home."

She placed the *wakizashi* on her right hip as well and then followed him as they walked to his home office door. "I'll take that from here," he said. He opened the door, walked in alone, and placed the swords in the left hilt position. "I'm placing them in this direction because they are at rest and will not be drawn in this home, and thus we do not disrespect the sword by making it ready if it is not required to be ready."

He then stood, closed the door, and listened for the whir before verifying that it was locked. "Any breakfast preferences before our usual walk?" he asked.

"Let's make a light farmer's breakfast," she suggested.

"I know all that sword stuff sounds *particular* but…"

"There's no need to explain. Rituals are sacred. Canon or not. So thank you for working me into yours."

"Farmer's breakfast it is, then, *azizam*," he agreed. "I'll prep the hashbrowns. And you're very welcome, my love."

≪•≫

That day they varied their walk to include a stroll across the Lions Gate Bridge. After returning, they returned home on the eastern side of Stanley Park along the Seawall, around Brockton Point, rather than circumnavigating along the western side, which would have brought them right past Third Beach. Although they had agreed to take their weekly Sunday walk after the morning meditation, they had decided their forays should be freeform, with the only constant rule being that they would never bring Brett's beeper or Manijeh's Motorola StarTAC with them.

When they returned home around three in the afternoon, they shared a shower and Brett finally allowed himself to check his beeper. When he did, he saw that Rostam had sent his cell number, which was rare, but not unheard of. He sat on the sofa with a cold bottle of Chinotto and then dialed Rostam's number from the wireless landline.

"Hey, thanks for calling back, Brett. Can you take a taxi to the Still Creek ravine?" Rostam asked. "Just you, please."
"What time?"
"See you there at four? The spot where we first met. Do you remember the bend right near the—you know, where you and I met the very first time. That place."
"Got it," Brett replied, the exact spot mentioned flashing clearly on the wireframe topology of his mental map of the place.
"Want me to bring anything?" he asked.
"Just yourself," Rostam replied. "And again, take a cab, not your car."
"Sounds good. I'll meet you there at four o'clock," he said before hanging up.
"What did Rostam want?" Manijeh asked as she sat with him on the sofa. No fan of Chinotto, she was drinking a Perrier.
"He wants me to meet him at the Still Creek ravine at four," he answered, placing the receiver on the coffee table.
"Did he say whatever for? I mean, I am almost certain this is going to be about what happened at Taraneh's place, but did he say anything?" She tipped back her bottle without losing eye contact with Brett.
"Just that I should take a taxi, rather than drive, and that I should come alone." He finished his drink and looked in his wallet to check his cash for the trip there and back and after having convinced himself that he had enough for the roundtrip, waited for Manijeh to finish her drink and carried the bottles into the kitchen bin they used for empty containers.
"It sounds ominous," Manijeh noted.
"Remember Tracie? You may not. It was around 1988, so the name may be a bit hazy."
As if the name rang in her inner ear, Manijeh hummed with her index finger on her chin, and said, "No, I don't remember that name. I had my own things going on back then and didn't keep track of other people's names and business. And just who was *Tracie* you're on about?"
The refrigerator fruit drawer was almost empty, but still had some good apples. He took out two, washed them both, and offered Manijeh one. "She was his *first* 'she's the *one*, man,'" he explained the relationship quickly.
"Ah," Manijeh acknowledged. "Those he indeed has had a few of," she said. "Though, that's surely no judgment on him. Many have. Why does *Tracie* stand out in your mind?"

Touched by Fortune's Shadow: a triptych

Through the glass door out onto the terrace, in the outside air with his freshly washed apple in hand, he waited for her to be beside him. "The last time he and I went to the ravine together, alone, just us, was after they broke up. As you say, there've been a few since then. They didn't warrant a Still Creek Conference, though. And life after Tracie was no picnic."

As if something he had just said lit a torch in the labyrinth of her recollection of life past, Manijeh's eyes suddenly jumped to an epiphany. "Tracie! Yes! He was *miserable* during that. Absolutely miserable. The next time he was *that* depressed had to have been when…" She stopped herself.

"… he realized that he didn't want to be an engineer even though he had blown four solid years of excruciating study and competition to become one," Brett finished for her, to be sure they were talking about the same history.

"Yes," she said. Her eyes were uncharacteristically sad. "In any case, we'll know what's up by the time that you come back tonight. You go do your thing you do so well with Rostam."

22

"I'm over here, Brett!" Rostam called out. He was sitting on the stonework at the side of the creek, perhaps ten feet from where he and Brett had first met back in 1981 all those years before.

Brett sat on Rostam's left, a yard at most from him, his legs also over the side. After adjusting his buttocks slightly to avoid poking himself in the ass with a rock, he said, "This place brings back good memories. All good."

Rostam said, "I come here twice a year. You?"

"Once in a while, on the way past, I think about it, but life has been like that for me, so not so much." He tapped his temple with his right index finger. "But it's always in the vault, man. Always inside my center when I need a place to find myself."

"Yeah, this place made us—all three of us—who we are today, don't you think?" his friend added over his breath and a mild slurring that made it clear that he was not entirely sober, which Brett took note of.

"It has certainly been a North Star in all of our lives, yes," Brett agreed. "So, why did you ask me to take a *taxi* here?"

There was a sound of paper rustling as Rostam reached into his inner jacket pocket about pulled out a brown paper bag. He unscrewed the top of a mickey and handed it to Brett. "It's not single malt, but here you go. I have my own," he then added, showing Brett his bag and bottle beside him on the ledge.

"Ah!" Brett said, taking the bottle. A quick swig later, he asked, "What's up, my friend?" There was a slight aftertaste that one might describe as toothpaste. "Why does this booze taste like Colgate?" he asked, wiping his mouth.

Rostam's left arm extended and he motioned Brett to scoot over to him, which Brett did, and then he put his arm fully around Brett's back. "Dad told me that he *finally* told you about the Cinema Rex fire in Abadan," he began.

Touched by Fortune's Shadow: a triptych

"He did. That night we were all over at your parents' with Taraneh. When I gracefully banged out that Bach on the piano," Brett replied. Although he was not sure he should have brought the topic of Taraneh and piano to the fore of their conversation, he suspected that, at some point that night beside the creek with their mickeys of nasty whisky, the topic would return.

"August 19, 1953. That's when Mosaddeq was ousted and Shah re-installed," he said. "August 19, 1978, that was the day of that fire. It's as if totally innocent people died so a square on some sick commemorative calendar could be checked off after twenty-five years of seething over it. What a truly *disgusting* world we live in, man. It's horrifying. It all makes it so damned difficult be believe in humanity sometimes."

"I read up about it all right after your dad told me about what happened to your family," he admitted. "I can't even imagine what that did to you all. Can't even *imagine*."

"It got us all to Canada," he replied. "That's what it did to us all. Got us all the hell out of what became Hell on Earth once the Iraqis hit Khuzestan."

"That it did!" he agreed, patting Rostam on the back. "And here we are, right here, come full circle."

"We *were* originally *all* going to go with my Uncle Farokh's family," Rostam revealed. "We would have all died with them if we had. Hundred percent."

Suddenly Brett's solar plexus contracted, and he was filled with a suffocating sense of existential dread as a vivid flash of an image, an actual visual mental image with such rare optical clarity that he was almost pushed over onto his back. It was Manijeh's beautiful face, completely obliterated by fire. He took a sip of his bottle, followed by a very deep breath. Finally, when he had recentered, he asked, "Why didn't you go?" Rostam had called him here to talk; he knew he must push his feelings aside until later if he could manage, so that he could be focused on his friend, even with the liquor in him.

"*The Deer*. It was a *complex* movie. *Way* too complicated and deep for children. My uncle's kids were older. Dad and Mom thought it wasn't something our eyes should see at our age. I saw it later in life and understood the point my parents were making about it not being for kids our age. So, anyway, Dad, Mom, and Farokh had a little family-style argument about it, and we stayed home that Saturday." He, too, took another draw from his bottle.

"That's some serious shit," Brett could barely muster, still horrified by the flash he had experienced when he'd found out what Manijeh's fate had almost been.

"That's sure some *deep* philosophical wisdom coming from your mouth, *Sensei*," Rostam teased. "You writing a self-help book using that material?"

"Why are we here *tonight*?" Brett finally outright asked. "Not that this isn't a good enough reason to talk, you and I, but why *here* at the creek? I'm trying to figure *this* out. Why are we *here* right now. At the creek where we met?"

"Just like you trying to build a mental map in your head about where you stand in the moment," Rostam said. "So perpetually situationally aware." Laughter erupted from his chest and almost fully left his mouth, but he chewed on the last few breaths of it. "She told me, man. Just up and told me."

This moment had an inevitability to it that Brett knew he could not escape. Brett's girlfriend had lost her composure, put her hand on his thigh, pushed past the embarrassment, and moved forward to regain her bearings. That was how he saw it, and that was how Manijeh saw it, having heard it told, but he did not yet know Rostam's understanding and decided to let him do the talking before he said much else. "What exactly?" he asked. "I mean, I know what you're talking about, but what exactly happened in *your* mind? How are *you* seeing things?"

"You're family now, Brett," he replied, pulling his friend more firmly to him. "Always have been. I know how it is with you and women, you were never shy about how you see relationships, and I have great respect for minding my side of the road about any of that. Does Manijeh know about…?"

"She knows all about what happened," Brett answered.

"That's good to know, but I mean, does she know about your views on open relationships? Is she good with…?"

"She agreed to marry me, man," Brett replied. "She knew about my openness the day she asked me to go steady because I felt I had to disclose to her. So yes, she knows all about it and she and I are good. It wasn't something I was going to hand her a book on a year down the road. Fair is fair. Informed consent." He pulled Rostam even closer to his side and said, "She and I both prefer to keep the practicalities and specifics of such intimate matters strictly between ourselves, confined within the privacy of our relationship's inner sanctum."

Touched by Fortune's Shadow: a triptych

"I understand that these are all deeply personal and private matters," Rostam agreed. "I appreciate your clarifying as much as you have." After picking up a small stone and tossing it into the creek, Rostam shifted about, as if to get comfortable. "It's not how I do *my* own thing," he then said. "And you know, I don't even really mind that a person has a slip or two early in a relationship. That happens. You saw what happened to my life after I cheated on Tracie back in the day. I destroyed *that* and hurt some people: her, her parents, the one I cheated *with*, me. Quite a graphic toll of relationship carnage. No medals for my honor on affairs of the heart, I'm prepared to admit. Not with pride, but I can face my maker on it. I've tried to follow *Humata, Hukhta, Huvarshta*,[31] secular humanist though I am. Maybe even more so because I'm not spiritual and just feel it's *right*. But I've slipped. So I can understand.

"So I *get* it. Life and love and lust are more complex than the futures markets, man. I don't judge any of *that*, but, if I'm honest about my take on the matter, I feel like Taraneh should have known not to mess with my *family*, at the very least, if she wanted to go that way for herself." He again emphasized his embrace. "You know? Context. Don't piss in the pool, as a matter of pure courtesy, at least. *Ta'arof* has bankrupted people for less social connection than this. You're *family*."

Dancing with a sharpened *katana* that could remove a limb in a single distracted moment never felt as dangerous to Brett as this single moment on a stonework creek wall with his lifetime friend, so Brett tried to be as careful as the whiskey in his blood would allow. "She *did not* mess with your family, man. So let's not go and make Brobdingnagian tempests out of Lilliputian teapots. We quickly made it clear like two grown-assed adults what the boundaries were and we put it behind us."

"But she must have known... *everyone* knows not to..."

"Modern human beings are far more complicated than a judgment based upon what amounts to property law written sometimes hundreds or thousands of years ago has any right to declare or describe," Brett said. Another swig of swill in him, he added, "Let's deal with one another directly rather than through the lens of a society that considered women as cattle."

---

[31] *Humata, Hukhta, Huvarshta*, (lit. "Good thoughts; good words; good deeds"), a principle Zoroastrian tenet, here in Avestan, the language of the Avesta, the holy book of Zoroastrianism.

"That's a hideous way to frame it."

"It's only as hideous as the truth of how history actually played out. You want to talk about stuff being *horrifying*?"

After a very long pause, Rostam replied, "On the plus side, Taraneh still *feels* like the *one*. And she told me *right away*—Wednesday night after it happened."

"These are good signs of mature adults being in the room," Brett commented. "What are your thoughts on how you're going to move forward with her, given all this? I suggest you keep at it if you can manage because I think she's worth it."

"I told her I would talk to you and think about her and my future after I got your side of it," he then said. "She made it clear that she wants to put this behind us fully and keep dating." He started to make like he was going to stand, and Brett took this signal, and soon they were both upright, though tipsy.

"So now you've talked with me about it. Any good come of it? How's your understanding *now*?"

Rostam hugged his friend. "I've already thought about it. As far as I'm concerned, it's water under the bridge going forward. Taraneh is a treasure, and I'm not going to be an entitled, self-righteous patriarchal jerk because my male-privilege nose got a little out of joint over a kerfuffle. I know what I did to Tracie, and she wasn't even the last I… well, you know. So I owe Taraneh grace if for no other reason than to not be *kur kurâneh*."[32]

"We should *all* always have our eyes open in a relationship, I reckon. We must take care. I think she's a *spectacular* match for you, Rostam," Brett added. "You're on the right path, man. I think you stand a good chance. Just keep it open."

"Open? You mean?"

"No dude. I mean your *conversation*. And your eyes. And your heart. Keep *those* all open. Share yourself with her and listen when she does the same with you as if these were the two most important gifts you could ever give one another and give your relationship. Because near as I can tell, brother, they are. We've already figured out that the *other* kind of open really just ain't your *thing*."

"Just making sure," Rostam added with a hearty laugh. "Now you think we can make it up the side to the community center and call a cab in our state?"

---

[32] k*ur kurâneh* (lit. "[the] blind [acting] blindly"), meaning in this context "for no other reason than to avoid being reckless and acting without looking first."

Touched by Fortune's Shadow: a triptych

"Loser pays the fare!" Brett called out as he started quickly on the trail toward the community center at the edge of the forested ravine that hid creek.

❦ • ❦

The moment he opened the door, Brett darted into the living room, where he found Manijeh sitting on the sofa, watching television. He walked up behind her and put his arms around her from behind, dropping to his knees to be able to do so, and he put his whiskey-soaked lips to the back of her ear and kissed her repeatedly, and then behind the other ear.

"Oh," she said, delighted. "Whatever have I done to deserve *this*? By the way, you smell mildly of The Yale."

The image of her scorched visage finally left his mind's eye. "I love you so much and *never* want to lose you," he surrendered.

"Oh yeah, you've been drinking alright," she said after the wafts of his words reached her. "Is Rostam okay?"

"He's *fine*. He'll make it. He told me that you almost went to the Rex Cinema with your uncle's family the night of the arson," he explained his exaggerated display of affection. "It made me want to hold you and kiss you and feel your breath and…"

"Cinema Rex?" Her hand touched his arm gently. "All the stuff with Taraneh and *that's* what he wanted to talk about?"

"That and Taraneh," he replied. He stood up, walked around to the other side of the sofa, and dropped slowly to his knees in front of Manijeh. He put his head on her soft lap.

"How did *that* roll over?"

"She told him. He's over it and is moving forward with her. We'll see how that pans out in reality. I may or may not have a piano lesson with Taraneh this Wednesday."

Manijeh's gentle hand ran along his hair, smoothing it as she stroked. "Would you like to go to The Yale?" she asked. "For some music and dancing?"

"I'm knackered and already a quite bit over-liquored," he replied. "Let's pick out a classic movie tonight. I'm all for next Friday, though. Used to love that place. Haven't checked it out for quite some while."

"Do you have anyone from work to invite? I could invite a few colleagues from Klein *et al*."

After a few moments of going over options in his mind, Brett replied, "Winston's a likely candidate."

"Winston?"

"Winston Rampersad, my assistant," he replied. "Life of the Christmas Party last year. He's a good bet. A true ninja."

"What about inviting Rostam and Taraneh?" she ventured.

A deep cough started in Brett's chest. "Might want to let them settle their feathers before being all of us in a single room together at once," he suggested.

"Or rip the Band-Aid off and push forward," she countered, gesturing as if ripping a bandage from her left forearm. "Ouch! But it's all *better* now.... See? Rip it!" She smiled cheerfully. "Because it's going to happen eventually. A week's *plenty* of time. And The Yale is semi-public. Besides, it's the *ta'arof* thing to invite them to any social gatherings they would notice not being invited to, no matter the tension we may be experiencing at the moment."

"What does the *ta'arof* thing say they have to do when they get the invite?"

"The exact same as *every* other culture: it says they should RSVP and decide whether or not to show up like the adults they are," she replied.

"I'll bring it up to Taraneh at my lesson," he agreed.

Within a minute, Brett was fully back on his feet and in the washroom brushing his teeth. With actual toothpaste so recently in his mouth, he concluded that what he had thought tasted like Colgate on the lip of the whiskey bottle probably was. Perhaps Rostam had taken a sip, right after brushing his teeth? The seal on the bottle had been broken and some was missing before Rostam had handed it to him, and Rostam already had his own bottle at that point. He put this into the vault of things to think about later if it occurred to him, and rinsed his mouth out thoroughly; it was time to put the nastiness away and move on with Sunday night in Manijeh's arms with breath that smelled *only* of Colgate and not of that mixed with half-a-mickey of Ballentine's Blended.

Touched by Fortune's Shadow: a triptych

23

Taraneh Khoshrangi pushed the sugar bowl toward Brett. "*Befarma'id!*" she said with a sweep of her right hand.

Brett took a cube, dropped it into his tea, stirred, and took a sip before saying, "Happy Canada Day, by the way. I had forgotten all about that when we made our plans to keep this Wednesday's practice session."

"I hope your day off with Manijeh wasn't ruined for this," she replied apologetically.

"We figured, given the situation, that there was a reason you called to keep this lesson," he explained before taking another sip of his tea. He watched her movements, which were graceful and calculated. She was dressed for dinner at a decent restaurant. "Are you and Rostam going out later?" he asked.

"Yes," she replied. "He and I have a dinner reservation at the Revolving Restaurant."

"Nice," he replied. "Since you'll see him tonight, could you ask if you and he would like to come to The Yale Friday night? Manijeh, a friend of hers, and Winston, whom you've met at the office, will all be there."

"I'll be sure to do that," she replied. "I would *love* to go, frankly. But I don't know Rostam's plans for Friday night." She took a sip, put the cup down carefully, and said, "Before we begin the lesson, I wanted to talk about last week's lesson."

Brett smiled, and motioned that she had the floor to speak.

"Rostam mentioned that you believe in open relationships," Taraneh said.

The tea he'd been sipping as she said this almost scalded his palate when he choked on it. "It's kind of an open secret in the hallways around a few watercoolers by now, but it's not something I show at the door unless the need to know arises," he explained.

"And Manijeh would know as well, I assume," she added.

"Yes. Of course. Why do you ask?"

She had been holding her cup with bent elbows, but put it on the table, and said, "I'm trying to understand the world I'm in right now. It is not what I'm familiar with. I'm here by choice, yes, but I want to better understand the landscape."

The macarons were still sitting right in the middle of the table, untested, and so he took one, and after a small bite said, "Delicious! I absolutely love macarons, and these are *very* nice." He washed the explosion of pistachio down with sugary tea and it felt good. "As for which world you're in, I'm pleased to be able to say that you're in *your* world, Taraneh. After all, *you're* living in it *now*. Is there anything I can do to help you navigate it, perhaps? Or are you just hoping for an understanding ear? I'm happy either way."

Taraneh nodded enthusiastically. "From my side, I've never had even an *iota* of what others would call a lover's jealousy, and so I *suspect* I would be fine with *your* way. I sometimes ask myself if that's because I'm so free and unjealous, or if I simply have not yet laid eyes on my Majnoun."

It was only by solidly reminding himself that he was a guest in Taraneh's home and that she had invited him to discuss matters, that Brett was able to allow her to direct the conversation where she was taking it, even though he would much rather have been rehearsing his phrasing at the keys. Taraneh was a fellow traveler, searching, asking, and he put aside his wish to be off the topic.

"That's how you feel now, but as you go along your path, you may find that what you believed of yourself needs adjustment," he began his reply. "I have adjusted my understanding of myself and what my limits and even core desires were in just the short time since Manijeh came back to Vancouver in April."

"How have you adjusted something as foundational as your core? Are you so *inconstant*?" She asked without judgment in her voice, but with pure curiosity. "You don't *seem* as fickle as that, Brett. At least I haven't seen you be."

"Not at all," he said. "I'm adaptable but have constant core values. My core *desires*, while *informed* by my values, are not my values. I value good thoughts, good words, and good deeds."

"Oh, are you a Zoroastrian, too, then?" she asked him. "I didn't know. How *lovely*!"

"No, I'm not a Zoroastrian by any means, although I have studied the Avesta, the Gatha in particular, in translation. But those *are* my values: good thoughts, good words, and good deeds. These core values provide a solid foundation.

"I *desire* peace, and that is consistent with those values. I cannot be revised or adjusted on these points. I will *always* desire peace. So while desires are not values, they can align so well that they are for all practical purposes as constant as values."

Taraneh nodded understanding and agreement.

"However, there are also desires informed by context. For instance, whether I desire to share myself in *any* capacity, not just physical, with another at any given point or time in my life is built about *where* I am in my life, *whom* I am with, *why* I am with them, and so on. These are not static and stagnant things. Why do I desire this *now*?

"People are astoundingly and wondrously complex beings. What is it about *this person* that I am craving, or think I want? These things are extremely context-specific, and we must adjust when we find our compass near such magnets. So, to answer one of your questions, this does not in any way make us *inconstant* or *inconsistent*. It makes us rivers rather than rocks. It makes us *contextually* consistent."

"How is that any different from standard moral relativism?" Taraneh sought clarification. "I must admit that I'm not a fan of morally relativistic arguments, though you won't find me going as deep as Kant into that arena. They seem slippery."

"Well," he began after giving it some consideration, "moral relativism typically suggests that moral truths are contingent upon cultural, societal, or individual perspectives, often leading to the conclusion that there are, in fact, no *universal* moral principles. In contrast, contextual consistency acknowledges the influence of context on our desires and actions without necessarily denying the existence of universal core values or objective moral truths. It is agnostic to the universality by focusing on locality and abstracting out the common basis."

"Your words sound *mathematical* rather than *emotional*," Taraneh noted. "It feels like reducing Rachmaninoff or Chopin to Sir Isaac Newton rather than Hafiz. I want your best *Hafiz*."

"Whereas moral relativism might well argue that what is *good* or *right* varies across multiple contexts, contextual consistency emphasizes maintaining alignment with one's core values while acknowledging the dynamic nature of desires within varying circumstances. This perspective does not actively encourage fence sitting or self-justification of one's actions based on some kind of inconstant view, as it puts its foundations on principles that are universally mutually benevolent, rather than self-serving."

Touched by Fortune's Shadow: a triptych

Taraneh nodded her head in agreement, smiling as she did, and said after sipping her tea, "Thank you, Brett, for explaining. I take it you're saying that contextual consistency acknowledges the influence of situational factors on our desires and actions while still maintaining alignment with our core values, rather than completely relativizing moral truths?"

"Indeed! Well put! What I'm really trying to get at here, if we go back to your original concern, is that you may find that meeting the Majnoun of your dreams will suddenly turn you into a jealous, spiteful, or otherwise angry person if that person crosses a line that somehow they and only they drew, whereas that didn't happen inside you until that particular relationship," he concluded his understanding of the topic at the depth that made sense to him to discuss. "Or you very well might still not be bothered one whit. The exact context has not yet arisen, and so the path is not yet more than a mental exercise."

"I appreciate your refreshing candor," she said. "It isn't often that one can have a frank discussion about such things that isn't wrapped in a thousand social expectations and innuendo."

The rest of the afternoon was spent with the recital of what he had practiced on his new Roland RD-600 electric keyboard, with its weighted full eighty-eight keys, at home in the spare room, and reviewing areas he would need to continue to refine his technique and interpretation.

❦ • ❧

"Was it worth ditching our Canada Day over? But if you think about it, Canada Day from this penthouse is pretty much the platinum standard, so I don't exactly feel put out much at all." Manijeh took a sip from her soda and put it on the table beside the *chaise longue*.

"I'd say so," Brett replied. "Though it could well have been a simple phone call, to be honest. Nice macarons, though."

"We tanked the day for *macarons*?" Her playfulness was clear on her face.

"Pistachio," he said with a huge grin.

She turned to face him. "Well worth it."

"I think they're going to be fine. Taraneh has an incredible capacity for self-awareness that more than compensates for Rost…. I hope the two of them can find their groove," he said. "Also, I did ask her to bring up Friday at The Yale," he added.

"I'm looking forward to it. Your place is spectacular. Such a breathtakingly almost painterly view."

Brett reached across to her hand, held it, and said, "*Our* place is spectacular. *This* we *can* own. Well, that is, as much as one can be said to *own* land that was never ceded by those who cared for it long before we even knew North America was a thing, let alone this part of Canada we happen to find ourselves enjoying this wonderful and enchanted evening. Happy Squatter's Day!"

"Happy Canada Day to you, too!" Manijeh playfully retorted but with no small degree of unease on her face about what had just been said.

At quarter past eleven, the fireworks were done and both were tired enough to turn in for the night, Manijeh's cell phone began to shake with an incoming call.

"It's from Taraneh," she said. "I *should* answer it." She placed the phone closely to her ear. "Taraneh-*joonam*, s*alâm! Khub-im, kheili mamnun. Hâl-e-tche tor-e?*" she said in Persian. "*Areh. Areh. Alân zamân khub-e! Gush mikonam! Gorbân-et-am, aziz-am! Harf begu!*"[33]

Brett went back onto the balcony and closed the door to give Manijeh and Taraneh their privacy. Although they were speaking Persian and he only studied it, he could understand some phrases, and he had been around the Yazdpours for almost twenty years and could differentiate the words more readily than from book study alone. Since he was hearing to only his mangled interpretation of Manijeh's half of the conversation alone, however, he knew that what his mind might automatically interpret her as having said was entirely likely pure fabrication on his part, given his very shaky formal understanding of Farsi. If Manijeh had anything to say after the conversation with Taraneh, she would explain it to him. He was happy that the call had come well after he and she had enjoyed an uninterrupted evening together.

---

[33] "Taraneh, sweetie, hello! We're good, thanks so much. How are you? Yes. Yes. Now's a good time! I'm listening! I'm here for you 100%, darling! Talk!"

Touched by Fortune's Shadow: a triptych

24

Trough-style urinals, no matter how esthetically pleasing the tiling might have been in any number of other contexts, were not among Brett Lloyd-Ronan's favorite places to rid himself of the consequences of the evening's stout, but here he was, at The Yale on his first go at it. Winston Rampersad stood to his right. "So how many did you count?" he asked.

"Five servings," Winston responded quietly.

"Thanks. Keep counting."

Winston nodded before zipping up, washing his hands, drying them thoroughly, and then leaving the washroom. Brett soon followed back to the table, where Rostam, Taraneh, Manijeh, and Ken, Manijeh's colleague, were also seated. He took his seat beside Manijeh. "What'd I miss?" he asked. After he was caught up, he asked Manijeh to dance on the next slow song, and when that came, they were on the floor, as were Rostam and Taraneh, as Winston and Ken from Manijeh's office meanwhile leaned back and swapped trading gossip.

"He's pretty much outright hammered," Brett whispered into Manijeh's attentive ear.

"How much?" she asked in reply.

"Five drinks in him so far near as Winston could tell, and he *may* have prepped, so I'm going to say that he's actually had more like *seven*."

She held him even more tightly. "Damn. That's a lot when you're trying to stay social," she said. Her right hand held to his French cuff like a handle as they danced.

On the distressed call Manijeh had received from Taraneh on Wednesday night, they learned Rostam had become offensively drunk while at the restaurant and that Taraneh had had to use her grace and manners to prevent an embarrassing call by staff that would not have played out well for anyone.

Touched by Fortune's Shadow: a triptych

Brett had noticed something was off with Rostam's putting back the liquor lately, but a public spectacle was an escalation unlike he'd known from him, and besides, he felt for Taraneh's having felt obligated to rescue Rostam from the consequences of his behavior.

Normally, Rostam would pretend it had to be single malt, The Glenlivet, or something equally pricey to at least seem like a special treat one gave oneself rarely, but Ballentine's Blended in a bottle with toothpaste on the broken seal, things like this suggested something was askew.

He remembered his father's struggle with liquor, where that brought him and his mother as witnesses to both Arthur Lloyd-Ronan's torment and that which this level of dependence rained down upon the bystanders, the mistakes it encouraged, and the eventual path he had to take to get out of his hamster wheel, and he worried for his friend, as did Manijeh. He remembered how back before they started VAI that Rostam had been riding the rails of binge drinking, but back then he had been able to pull his sails in for the high winds and ride out the storm. Brett's experience with his father had helped him be supportive during that patch. A patch he thought had passed. The sea was changing lately, though, and Rostam's trusty sextant had been soundly dropped and was now reading as if bent from the tumble.

As for Taraneh, she had taken her and Brett's conversation from earlier that Wednesday to heart and reached out for help and advice to Rostam's family, his sister, to at least try to make sense of his recent spike in disruptive drinking. She chose to make her new understanding one of a union between Rostam's and her groups, rather than an insulated intersection. By reaching out to Manijeh by phone that night, she had begun to build her own place in the new world she had been struggling to understand, giving her some agency in its outcomes, as those outcomes were now shared by her. Upon speaking with both Manijeh and Brett about Rostam's drinking, she learned that this level of excess was something that everyone had thought he had made his way through. Even then he had *never* made a public scene that anyone had ever heard of. This gave everyone hope that it was an acute local disruption in his patterns and wouldn't become chronic.

The song ended and all returned to the table. When Rostam called out for another round, Brett spoke out. His tone was gentle, but his message was clear. "Let's *not* and call it a night."

Rostam laughed, glanced at Brett, and said, "You do *you*."

Taraneh glanced quickly into Manijeh's eyes. It had already been agreed between the three of them, and Winston, who was sworn to secrecy and was completely aware that in their line of business, business and personal matters when in public were one and the same thing, that, while they were not going to interfere in any kind of excess on Rostam's part, they were going to run ground and air cover for him and collectively stay sober enough to keep the night safe and enjoyable, which it had been to this point. Ken, of course, was none the wiser about any of this and seemed to be having as fun a night out as he'd had in at least a year.

The night ended pleasantly, everyone went home in taxis, and two conversations in The Yale restrooms, between Manijeh and Taraneh in theirs and Brett and Winston in theirs and it was agreed upon unanimously that Rostam probably needed a few weeks of vacation to deal with whatever his soul seemed to be struggling with. In all his time at Vector Affinity Insights, he had only ever taken three weeks' time off, which he often announced as a matter of pride. Taraneh was given the duty of convincing him that such a holiday would be a good thing not just for him, but for the two of them. She was to report back to Manijeh directly on the success of their first, response to Rostam's return to a pattern of intemperate drinking.

◈ • ◈

On the westward facing arm of the balcony, overlooking the Park, Manijeh huddled into Brett's chest as they shared a *chaise longue* over orange juice. The evening's dancing and socializing was slowly beginning to leave their frames and be replaced with the cool sparkle of the July sky. Through the outdoor speaker, the stylings of David Bowie's *Low* decorated the summer wind.

Manijeh pulled the light blanket they had over them to her neck and pressed even more firmly into him. "I really thought he'd run that race and won it," she finally said.

Before speaking, Brett inhaled, held it, exhaled, held it, and then finally said, "It's been six years that he's been moderating his alcohol well. Things in his life have changed over that time, and for the most part, that has been a slow process, given the speed that some things move. So he's been able to adapt. But things have been shifting around lately *very* quickly."

"A hectic mess," Manijeh agreed.

Touched by Fortune's Shadow: a triptych

"On multiple fronts: business, family, close relationships." He pulled her in even more tightly. The stars also comforted him. "That's why these things require regular attention and a thorough search and fearless inventory to keep track of today's stresses and triggers rather than just relying on yesterday's successes."

"Brett, did you mean to say *searching and fearless moral inventory*? It sounds like you have had some exposure to the Program. I had a dorm mate who was in it, and I went to some of her meetings with her to support her, while I was at UBC."

Although he had, across the span of his years of having known the Yazdpours, never spoken about his father's battles, Manijeh was now his life partner, making Arthur Lloyd-Ronan her future father-in-law, and he opened that door inside him, took a very quick look into the long-locked chamber he was about to show her and invite her into, and finally said, "My father is a recovering alcoholic. He's been sober since I was fourteen, but he was *heavily* in the problem by the time *he* was fourteen himself. Just over fourteen years he's been without a drop. I don't count the days, that's for him and Mom, though I do attend his yearly birthday to show him I'm proud as hell that he pulled out in time to save his marriage and his and my relationship. So I have some direct personal experience with that world."

The stars did not fall and destroy the Earth. The sea did not swell and overcome the shores all about them. The words simply left his lips, flew to her ears, and found their resting place in her consideration. Her expression showed she was, indeed, giving what he had said thought.

"Oh, sweety, why did you carry that burden *alone* all these years?" She kissed his cheek.

He first kissed Manijeh's forehead, and replied, "It wasn't a burden for *me* to carry, as much as it was *his*. For years before he finally hit rock bottom, he was in and out like a fiddler's elbow. It ran roughshod on Mom and me. *Our* burdens were between her and me, so I didn't talk about any of those with my friends. Dad hid it well from everyone but us, and we learned to cope as well as we learned to keep it in the family."

"Seeing Rostam fall so hard into binge drinking back when he was struggling with his career choice must have triggered some things," she said. "I mean, I know how it made me feel, and my dad and mom are practically teetotalers. So I can only imagine how it might have made you feel, given what you just told me about your father and how it affected you.."

Brett tried to remember how it felt when he realized Rostam was falling fast just before they started their business together. "He was searching for something that was *his*. Your dad, the chemical engineer who rescued his family by bringing you all safely out of the chaos after what happened to your uncle and his family, was guiding him down the engineering path. It was when he finally had something that was his and my path alone, and not put on him from expectation, that he found the light." He paused for a while before adding, "But we must constantly take that inventory. Things change. We get comfortable. Our muscles lose tone. Our daily self-care falls into disrepair. That's honestly where I think he is right now. It's an awful place to be, speaking from dark personal experience."

"Have you ever been a binge drinker at all?" she asked.

"I rode the rails to the slivers a few times in my life," he admitted. "Came mighty close to those tracks. Back when I was in Port Coquitlam, I spent a lot of time at the Golden Ears Pub with my hand on the counter and a tumbler tapping for another. Pulled through it by sheer youthful constitution most days, bright-eyed and bushytailed on the outside and hammered shite on the inside. But I eventually found that for me is what about wanting to shut the world down around me. So I leaned into my meditation and that worked for *me*."

"Good. This stuff with Taraneh must have also been quite a distraction for him," Manijeh suggested.

"Honestly?"

"Of course. I wouldn't have it any other way."

He pulled together what he wanted to say in his mind before letting it leave his lips. "He's been in trading and finance for a while now, and he has nerves of steel, and it never so much as *baffled* him. He's got perfect pitch when it comes to stress at levels that I have no idea about. I've seen him close deals that, had he not, could have *broken* us early only. Without even breaking a sweat. Girlfriend's hand slips during piano lesson is a very small item on his list of worries. It seems deeper to me."

Manijeh hummed, "Yes, me too, I saw Rostam *slay* during my time at VAI."

"He's also honest about his own walk," Brett added. "He broke his share of hearts in his time with behavior that he now calls himself out on. Hhe's not emotionally *fragile* about a hand landing on my lap at a practice over at Taraneh's, near as I can tell. That's all par for his course."

Touched by Fortune's Shadow: a triptych

With a sliding motion, Manijeh slid so that she was on top of him, facing him, her hands on either side of his face. "We'll let her try to get them to take a vacation," she said. "Taraneh suggested Harrison Hot Springs, but I told her they should drive all the way to Alberta and hit Drumheller. They need time with him sober on the road, away from opportunities to be constantly sauced. At least long enough for him to catch his breath."

"Life is what happens to us while we are making other plans." Brett then put his arms around her, pulled her in, kissed her deeply, and didn't say anything else. They made love on the balcony, under the summer stars, pulled the thin blanket over themselves, as the record next on the pre-arranged stack fell down, and they fell asleep huddled closely together, brought to Morpheus' serene inkiness by Bowie's *The Man Who Sold the World*.

/ Quinn Tyler Jackson

Vancouver, mid-July 1998

Touched by Fortune's Shadow: a triptych

25

At the large table at Cazba, the Yazdpour family's favorite Persian restaurant, sat Ardashir and Mahnaz Yazdpour, the proud parents of Manijeh, who had finally received her registration and license to trade at fullest capacity. She sat beside Brett, and also at the table were Brett's parents, Arthur and Siobhan Lloyd-Ronan. They had received the news in the mail on Wednesday, and now it was Friday. Her brother Rostam had been given the news by phone call as he and Taraneh drove their road trip from Vancouver to Calgary, Alberta, and then up to Drumheller, and they insisted that everyone else not wait to celebrate Manijeh's promotion. With this change in her status at Klein, Holdum, and French, one of the most prestigious house's in the Vancouver scene, her salary had tripled with the flick of a letter opener, and it was time to be merry.

"I remember when Brett got the license to trade," Siobhan said to Manijeh, as if speaking to her directly, rather than to the whole table. "The call. The excitement in his voice. Surely, you must feel the same way."

"It's liberating to *finally* be able to do what I'm trained to do," Manijeh replied.

"But you must have felt that for the six months you were at in Toronto," Mahnaz noted. "We weren't there to celebrate together like this. What was Toronto like? You never really said."

"I'd rather not—"

"Like apples and oranges," Brett interjected. "Completely different situations in Vancouver and Toronto. Vancouver is a career *coup*." Though it felt awkward to interrupt Manijeh, he knew from recent conversations with her that Mahnaz was disappointed with her drop in presentational career status and salary as she toiled at Klein, Holdum and French at the more junior work until registration.

Touched by Fortune's Shadow: a triptych

As parents sometimes will, although she loved Brett and was ecstatic they were together, she could never quite reconcile the loss in status she perceived Manijeh had put herself through in leaving her very decent fledgling career in Toronto, and her own social circles had made an annoying point of returning to this topic occasionally, which did not at all lighten Manijeh's load on the matter.

So when Brett had offered Mahnaz some justification of the sacrifice Manijeh had made not being about *him* or *love*, but about career path progression, Mahnaz' eyes lit up in a way that Brett had often seen in Manijeh, and this was the first time he had noticed the correlation in their gazes. "So, you think Vancouver is better than Toronto was? How is that?"

Brett wanted that track of conversation to end, for the topic of trading in Toronto to go away and never come back. He felt that perhaps not being around Manijeh as much as she once had, and now that she had access to her to discuss topics that might help them reconnect and affirm their bonds, Mahnaz dove too deeply with her probing. He concentrated on his next words and his intent in uttering them. His goal was to close the topic without follow-up, without seeming to be in a hurry to go on to something else, and to do it with discretion and honesty. Such delicate social calculations were more difficult than any occult equation he could muster against the markets.

He quickly reviewed Manijeh's position description in his mind so that he would not say about her what had not already been said in public. "Manijeh is now with Klein, Holdum, and French, probably the most reputable and solid house going, and that's here in *Vancouver*. Manijeh's role now involves hedging investment portfolios with EU and US instruments, and to expand and develop relationships and best-practices that facilitate this. All of this is happening on the cusp of the euro getting the lights switched on for banking and trade in the EU this coming year, and that will turn the disco ball on to light up the whole room. Because of this extra agency allowed by the *Vancouver* situation, we can safely say that it's apples and oranges with respect to what Toronto felt it had on offer in *theory* and what it could actually *deliver* in practice compared to here, where we can all sit around a single table and share our collective joy."

Both Ardashir and Mahnaz nodded, fully in agreement with this, smiled, congratulated their daughter, and talk moved on eventually to the perfect *tah-dig* presented by the restaurant.

Manijeh leaned into Brett's ear, holding his hand, and said, "Thank you. I love you."

Brett kissed her cheek. "New team project: let's try to perfect our *tah-dig* together."[34]

"Mine sucks," she replied.

"Pardon?" Mahnaz asked.

"I said every attempt I've ever made at *tah-dig* is an utter trainwreck. I can make a perfect beef Wellington, but I'm lost with *tah-dig*."

"I've tried making *tah-dig* and can say without any shame that mine's not *any* better," Brett confessed. "And yeah, Manijeh's beef Wellington's amazing."

"What's the secret?" Siobhan asked. "I imagine I'd burn more than a few attempts to get it anywhere near this golden."

"Now that you're family, Siobhan and Arthur, I will reveal the Yazdpour family secret," Mahnaz began.

"I assure you that this is truly our best kept secret," Manijeh punctuated her mother's point.

"Just as with Manijeh and Brett, my *tah-dig* is substandard. I am a nurse, not a chef. But Ardashir… he's a chemical engineer. Rostam also makes excellent *tah-dig*, crisp, golden, aromatic. Ardashir and Rostam have saved many formal dinners at our house from certain disaster."

Ardashir did a sitting bow. "What is food but chemicals? It's all a matter of figuring out the correct reactions. I accept my Master's Diploma in *Tah-dig-shenâssi*[35] and remind my lovely wife that her *kabab soltâni*[36] lives up to the fancy name." Then, he did something unexpected by lifting up his hand, pointing over at Arthur and saying, "Everyone, Arthur has something for you all to hear. Arthur, you have the floor."

Arthur Lloyd-Ronan then gave a small cough before saying, "Everyone, I've got very good news, as well. I got word back from the four Japanese fellows who were taking a look at my alloy.

---

[34] *Tah-dig* (lit. "bottom-pot") is a prized component of Iranian cuisine, known for its crunchy texture and the skill required to perfect it. This crispy layer of rice, which can also include potatoes or bread, symbolizes hospitality and the joy of shared meals.

[35] *tah-dig-shenâssi* (lit. "crispy-rice-ology"), clearly something he made up.

[36] *Kebab soltâni* (lit. "Sultan's Kebab") is a luxurious Persian dish combining ground meat kebabs and grilled pieces of meat, served alongside rice and vegetables, epitomizing royal indulgence and culinary craftsmanship in its preparation and presentation.

Touched by Fortune's Shadow: a triptych

The sword sets they asked for are not quite ready yet, but they asked me if I'd consider licensing the alloy for any other use, since I hold the patent. Of course I said yes. And so, we—Ardashir and I—prepared a prototype quickly using his tooling and got it to them. They loved it, and suggested we introduce the alloy to Japanese metallurgists first through the licensed manufacturing use in law-enforcement-restricted telescoping batons. This small penetration into that market would then position our four friends, the ones who were at Brett's *kenjutsu* ceremony, in their petition to consider the alloy for eventual *nihonto* use."

At this point, Ardashir started talking. "The idea is that we first introduce the alloy in other related contexts, prove it out, and then build our case with the regulators. It's a long endgame, and so Arthur and I formed a small company around the baton project, which we own together. We are now business partners, tying our bonds as families even more closely."

Manijeh reached for her napkin to wipe away some tears, and Brett almost felt the need to do the same. Never had he been at a business announcement presentation that had done that to him. To see his father's hard work as a machinist finally come to fruit like this shook him about. He regained his composure slowly, and just continued to sit there.

"That's so lovely!" Manijeh finally ejected.

"It is!" Mahnaz agreed.

"Arthur told me not to tell you until the papers were through," Siobhan explained. "Or you know I would have. What a great thing we all have."

"A thing like that could really grow," Brett said. "I mean, truth told, I wouldn't mind carrying one of those things myself. Especially when walking through Stanley Park at night."

"Beats the hell out of an umbrella!" Ardashir exclaimed. "I think we have our new tagline!"

"Today batons," Arthur closed, "tomorrow *katana*."

∽•∾

"I wanted to hide under my napkin," Manijeh said when they were halfway back on the route home over the Lions Gate.

"I think your mom just wants to reconnect," he replied, remembering how uncomfortable that part of the evening felt. At least his and her father's announcement had completely put that into the rearview mirror.

Her loud sigh filled the front seat cabin. "'How did Toronto make you feel?' One day I'll tell you, Mom, but for now, pass the *sumac*, please. But you at least redirected her without telling her not to ask. I was halfway to telling her to shut up."

"Oh, I know you were, which is why I jumped in with all the extra *gravitas* you have here now that the license has arrived. It was either the tack I went with or bring up all the anti-comingling and other conditions they put on you and me in detail and moan about that instead," he said. Separate checking accounts. Any shared accounts are to have deposits only directly from those two accounts. No undeclared personal gifts over five-hundred dollars. All physical and other firewall separation already in place at time of application to remain implemented. "Albeit that the conditions are nothing too draconian, considering what we do and what we do it *with*: that being other people's money. We must be *seen* to comply, as Margaret put it. What was it you said about that?"

"O brave new world, that has such cynicism in it," she said.

At that instant, Dylan's "Gotta Serve Somebody" came on the car radio, and he turned up the volume and they listened to it without speaking the rest of the way home, except that when Dylan reached that part about being a businessperson or thief, being called Doctor or Chief, Brett sang along, and in that spirit, Manijeh joined in and the mood in the car lifted.

They were halfway up the elevator to their floor when Brett asked, "How do you think they're doing over there in Alberta?"

"I got a nice text message this morning from Taraneh that they were doing well," Manijeh replied. "I'm sorry that I forgot to mention it earlier. They're enjoying long hikes together and counting cacti. Healthy stuff to let him find himself again."

"Maybe she'll find herself out there, too," Brett added. "From what I've seen, she has a world of thinking going on in her head, so the dry, fresh air might be good for them both to sort it all out."

"Don't we all, though? Have a lot of thinking going on in our heads, I mean."

"Indeed we do!" he said as they arrived at their floor and the doors opened, letting them enter the rest of their evening together.

Touched by Fortune's Shadow: a triptych

26

"I really needed the break," Rostam volunteered from across the table at the very back of Taf's Cafe. "I was putting it back pretty hard for a while," he admitted.

"There were signs," Brett replied. "But I missed them until what happened on Canada Day."

"When we were on our way back, when we hit Lake Louise, Taraneh told me she told Manijeh about Canada Day," he said. He sipped from his cola and then spooned some soup to his mouth.

"How are you now? Are you fully on the tracks, or are you a slow trainwreck?"

At this, Rostam stopped eating and sat up straight. "How do you keep yourself so together, man?"

Brett put down his coffee before saying, "My friend, my life is complete disarray and has been since Manijeh came back." He smiled as he considered how Manijeh was *actually* in his life.

"I need a smoke. Do you want one? I know you don't usually smoke with me, but I could use to feel not like a freak standing alone out there," he pleaded.

"Sure thing." He then turned to the waiter and said, "We'll be right back; going for a smoke."

The waiter nodded an acknowledgement.

Once they were outside in the front, Rostam handed his friend a cigarette and then lit his own. Once Brett was lit, too, he started to talk. "Disarray? Tell me about that."

"Good stuff. I didn't plan for the woman I loved much of my adult life to literally show up on my doorstep, man. I had no Plan B, C, or D for that matter, that included any of what has happened recently. I mean our dads are now cofounders of... well, you know what I mean. I had no *plan* for *any* of this to happen. Getting married to Manijeh?"

"It has been a bit of a ride lately, hasn't it?" Rostam agreed.

"Come on, man, when was any of *that* ever on anyone's radars? Except in my deepest heart, that I hardly even trusted at times, from insecurity and fear. This stuff was just pixie dust and fairy tale material. In the lands where Love's First Kiss reigns supreme and makes all the chaos go away to hide."

"Unbelievable, man," Rostam sighed more than said. "Aren't you also a philosophical master as well as sword master, with a mandate to guide others along *their* journeys?" His eyes were sincere. "Isn't that all part of who you've been becoming all these years with your *kenjutsu* journey? *Sensei* Brett Lloyd-Ronan. And all you have to show for your barefoot journey on glass shards is chaos and *fairy tales*? Put your *back* into it!"

"So, I take it what you're saying is you want some master level philosophical musings? Sure, let's give it a shot...." After taking a drag from his cigarette, Brett continued. "Sometimes, like the day we met, life is a Creek. We risk falling in and getting wet, getting stuck, getting our socks wet, and rotting out our boot." He patted Rostam on the back when he saw that this brought back memories to his imagination. "Sometimes life is putting a pointed stick at someone's Adam's apple, so they shut the hell up." He swept his hand across the vibrant flow that was this section of Granville Street.

"And sometimes life is a River, each next thing to flow past us completely catching us off our guard," he continued. "Just like Granville, Hastings, or any other street of a dozen you can name around here."

"Seems like more and more of that crap to me these days," Rostam agreed. "I mean, being told by my girlfriend about... you know. And any number of other things that are starting to catch up on me at the office. Not the least of which the decision about adaptive vector attunement and whether we take that to patent or lock it up as a trade secret. We have to get back on that with Gerry, by the way," he added as an side to be noted. "You don't seem to be in *disarray* compared to how I'm performing in public places like on Canada Day. I feel awful for what I did to Taraneh there."

Brett took his final drag from the courtesy cigarette before saying, "What I'm saying is that life doesn't care one whit about my philosophy. Creek or River: I don't choose which my raft gets sent down on any given day. "I can tell you what the Seven Virtues are, and listen when you need an ear, but *self-control*, one of those Virtues, is what we find when we stare into the water: be it river or creek water, or our personal *koi* pond.

"It's up to *me* to put aside things of the past I have outgrown and pull toward me those new people and things in my life that are made for *today*. Don't remember how well you handled the turns of the river upstream that you've *already* flown past. Keep your eyes open for signs of *coming* waterfalls, and enjoy the rapids right under your paddle, right here, at this particular turn. I find this works for both creeks *and* rivers. And tranquil ponds."

With that, they flicked their butts discretely into the curb, as if by their small discretion they had somehow magically not littered, and then returned to the café.

"Real life takes daily curation and diligence," Brett added. "Is there anything I can carry for you right now that might make your load lighter? Really, Rostam, what do you need from me that I can give you to help you weather this storm?"

"You *could* give me some outright advice, to be honest," Rostam replied. "I won't take it wrong. It doesn't even have to sound mystical and wise. You may say you're in disarray and messed up, but I still trust your advice."

"Give my dad a call," Brett suggested.

"Pardon? Arthur? How does this?"

"Tell him you're looking for a friend of Bill's," he then added.

"Bill? Who…?"

"Dude, just do it. You asked for my advice, and there you go, the best advice the *Sensei* has on offer right now, man. Now… tell me about your worries with adaptive vector attunement's status."

While he still appeared completely confused, Rostam sat back. "My concern, as always, is that patent disclosures will open us up to adjacent but non-violating competition, whereas keeping it a trade secret will lock that up."

The conundrum of committing resources to researching and developing innovative intellectual property in their space had hit them again. To date they had kept their advancements under lock and key and need-to-know, but in doing so, they had opened their competitive position up to eventual duplication of their methods by outside concerns.

"We already claim SR&ED[37] credits for much of our more innovative work," Brett began.

---

[37] Scientific Research & Experimental Development (SR&ED) tax credits are a Canadian government incentive designed to encourage businesses of all sizes and in all sectors to conduct research and development (R&D) in Canada.

Touched by Fortune's Shadow: a triptych

"That's another thing," Rostam replied. "Claiming *that* tax credit has required us to submit information outside of the company to substantiate our claims. I can't help but feel that keeping things under the hood has longer term benefits then we gain from the paltry tax benefits. Patents expire. We have to watch the bottom line and protect it from risk of disclosure, which could devalue our differentiators."

Brett started to laugh. "I can't spend all *my* money, man, and I'm not even wealthy by *any* standard. Can you spend all *yours*? Could you spend it all even if you spread it around to friends and family to make *their* lives better? Aren't you 'there' *yet*?"

Rostam shuffled about at this. His sandwich almost done, he started organizing his empty plates and cups for easy bussing. Brett knew that he did this because he had once been a busboy in hi university days and thus absolutely hated when customers left their tables in disorder.

"I'm responsible for the shareholders, profits, and the firm, and all of that in ways that require me to think about it as I do whether I personally am 'there' or not," Rostam defended his position. "But I certainly get your point from a purely *human* perspective; yes, I am content with my current level of affluence and the lifestyle it gives me. I've protected myself as much as you have in this regard, and already have a portfolio that goes leaps and bounds toward securing my retirement, as long as I keep it just for that and don't piss it away in a trough urinal."

"We're not even thirty-years-old," Brett said in a solid voice. "Let's remember how much time we have to figure out all of this stuff with our lives and not be in a hurry to forget about today. Yeah, you *must* think about the shareholders, and that weighs a lot more than many realize. As an officer of the company, I do, as well. You and I are called on to always be mindful to any number of higher powers. As is Manijeh in what she does. When you wake up in only your shorts and stumble to look yourself in the mirror, you have to ask *why* you struggle so much."

"Most of the time I feel quite able to handle it all myself," Rostam said.

"That was then, this is now, and you must figure out how much of that load you might put aside or let others carry if it *must* be carried now. Sometimes everyone *must* let the weight of the day humble them."

"Are you saying I should hire an assistant?"

"Yes. I'm saying you should look into finding an assistant. And give my father that call." He signaled that he wanted to pay the check, and soon they were on their way back to the office. "I'll even get Winston to start looking for someone for you."

"Please do," Rostam replied. "I'd do it, but don't even have the time to find an assistant myself. I got some good rest with Taraneh in Alberta, but I'm not *really* firing on all cylinders yet. I only play a competent CEO on television."

When they got back to the office, Brett called Winston into his office and told him to start looking for an Executive Assistant to the CEO for Rostam. In the life of VAI, Rostam had never asked for an assistant, even when Brett had hired Winston Rampersad, as if admitting that he needed support seemed to be an admission to failure. But those were yesterday's ways. Today suddenly became all there was for Rostam Yazdpour.

Touched by Fortune's Shadow: a triptych

Quinn Tyler Jackson

Vancouver, mid-December 1984

Touched by Fortune's Shadow: a triptych

27

Brett sat in the night air on the steps that led up to the front door of the main floor of the finished basement three-bedroom corner bungalow in the quiet Hastings-Sunrise neighborhood of Vancouver. It was cold but he was making do. He'd left the door open so he could hear when the racket inside the kitchen had stopped without having to get up to put his ear to the window, although the sound of pots, pans, dishes, and who knew what else smashing probably would have made it through a closed door anyway. But the racket did not stop, except once in a while to be interrupted by Siobhan Lloyd-Ronan pleading with her husband Arthur to calm down. He would slur something in return and proceed. Eventually, she came out on the front stairs and joined her son in sitting on the steps.

"I'll do them tomorrow," he whispered to his mother.

"Pardon me, Brett?" she asked, putting her arm around him to comfort him.

"He asked me when I was going to do the dishes in the sink," he explained. "I simply replied, 'I'll do them tomorrow' and *that* set him *right* off."

"He's been drinking," was her reply.

To his ear, it sounded as if every dish had been smashed, every pot and pan bent. Every single one in the house. That his mother would explain this all off with just four simple syllables made his abdomen ache and his heart constrict as the tears rushed to the edges of his eyes and his ears were pounding both with the beat of his own heart and the slowly diminishing chaos his father was wreaking on what was left of the kitchen.

"If *this* isn't rock bottom, Mom, what is?" he asked. "And what kind of question is that for a fourteen-year-old *child* to be asking his *mother* a week before Christmas?" he added.

He got up and started what turned out to be a two-hour walk around the block. When he returned at ten-thirty, all lights were out. Cardboard boxes filled with the trash that had been created by Arthur Lloyd-Ronan's explosive episode sat on the porch out back. He quickly walked across the kitchen, careful to avoid any pieces of glass in case all had not been cleaned yet, and shot downstairs to his basement bedroom, walking as quietly and quickly as he could so not to be noticed.

An hour passed before he admitted to himself that he was not going to fall asleep anytime soon, and so he positioned himself in the lotus position beside his bed and then started to regulate his breathing into a pattern towards inner stillness. He slowly let the mass of tangled strings loosen and fly away from the spinning center until all that remained was a single point: *him*.

Having let go of the night's duress, he returned to his bed and quicky fell into a deep sleep. When he awoke, he did not care what time it was, since the winter break had begun at school and time was irrelevant. As much as he did not want to, he forced himself to get dressed and walk upstairs and push the basement door open into the kitchen.

Arthur and Siobhan were both there, at the table, with two take-out cups of coffee one of them must have fetched from the store down the street, since there were no cups left in the house. Siobhan looked miserable, as if she had been up all night, and Arthur was three shades-of-hungover.

"I'm sorry about last night," Arthur said.

"Well, that's a start," Siobhan replied with a grimace.

Brett knew that his father probably was, in fact, sorry, since Arthur wasn't usually one to say things he didn't stand behind. Because of this, he didn't expect more by way of apology than this, and *word* sorry itself might very well be the entirety of the amends offered. He wouldn't have accepted it as a legitimate apology in any case, but he would have at least pushed one foot in front of the other for his mother's sake, and for family peace, and to let them have enough absolution to clean up the rest of his mess now that the glass was mostly swept away from underfoot.

He would have kept right on his way out the door to go buy breakfast somewhere cheap now that they had nothing to prepare food with, but before he could get out of earshot of anything he had to say, his father decided to keep talking.

"I'm sorry, but I wasn't wrong in *why* I did it."

Halfway on his trajectory out of the house, Brett turned to face Arthur squarely and said, "You're an idiot. You've a lot of nerve making this about *my* behavior. A lot of Goddamned nerve."

In a heartbeat, Arthur was on his feet with his clenched fist ready to hit Brett. "You ungrateful bastard!" he hissed. He started to swing and move toward Brett.

"Stop it, you two!" Siobhan screamed.

Years of judo training took over for Brett. Though he held a brown belt, his *sensei* had said that was only because of his age, and that he would be elevated to first *dan* black belt on his next birthday. He positioned himself slightly off to Arthur's side, catching him mid-step as he advanced. Brett seized Arthur's right arm, pulling it across Arthur's body to further unbalance him. At the same time, he placed his right leg behind Arthur's left, his nearest leg, effectively blocking Arthur's ability to step back and regain balance.

With a swift, clean movement, leveraging Arthur's forward momentum and his own leg as a fulcrum, Brett executed the *O Soto Gari*. He reaped Arthur's leg out from under him, causing him to fall heavily onto the kitchen floor. Before Arthur could react, Brett transitioned fluidly into a solid *Kesa Gatame* hold, securing Arthur in an only moderately uncomfortable grip.

Arthur's raw aggression, having been met with a controlled, measured response, almost as quickly as it had begun, led to him tapping out, signaling his submission. Brett, respecting the tap-out more from years of conditioning than from compassion, immediately released his father from the hold.

"If this isn't rock bottom, *what* is?" Brett asked.

"I've been considering going back to meetings," Arthur said, his head hung down.

"Enough of that! Dad, you're in and out like a fiddler's elbow. You're going to a meeting *tonight*, after going out with Mom and buying replacement dishes and pots and pans. Spend as much as you might have on the horses at a good day at the track. Skip all the first steps right now except the one about making amends. Fix what you did here."

He looked his father directly in his eyes and said, "Dad, I love you, very much. You mean the *world* to me. But I'm not going to hear anything you have to say about *anything* until you're saying it with a thirty-day token in your hand. I *am* grateful for all the support you have given me, but that gratitude does *not* buy you a ticket to treat us the way you do when you drink."

Touched by Fortune's Shadow: a triptych

He stood with one foot out the kitchen door and the other inside, and he added, "I'm *making* this your rock bottom. You're sober from *this* moment forward, or the next time you raise a hand against me, I won't just let you tap out. This isn't cricket." He left to spend his last ten dollars on breakfast, hoping he would have the stomach to hold it down.

Part Three: *Tacere*

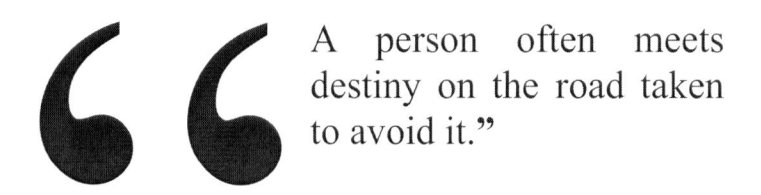

> "A person often meets destiny on the road taken to avoid it."

—Jean de La Fontaine (attributed)

Touched by Fortune's Shadow: a triptych

San Francisco, late September 1998

Touched by Fortune's Shadow: a triptych

28

The third annual *International Symposium on Quantitative Risk Management*, which was held at San Francisco's Palace Hotel as it had been the year before, found both Brett Lloyd-Ronan of Vector Affinity Insights and Manijeh Yazdpour of Klein, Holdum, and French, both from Vancouver, presenting each on different topics on different days. Manijeh was to give one of three keynotes, each held at the start of the three successive days of the symposium, hers to be on Tuesday the twenty-ninth. Given their representation of different firms, they were booked in separate rooms to maintain the firewall their profession demanded, since they each carried their own share of company sensitive material with them.

It was while she presented her keynote, "Dawn of the Euro: Preparing for Currency Transition Risks," that Brett received his first real taste of what she was up to at Klein *et al.*, since they had a number of covenants that kept these matters from their tongues over evening conversation. Her take on transition risks fell into many of the same places he'd explored in his imagination and some even with his coding dexterity, but not always exactly, and for that he was pleased, with his own ideas for where Vector Affinity Insights might take their adaptive vector attunement system, on which Rostam had ultimately made an executive call to hold as a trade secret rather than patent.

As a trade secret, he was not at liberty to even suggest to *anyone* outside VAI that it even existed, let alone provide the slightest hint of how it functioned, and thus he could only refer to it by its codename "Proteus." Proteus. The face of the sea-god, there out at Prospect Point along the Seawall. Where mathematics met metal. From out of Proteus, functions came, taking many forms, predicting changes in the wind's direction. Those changes had a monetary value assigned to them.

Touched by Fortune's Shadow: a triptych

The shifting forms of Proteus were spun upon manifolds, from reality, to data, to electron movements not unlike the mist, against a soundscape perhaps not too unlike water crashing on rocks, revealing the future to those who could overpower the mathematics by forcing them into applied algorithmic order. Which Brett had done. An occult truth, hidden from all except those who could profit from the coefficients of adjustment and market price of risk.

If this was only *his* god, then it was no god at all, he had told her at the place he had called the Face of God. Where else might the Proteus modeling algorithm take thinkers? It did not matter in his world. That knowledge existed as a mere spark, as paperwork filed, source code archived and secured, notes sealed. If the markets changed enough to remove the need for it, or if simple disinterested time faded it into deprecation, it would never lead to better avenues of human understanding. Proteus was at the beck and call of the shareholders as VAI saw fit to turn silver into gold with its foresight. This was the life he accepted: a risky, secretive world where achievement often existed only for a brief moment, and then vanished when it no longer continued to be profitable to be notable, without ever having been considered by another soul for their own insight.

The great paradox of this endless wash cycle of Industrial Autoerotic Innovation was that those captured in its throes had only assumptions, triangulations, guesses, and intuitions about the *true* novelty of their work, not knowing even if today's latest wonder wasn't already in mature adoption across the sweep of the competition. Just because one hadn't heard of it didn't mean it wasn't already state-of-the-art; since the Art was immense in its overall scope.

That feeling of *sui generis* uniqueness and of being on the vanguard, however, powered many a potent session around the conference bar during the ceremonial pounding of the shields as old salts sang like the victorious warriors of Beowulf reporting to their Chieftain of all their glory in filling coffers and slaying foul, non-profitable beasts. To Brett, it seemed that these symposiums were in large part an attempt to be seated at the right table when someone let slip what they were *really* doing behind their own curtain, that one might best judge one's own *true* position in the field, and in so doing, find kinship in the knowledge that other ships sailed those same lonely oceans guided by sextants not dissimilar to one's own.

As a setting designed for speaking, it was a good place to keep quiet and long for such sparks of connection. And even with all this, this world, though occult and arcane, was the scaffolding of entire economies held constrained by the same models the systems were shy to reveal even to the most faithful seers.

"That's a gorgeous watch," a familiar voice from behind his barstool noted.

Brett turned to see Elle Loughlan-Kent, a journalist, as she leaned in to give him a quick kiss. She sat on the stool beside him.

"Thank you, Elle," he replied. "My fiancée gave it to me. How have you been?"

For a moment, Elle was quiet, until she replied, "Engaged? What news! Congratulations, Brett!" she offered her hand lightly as if for a handshake, which Brett took before returning to his gin and tonic. "Did she come with you to the Symposium, or did she stay up in Vancouver?"

"Actually, she presented about an hour ago," he said. "'The day's keynote: 'Dawn of the Euro.'"

Elle's eyes lit up at this news. "Nice! Manijeh Yazdpour, yes? A *wonderful* and very timely and interesting keynote. I'm doing fine—spectacularly well in fact—thanks for asking. Other than getting engaged, how have *you* been?"

Brett nodded with a warm smile, proud that Manijeh had impressed upon Elle's recollection so readily on her first major presentation since her full solid entry into the industry; he considered Toronto to never have happened as much as he was able. "Spectacularly describes me, as well, thanks," he replied to her query.

Elle leaned in very close, putting a hand on his right forearm, "If you don't mind my saying so, I took you for an incorrigible dandy." She touched his adorned ring finger. "I *certainly* wasn't expecting to see a band on *that* finger for *you* of all people." She lit up a cigarette. "Would you like a smoke?" she offered, holding out her half-empty pack.

"No thanks," Brett replied uncharacteristically. He liked Elle and enjoyed her company, but he felt it was time to start putting up walls with people when it came to accepting offered cigarettes. What Rostam was going through back in Vancouver was enough to convince him of that.

"Did you *quit*?" she asked. She sipped her rum and Coke, which had finally arrived in front of her.

"Never started," he replied.

"But you smoked last year here."
"I used to have a rule never to turn down an offer," he said. "I've been changing up a few of my rules of late."

Elle smiled and said, "Does that go for…?"

At that moment, Brett felt another hand on small of his back as Manijeh landed on his left side. "Elle, I would like you to meet Manijeh Yazdpour of Klein, Holdum, and French, my fiancée."

The two women reached across in front of him over the bar counter and shook hands, their clasp right in front of his tall cocktail glass. "So nice to meet you!" Manijeh said. "I've read your work."

"I was quite intrigued by your keynote today, Manijeh" Elle replied in turn. "You clearly have your head around the euro."

After a few more minutes of talking across the front of him as they sat three in a row in front of the "Pied Piper of Hamelin" painting, Brett suggested that he needed some air. Once he and Manijeh had politely left the hotel bar and made it to the front street, they talked.

"Wow. *The* Elle Loughlan-Kent. Have you two ever slept together?" she asked him.

Brett tried to guess from her eyes and smile why he was being asked this but could not. Finally, he simply replied, "Indeed. Once or twice, plus or minus, back in the day."

At this reply, Manijeh could not restrain her laughter. "Are you a quant or aren't you? What's up with this 'once or twice, plus or minus' nonsense? Confidence intervals don't apply here."

"She reports on a lot of these conferences," he replied. "I have been to a lot of these conferences," he then added. "I'm not sure if we would call that mathematics or arithmetic."

"She seems *really* nice. I think I understand now what you meant when you said you only sleep with people you like. I would sleep with her in a heartbeat, I like her that much already." She put her arm around his back. "So what did you think?"

"Your presentation?"

"What else?" Manijeh asked, poking Brett in the ribs. "I'm not talking about *her* impeccable presentation. Well, at least we're not anymore; we've moved on from that for now." She shifted about as if her Blahniks were becoming uncomfortable on her feet.

"You made a real splash. Working in Russia's debt default from last month really added emphasis on the right syllable. I found your story convincing, and it made me want to hedge all my bets in French aerospace. I'm using that as a placeholder."

"Wow, so many business clichés in one breath," she teased.

"Clichés are, after all, a dime a dozen, and I've got a million of them here in the naked city, Sarge," Brett teased in return.

"You are incorrigible!" Manijeh laughed.

"But seriously, I think Holdum's going to be pleased with the buzz your keynote generates. Especially if you can persuade Elle to give it pride of place in her final write up on this year's shindig."

∞ • ∂

"In examining Heston's seminal work on the closed-form solution for options pricing under various stochastic volatility frameworks,[38] we are compelled to explore the potential for more targeted applications of volatility models. Specifically, the feasibility of using such models in a constrained, directional manner warrants investigation," Brett initiated his discourse during the ten o'clock session on Wednesday. "Today we will be looking into how we have begun to do this at Vector Affinity Insights, offered to the community here today in the spirit of open discussion of what we feel are up-and-coming notions in the trade that will one day have application, and as part of Vector Affinity Insight's mandate to share perspectives amongst others in the quantitative analysis arena as it grows. I will be answering any questions after my presentation, which should take about three-quarters of an hour to get through."

He then coughed after turning away from the live mic and continued. "By implementing a bifurcated approach within our modeling architecture—segregating risk management and return optimization through a structured partition, akin to a firewall, we enforce risk-return separation. This allows for a disciplined application of these isolated strategies within each domain. Moreover, by enabling a mechanism for risk-adjusted dialogue between these compartmentalized models, based on client risk tolerance levels, we propose a novel framework. This framework not only preserves the integrity of risk mitigation and return enhancement independently but also facilitates a synergistic interplay where necessary."

He looked out into the audience for Manijeh and saw that she was seated directly next to Elle.

---

[38] Steven L. Heston, "A Closed-Form Solution for Options with Stochastic Volatility with Applications to Bond and Currency Options," *The Review of Financial Studies*, Vol. 6, No. 2, pp. 327–343, April 1993.

Touched by Fortune's Shadow: a triptych

"The essence of the utility of this approach lies in its ability to harmonize the dual objectives of optimizing returns while also simultaneously effectively managing risk, thus encapsulating the adage that allows us to have our cake and eat it, too," he then added. His presentation went on in a much similar tone for a further forty-five minutes, after which he answered his audience members' questions. Though most questions were brief requests for clarification or definition, one caught his full attention and returned his full mind to what he was presenting.

"Hello, Mr. Lloyd-Ronan, my name is Ali Mirza. Thank you for taking my question. Your discussion on your approach to segregating risk management from return optimization really interests me. Specifically, I'm wondering if you are suggesting that this proposed structured partitioning, and the introduction of risk-adjusted dialogue could potentially redefine the frontier in near real-time portfolio management by allowing for a more dynamic adjustment to risk tolerance levels than we might be permitted in a BSM or similar framework?"

He composed his thoughts before replying.

"That's a good question and that is exactly why I mentioned the concept of 'risk-adjusted dialogue' between the two models. We strive to advance the more traditional methods of portfolio management by challenging the first principles themselves; we are fundamentally questioning the static nature of the efficiency frontier as it has been understood."

Mirza nodded and Brett then continued after composing his thoughts on an answer to his question.

"But of course this level of innovation has to still answer to both practical economic mathematics and regulatory practice. In response to changing market conditions or more fluid investor preferences within a client base, we aim to navigate more closely along—or even possibly extend—the frontier. This not only allows for more precise risk management but also opens the door to uncovering return opportunities, all within the bounds of our clients' risk appetites, and even, if one minds what one does, without cross-informing training, and thereby maintaining entity isolation at the regulatory level. Which is to say that we won't find Peter paying Paul using this framework. It's a move towards a more responsive form of portfolio management that leverages volatility to our fiscal advantage, with built-in safeguards."

Afterwards, Brett attended the eleven o'clock presentation. That out of the way, he was approached almost immediately by Manijeh and Elle, who had also attended the same session he had.

"I hardly understood a single word you said, as usual," Elle commented. "And I go to *enough* of these things to groove the lingo. But that's exactly why I come to these things in the first place," she admitted. "Keeps me confused enough to figure I'm learning something new. Also forces me to ask questions."

"We're headed for lunch," Manijeh said, putting her arm lightly around Elle. "Would you care to join us?"

"I truly wish I could," Brett returned with a sigh. "But I've got a truckload of handshaking to do on Rostam's behalf since he couldn't make it."

Manijeh nodded.

"Why couldn't he make it?" Elle asked. "This stuff is his one true religion, isn't it?"

"Something came up at the last minute," Manijeh explained as the two women headed for lunch.

Brett walked out into the hallway at the gathering around the coffee carafes and found faces he recognized and began shaking hands, answering questions, and handing out cards. This went on for another forty-five minutes before he tired of it and returned to his room for a nap. He had no other sessions to attend on the last day of the symposium and decided to let this give him a moment to collect his thoughts before his dinner plans with Manijeh, who was attending sessions for the entire afternoon.

When he exited his room upon receiving her text message Manijeh sent asking him to meet her at the Pied Piper Bar, he was expecting to walk down the hallway, around a few corners, and into the bar, where he would catch up on the afternoon's events for her over a cocktail before having dinner. He was not expecting Elle to still be with her, especially with a Cheshire grin on her face.

"You really should introduce me to more of your friends," Manijeh teased as Brett sat beside her. "Elle and I talked forever and *day* today."

Brett laughed and asked, "You do *know* that she's a freelance *journalist*, right?" He winked at Elle. "Unless you're off-the-record, she takes *notes*." He tapped his right temple with his index finger as he said this.

"Off-the-Record Elle, that's what they call me," Elle said.

"Oh, really?" Manijeh returned.

"At least that's what those who *remain* off-the-record call me," she added. "And of course I can't tell you who *they* are, or I'd be run right out of town!" She winked back.

Brett leaned over to Manijeh's ear, even though he was in plain sight, and quietly but audibly said, "Whisper, whisper."

"To answer your question," Elle said, "we've decided to go to my room and order dinner in. Apparently, due to *your* rules and regulations, *my* room somehow has the fortune of being the only DMZ we've got around here."

Manijeh leaned into Brett's ear, saying, "Whisper, whisper."

"Sounds like a plan," he agreed.

◈ • ◈

"We should do that more often," Manijeh said, her hand in his as they sat in their seats on the flight back to Vancouver.

"Feel free to figure out how we might, but you might want to hold off for a while on any new ideas," he replied before closing his eyes to let them finally rest. "Doing both Rostam's and my job is starting to tire me out. Not that I *mind* carrying his bricks, mind you, but I'm *bushed*."

"For sure." Manijeh put her hand on his neck and stroked it. "Two more weeks before he's back and then hopefully things will settle down for you."

Quinn Tyler Jackson

Vancouver, mid-October 1998

Touched by Fortune's Shadow: a triptych

29

Back in July, when Brett had suggested Rostam call his father and ask him to talk to Bill, his father, being a recovering alcoholic who was familiar with what was really being said, invited Rostam to his Wednesday evening meeting, and Rostam there began his walk on the craggy path of recent sobriety. Once he'd had his thirty-day token by the end of August, he'd relapsed and binged heavily with some brief but pronounced amount of drama along with that, and following this, checked himself in to a private clinic for a more thorough look at what was pulling him in this direction so insistently. It was now the third Friday of October, and his stay at the clinic was coming to an end.

Rostam and Taraneh had officially broken off their romantic relationship by mutual agreement back just after his relapse, and since she and Brett had agreed to continue with his piano lessons after that, and since she and he had discussed the matter in some depth, he knew that the breakup was indeed amicable and was not only being represented as such. It was made clear to those who asked that it was a final break and not a temporary trial separation. Manijeh, however, not only maintained, but also actively nurtured the relationship she had built with Taraneh, although Rostam's parents had politely cooled to her since the breakup.

A month in treatment passed, and Rostam was back home, set to attend meetings close to him, and ready to resume work at Vector Affinity Insights the following Monday. Monday morning came, and he and Brett went to the fencing club to practice on the *pistes*, something they hadn't done together for quite a long time, though Brett had maintained his personal weekly fencing session on Tuesday mornings come rain or shine for some years. Rostam soundly thrashed on the *pistes* Brett at both épées and foils, even though Brett had put in his full effort.

"Why so off?" he asked, lifting his mask on the final touch of their bout.

"Just *tired*, is all," he admitted.

"Well, I'm fully back," his friend said as they headed out the door. "I'll carry my own baggage from here on out."

"One day at a time," Brett replied. "So, if you feel like you are juggling too much, remember to get Katja on it. She's great and totally up to speed on nine-tenths of your office's flow. Take time to be holy."

Rostam smiled. "Oh, I plan to. Definitely. Katja was a *great* hire. She shows sharp judgment and initiative. Doesn't need even the tiniest bit of handholding, even after so little time on board. I'm impressed."

"Ekaterina completely landed on our office door the day we needed her most," Brett agreed.

Back at the office, Katja, Rostam's new executive assistant, handed Rostam a single sheet with a bulleted list of things on his agenda for the day, and returned to her own desk once she did. Rostam looked at this and said, "Give me a place to stand and with Katja I will move the world."

From over her privacy wall, Katja popped her head up and said, "You're very welcome, Mr. Archimedes!"

∽•∾

Things at the office ran smoothly over the next week, with Rostam and Brett catching up on lost time during their lunch hour every day. On their Friday stroll down Granville Street, as they walked very slowly southward toward the bridge, in the direction of The Yale, Rostam shifted from talk of business to more personal matters. He lit up a cigarette and Brett decided to ask for one himself and join him just to see what it was like to smoke one without having been offered. He made it a quarter through before putting it out on the curb and flicking the mess into a drain.

"Brett, what would you say to my taking a year's sabbatical?" Rostam offered what he had been considering as they strolled. Brett put his arm on Rostam's shoulder, held him, and stopped walking, which stopped Rostam's stride as well, at which point Rostam added, "I've had a lot of time to think it over this last month, with the therapy and meetings, and I want to backpack around the world—or at the very least, Europe—and you know, proverbially find myself."

Brett remembered back to the early nineties, when Rostam was in similar condition, speaking of similar travels, back when such trips were common right after getting an undergraduate degree; the year off to travel. Rostam, however, opted to start up Vector Affinity Insights with Brett at that time instead, and it had consumed both of them from that decision forward, until this moment as they walked toward Granville Island.

"I'm ideologically on board for your taking a sabbatical," Brett began, "but I was just left to steer VAI for a *month*, and frankly it utterly *exhausted* me to do both our jobs. I'm at the limits of my ability and don't know how long I can sustain the current level of demands I've been under without you. So, if I'm being honest...."

"Oh, you're always straightforward, unless you are purposely dancing around the topic, but that's for another time," Rostam laughed, starting to walk again the direction they had been headed before they stopped. "I had *daily* therapy time at Circle Forward," he said. "That and the daily meeting pulled a lot of baggage out of my closet into the light of day."

"And convinced you to take a sabbatical to do the travel thing?" Brett asked.

"It showed me where I had been putting all of my major pain throughout my adult life," Rostam returned, glancing over his shoulder, and looking into Brett's eyes with his own glassy regard. "And pushing down the pain is what the drink does for me. Except that it ultimately *causes* more grief—and some of that to others—than it pushes down."

"Let's sit down there and have some cola or something," Brett suggested, pointing to a set of chairs and a small table that were still outside in front of the café they served despite the lateness of the outdoor dining season. They sat, and within a few minutes were handed colas and a shared plate of calamari. A few bites in, Rostam began to explain himself.

"You ever heard of survivor's guilt?" Rostam asked.

Before replying, Brett tried to imagine why he was being asked this, given everything Rostam had said since the walk started. "Yes, I have. I suspect you're as likely a candidate for it as anyone *can* be."

Rostam nodded as he speared another piece of crisp squid with his fork. "Yes. I really *wanted* to go that night with my uncle's family to the Cinema Rex," he admitted.

"Close calls like that are something I'm also familiar with."

"And then, afterward, when Dad and Mom decided to flee to Turkey, I threw a holy *fit* trying to keep us in Khorramshahr. Like the *child* I actually was. We know where *that* would have gone soon enough. *Zero-for-two*." His head dropped with eyes closed when he said this.

"I know all about survivor's guilt, Rostam," Brett said. "My own version, though. Did Manijeh ever tell you that I told her what drove my dad to offer me self-defense lessons?" he asked.

At this, Rostam tipped his head. "No, she didn't, but Arthur did. Early in my first try at sobriety, when he was driving me to his meeting with him. I was horrified when I heard about what happened to you, but decided to let you tell me when and if the time came. It made a lot of things suddenly make more sense."

"My friend Richard was murdered, and I was literally stabbed in the heart and left for dead," Brett said. "Like I said, survivor's guilt and extremely close calls are something I've traded in for much of my short life, it seems. I swam through *that* swamp, in my childish way, for years. I don't wish that kind of darkness on your soul. Do you think traveling the world might lift it?" His cola was almost empty, so he held up the glass when the waiter passed the window and smiled for a refill.

"Well, you know, Brett," Rostam began, "I'm certainly *not* looking for a geographical cure. Wherever I go, that's where I will still be when my head hits my pillow, after all. I'm not looking for any easy answers or distractions."

"It's reassuring to hear you've given that some thought," Brett agreed with this friend. The waiter came outside, refilled their glasses, and asked if there would be anything else, to which Brett replied, "Just the check, thanks. I'm paying."

"I felt really great when Taraneh and I were in Drumheller, running around, exploring," he explained. "I enjoyed hiking and she and I even camped in a tent for two nights out there, though I'm not sure we picked a legal site for that. But we did it anyway, and we had a *good* time. And I found time to settle my mind, to put the hamster in its wheel in a state of gentle peace, so it stopped running circles in there." He frowned and then added, "Of course I wouldn't be doing this with *her*, but you get the idea. It reminded me about my earlier goals in life."

"So you want to close the circle? Finish what you never had the chance to start?"

"I want to focus on my side of the street," Rostam finally replied. "Without having to always be closing."

The waiter came with the check and Brett handed him a twenty and told him to keep the change. Once the waiter was out of earshot, Brett said to his friend, "What about your meetings, therapy, *et cetera*? It's going to be hard to do on the road with any kind of regularity. I know from Dad's recovery that regularity is a *key* driver of ongoing success. One day at a time, after all is said and done. It's *your* program, so I'm not going to tell you what to do, except that I do know that you *must* work it if it's going to work. That's *not* a cliché."

Rostam took out his fat wallet. "Dude, I'm not a poor student, with loans piled on, running around with a backpack full and hopes and dreams and nothing else to show for life." He opened his wallet and showed the many bills in there. "I've got a great tool for dealing with everything I need during my year: white privilege. And by *that* I mean all the white people on the front of all my money, which will give me access to a ton of *options* for meetings and therapy. Hell, I'll be able to do my weekly therapy by long-distance telephone call without breaking a sweat. Far fewer logistics than what I deal with at VAI on a regular basis. I'll find meetings."

They stood to resume their walk. "Yeah, having money won't hurt your options as you travel about."

"Hey, you know me. I am *not* looking to sleep rough," he said. "I'm looking to finish what I started while I get my aching head around a lifetime of running away from the fact that I…." He didn't seem able to find his next words. "Running away from the fact that I for some reason lived and others I loved did not, even though, had it been my *own* wishes that were heeded, I would most likely have joined the dead."

"Let's head back," he suggested before responding to what Rostam had just said.

"So what do you think?" Rostam finally asked.

"Give me some time to think about it, Rostam," Brett said. "I've nothing against your plan yet, except that I am not certain I can pull both our carts for a full year, *even* with Katja to help me in her quite capable way. That said, let me think. Do you mind if I talk with Manijeh about this, or would you rather do that yourself? I think she should know, so she and I can reason through how we'd carry this off as a team."

"Brett, brother, you are *always* my welcome guest to share with Manijeh *anything* personal I tell you, *unless* I explicitly ask you not to," Rostam said.

Touched by Fortune's Shadow: a triptych

"It's still your private business, man, so I just wanted to make sure you were okay with my talking about it with her as I try to sort out how I might manage things if you do go," Brett explained.

"This impacts our business plans, which we *must* avoid getting into detail with her about, but I trust your judgment on how you skate around that. Because it also impacts our personal lives, and I respect that this needs some coordination and discussion. I'm keeping it from Mom and Dad until it's final, though."

"Okay," Brett agreed. "We *will* figure this thing out, man." He slapped his friend on the back.

"Let me know when you have done some of your famous analysis on it," Rostam said.

For the rest of the walk back to the office, they talked about work, the future of Proteus now that it was about ready to go live on streamed data in alpha runs, and other matters that were not so sensitive that they couldn't be talked about in the open street.

30

From the north-facing part of their balcony on a Friday night, North Vancouver was a jewel more magnificent than those found in the entire Pahlavi royal collection, and it was there for all of Vancouver to see who came to look. Brett leaned on the railing, sipping his gin and tonic. His cashmere sweater overtop his polo shirt protected him still from October's chill, but he knew that soon it would be season to turn on the electric heat lamp, as being outside on the balcony was a year-round thing for him.

After Brett had been outside for only ten minutes, Manijeh returned from work, and came to join him, holding his note in her hand, which he had left on the kitchen counter for her to find. "Make a tall cold drink for yourself and join me on the balcony," it read, and she did.

"How was your day?" he asked her as she stepped through the open glass door. He then approached her, kissed her cheek, and returned to the railing with her beside him.

"Pretty good," she replied. "Pulled in a solid cut today," she said. "If we ever go on a proper vacation, then the next one is on me. Reassured me that I chose the right career path."

"That's *awesome*!" Brett replied.

"All that prep I had to do while I was busy waiting on my registration has actually paid off a lot," she replied. "I got all that time to learn their particular portfolio flow, and *then* I could trade, rather than being expected to get it right from day one. So I'm kicking ass. Charles Holdum is beside himself pleased, near as I can tell." She kissed his right ear. "And how about you, my love? How was your day?"

It never ceased to overjoy Brett's heart and fill his chest with fire when he heard of love from Manijeh's lips. He let that feeling fill him before he continued with the topic that had been on his mind since his return from work.

"Your brother, may the gods all bless him with overflowing abundance, wants to do the whole trip-around-the-world-with-a-backpack thing," he outright declared. "Needless to say, this is not to be shared yet, even with your parents."

For at least thirty seconds, Manijeh fell silent at this. She took a sip from her screwdriver, and finally said aloud, "Sounds like something he would consider doing, given everything that's happened recently with him. Can't say I'm caught off guard. Not sure what it *means*, though." After another sip, "Though, it could just be his chasing an external answer solution to an internal conundrum. But I'm no therapist, by any measure."

"Whatever it all ends up meaning for him, and I truly hope it means he'll find what it is he's really after, for me it means I'll be *overwhelmed*," Brett suggested. "We can't simply rent a CEO from somewhere for the time being, and that means that I'd be doing two jobs. We saw how *that* pans out over even a short time. I start to fray all around the seams."

"Isn't his assistant fully on board now? Didn't she help a lot?" Manijeh asked before sipping her drink. She put her free hand on the small of Brett's back, and he did likewise with her.

"Katja? She's a *godsend*. But she can't make executive calls. Only I can," he said. "And again, we know that I can't keep up with both our responsibilities for any length of time like that. The markets keep turning daily, and we can't just put our clients on hold in the freezer."

Hearing this, Manijeh let out a protracted sigh. "Have you considered putting down just a few of your other things for the year?" she finally asked.

"You mean like piano lessons?"

"Well, there's that, sure, but honestly I think that's healthy for you. And Taraneh says you are progressing very well and will likely be nearing time by the middle of next year for Grade 10 completion if you keep it up."

"You mean what? Fencing? Judo?"

"There *are* those," she said. "It's not for *me* to triage."

Brett thought about what he was being asked before saying, "I did consider dropping fencing, since, to be honest. I'm *done* with competition. The trophies are all in storage, after all."

"Giving up fencing after *twenty* years? Didn't you qualify to join the Canadian team in Atlanta or am I misremembering something?" she asked in near disbelief at his suggestion. "That was while I was in Boston."

"What I qualified for was the final set of tryouts," he said. "But I couldn't commit the time away from VAI, so I withdrew after giving it a great deal of thought. I don't regret my decision to let it go."

Manijeh's face was awash with her astonishment. "My God, Brett. While I was off in Harvard getting all my shiny baubles, you picked the world of finance over a chance to compete at *that* level in a lifelong passion of yours. And I bet you did it out of loyalty to Rostam's dream for VAI, too, knowing you. Maybe *you* are the one in need of a sabbatical. Sometimes it's allowed to be just about you, *Jân-e-jânân-am.*"[39]

"All of this isn't a one-sided venture," he gently reminded her. "The company was our *shared* dream," he insisted. "And we—all three of us—had our particular part in realizing it. For all that it did for everyone else, it pulled *me* out of the blue-collar rut and let me pay of my parents' house and give them a chance at a decent retirement. Dad's back is buggered from all that work with heavy iron. He's ready to relax soon. Now he doesn't have to worry about how that's going to come about. So I didn't pass up Atlanta to keep Rostam flying straight. I *do* have my *own* drivers and I do try to *avoid* regret, although I've missed that goal more than a few times in life, I'll confess."

"Maybe I put more sentimental value into your fencing than you do," she then admitted. "And this isn't about me; it's about your finding a way to streamline your life so you can run the show for a year without burning yourself out in the process. But please let me grieve how much of your personal glory you've poured out for the fortune and benefit of others, my *Huma*. Humility may be *your* chosen walk, but I still take great *pride* in your ascent into the skies, and you can cast that lucky shadow of yours onto others only because *you* have made that ascent, let's remember." She smiled softly. "Rostam very well may have been the rainmaker, Brett, but you've always been holding up the sky as he taunts the clouds. Don't tire your arms, *Jân-e-jânân-am.*"

"I still have *kenjutsu*, and fencing feels redundant in my life. I was only staying with it for Rostam's sake; he's been a star on the *pistes* this last year, not me. My heart just hasn't been in the épée and foil lately."

---

[39] *Jân-e-jânân-am*! (lit. "soul of my souls") A devoted term of endearment, much as saying "My very *dearest* heart and soul."

The birds called out to fill the night with signals and songs only birds knew. With her own sweet voice, Manijeh said, "And if he goes away for a year, why not just put that aside, rather than outright quit and retire from the whole circuit, and use the time to relax in your busy life?" She stroked his back and he hers. "Makes sense to me."

So many things had changed since April. Since Manijeh had entered his world. Since they had joined hands on the path life presented them. With all the change, at first he hesitated to accept any more disruption, but where he was now as a result of having allowed commotion and adjustment and change into his life far surpassed where he had been even ten minutes before getting that call from Manijeh at Vancouver Airport back in April. Change had been a necessary and *good* thing.

"You do make a *lot* of sense on that," he finally admitted. "That frees up a Tuesday morning right there. I'll stand back from fencing, rather than quitting it outright."

"Enough is okay," Manijeh replied.

Brett took a moment to appreciate what she had just said and replied, "Yes. That's beautiful. Enough *is* okay."

"It's a start," she noted. "We can figure out the rest as it comes along. I think if Rostam is asking to go on leave, we should help him as much as possible in that direction. He really seems to be searching for *something*. I was able to do that in my adult life. I made some wrong decisions and dealt with the outcomes and figured myself out all in due time. Stuff that has *nothing* to do with derivatives, whether they be VSE, TSX, NYSE, or even Newton himself. It's time for him to start thinking about what he *needs*, rather than tracking the stuff that's distraction and filler."

"Yeah, he has basically set us all up for life," he said. "It's time for him to have a life. Or a fair attempt at the kind of life he has been craving so all this time."

"Yes, it's time. What else has been going on?" she asked.

"Our fathers have officially entered the telescoping *Keibo*[40] market with Dad's alloy as of last week."

"They were approved? That was fast. Wouldn't it be great if our bureaucracies were as smooth as that? That's great news!"

---

[40] *Keibo* (lit. "baton"), a specialized police baton used in Japan by law-enforcement officers.

"Yes. Nakamura also has received the *daisho* sets from Dad, and *Soke* Hashimoto informs me that that, with the alloy being produced and studied under license by several Japanese-based metallurgists now, the future, while anyone's guess, looks brighter every day."

"Wow, that's wonderful!"

"Worst that can happen is that they make serious bank with the baton market. Dad gave me one of the batons. It's a work of art. Anyway, my point is, everyone's all set up to do their own thing, so it's time for Dad to give doing something just for *himself* a shot. A belated shot at that, but a shot nonetheless."

The buzzing sound of Manijeh's phone caught them both off guard. She pulled it from her clutch, looked at the text message, and said, "Taraneh wants to do some serious shopping therapy at Pacific Center and Robson Street tomorrow. Do you mind?"

"Of course I don't mind," he replied.

Hearing this, Manijeh typed in a reply on the numeric pad, and sent her reply, after which she received another text and put the phone back in her clutch. "I'll be heading out at eleven," she said to Brett, "to meet her there."

"Great. How about let's say we go to the Water Street Café and celebrate your solid returns at work?"

"I'd rather order pizza and watch black-and-white movies," she said. "It's been a long week."

"How about Ozu's *Tokyo Story*?" he asked.

"I've never heard of it. Well, I saw the VHS tape on the shelf. So, what's it about?"

"It's a subtle, early-fifties Japanese film that explores the complexities of family relationships and the passage of time. It's more about the emotional journeys of the characters rather than a plot-driven story. The way Yasujiro Ozu captures the essence of life's transitions is truly remarkable. It has a certain serenity and depth that's compelling without being onerous," he explained, hoping to pique her interest without revealing too many details that might spoil it for her.

"That does sound intriguing," Manijeh replied. "Let's give it a try. A film that gets us thinking could be a nice change of pace from the usual crap on television. And it seems to fit the mood tonight—pizza and a thoughtful movie. Perfect."

Brett smiled. "Great. It'll be a nice way to wind. I'll get the pizza ordered. Any preferences?"

Touched by Fortune's Shadow: a triptych

Manijeh thought for a moment, then replied, "How about something with a bit of everything? A supreme? And maybe some garlic knots on the side?"

"Done," Brett said. "Supreme and garlic knots it is. This is shaping up to be a perfect evening." They both returned inside, where he went to the phone receiver on the coffee table.

As Brett dialed, Manijeh settled into the sofa, tucking a throw pillow under her arm. The promise of a quiet night in, a classic film, and the comfort of each other's company felt like the perfect antidote to the week's hustle and bustle, and both expressed this in an almost synchronized exhaled breath of content satisfaction.

31

It had been months since Brett had the apartment to himself on a Saturday afternoon, and he found as he sat at the kitchen counter and ate the sandwich he had made himself for lunch that he did not miss his solitude. Manijeh had, since moving in, more than provided enough difference to supply a Moiré pattern describing the change. While she had not altered much, she had noticeably refined his world—*their* world—with the painterly esthetic precision she had been imparted by her artist mother.

The silk-screened piece he had made himself, which once had pride of place beside the art niches, beside the Robert Held vase and its matching *kintsugi* bowl by Raku, was now leaned up against the wall in the spare room and in its place sat a work she had bought by New York artist Rueben Hurst. Unlike the abstract piece that it replaced, Hurst's work, "Nude Study #75" called to mind Klimt. When she'd asked him if she could replace his own piece with Hurst's, he said yes without even first looking at the Hurst himself, trusting her judgment completely.

His trust in her esthetic was not misplaced. Upon seeing the piece and looking the artist up, he discovered that Hurst walked in the same circles as Cyrus Drake and was a lifetime friend of his, and upon learning this, he immediately understood. He tracked down Drake's agency, selected a smaller work that would complement it, and that, too, was now up on that wall, having cost him to acquire, but well worth the cost to see there.[41] In another niche was the Persian New Year's painted egg that he had given Manijeh the first time he'd visited the Yazdpour house, and to the right of that, one of Mahnaz' exquisite works. That his own amateur offering was a spare room castaway did not bother him in such company.

---

[41] *The Ancestral Sea*, Knight Terra Press, February 2024.

Throughout the apartment other optimizations had been carried out, many which, he was sure, he had yet to discover as he went about his day. He had committed his time and his space to her, and she had not taken either for granted. He went over in his mind his own behavior to determine, to the best of his own insight, if perhaps he had somehow taken *her* for granted. Though he knew there might be something as yet unexpressed or unknown or unseen, he did not feel, at least in this moment, that had had. He closed his eyes and released the thought to the four winds as he rested his head on the sofa pillow, pulled the furry blanket over himself, rolled onto his side, and had an afternoon nap to the sound of bird calls carrying through the ajar balcony door.

⊷•⊶

"It looks as though we caught him sleeping," a soft voice, not Manijeh's, noted from above Brett's right ear. He then yawned as he rolled onto his back, stretching his arms as he did so, and opened his eyes.

It was Taraneh looking down upon him as he awoke from his slumber. He could see that she had a number of bags in each hand. Manijeh then peeked over the edge of the sofa, she too, carrying many bags clearly marked with their store branding, most of those being, from his recollection, on Robson Street. Neither of them had resisted the urge to bring home too much from their day out. He lifted his arm to look at his watch, and through still blurry eyes saw that it was half-past four. He then rubbed the sleep from his eyes and pushed himself to sit up.

"Did you two have fun?" he finally was able to ask through his sleep-sticky lips.

Manijeh quickly put her bags down and fetched him a cold glass of water, saying, "We did. More than you'll *ever* know!"

"I invited myself over to play some *Pasur* with you two," Taraneh explained.

Brett sat up and took a long sip of the water Manijeh had given him. "Wonderful. Welcome. Have you seen our place?" he asked. "*Befarma'id!*"

"I'll show her!" Manijeh said, taking her friend by the arm and leading her around, speaking Persian the entire time as they went everywhere except the home offices, which were off limits.

"You two have a truly gorgeous home! And the Roland really works in the spare room."

"I've considered a proper piano, but I think the Roland is sufficient for now," Brett commented.

Taraneh smiled. "It's carried you through our lessons to date," she agreed. "I think you'll be ready for the exam by June next year, right near your wedding," she then added. "What kind of piano you play on once you pass the Conservatory exam is something to think about then."

Brett neatly folded the blanket he had been napping under and placed it back over the arm of the sofa where it had been. "I'm peckish," he then said. "I ate a sandwich earlier, but that's not going to push me through a couple games of cards."

"Let's say we all make dinner first!" Manijeh suggested.

"I'm all for that!" Taraneh agreed. "Let me show you two how to make *tah-dig* the *right* way. Manijeh tells me that neither of you has yet figured it out."

"I'm game," Brett said. "Let me just freshen up from my nap. I'm still groggy and disheveled."

He got up, went to the ensuite bathroom, closed the door, and brushed his teeth and washed the drool from the left side of his chin. A test of his underarms said he was acceptable to present as is, but he washed under his arms with soap and rinsed anyway, following up with antiperspirant. Walking back through the walk-through closet, he found a fresh polo, put it on, and returned to the living room.

Taraneh and Manijeh were already organizing the kitchen for making dinner, which they had decided was going to be a combination of Manijeh's *kebab soltâni*, using her mother's guarded family recipe, and which Brett knew to be delicious, and Taraneh's basmati rice, which would include her reportedly perfect *tah-dig*. When he asked what he could do to help, Manijeh insisted that his primary job during this was to do prep and active clean up as garbage was generated by their cooking, which he gladly did as they went over the details of each of their techniques in Persian to one another.

With an almost instinctive coordination between the three of them, they had produced a flawless presentation of *kebab soltâni* with saffron-adorned basmati, deliciously aromatic and perfectly shaped, each grain separate from the others, atop caramelized *tah-dig*, and they had done it in a way that no one person had actually been responsible for any single part of the dish, thus allowing them to declare their shared victory in this kitchen conquest.

And it went well with two bottles of wine between the three of them, chatting and exploring as they dined together. Dinner done, it came time to bring out the cards, and from this point forward, the conversation became more serious, as is sometimes the case when one moves from dinner talk that can happen near food and talk best kept for calmer oceans.

After having counted up her latest move's points, Taraneh said, "I have a question for both of you, now that the three of us are all in one quiet place."

"*Befarma'id*!" Manijeh exclaimed.

Brett, too, nodded his agreement to proceed.

"I now understand Brett's position on open relationships," Taraneh said. "And I know you, Manijeh, are fine with everything. And yet you feel you are one another's *soulmates*, don't you? I expect when and if I meet *that* person somehow I will be expected to advance from where I stand now, comfortable with openness, to where I am after that moment. As we have discussed, Brett," she handed at least some of the conversation to him.

"As much as I have to say on this, I think maybe Manijeh's views might offer you a fresh perspective, since you and I have already talked. Manijeh?"

Manijeh took the torch cheerfully. "I'm not actually sure I personally *believe* in such a thing as a soulmate. At least not the way they are often put forward. I think there can be someone you *absolutely* love and adore and want to be with *forever*, and I know this because here we are right now right here in this apartment together." She leaned across enough to be able to brush Brett lightly with her hand, and then returned fully to her seat. "But this idea of rules of what a soulmate *should* make us feel and how this or that kind of love *should* make us behave and feel, these are social constructs, not intrinsic truths."

Brett lifted his finger to signal a brief polite interrupt and added, "And all of those constructs, or most of them, anyway, were put in place by a patriarchy of privileged owners of other living, breathing human beings, so who's to say that soulmates should feel a certain specific way? Some old white dudes with clay tablets and too much time in front of them back when the harvest season was done and they had free time to confirm and entrench their position in the hierarchy onto their mud tablets, writing the fates of entire intersections of populations with twigs, backed by a brutal sticks-and-stones hegemony?"

"Ouch, but absolutely *yes*," Taraneh agreed.

"Exactly!" Manijeh agreed. "So, given all of that, I walked into this knowing what Brett was saying was seriously what he was about. If that had triggered an alarm in me, at or near my heart, that's a different narrative. As it stands, it didn't—and doesn't—bother me or concern me in the *slightest*. He's old enough now to know what is coming out of his mouth in a situation like that requires some mindfulness. If something comes along in life that makes me think about this again, then that makes it a *life* instead of a *history*. There's no need for a *soulmate* construct to be in genuine love in an open world."

"Seize the day, but consider the end," Brett said. "Speaking of which, more wine everyone?" He stood, went to the rack, and opened a bottle, filling their and his glasses. "I mean, what the hell, tomorrow's Sunday...."

Touched by Fortune's Shadow: a triptych

32

His brain was pounding against the raw red and pink flicker of daylight against his eyelids. Through the spiderweb sky he flew, across ridges and valleys beyond lakes to tree peaks, and around again, golden silk carpet weaving strand, and then upward, beyond the valleys, toward the stars of the starless skies, and into today across the threshold of yesterday, he reached for his coffee mug, fumbled about because it was not where it should be, and took a sip, opening his eyes.

To the left of the three-point constellation they had formed in their crossed-leg meditation group, sat Taraneh, and to his right, sat Manijeh. When they had both opened their own eyes he said, "Happy Sunday. Does anyone else have a hangover?"

Both nodded yes.

"Coffee all morning if you want it."

"Should we still do our walk today?" Manijeh asked.

"Oh? Walk? Were you two *planning* something?" Taraneh asked. "You needn't worry about me. I can find my way home." She pulled Brett's Burberry check wool shirt more tightly over her shoulders, as Manijeh's thin blue lace babydoll, which she was wearing underneath the unbuttoned shirt, was not enough to keep her warm and she was clearly shivering in the October morning chill, even with the heat lamp.

"No, no," Manijeh insisted. "I have walking gear you can wear. On Sundays, after our meditation, we walk the Seawall and come back past the Lost Lagoon."

"I'd love to join you both," she said.

"*In etafâq qablân oftâdeh*,"[42] Manijeh replied, winking.

At this, Taraneh smiled in return and said, "I can use your gear. I'm ready when you two are!"

---

[42] "That's already happened."

"Sure. Let's just fix some hangover breakfast and head out afterwards," Brett suggested. "It's too chilly to sit out here in a state of half-dress."

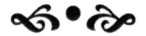

◈ • ◈

First thing Monday morning, as Brett readied himself at his desk, Rostam popped into his office and closed the door. "So did you give it some thought?" he asked as he sat down.

"Do it. Find yourself. Run like the wind into the horizon. But on one condition."

"What's that?" he asked, his face showing his concern.

"I'll need one hundred percent control while you're off doing your thing. I don't want to have to hunt you down for so much as *one* signature while you're gone."

Rostam started to laugh. "I would expect no less. You know I trust you. As far as I am concerned, if we get a buyout offer that you and you feel is fair, you can sign on the line." He made motion with his hand. "I'm heading out for a year. A lot can happen in the weeks after I'm out the door, let alone in a whole year. The helm will be *completely* yours. I don't expect you to chase me down to sign permission slips."

"I appreciate your trust. And yes, a *lot* can happen quickly in our line of work."

"Again, I trust you with my *sister* and my fortune. Every day, so let's move past that now and talk about the coming transition timeline. What are your thoughts on when you'll be ready to make this a reality?"

Brett readied himself to speak. "You already spent a month off and we had a rhythm going in your absence, so I see no reason to drag our feet on a timeline. I *assume* you've already flown this all by Margaret, or we never would have mentioned any of it in the first place?"

Rostam again started to laugh.

"That's why I *trust* you, man. You think of these things. Of course it went by her. I already guessed you'd want *full* powers and given that this might have been a compliance issue, and in some ways it is, I have a stack of paper for us to go through all this week already. I can hand over the torch by next Monday. Time being of the essence, that seems pretty soon, but like you said, you already had a rhythm going around here without me and my being back this short time hasn't thrown that off by much. So let's get it in full swing."

"I'm going to keep both the assistants," Brett said. "But not as such. I'll be promoting Winston to COO."

"Makes sense to me. He's tracked both of our executive decisions for some time now and knows our ropes."

"Yes. He can take over a large number of things that are well underway and have systems in place and just need someone to mind the flow. He's quite good at minding the flow. And he's registered to trade. That alleviates my concern about getting more personally overwhelmed than I have been this last while."

"Like I said, makes sense to me."

"Lunch at Taf's later?"

"Sorry, man, but I'm totally booked solid literally *all* day," Rostam apologized. "But since we'll be starting to go over those papers tomorrow…."

"Sure thing. I really hope you have a great time hopping all over the globe," he said. "If you'll ignore the pun, I think it will do you a world of good."

"You should do it one day, too."

"Plan to one day," Brett said, "but today is not that day."

∞•∞

"Wow, that happened fast," Manijeh said upon discovering the news of the rapidity of the start of Rostam's sabbatical. Brett had told her the details as the two of them attempted *tah-dig* together without Taraneh's assistance, an experiment that had been a resounding success, making Manijeh capable of finally outcooking her father and Rostam by producing a perfect entire *kebab soltâni* singlehandedly, a feat no single Yazdpour had yet been able to master.

"He has been considering this for a very long time now. He had Margaret put together the paperwork for compliance and so forth before he even asked me last week. So it only *seems* fast. He has lot dials to turn, machinery to kick, t's to cross, and i's to dot."

"Did you go over all your scheduling how we discussed and consider what you might adjust so you're not so tired?"

"Well, I did that, sure, and think I can honestly put my judo time to once a month rather than weekly and take out fencing altogether. I could have kept both of them, but I think it's time, honestly, to put aside the things of the past. *Kenjutsu* is far more important to me than either of those, so that frees me up. I can adjust and take on more judo sessions as I get my balance on this."

"Okay," she said as she prepared their plates and he set the cutlery down on the table.

"I also plan on promoting Winston Rampersad to COO from EA. He'll still report to me, but he'll have so much more mandate to act that I can delegate a large amount of my actual executive load to him, and he knows how we party."

"Here's to always moving forward rather than sideways or backwards," Manijeh toasted. After clinking and sipping, the both started eating. "Taraneh asked me to check if you wanted to plan another round of *Pasur* for this Saturday."

"That would be great," Brett replied. "And could you let her know that I'll have to miss this Wednesday's piano lesson at three? But only this one week. Between you and me only, it's because I have paperwork review with Rostam literally all week going forward so we can do the hand-off on Monday. That's in the vault, though."

"Will do. Cards for Saturday, skip this Wednesday."

"And let's put together dinner for her, ready just before she arrives," he added. "So she sees just how well you totally *nailed* the *tah-dig*."

Manijeh agreed wholeheartedly with his plan.

That night they fell asleep on the sofa watching television together. Rather than wake her, Brett covered her in the fuzzy blanket and set an alarm early enough that they could get ready for work the next day, if she didn't wake up sooner, and he fell asleep curled up on the end of the sofa she'd least occupied. It was not a comfortable sleep, but he didn't mind in the least.

33

Rostam, Brett, and Katja spent all Tuesday, Wednesday, and Thursday locked in the board room, except for lunch, reviewing all of the paperwork involved in having Rostam take a year, or even more if he chose, on a leave-of-absence. Brett was to be made acting CEO of Vector Affinity Insights, with the understanding, but without the obligation on the part of the firm, that Rostam would return to this role upon his return. This was upon the insistence of the Board, as some voices there were concerned for Rostam's health and well-being and how these would impact on his ability to fulfill his obligations upon his return, and so they asked for a safeguard. They finished the review and paperwork early, and so announced on Friday rather than Monday as they had planned, and executed accordingly, leaving Winston Rampersad promoted to COO, announced before all his colleagues.

Rostam Yazdpour, everyday citizen, free of encumbrances, headed out of the office Friday afternoon with a smile and a wave for the company he had built so skillfully. When Manijeh returned home that Friday night, Brett showed her his new business card, with his additional title, as he continued to also be the Chief Analyst at VAI. Though one might have thought it was not truly a time to celebrate, Rostam seemed much happier to everyone in the family since his decision, and so Manijeh suggested they celebrate at the Water Street Café. They reserved a table for later in the evening, dressed for dinner, and walked to the restaurant.

"I truly love where we live," Manijeh said as they finished their *rasmalai*.

Brett finished signing the credit card slip and replied, "I put a *lot* of thought into where I sunk my first major returns. It was my Fortress of Solitude until you joined me."

"Speaking of your Fortress of Solitude, I never asked if you have more property," she noted.

"I actually own *both* north facing penthouse apartments," he replied. "The northeastern corner suite is entirely managed by a property management company. Fully paid up. I'm not a fan of mortgages if I can avoid them. I do understand why mortgages make sense, or I wouldn't have passed my registration to trade, but there's nothing like a clear strata title clause under your feet to ground one in a feeling of stability. If shit ever hits the fan."

Manijeh's alert slate-gray eyes opened more widely than usual. "Seriously? You own the adjacent penthouse as well? Why didn't you mention that before? Wow. And yes, that fan has way of periodically getting hit and spreading the joy."

"It slipped my mind. I chose the one I did to live in because of the additional view of Stanley Park. I never even deal with any of the details, it's so far from me given that the management company deals with *everything* to do with it." They stood, put their jackets on to avoid the cold outside, and started to button up their coats.

"It must have been odd, growing up in the working class, and ending up wealthy so young," she noted.

"I'm not *wealthy* by any stretch or definition. I'm *rich*."

"What's the difference?"

"I assure you that, except for my interests in VAI and the holding company, and except for my personal portfolio and the usual stocks, bonds, and annuities one might find in such a beast, it's just the two penthouses here. Oh, and the sword collection, which you saw the price on when we loaned it to the museum." He wrote a number on a paper napkin and showed it to her. "That's my total net worth. Left-hand side, more or less liquid; right-hand side, total. Four-and-a-half, all day long; five leaning towards five-and-a-half after a yard sale." He then added, "And the difference is that the wealthy sign the paychecks of the rich. I, on the other hand, sign only credit card slips at restaurants and NDAs at work. You see now that I am *blessed*, and grateful to you and Rostam for it, but not wealthy."

Manijeh looked at what he had written down without a change in her expression, and then took his pen from him and wrote her numbers down and showed them to him. "Fair is fair," she said. "My particulars." Their buttons done up, their numbers shared, Brett started to hum.

"Why so happy, my love?" she asked.

Brett stopped, turn to her, kissed the tip of her nose and said, "I'm just happy."

Manijeh kissed him back and they resumed their walk on Water Street. "Remember, some games of *Pasur* and our *tah-dig* victory dance, tomorrow night with Taraneh."

"Oh, I've been waiting to show her our A-level rice making skills all week," Brett returned.

"Me, too!"

༄ • ༄

"You two certainly did it!" Taraneh exclaimed when she saw the rice they had made together before her arrival. "When Manijeh told me that you had mastered the technique, I was wondering, but you *got* it. *Mobarak*!"

"We should all try something *new* next Saturday," Manijeh suggested. "Like *fesenjân*,"[43] she suggested.

"*Fesenjoon*? What are we celebrating?" Taraneh asked. "I would have to come over earlier, unless we plan on my staying over again, as it takes forever."

"We're celebrating Brett's new position as the CEO of Vector Affinity Insights," Manijeh declared. "This will all be formally announced on Monday, but it's already official, jut not publicly so. So we can *finally* tell you about it." She put more stew on her current plate of rice. "We'll fetch the things and make it next Saturday night. Taraneh, you know by now that you are *always* welcome to stay overnight with us," she added.

"CEO?" Taraneh replied, some confusion visible on her face. "But what about *Rostam*? I thought…." She shifted about as if she were uncomfortable.

Brett sipped his orange juice. He had decided not to overdo the wine as they had the weekend before. "Rostam has taken a year's leave-of-absence," he finally explained. "That leaves me running matters at VAI." He found a card from his wallet and pushed it across to her.

"*Mobarak*!" Taraneh said. "How's he doing?"

"Well, he handed me the keys to the kingdom he built," Brett answered. "That speaks volumes. But I'm thinking he's going to be alright if he keeps going how he is now."

Taraneh closed her eyes. She let out a sigh, and then opened them once more, and asked, "Duck or chicken?"

---

[43] *Fesenjân* (or *fesenjoon*) is a chicken or duck dish, slow-cooked in a sauce of walnuts and pomegranates, giving it a sweet-and-sour flavor, served with rice, often considered a celebratory dish.

"Pardon?" Brett asked.

"For the *fesenjân*," Manijeh explained. "I vote for duck."

"For a team cooking challenge we're going to start with the difficult bird straight up?" Taraneh asked.

"We got the *tah-dig* after years of failing with your help," Manijeh replied. "You're our Persian food ninja."

"Let's try with the duck," Brett agreed. "The three of us can manage it."

They cleaned up the table, put all of the night's dishes in the dishwasher, and sat down to play *Pasur*. Three games in, Manijeh suggested a movie. After the movie, they stayed up and talked over wine, with Brett still opting for orange juice to remain sober.

"Do you know how I ended up with you two here tonight?" Taraneh asked well into their conversation. "There I was, sitting at my piano, minding my own business, when I got a call from my mother," she said. "Rostam Yazdpour from back in my UBC days, which I had pretty much hung up on a wall and forgotten about, had gotten in touch with them and asked them to let me know he wanted to talk."

"That's what he told me back when you and I first met at the Yazdpours' get together," Brett said.

"Despite how it all turned out, I'm actually glad that he called my parents," she said.

"It brought the three of us together," Manijeh agreed.

"Yes," Taraneh replied with a smile. "I hope he finds what he's looking for out there on his sabbatical and doesn't bring chaos while doing it."

"He's carrying some complex burdens," Brett said, and when he did, everyone nodded.

Taraneh again stayed the night, and the next day, after a group meditation, they walked the usual route around the Seawall before Taraneh headed home and Brett and Manijeh settled into their quiet afternoon together.

"Are you ready for tomorrow's big reveal?" Manijeh asked as she slid beside him while they watched *Henry & June*.

"It shouldn't change much," Brett replied, clicking pause on the control so as to not miss Uma Thurman's dialog. "Are you in any way concerned? You sound apprehensive."

"I don't want Rostam's departure to put him in any kind of bad light in the trading community," she admitted with sadness. "He doesn't deserve that, after all that he has done for VAI and the Vancouver trading scene in general since he started."

Before answering, Brett went to the refrigerator and found two bottles of Perrier, which be brought over to the coffee table and rested there. Presenting one to her, when she nodded, he opened it and handed it to her.

"The formal announcement takes care of a lot of the optics around this situation, and I trust the judgment of the powers-that-be who produced that work of art," he said. "I have every reason to believe that Rostam's reputation within the trading community is quite safe despite his taking an unexpected break, and that VAI and Mind Flame Holdings, being privately held, are also safe since they won't be subjected to speculation. And in a few weeks, Proteus will be announced and…"

"Pardon? *Proteus*? What's that?"

It happened very rarely that Brett's tongue let slip a company secret even in codenamed form, which was exactly why such secrets had obscure monikers like "Proteus" in the first place. He had revealed nothing to Manijeh but felt like an idiot for letting a personal conversation slip into highly sensitive confidential proprietary business. He searched for an honest and quick way to put the matter of Proteus solidly away with her.

"Please forget you heard that. Forget in the regulatory sense."

"Understood," Manijeh immediately replied, gesturing that her lips were sealed.

"Let's hit Pacific Center and dress me up as a proper newly-minted CEO, what say?" he suggested.

"Don't you usually go made-to-fit for this level of thing?" she asked. "We're not likely to find anywhere that can do that on a Sunday. You want this ready by tomorrow, I assume?"

"I'll risk buying the closest fit and driving it over to Mom later today for alterations," he said. "We can invite ourselves over there for dinner in the meantime," he then added, leaning to the phone.

The phone rang, and Siobhan Lloyd-Ronan answered at the other end. "Hello, Mom!" Brett greeted her. Within ten minutes, he had arranged to go over to his parents' house, get his as yet unbought suit altered so it would present as a perfect fit, and have dinner with his parents there. Shortly, they were out and about and looking for his next Armani *prêt-à-porter*.

They found what they were looking for, and soon headed to his parents', where they treated everyone to their lasagna, and afterward headed home with a perfectly executed charcoal gray Armani, vest, and pocket square, ready for his Lobbs to walk him into Monday morning.

Touched by Fortune's Shadow: a triptych

34

On his first day as full CEO of Vector Affinity Insights, Brett Lloyd-Ronan unmistakably fit his new role. His mother had altered his suit perfectly, and he felt ready for whatever he needed to handle. The release had hit Reuters and Bloomberg at the opening of trading on the NSE, thanks to the early finish on the paperwork the week before and Katja's diligence and extensive experience with the newswire services, and calls to talk had been starting to trickle in. Brett handed Katja a list of those he would be interested in talking with and asked her to field all of his other calls at least until Wednesday.

It was by two-forty-five that afternoon that his desk phone started to blink on Katja's line, and he picked up. "Yes?" he said. "What's up?"

"She's not on your list, Brett, but Elle Loughlan-Kent is on the line, and I know she did that great piece on you and Ms. Yazdpour from the San Francisco Symposium, and that was such a nice article that I just assumed you'd want to talk with her if for nothing else than professional courtesy. Shall I put her call through?"

"Very good catch!" he said. "Yes, please put Elle through. It was pure oversight on my part that I hadn't already added her to my list this morning."

"Hey, Elle," he greeted her when the call transferred in.

"Congratulations, Brett!" Elle replied. "And I have to say, I didn't see that coming when we all hooked-up at the Palace at last month's symposium."

"Thank you," he replied, his thoughts all drifting to what Rostam might be up to at that exact moment now that the was on sabbatical. "And thank you so much for all the kindness you showed Manijeh and me in your piece! She loved it, too! To what do I owe the pleasure of your call?"

Touched by Fortune's Shadow: a triptych

"I'd love to do a phone interview with you. Just a fireside chat piece about your new position and what it might mean. That kind of thing. Are you up for it?"

The desk drawer in front of him opened, Brett fumbled with paperclips, finally saying, "Sure. Sounds good."

"Great!" Elle said. "I'll gather my thoughts, and you gather yours, and I'll call you early next week," she said.

"Wonderful. Please set it all up with Katja Fedorova, my assistant. She's the one who sent you to my line just a minute or two ago," he said.

"Looking forward to talking," he started to close.

"A plan it is, then," she replied before the two said their goodbyes and Brett hung up.

Brett then got up, walked out to Katja, and informed her, "Ms. Loughlan-Kent will be interviewing me on the phone next week. She'll be calling to set up times."

Katja closed her eyes, moved them back and forth behind her eyelids as if reading and said, "I've already got three blocks of time I'll hold until she calls and picks one."

"Let her pick all three if she needs," he added. "I'm not sure how long this interview is going to be."

"That works. Meanwhile, I meant to ask if you plan to keep your piano lessons at three on Wednesdays now that you have shifted roles here."

As Brett was returning to his office, he replied to Katja in a firm but pleasant voice, "That Wednesday spot is sacrosanct except in the case of a kitchen fire."

"Also, have you dug into the Klein, Holdum, and French contract pile since coming on?" he asked.

Katja's face scrunched at this. "I had to quick look at it two weeks back," she replied. "It made me dizzy, to be honest."

"Yes, it's a paperclipped mess. They've been our client since 1994. Over the years, that agreement has been amended, revised, redacted, extended, you name it. A real mess."

"I'd call it *organic*," Katja suggested. "Rather than *mess*."

"Yes, *organic*. Like that sandwich in school one finds in one's backpack six months in. Anyway, please gather it all together, put all the changes, *et cetera*, in chronological order, and get me a full consolidated summary of the thing. Be sure to label it clearly as a consolidated version, not the original, and include the dates and a very brief summary of each change that has been made."

"Sure. That's about a week's work," she said.

"Take two weeks to get it *triple*-checked right without having to rush through your other things," Brett said. "Just to be clear: the triple checking is for standard due diligence, not because I don't think you can't do it in a week. And then get it to Winston when you're done, with a copy to me, of course." He smiled. "And speaking of Winston, when he gets back from wherever he is, send him my way."

"All good!" Katja replied with a smile.

◈ • ◈

"Katja said you wanted to talk," Winston announced as he looked around the corner of Brett's open door.

"Come in and sit down for a while," Brett returned as he looked up from what he was doing before being interrupted. "And close the door, please."

Once Winston had sat down, Brett opened his drawer and pulled out a thick folder. "I'm giving you a wide berth on what I'm about to hand you. Please keep all of this between you and me, Margaret, and Gerry. When you need to get either of those two involved I leave up to your judgment."

He stood, walked over to Winston, handed him the folder, and sat on his desk, with one of his legs up and the other on the ground, as Winston started to slowly flip through the pages he had been handed. Periodically, as he read, Winston looked up at Brett as if to gain further information from his face or body posture as Brett sat on the desk.

"I've asked Katja to put together Klein *et al.*'s consolidated agreement. She'll have it in two weeks. Do you think you can time your first part around that milestone? By the way, please don't hint to Katja what it's for yet."

Winston looked over his shoulder at the closed door, as if being certain it was closed, then back to Brett. "It's hard to say with just a cursory glance and until I at least fly some of what you're asking by Margaret, and you're right, probably General Counsel. But yeah, I can hit the two-week milestone if Katja does, while reserving the right to adjust timelines accordingly, given the complexity of the moving parts involved here."

"Great."

"Just one question," Winston put forward.

"Of course," Brett replied. "Asking as many questions as you feel necessary while we do this is important."

"Is Rostam backing this?" he asked. "I mean…"

Touched by Fortune's Shadow: a triptych

Brett inhaled, waited a moment, and then exhaled. "Rostam is on sabbatical. Rostam is my friend of many years, in much need of rest, recouperation, and soul searching. I'm engaged to his sister, and his father is my father's business partner. We are entangled across *decades*. You were there with us at The Yale, counting his drinks as we steered him to not turning his world and ours into a tip fire by going down the path he was. We *all* love Rostam."
Winston half smiled. "Yes, but…"
Instead of a direct answer, Brett hummed and finally said, "You've exercised every option you've ever been issued, yes?"
Winston nodded yes and swallowed hard.
"And that stock grant you got when you were promoted?"
"Pretty sizeable. Thanks again for that. More than I would have ever asked for, if I'm honest."
"And when I handed that folder to you, you felt your pulse race about what all your stock suddenly *meant* in the grander scheme of things, am I right?" He smiled and approached his liquor cabinet. "Numbers that were once just numbers in vested option counts in your portfolio's summary column suddenly and clearly meant 'skiing trip' or 'braces for Samuel,'" he said. "I'm not trying to be flippant, please excuse my examples."
"I got to admit it, yes," Winston replied. "I used some of my COO promotion bonus to get Samuel's orthodontist started on that adventure. Thanks again for that."
"It's close of business," he said, opening the cabinet and then pouring two tumblers of The Glenlivet. "Ding!" he mimicked a bell as he handed Winston his drink. "Then you can imagine the smile Rostam's going to have on his face when and if Operation Proteus pans out."
"To moving forward!" Winston proposed the toast as he stood, folder in one hand, tumbler in the other.
"To moving forward!" returned the toast as he put back his shot in one tip.

35

As Brett finished the fiery Third Movement of Beethoven's "*Appassionata*," he allowed himself finally to breathe. His eyes were closed; he could still see the silver and gold notes drifting about on the surface of his recollection. He could feel his pulse race, both from the piece and from Taraneh's proximity.

"Where do you find *your* passion, Brett?" Taraneh asked from her heart. She had been quietly writing notes as he played, tracking his progress.

Brett turned his head to face her and replied, "Pardon? My passion in what sense?"

She stood, approached the bench, and asked, "May I?"

"Please do," he said, waving with his hand that she was more than welcome to join him on the bench. "I welcome your feedback on anything you might feel will help."

After closing her eyes for a moment, she replayed a section of the Third Movement. The notes resonated through Brett, and he could feel subtle interference patterns in his inner echo chamber between what he had just played, and what Taraneh soundly defeated with her perfect execution. But it was not just technical perfection that he was hearing; her passion with the phrasing was almost haunting. He could not tell if he was actually hearing this with his ear, of if this was an effect of his creative mind.

When she was finished, she took her hand, lifted it, and placed it over her heart for him to feel. Then, she lifted his hand to her neck, so that he could feel her pulse more directly. It was speeding. Brett nodded his understanding. He could feel his own heartbeat speed up until it was almost in pace with hers. The warmth of her skin, the exquisite sound of her breathing, the gentle movement of her chest as she inhaled and then exhaled. He wanted to lean toward her and could feel himself off-balance enough for this to happen.

Touched by Fortune's Shadow: a triptych

"When you're playing this same piece, I'm not feeling your heart racing in your notes," she commented. She placed his hand back on the keys. "I find mine in many places. My passion I mean. In remembering a Rumi poem being read. In the sound of birds some mornings while I'm on a walk. In love making, when the passionate kind. *Somewhere.*

"As I go for a *crescendo*, it flows through me, and I push to the climax with each beat of my pulse. That's the point. Where do *you* find *your* passion? When you sit on this bench, it is your *passion* that we must connect with, through a composition such as Beethoven's. If we do not, you will soon lose the listener, having mastered the *execution*, but not the *ecstasy*."

She got up, went behind him as he remained on the bench, and then stood behind him. Her left hand she placed over his heart on his back, resting her right on his right shoulder. "Play through the whole of the Movement again," she directed. "Oh, your heart is *sprinting.*" Her face flushed noticeably. "Someone as fit as you would normally have a much slower pulse, I would think."

Brett glanced over his shoulder and saw that her eyes were closed, and he then began to play again. While a bit difficult to play with her hand on his back and shoulder, he set this out of his mind and instead went into the same cool, dark, pool he went during his Sunday morning meditation sessions. When he was in that place, he could feel her touch on him, and her response to his efforts when he released his guards and let himself feel the Third Movement as it pulsed from one bar to the next. He and she were entwined in that moment, lost in one another like lovers on silk, if only in his sacred self, and he could hear what he felt, mixed with their synchronized breathing, and he could feel her in the soft amber static of her.

"Right *there!*" she said, pressing more firmly on his back when he executed an emphatic passage as if for the first time, and in that moment saw what he could only imagine was a conflated projection of passion incarnate, but which defied a label or name, and only existed as a phantasm in his private metaphysical ether.

Before he was done, Taraneh tapped his right shoulder twice with her right hand, her other still on his back. "That was *much* better than before. Especially when I spoke out; *that* moment was *ecstatic.* Not only for you, as the performer, but for *me*, as the listener. That is the moment you are aiming to create in an entire *audience.* All of them at the *edge* of *ecstasy*, right *there* with you and Beethoven in *that* passion."

Brett wiped down the keys, closed the top, and then wiped it down as well. "Manijeh's really excited about the duck *fesenjân* this Saturday," he said, struggling to regain his composure, almost unable, almost reaching out to hold her and be awash in the scent of her. The whitecaps inside his chest slowly subsided to a calm again, but only slowly.

Manijeh smiled. "So am I! Oh!" She ran upstairs and soon returned with a small box. "Pistachio macaron's for Manijeh! She was asking about these, and I finally was in that neighborhood again and they were well stocked."

Brett took the box. "These are the best. She'll love this." He placed all his notes and sheet music in his briefcase and snapped it firmly shut.

"Would you like to take tea?" she asked.

"Of course!" he replied. He stood and headed up the stairs behind her as they went to her kitchen.

The tea made and poured, Taraneh at last began to speak, as Brett had suspected she would, as after-session tea was typically their time to talk about whatever was weighing on her without her having to hold her tongue too much.

"I've been carrying around some amount of private guilt," she admitted after her first sip.

"Guilt? About?"

"I didn't want to say this in front of Manijeh, since Rostam is her brother, and I didn't want her to feel some kind of slight, but the whole relationship with him the second time around felt one-sided on his part, as far as I was concerned. This was *actually* why I broke up with him."

Brett put one more lump of sugar into his tea, stirred, and replied, "Feel free to unload. I won't share this."

Taraneh smiled, but it was not her usual smile, but rather, a half-uncomfortable one. "When he first contacted me after the years, I was quite willing to give it another shot, thinking that perhaps I may have grown, he may have grown, and there might be something that wasn't there the first time we went out years before. My optimism was exaggerated, it seems."

"Was there anything in particular that soured things the first time around? He and I didn't catch up as much on such things in those days, due to demands on both our time."

Her breathing was almost audible. "Our first breakup was *never* about anything being in the slightest bit *sour*. We got along on many levels," she conceded.

"There's a lot about him to praise," Brett said.

"His deep love of classical music, for instance. Many things to praise him for, but I never found myself in…"

"Limerence?"

"Pardon?"

"Limerence. The state of being infatuated or obsessed with someone so much that you wish of all wishes that they, too, feel the same way about you."

"Is that what you feel for Manijeh?"

"I had my share of that, and perhaps it ripples through me still, yes," Brett confessed. "Giddy chills."

"I didn't feel *that* for him," she admitted. "I felt *affection* for him. I enjoyed his company very much. But I didn't feel limerence or even *lust* if I'm being honest."

"These things don't come lit all brightly aflame on delivery," he replied. "They take time to develop. There's no equation."

Her eyes darted down modestly, and then she looked up. "But like I said, when he called my parents I thought, 'Maybe we've grown and changed and now I *will* feel those things.' You know? And suddenly there he was in my life again, all sails in the wind, declaring that I was the *one*, his *soulmate*, and there was I, not feeling able to say I reciprocated that. But of course my mother and father *absolutely love and adore* him and that carries a lot of weight; especially with our community, as you may have learned. He checked off all the boxes except the most important one; I was Shirin, and he was Farhad."

"That's not one I'm familiar with," Brett replied.

"It's a classic Persian tale of complicated love. King Khosro and Princess Shirin, and the sculptor, Farhad. A love triangle, except that Farhad dotes over Shirin, but she does not feel *that* way for him, and he goes to great lengths, but it just doesn't work out. She does, however, fall into love with Khosro; the actual full tale is complex and nuanced. Suffice it to say that I was Shirin and Rostam was Farhad."

Without a word, Brett put his hand on top of Taraneh's and comforted her, for he could see that she was almost at tears from her confession to him about how she and Rostam had really gotten along.

"And through all that, there was the Canada Day incident at the restaurant," she added. "That was *almost* my limit, but I rallied and pushed through it; perhaps so not to lose you…." She stopped herself and then smiled softly.

"I never was told what triggered that," he said.

Her face contorted slightly, and then she said, "You had asked me that Wednesday afternoon to invite us to The Yale for Friday, and over his and my dinner, I did that. He'd been putting back more than I was comfortable with. From that point forward, it got ugly. *Very* ugly."

"Sorry to hear that!"

"Well, Manijeh was such a darling to answer my call for help and advice that night, so I was able to figure that out. But it put me on *high* alert. I was surprised he agreed to The Yale."

"He didn't dance much, except with his beer glass," Brett replied. "Not to throw him under a bus he already didn't decide to jump under without any help from any of us."

There was a brief moment of anxious laughter of the kind that signaled an end to a topic. Brett pointed at the box of macarons and said, "The last time I ate those with you over tea, if I recall, was that same day. Much more pleasant!"

"I have more *just* for us if you'd like!" she said. She stood, found some more macarons, and approached the table with them, "Sorry I didn't offer sooner!"

Brett took a macaron, bit in slowly as the smooth surface started to dissolve, and said, "Amazing!"

"Any thoughts?" she finally asked.

"My answer *will* very likely be biased, since you've plied me with pistachio macarons," Brett teased. "You also have me at a disadvantage, since I don't really know how much of the past Rostam's shared with you, and some of it is not mine to share."

She nodded in agreement as she sipped her final sip from his first cupful. After refilling and stirring in the sugar, she said, "The fire in Abadan? His struggles with career choice? His *many* failed relationships? Remember, he said I was the *one*, and he treated my ears like I needed an entire life recap. I pretty much know what I need to know about *most* of his history, as a man might tell a woman he believes to be his soulmate. I think we're pretty safe; unlike you, who tends toward reticence, he was an open book. Except about business."

"How did it *really* go over when you told him about putting your hand on my leg?" Brett asked outright. "From my side, it looked to me as if it triggered a drinking session on Rostam's part, and I never really found out how that all went. Knowing might help me fit things together in my mind more before I start offering any insight into all this."

Taraneh blushed at this, putting both her hands up to cover her flushing face, and then said, "Oh. *That*." She found her composure and continued, "He wobbled, but then declared that he put the matter aside, and that was pretty much all that was said of the matter. He was angry, but we worked through that together."

Brett composed his thoughts and finally said, "It sounds to me like normal human relationship things here. From his side, he became obsessed with you. It's no insult to you to say that you're not the first he's called the *one* and probably won't be the last. But that could describe a number of people. I suspect many who *seem* less flighty are just *really* good at reticence, but in fact keep their lists of absolutely-the-one's in a diary."

She started to laugh. "Yes, I also have friends like that of both genders," she agreed.

"First off, you're not the only lady who just wasn't all that into him," Brett added, "whereas others thought he was Iran's answer to Antonio Banderas. Chemistry works that way. Every pot has a lid, I've heard."

"Yes. I always understood that. I just felt over the journey of my own failed relationships that either my soulmate would cross my path, or I would develop deeper feelings for the one I was with. Are you like that?" she asked. "Do you run around declaring the-one-ness with those who aren't as into you? I don't take you for being that fickle."

"Me?" His cup, too, was now empty, and he poured some more tea and added two sugar cubes. "I've lived an active life, but if I'm honest, Manijeh is the only woman I've been involved with whom I have felt as deeply as I do, and it took me forever and a day to confess the *true* depth of my feelings to her. I can feel attraction, certainly; I'm a healthy male when all is said and done. But despite my active history as free agent, that *level* of emotional romantic connection isn't something I'm incredibly familiar with, and so, I wouldn't say that I'm living with a trail of failed soulmates behind me on my walk."

Taraneh nodded. "Thanks for listening."

"I don't know how useful anything spewing out of my mouth has been," Brett said.

"Whatever got said," she replied, "I now feel like I have full permission to feel the way I feel about the whole situation. I'm happy to have met you and Manijeh from it."

"That's a great start," Brett said. "And we're as pleased to have gotten closer to you, as well, Taraneh."

They finished their tea. As Brett drove home with the box of pistachio macarons, he couldn't help but feel sadness for Rostam. Although Taraneh Khoshrangi was the most openly expressive romantic interest Rostam had ever had when it came to coming to him for advice after or during their relationship with him, she was not the first who had expressed similar feelings about being less interested in him than he'd been in them. He wasn't sure how he might process this and remembered that he had sworn not to share Taraneh's thoughts or feelings with anyone, and so he compartmentalized his thoughts and observations about the matter, and prepared to get home, rest, and finish off his first week as CEO at VAI.

Touched by Fortune's Shadow: a triptych

Vancouver, 31 October 1984

Touched by Fortune's Shadow: a triptych

36

Plastic swords, eye-patches, satin sashes, and coffee grounds sticking to the face with petroleum jelly. This would be the last Hallowe'en tour of the neighborhood that Brett and his two friends, Rostam and Manijeh, would ever celebrate, as they were now too old to be going door-to-door without arousing resistance from the adults handing out the candy. Siobhan Lloyd-Ronan, Brett's mother, had made each of their costumes, and although they were all sewn perfectly, they were intentionally exaggerated rather than an attempt to get the pirate attire to movie costume quality, as she was sometimes asked to do in her work with clients. They were out to have fun on a budget, not look like the cast of *The Pirates of Penzance*, and until nine that night, everything was pure Samhain fun, with their bags filling slower than usual, but taking on booty nonetheless.

The Hastings-Sunrise neighborhood was rife with spoils, and they had gathered many. One or two at the door questioned the group on their ages, but when they insisted this would be their last year trick-or-treating, the reluctance cooled, and treats were offered one last time. Until nine, other children in the streets left them alone. As they were headed back to Brett's house, where the Yazdpour children's father would be meeting them to drive them home, they were met by group of three ghosts who were taller than them, and who had pillowcases with them, rather than bags. One of the ghosts was carrying a broom, as if he considered himself to be a witch rather than a ghost, or perhaps he was dressed as a hybrid of both. The simplicity of their costumes: three sheets with sets of eyes cut out, and nothing else to speak of, betrayed the lack of care they had all put into the night. When the two groups were about three yards apart, they stopped and faced one another under the light of the streetlamp.

Touched by Fortune's Shadow: a triptych

Brett went through several scenarios in his mind if the situation were to become threatening, as he felt uncomfortable with these ghosts. The swords they had on them were plastic costume accessories at best and would be more useless than a twig to keep them at a managed distance. His mind was already considering the situation they were not facing if these three were going to make trouble.

His inner vision glowed like an amber screen, putting the world around him into a *Tron*-scape in his mind, with the three sketchy ghosts on one end and the three pirates on the other. The sidewalk lit up in his mind as the path for an extended breakfall, the *Mae Ukemi*, which he knew from experience would put him right in front of the one with the broom. He would be back on his feet, right in position, and could grab the broom, unbalance him with an *Uki Goshi* floating hip throw, putting the ghost to the ground and giving Brett the broom to work with as a makeshift two-handed *bokken* from there. As the six of them shifted about under the streetlamp, he adjusted the scenario to accommodate it. His heart was racing, but not excessively. He regulated his breathing and remembered to be careful not to start seeing the current situation with tunnel vision.

Finally, one of the ghosts called out, "Hey there! You sure had more luck than we did." He held out his pillowcase, turned it upside down, and shook it to show that it was empty.

"We can share some of ours with you," Manijeh offered.

The tallest of the three lifted his blanket, showing his face, which Brett recognized from school but could not put a name to. He called back, "Manijeh? I didn't recognize you with all that dirt on your face!"

"That's coffee!" Rostam explained. "It's *supposed* to be face stubble. Hey, Michael!"

Michael responded with, "Hey! You'd share yours? That's great! We got *nothing*, man! *Bupkis!*"

"We had to *beg* to get what we got," Brett added to show that he understood their plight and had almost shared it.

"Why didn't *we* get anything when *we* begged?" Michael asked his two friends.

The one on his left lifted his sheet, and Brett recognized Luke from his shop class, and said, "I *told* you these sheets were *lame*. Their costumes at least have some effort put into them."

"Brett's mom made them for us," Manijeh said. "Yeah, you guys can have my bag, and we'll split our other two."

Michael smiled, "You'd do that? And wow, Brett, your mom can really put together some nice stuff."

"She's a seamstress," Brett said proudly.

Manijeh reached out her hand with her bag and said, "Sure. We can give you some of ours."

"That's great, guys!" Luke said, stepping forward to take her bag, which they then split between the three of them. "My dad told me this was absolutely the last time I was going out on Hallowe'en except to take Sarah—my little sister. That's next year for me, I guess."

"You guys are lifesavers!"

"Does your mom do graduation dresses?" Michael asked. "My sister needs one this year."

"Yes, she does," Brett said. "Talk to me at school about it."

The three exchanged small talk about school for a few minutes and started back on their way home to meet up with Mr. Yazdpour, who would be waiting for them, and they were now a little late. Well away from the boys dressed only in sheets carrying a broom, Rostam finally spoke up.

"Why'd you go and give away your candy?" he asked.

"I recognized the blue Reeboks that Luke was wearing," Manijeh explained.

"Do you keep track of the color of Luke Dafoe's Reeboks?" Rostam asked.

"He's cute! Of course I do!"

"He's in my shop class," Brett said. "And I think Manijeh did absolutely the right thing by offering them some of our candy," he then admitted.

"You and your martial arts philosophy, I guess?" Rostam said.

"Maybe," Brett replied. "Or maybe it's just that they all were so pathetic that they needed some charity. Not *every* group of boys in the street is Hinton's *Outsiders*' young thugs."

"Stay gold, Ponyboy. Stay gold," Manijeh then added at this. "Their costumes were *truly* pathetic," she then agreed.

"When their parents realize they destroyed those sheets, at least now they'll have loot to show for it," Brett said.

They started to laugh together and were soon back at his house, where Rostam and Manijeh's father was waiting to drive them home safely.

Touched by Fortune's Shadow: a triptych

Vancouver, mid-November 1998

Touched by Fortune's Shadow: a triptych

37

"I have actually gotten jealous over you once or twice over the years," Brett admitted to Manijeh as they approached being awake on Saturday morning. She lay naked against him, under his arm, her head resting lightly on his right shoulder under their covers. The nine-hundred thread count Egyptian cotton under his back was smooth on his skin, but she was infinitely more so, and he wanted to just be with her, in the sheets, forever.

"You? *Jealous*? Mr. *Open*?" She turned her head, her gray eyes almost mystical in the low light of morning and with the lights off as they were. "Do tell."

"Do you at all remember that last time that we all three went out on Hallowe'en together?" Brett asked, stroking her shoulder as he spoke.

After a short silence, she replied, "Shiver me timbers!"

"Yes, *that* year. *Pirates and ghosts*."

Again there was silence. "Oh, do you mean Luke Dafoe?"

"Bingo. You *do* remember. The ghost with the most."

"Yeah, I kind of thought he was cute for some reason."

"I picked up on that and brooded over it," he admitted.

"Normal teen stuff," she noted. "Classic, actually."

"He was hopelessly *lousy* at shop; always asked me to help him," Brett confessed.

"Which of *course* you did," Manijeh commented, stroking the hair on his chest.

"Which of *course* I did," he admitted. "All told, Luke was actually a very nice kid. Do you have any plans for the day?"

"Taraneh wants to go hiking at Lynn Valley with me," she said after some thought. "Care to join us?"

"I can't today, but you two have fun."

"You can't come?" she pouted. "I thought all *three* of us could go. Like a grown-up version of the Renfrew Ravine."

"I *totally* wish I could join you two, but I'm getting ready for a very big meeting on Monday," he excused himself. "At least it's not a filler meeting I'm preparing for. I still would rather go with you than prepare, but one *must* press on."

"What's that about, anyway? You've dropped hints the last while, but not so much as a word."

"I'm not at liberty, *yadda yadda*," he said. He wanted to tell her what had been going on at the office at VAI, but it was absolutely critical that not a word of it be shared outside of a small bubble of regulated confidentiality. "But if you want to play gin tonight or something, feel free to invite Taraneh over when you're done. I should have all my stuff out of the way by four at the latest. All work and no play turns us into salt."

Once showered and awake, Brett made breakfast for them both, which they ate on the balcony in front of a heat lamp. Manijeh was out in the Lexus to fetch Taraneh for their hike by ten, and Brett was soon in his home office in front of the freshly made slides he would be using for Monday's meeting. It had taken almost a month to put together, having been more complex than he had at first anticipated, but Katja and Winston had made best use of everyone's time and every research at their disposal to present the case he was going to be making as convincingly as pitch as he had ever given or attended.

When lunch came, he opened a tin of Campbell's chicken noodle soup and made that, eating it with toast and the last non-decaffeinated coffee he would allow himself that day. Lunch and its pangs out of the way, he returned to his office until three o'clock. At three, his work finally completed, he went to the living room sofa, pulled the blanket over himself, and fell into a deep nap.

~•~

The smell of basmati on the boil filled Brett's senses as he awoke from his slumber. His head spun about as he sat up and got his bearings. As he turned his head from left to right, his eyes closed, he could both feel and hear the pops in his neck, and brief flashes filled his inner vision. None of it was real. It was how he perceived it to be, not how it was. Only the present moment was real.

Taraneh approached him with a full glass of water, handed it to him and said, "Good morning, sleepy!" She gave him a quick kiss on the cheek and then returned to the stove in the kitchen.

"What did I miss?" he asked quietly as he came more fully to his senses.

"Manijeh had to go out to find us a few ingredients we were missing," she explained why they were alone in the suite. "She's probably in the elevator by now, on her way back."

"Thank you," he said. He sipped the water, feeling refreshed as it poured down his throat like water from a glacier lake up in the Rocky Mountains. When he was halfway done, the phone rang, and he picked it up without checking who was calling first.

"*Moshi moshi*," Soke Hashimoto greeted him.

"*Moshi moshi*," he replied.

"I'm so sorry to be bothering you on Sunday," Hashimoto apologized. "*Moshiwake gozaimasen*," he apologized again.

"It's no bother at all, *Soke* Hashimoto," he replied. "I wasn't expecting your call, but no worries. To what do I owe the pleasure, *Soke*?" he asked. Calls from *Soke* Hashimoto were *very* rare and lately had been about updates on the *nihonto* alloy project mostly when they did happen.

"Brett, could I impose on you to take over my Tuesday and Thursday classes for the next little while? Until about the end of January. I figured, since you already attend and assist with the instruction, that taking them over more fully would not impact your busy schedule."

Before answering, Brett considered his schedule. After the meeting coming for Monday, things might be busy, but he didn't anticipate they would put out his timetable, given how effective Katja and Winston had both been with doing all of the critical, meticulous detail work that would have required him to work overtime in any other setting he could imagine himself in.

"I suppose I could do that, *Soke*," he replied. "No problem at all. Is everything okay?"

"June and I have some serious family matters to attend over in Ottawa," he said. "You see, Brett, my son's wife, Elizabeth, has been diagnosed with late-stage breast cancer."

"I'm *so* sorry to hear that," Brett immediately replied. He did not recall the *Soke* ever referring to his own wife as *anything* other than Mrs. Hashimoto, let alone by a simple *June*, and he could hear distraction in his voice.

"Thank you, Brett," he replied. "We are going there to help them arrange her treatment plan, and to spend Christmas with the grandchildren. You're really doing us a *huge* favor."

"No problem at all. You take as long as you all *need*," Brett volunteered. "I'll keep everything going smoothly, *Soke*."

The two finished their conversation after setting up specific details of what Hashimoto had been doing recently with the others' curricula at the *dojo*, and then Brett hung up the phone.

"I'm back!" Manijeh called out from the kitchen, holding a brown paper bag full of various ingredients for dinner. In his conversation with the *Soke*, Brett had not noticed her enter the apartment. "Did you *miss* me?"

"You two need any help?" he offered.

"We're good for now," Manijeh replied as she gingerly took the package of chicken from the bag. "We'll let you know if we need you. Who was that you were talking to?" she asked.

"*Soke* Hashimoto."

"I meant to ask, is that his first name? *Soke*?" Taraneh said.

"That's not a name, that's his title," Brett explained. "He's the head of the school. He's more fully the *Shodai Soke*, which means he founded this particular branch of *kenjutsu*."

"What did he want to discuss?" Manijeh asked.

"He we be visiting his son's family in Ottawa with his wife for a few months, and he wants me to take over the class fully until he's back. It will be Tuesday and Thursday nights, which I've already set aside anyway for *kenjutsu*, so I said yes."

"That might jam our winter break this December," she said.

"We'll figure it out," Brett assured her. "Without breaking so much as a sweat over it. Plenty of *us* time."

ൠ•ൠ

"Have you heard anything from Rostam at all recently?" Taraneh asked as she cut her chicken.

"He checks in with Mom and Dad more than with me," Manijeh replied. "I think he's in Luxembourg or something."

"Still? I figured he'd made it to Berlin by now," Brett said. "Basically, Taraneh, he's visiting museums and having a blast over in Europe with his copy of *Lonely Planet* and a ton of rolls of film. Dry as toast last I heard."

"Good to hear he's having fun," she said. "Say, I've got a favor to ask you two. Maybe you can help me out."

Brett and Manijeh nodded in the affirmative at the same time, triggering them to smile at one another for having been so synchronized in their response.

"I *need* a place by February, at the very latest," she said almost contritely. "My landlords—a *lovely* couple—just gave me notice that they are moving the husband's in-laws in."

"That's no fun," Manijeh said.
"Definitely not," Brett agreed.
"We'll keep our eyes and ears open," Manijeh finally said. Brett chewed, swallowed, and said, "Definitely."
"Thank you," their friend replied. "It's been rough on me since I found out I have to move. I found my current place after I decided to teach full-time, and it's perfect for that."
"It really is a great place in a great location," Brett agreed. "I've always been meaning to ask why you walked away from being a concert pianist to teach."
Taraneh smiled before replying. "It's not so much that I 'walked away' from performing in concert as it is that I 'walked toward' teaching," she began. "As much as I *absolutely* love the applause, and I do indeed, I love my financial independence *far* more. I could not achieve that while building my reputation on the lean concert circuit. Teaching has been a fair balance I've struck with reality. I prefer eating to being hallway famous."
"Being able to survive on one's own merits as a woman in what is still pretty much a man's world definitely informs one's work-a-day choices," Manijeh then agreed with animated vigor. "Which, considering we're at 1998 now, is *codswallop*. But we *must* play the cards we're dealt at the table."
"I've found myself far more suited to life as a piano teacher who once played for VSO, and who now helps guide others on *their* journey with classical piano, than I was to chasing that other dream, as daring, charming, and romantic as it was."
"I must admit," Manijeh said, "I spent a bit of time at the Vancouver Library main branch catching up with where your career as a concert pianist went and was going before you retired from that life." She smiled at her friend appreciatively. "Stepping back must have been a *huge* change from all that."
"For me, though, teaching is significantly more satisfying, even beyond the mere money. Although I don't get the almost sensual rush I once did giving a live performance for multitudes at the Orpheum, I get to see progress in others as they pursue their own versions of that." She stopped herself almost as if embarrassed. "If you'll pardon my exuberance. I sometimes miss it, but not often enough to ever regret putting it behind me. Fond memories and recordings from then are sufficient for me."
"Well, as I said, we'll both keep our eyes and ears open for a place for you to be able to teach, and also somewhere you'd enjoy living," Manijeh repeated her promise.

After finishing their meal, they played gin, and then a long game of *Trivial Pursuit*, which Manijeh won, and finished the evening by watched *The Fifth Element* on DVD, which they all agreed was well worth it.

≪•≫

The next morning, after Taraneh had walked the Seawall with them and had headed home, as had become their weekend routine, Manijeh sat beside Brett on the sofa and said, "What about your other penthouse? Didn't you say the tenant gave notice for the end of December? Or was I imagining that?"

"Pardon?" he asked.

"Your other suite. Down the *hallway*," she said.

"Are you suggesting Taraneh live next to us? Down the hall?" he replied, putting down his copy of Goldblatt's *Topoi*.

Manijeh's face lit up. "It's really a formality at *this* point, isn't it, though?" She had turned on the television with the volume muted and was flipping through the guide to see what was on that afternoon. "She could teach from there; the piano would go up the service elevator with some professional packing. Her parents and friends could easily visit, and she'd have all the privacy—and the best view of Vancouver—she needs to be the wonderful, lovely fully financially independent person she is."

"Let me think about it a bit, Manijeh," he finally conceded. "Please don't breathe a word of it to her until I've run it through my mind for a little while. The management company insists on locking tenants with a one-year lease to make it worthwhile for them fiscally, and though I own it, I cannot just override that contract. And besides, they're excellent property managers."

"Are you thinking of asking Rostam what he feels about it?" Manijeh inquired. "Because if you are, it's *none* of his business."

"I agree with you on that, Manijeh. I have so much going on this week, what with tomorrow's big meeting and with taking over Hashimoto's role for a while, that I just want to make sure I'm thinking about this with a clear mind."

"Sure," she said. "Just don't take *too* long to decide. It's too wonderful an opportunity for everyone to have it fly away from us. Don't be Hamlet."

"Let's take the Sea Bus to the Quai and find somewhere to eat over on the North Shore," he suggested.

"I want to relax today," she replied. "Holdum has me doing a bunch of inexplicably weird things in the office tomorrow."

"Not even a walk?" Brett asked.

"That I *can* do. A walk would be much more relaxing than the Sea Bus. Where to? The Seawall circuit?"

"We did that this morning with Taraneh. How about we walk down toward Graville Island and just take it in as it comes by us? One intersection at a time."

"Great. I'm going to wear comfy sweats and a messy scarf," she suggested. "Are you okay with coordinating with lazy Sunday chic? Because today tells me to be cozy."

"Wonderful. I was built for it. I keep a few extra pairs of jeans with worn out knees for just such occasions. And I didn't even *buy* them in that condition."

Manijeh started to laugh lightly. "Oh, blue-collar core is my *favorite*. And throw on a that sexy denim jacket… the one with the sherpa lining."

Touched by Fortune's Shadow: a triptych

38

"Holy shit!"

Charles Holdum stood up, looked to his left at his own team, to his right at Brett Lloyd-Ronan's team, and said, "What more can I say? I was not expecting that when I was driving to work today," he said. He walked up to the whiteboard and drew a big arrow that pointed at an illustration that Brett had drawn there during the meeting.

"Like *Jeopardy*," Brett said, "we need that arrow in the form of a question." He checked the faces of Margaret, Gerry, Winston, and Katja, and they all appeared relaxed. On the other side, the Klein, Holdum, and French team were flipping through handout sheets that Katja and Winston had passed around at various stages of the presentation they'd all just participated in. "In other words, what are you asking, exactly?"

"Brett, what you're describing here is all well and good as skyhooks and left-handed monkey wrenches go at the Dog and Pony, but my biggest question is whether or not that thing—this Proteus-what-have-you—really exists as represented here or is just smoke and mirrors." He returned to his seat and sat down.

"Thank you for your infamous dose of healthy skepticism, Chuck. When have you ever known us to show you a Potemkin's Village?" Brett asked outright. He turned to Katja and nodded. She stood, moved some papers from the path of the projector, and then turned out the lights. "Thank you, Ekaterina."

On the screen was live data that everyone there recognized at a glance, as it was part of their day-to-day business to be able to spot a slight market fluctuation on such screens. "I'm clicking on the present market state," he said. "The present is training the Proteus model." He switched to another keyboard, typed in his password, and a second screen occupied the presentation area on the wall of the VAI meeting room.

"The model is now trained," Katja said. "The purple line is your seeing into the future, based upon how the moment of training represents that future. Note the confidence bands and how they widen as we pry further and further forward from the present, which is how mathematics accounts for the fact that uncertainty about the future state of the market at this level grows as we go further forward. We could be here for a minute or two as we build an intuition about what we're seeing. Please keep in mind that the computational resources we have given this demo are more limited than we would in actual use."

A minute later, the purple line started to flash, and Winston started to speak. "This is what we were waiting for: a market change point has been detected. One element that was making the future uncertain has now manifested in an actual shift in the market's predictability under the existing model. The prior model will start to lose predictive fidelity very quickly from this point forward, but as you can see in the yellow adjustment lines now starting to appear along the bands, it is already retraining to the current conditions and correcting its path." When the line went purple again, he added, "And we now have stability within the confidence interval. Moreover, the prior model, or models for that matter, can be reactivated should past conditions reappear in the market. It both learns new patterns and remembers prior models and resurfaces them if suitable. The rest is outlined in as much detail as Legal and Compliance would allow us in the paperwork you've been given."

Brett used his mouse to put the pointer over a counter on the bottom right of the screen. "In total, the dynamic Proteus model showed this profitability gain over the non-adaptive baseline. This, Chuck, is where you can say 'Holy shit!'"

"I used that one up already this meeting, which is frankly two over my usual budget." Charles replied. "But I *can* throw in an 'I'll be damned!' on the house."

Katja turned the lights back on and started shutting down the screens that were being projected. "What we all just witnessed was a live real-time demonstration of the actual technology being discussed, with to-the-second market data, but for confidentiality and compliance, the portfolios being monitored and used as client risk exemplars were deidentified and are historical in nature. Because of this, the results we saw may not reflect performance with live portfolios. This disclosure was legal and compliance talking. Now back to Brett."

Brett put the consolidated agreement in the center of the table, face up, with its cover page clearly denoted and said in his most non-threatening but nonetheless commanding voice, "This represents the consolidation of our original agreement and all subsequent amendments and schedules. You were amongst our first clients to license our technology. As early-adopters, you helped us get our chips in the game, and we were able to leverage those chips toward considerable growth, and substantial returns to you for your early faith in us. This document represents the current agreement, as consolidated and put in front of our General Counsel for review. It serves as *the* place to go as we move forward. We thank Ekaterina for this."

"Just where exactly are you hoping we move forward *to*?" Holdum asked. "I'm seeing a lot of amazing things here, but what I'm not seeing in the *direction* we're trying to steer."

He walked to the window. "Back then, we fought over a few clauses in there. I can't remember how many nights of sleep I lost to verbiage such as seen in the form of the Binding Arbitration Clause we were able to at last agree on. But we always believed that as such an early adopter, there was one clause Klein, Holdum, and French absolutely deserved to be the one to get exclusive rights to." He turned to face the room and said, "And that would be the Right of First Refusal clause, of course."

"I'm just going to assume I heard that right and ask, what exactly is on offer *here* and *now*?" As he said this, his team started flipping through their papers as if they might find the answer there somewhere before Brett replied.

It had all come to this. Rostam was lost in Europe, sending post-cards to friends and family, finding his bliss, and enjoying every minute of it. He'd given his blessing over the phone during a recent call. Because she worked for Klein *et al.*, Manijeh could not yet be told anything. But they had talked directly, and Rostam was more than happy to walk away from the whole thing with a bag of cash and a solid asset portfolio. It had all come to this.

"You only hold right of first refusal on *one* thing. But so that everyone here is exactly aligned on the matter: what is on offer is Vector Affinity Insights, Inc. The one thing you get first call on."

After saying this, Brett waited for everyone in the room to fully process what he had just revealed, and then continued slowly. "We're obviously not offering Mind Flame Holdings, which was incorporated and trading before VAI even came into existence as a corporation."

He sat at, at which point Gerald Cheung, General Counsel for VAI, clarified with, "Mind Flame Holdings is making the offer of sale of Vector Affinity Insights, Inc., which is fully owned by Mind Flame. This offer is being made first and presently *only* to Klein, Holdum, and French, under the many consolidated provisions outlined in our current consolidated agreement which guarantee Klein, Holdum, and French the right of first refusal."

Brett watched everyone Klein, Holdum, and French had sent to this meeting, and saw that they were still all caught off guard by the outright offer of sale of VAI. After another period of silence, he continued.

"Gerry said it like the lawyer he is. Lock, stock, and barrel. After the acquisition, I would be transitioning my role as CEO to Winston Rampersad, so that by spring next year he'd be running the show. I'm not pretending to tell you how to do your business, only how ours worked well: you might just want to put VAI, once you acquire it—you'll pardon my presumption about that detail—under its own holding company and keep it insulated from yourself the way we've kept it quiet and easy-to-manage here."

"Do you have a price in mind?"

"It seems that I missed the History of Negotiation class that talks about how we should jump directly to closing numbers during the initial pitch," Brett replied playfully. "If you want to know whether or not to buy the car, you first must walk around it and kick the tires, Chuck."

"We're not hedging here," Winston interjected calmly. "Our initial ask is already in sealed escrow to be revealed only when you've reviewed the paperwork you've been presented to date."

"We *really* want you to kick those tires," Katja added.

Charles Holdum started to laugh to the point where he started to cough lightly, prompting the person from his firm sitting beside him to open a bottle of Perrier on offer and hand it to him. Once he had cleared his throat, he said, "Fair enough. This *is* going to take some sophisticated projections to figure out in terms of its value proposition to us."

"We have provided a large number of projections you might consider using as templates," Katja interjected. "If you wish, please have your people email me and I can get the scripts we used to generate those to you and then you can modify them to your own practices and needs."

"That would be lovely!" Karl Todd from the Klein *et al.* side of the table replied.

Brett finally continued. "Wonderful. All of you get into your respective rooms and figure out what all of that paperwork we've handed you means in light of what you have seen us demonstrate today," Brett suggested. "The business model is right there, more or less, if you get creative with it after half a bottle of chardonnay. You can use it as a starting point and take it where you want Klein *et al.* to go moving forward."

Charles Holdum pulled his papers to himself and sighed. "What are you planning on doing after you phase out and move on, Brett?" he asked.

"I'm not walking away from anything, Chuck," he said. "Not really. Manijeh works with you, and she and I live right downtown at Coal Harbor. I will adjust and adapt."

"I forgot to mention this to my team: Brett and Manijeh are engaged to be married next year. For compliance reasons, not a *word* of what we've discussed here today can go by her at our office until further notice," Charles reminded everyone present.

"Let's call this a day and go have a few beers," Winston then suggested as he stood and started gathering his paperwork.

The meeting officially over, they all wandered to a local pub, had a few icy cold beers over small talk, and then dispersed. Ten minutes later, his beeper alerted him to the need to call Katja on her mobile, and he found a payphone and dialed.

"What's up?" he asked.

"Just wanted to say that was very cool to finally see it all pulled together in real-time like that," she said. "Thanks for a milestone day in my career."

"Thanks for a job *very* well done!" he said. "Why don't you draft some appropriate bonuses for you and Winston, and I'll sign them tomorrow?"

"That's so kind!"

"You put in a ton of work on this," Brett replied.

"Can we meet at Taf's Café for a minute?" she asked.

"Sure, I'm just around the corner from it."

◈•◈

Katja arrived within five minutes, greeting Brett through the window and then joining him near the front of the café. She ordered a coffee as she sat down across from him.

"What's up?" Brett asked.

"I wanted to follow up on Charles Holdum's question about what you're planning on doing with yourself once you phase out of your CEO role at VAI," she explained.

"I have a number of things that I'm interested in pursuing," he replied. "Is there any particular reason for your interest?" He sipped his coffee and smiled.

"I've worked at a few places in this field now," she replied. "You've been the most interesting to work with, by far. As much as I think Winston is a great choice for the next CEO, I think your and my professional styles mesh more naturally."

After about fifteen seconds of silence, Brett replied, "Are you asking me to *poach* you when I leave?"

"Clearly it wouldn't be *poaching* if you are getting out of trading. It would just be me, a free agent in the free market with exceptional executive administration skills on offer, moving on." She smiled a smile of exaggerated innocence about the topic of their conversation and gave a small theatrical shrug. "Winston is extremely resourceful, or he wouldn't have climbed from EA to CEO in less than a year. You made those decisions, but you made them because of his ability. He'll find someone to help him out when the time comes."

"I have really enjoy working with you, as well, Katja. Very much." He made humming sounds to show that he was deep in thought. "How does 'Executive Administrator' sound to you? Essentially, the same role you have now, pretty much, taking care of all the fiddly-bits of what might be a few small very grass-roots ventures. All handled through the umbrella of the private service corporation that I set up a while back and never really got running due to other distractions. Would that work?"

Her eyes opened more widely than they had been and she said, "That sounds almost exactly like what I was thinking." She took a napkin and wrote a figure on it, and then pushed it to him. "Does this sound like what you were thinking?"

After carefully looking at and considering the figure she had put forward, he reached across the table to shake her hand and said, "It does now. With the usual embellishments once we get that in the form of a real offer. If this deal flies—and every sign is that it should, insert disclaimers here about forward-looking statements—then we've a deal."

Ekaterina Fedorova accepted his hand, and they shook firmly on it. "*U nas sdelka*," she said in Russian. "We have a deal, Brett. I'm looking forward to it."

39

From order to chaos. From rest to exhaustion. From then to now. The blown glass trees and the branches and their leaves shimmered through chaos and exhaustion and lost their beer bottle brown and went green, then clear, like ice before a melt, at that decision point just before the tree became water, he lifted his coffee to his mouth and opened his eyes.

This Sunday morning, he was all alone. It had been many months that he hadn't been, but today the women had awoken first and gone on the Seawall walk without him. He took his *katana*, placed it on his hip, and carried it to his office, where he properly presented it and locked the door behind him. There were a few clothes here and about, and he sorted them into small piles, careful not to mix anything, and then put the three piles on the enormous dresser.

After showering, shaving, and clipping his nails, he sat in front of the television and hunted for anything mildly bearable but found nothing. He discovered a novel he had been meaning to finish reading and set to turning through the pages slowly enough to follow the almost deliciously indiscernible plot. A while in, he decided to restart from the beginning, as it had been a long time since last he'd last picked it up.

When they returned, he gave each an extra affectionate kiss on the cheek and asked if they would like a class of orange juice, which they both accepted. With them all seated in the living room, Manijeh was first to speak.

"Have you found a place you can relocate?" Brett asked.

"No, unfortunately" Taraneh replied. "It's turning out that the concert grand's an issue. All the movers I've called say they can't transport it on elevators of older buildings, and landlords living in basement suites don't want 'noise' as students practice. But I won't be downgrading to a baby grand if I can avoid it."

"*This* place is *soundproof* by design," Brett said. "Well, at least the penthouse level is."
Taraneh's face ignited at this. "What do you mean? Are you suggesting…?"
Manijeh put her hand on Taraneh's forearm. "Clearly *this* place is too small for the lot of us," she said. "But listen to Brett for a moment."
"You see, I own the northeastern penthouse suite as well, as a revenue-generating investment property," Brett said. "There's a huge service elevator that can handle concert grands. And these units are designed to be soundproof."
Taraneh covered her face as tears formed in her eyes.
Brett handed her a napkin and then pushed a sheet of paper across the table. "We put this together. It covers the base fixed costs, such as strata fees and property taxes and such. All said, Manijeh and I figure it is probably about what you are paying for the house you are at now. I have to charge you a *tiny* bit of margin for taxes, but that was kept to a minimum."
Taraneh looked at the paper. "It's slightly *less* than the rent on the house was. I assume the heating bill will be less, also."
"Well, there's that," Manijeh said.
"Shall we celebrate?" Taraneh said.
"What do you have in mind?" Manijeh asked.
"I can tell you," Taraneh said, "that I have been so damned wound up about this whole move that I quite literally just want to get *roaring* drunk and work it out in a tangled pile on the floor."
"I'm all in for calling in hungover tomorrow," Manijeh said with a tone of high enthusiasm.
"Count me in, as well," Brett agreed.

⇜•⇝

Two-fifteen in the morning shone red on the clock across the bedroom. Brett slid so as to not awaken anyone, and quietly went into the bathroom and emptied his bladder. He put the robe that had been hanging on the bathroom door over his shoulders and slid his arms through the sleeves and walked out into the hallway as quietly as he could manage. At the kitchen sink he let the water run until it was as cold as it could get, so he could have cold water without triggering the noisy ice maker on the refrigerator, as the pitcher in the fridge had been left empty on the counter. He then turned off the tap and went to the couch, where he sat and slowly sipped the cool water.

The lights from across Vancouver Harbor filled his mind, proving points in space that flickered without need for his brain. Images that provided the lattice strands of his mind with purchase, without his having to concentrate on their form. From chaos, order. From exhaustion to rest. Always from then to now. That never changed, even when the other rivers changed their wind in time.

As he sat there, staring into ecstasy, he felt the soft, familiar hand at his neck, sliding behind his robe, over his heart, placed there as if an ear to listen, and he let his eyelids drop as she leaned in and kissed his neck behind his ear.

"Thank you," she said, very quietly.

He reached up and her right hand met his. Their fingers clasped together, and they made love on the sofa, and when they were done, returned to bed, careful to avoid waking her.

◈ • ◈

"Breakfast time!" Manijeh called out in her most cheerful morning voice.

His eyes wouldn't open. Eventually, they let in some light. The sound of the ensuite sink running, and teeth being brushed overwhelmed him. He slowly rolled out of bed. Manijeh was at the bedroom door, smiling. "You should brush your teeth, too," she suggested. "Don't want hangover mouth."

"You certainly don't!" Taraneh agreed as she walked across the room to join Manijeh. "Or there will be no good morning kisses for you."

Taking their suggestion, Brett went to the sink and washed up as fully as made sense to do, and then walked to the kitchen.

"I already called in sick for you to Katja," Manijeh said to Brett as she handed him a plate of scrambled eggs. "Charles really wanted me to come in sick today for some reason, but I insisted that what I have may be *contagious*."

Taraneh sat the at the kitchen counter and said, "Yes, it *is* contagious. You mostly catch it from sharing a bottle of… what exactly did we end up drinking by close of bar?"

"Ouzo," he replied. "Off midriffs if I recall. My memory is all a blur on the matter, however."

"*Ân râ az yâdet na raft*,"[44] Taraneh said.

---

[44] "You haven't forgotten *that*."

Touched by Fortune's Shadow: a triptych

By noon, Taraneh returned to her home in Kitsilano and Brett and Manijeh were left alone to clean up the disorder the three had caused. As he put away the dishes that had already been washed in the machine before he loaded it again with more dirty dishes, Brett popped up his head and asked, "So what led you two to head out yesterday morning instead of spending our Sunday meditation session together?"

"Were you lonely?"

"You know it," he replied. "Of course, I don't mind at all that you did head out without me, I'm just curious, is all."

"She wanted to talk," Manijeh said, fluffing the sofa pillows. "Let's put together some tea."

She started for the essentials needed to make a decent round of cups, and soon enough they were out on the balcony beside the heat lamp, sipping tea.

"You are the *Huma*," she said.

Brett started to laugh. "Oh, *that* again!"

"My love, you do not know it, which makes it *so* much more beautiful to behold. But with all that also comes a great burden."

These words he had not expected to hear.

"People crush on you. They fall right into love with you. They want, they want, they want." She smiled over the edge of her China cup and then took a tiny sip, her slate-gray eyes shining with insight and the occult. "This is your fate as the *Huma*."

"You and I have been sharing our lives since April now," Brett replied, "and I've *never* been happier, though I have been *far* more organized and on a predictable path than of late. But that's where my happiness comes from: being messy but hand-in-hand. That's me, just a cluttered tinkering type who tells the time correctly twice daily. Nothing at all like that *Huma* bird that you're always going on about."

"You were always so meticulous and organized," Manijeh agreed. "But hell, I knew better that day you took out Willard in the ravine. I saw that spark in you then: that need to protect. That adventurous core willingness to risk it all, but to be careful doing it. I saw it all," she said.

"You were a wee bit young to have seen all that in *one* day, can't we agree?" he asked.

"Details filled themselves in over the many years, yes," she conceded, "but the essence of that was all there, that day, at the end of a pointy stick."

"You fell in love with Erol Flynn?"

"Robin Hood," Manijeh replied. "The Three Musketeers! Oh, D'Artagnan! Vanquish that rapscallion, thou beamish boy! Begone or taste thy death at this pointy stick, thou scoundrel!"

"We had some great times, eh?"

"Taraneh told me she *totally* sparked on you that day at my parents'. With Rostam *right* there, too! It didn't matter. You two talked, you played Bach's 'Prelude.' I told you that night on the way home, *right*? You *are* the *Huma*. There's *no* mistaking the gaze of the smitten."

Having nothing more whatever to say on the subject in that moment, Brett remained silent, until Manijeh finally continued to speak. "So yesterday, she wanted to talk out of earshot, and I suggested the Seawall. And she explained that she has fallen in *proper* love with you, and she wanted my blessing on whether or not she come to you with that."

Hearing this, Brett let his mind fall empty of thoughts and took a sip, so that he could fall into the sweet, scalding tea at his lip and be free of distraction and self-misdirection.

"And what did you say?" he asked.

"There's no course for any degree I've ever earned or even *considered* earning that covers *this* stuff in the slightest bit. So I went with the simple truth, and I told her I am overjoyed, which I am—she's such a wonderful, talented, authentic human being and a blessing to be around—and that she should feel utterly welcome now and in future to bring such matters directly to *you*, since I probably won't play well as her de Bergerac."

She smiled and put down her cup. "Which is a fancy way of saying I passed the proverbial buck to you."

"If *you* are de Bergerac, does that make her Roxane or the Christian? Anyway, let's say for the sake of argument say that I *am* this *Huma*," he conceded. "So I ask you, what should I do so that this situation doesn't turn and around and bite anyone, myself included, in the ass?"

Manijeh was quiet for a while, and then replied, "Do I look like some kind of philosopher to you? That's a *tough* question. That being said: 'good thoughts; good words; good deeds' will probably *never* steer you wrong. I've been reminding you to stay gold, Ponyboy, for some number of years now, if I'm not mistaken."

"Maintaining the Ponyboy Curtis' state of Goldenness has, indeed, been a leitmotif in our life," Brett replied. "Which is subtly ironic, given the common theme of switchblades."

Touched by Fortune's Shadow: a triptych

"You're aware that I had no idea about your tragic encounter and the loss of your friend when I started quoting *Outsiders*, right?" she replied.

"Absolutely aware. And it's all good, in any case. I spent my whole life coming to terms with blades, after all," he replied.

"Anyway, as for this turning sideways to bite you, my job as your advisor on these matters ends with the Grade 8 English curriculum. They don't push this kind of thing—whatever it's called—at UBC *or* Harvard. Not even as a progressive elective. The subject matter is hidden behind the walls we put around our hearts and the locks we put on our tongues when in mixed company. We're never given an opportunity in life to prepare for how to address any of it should it arise in one's life."

"So what you're saying is," Brett began, "is that…"

"… you should figure it out for *yourself*. That's what I'm saying." She grinned at him mischievously. "I only suggest that you do *not* make her sit in her feelings about you too long now that she's vulnerably made her feelings *roshan mesl-e ruz*."[45]

"I'm all for shacking up until Wednesday morning," Brett offered. "Though I *will* still have to lead *Soke* Hashimoto's group tomorrow night at the *dojo*."

"I'm all in!" Manijeh agreed. "And I'll even come watch you teach tomorrow night! And as for Taraneh, well, just remember: Be brave. Be kind. There, I gave you an aphorism that does not in any way involve switchblades."

---

[45] *roshan mesl-e ruz* (lit. "bright like day"), "as clear as day."

Port Coquitlam, mid-April 1993

Touched by Fortune's Shadow: a triptych

40

After finding a place to watch the river flow by at Coquitlam River Park, Rostam and Brett started tossing stones and listened to them ricochet. A few minutes in, Rostam spoke.

"I want to talk about what you're planning on doing, Brett," Rostam said.

"Planning on doing *when*?" Brett asked. "With *what*?"

"With that correspondence diploma you got at the end of last year," he explained.

"I plan on finding a job as a programmer so I can get out of this life of mucking toilets I seem to have fallen into." His voice betrayed his exhaustion, though he suspected Rostam may have interpreted this as indignation. "What about you?"

"I tried for a whole year *solid*, man, but I just can't do the whole 'engineer' thing," Rostam said, almost groaning under the weight of his confession as he put air quotes around the word *engineer*. "I *cannot*, for the life of me, shake the feeling that Dad's *so* disappointed about it, but I also can't let it turn me into a salt pillar, and I think he understands that."

"Your father is very much all about you and your sister's happiness in life, man," Brett observed. "It's perfectly fine to get a degree in engineering and use what you learned there for something completely different." He tossed a stone across, hit a large, pointed rock that poked up out of the river, and the stone clacked, skipping into the bushes on the far bank.

"Hey, have you been following any of what Manijeh's been up to in the Faculty of Commerce?" Rostam asked. "I mean, have you gotten a taste of formal economics theory?"

Brett tried to remember the last time he and Manijeh had gotten together. It had been at least six months since last they had coffee while he happened to be down in her part of town.

"I've read a few of her textbooks, but I can't say it made me as good at math as the stuff you gave me from *your* courses."

"Mmm-hmm," Rostam hummed. "If I get them to you... her books... do you think you might give them a look?"

Before answering, Brett stood and brushed off his jeans. Rostam stood up as well and they started to slowly walk along the river path. "I'd love to read anything you throw at me, to be honest," he said.

"I have a huge *pile* of books to throw your way, man," Rostam warned his friend. "Be careful what you wish for!"

"That's fine by me," Brett conceded. "I need to have as much exposure to coding applications as I can get if I'm going to get into the industry with only a two-year programming diploma behind me to show."

"Yes, that's also what I'm thinking. If you could make a model and compile it into executable code so it remains a secret, for instance, can you see what I'm getting at?"

"You mean applied mathematical modeling implemented to allow competitive exclusivity?" Brett asked.

"Have you been thinking about this stuff as well?" Rostam asked. He bent over, picked up a small twig, and tossed it into the water. "Sounds like it."

"A bit. My dad's a handicapper, so I spent a lot of time at his side at the paddock watching horses getting ready for the race at Exhibition Park. What you're talking about has been coming out of his mouth for *ages*, in some form or another. 'You got to have a system,' he says. Once you have the system, you have to gain trust in it over time, or adjust it if you must until you can trust it. And if you can *automate* that system, you remove the emotional driver behind speculative failure. I never heard an end to his stories about the losses that came from emotions pulling one away from one's own tested system."

"Damn. So I'm thinking we will figure this all out together. I'm going to raise funds to get us going, and all of that. I've got a good buddy who went to UBC with Manijeh in a few of her Commerce classes who now works for a firm called Klein— and so on, I forget all the names—and he thinks if we can get this up and running, we might be able to get some traction by early next year. He'll get us a pitch meeting when we're ready to pitch, anyway, which is the most we can ask for in a situation like this. That would be a huge opportunity for us both."

"So what do you want from me?" Brett asked.

"You just give me some of that wattage you carry around on your shoulders when the time inevitably comes to pay the piper," Rostam explained. "So, let me know… we in?"

Brett's hand was slapped against Rostam's in half a second, as he said, "We in."

"Great! I'll ask Manijeh to get you those books of hers now that she's out of the dorms," he said.

"Is she moving back home now that she's got the degree?"

"She's doing her thing, as always with Manijeh," Rostam said. "Not sure what it is."

"I'll read them. Just get Manijeh to call me to set up a time to drop them off."

"I sure will, man. And now for that *other* important matter. Happy Birthday!" He reached into his jacket inner pocket and pulled out an envelope. "I know it was on Thursday, but let's ignore the fact that I'm late."

"Thanks, Rostam!" he said. He gave his friend a hug and took the envelope. Inside was a card, delicately illustrated by Rostam's mother, Mahnaz, in her unique and beautiful style, and signed by all the family. A crisp one-hundred-dollar bill, a lottery ticket, and a pair of tickets to the Vancouver Symphony Orchestra were included in the envelope. "Let everyone know how much I really appreciate this. Your mother did a wonderful job on this card; it's an artwork worthy of putting on the wall."

"Who you going to take?" Rostam asked. "To the VSO, I mean. I'm pretty sure you'll love the pianist. She's well-known for her Liszt and Rachmaninoff. This night will be the Liszt."

"The *pianist*? Liszt? Then I'm taking Mom, of course," he replied. "I'm sure we'll both absolutely *love* it."

⁂

The pile of economics, finance, and assorted texts before him was daunting, but Brett had promised he would read them through, and he intended to keep that promise. "I can't thank you enough," he said to Manijeh.

"No problem at all," she said. "Nice place you got here," she then commented.

"It's not bad. Just wish it wasn't all the way out here, but that's where the work took me."

"Port Coquitlam is nice," she said.

"It's absolutely beautiful out here. I love it. I just prefer being closer to the pulse of the city."

Touched by Fortune's Shadow: a triptych

Brett wanted to tell her the full truth; that he preferred to be nearer to her so they could meet up more often than his current location allowed, but these were not confessions he felt ready to make. It took enough from him to gather the courage to call her to arrange to have her drop off her textbooks.

"I get it," she finally agreed. "If you have any questions at *all* about *any* of those books, Brett, please ask me to explain it and we'll set up a time. It would give us time to catch up, too. Feel free. It's no hassle for me at all. Also feel free to ring me up any time at all if even if you just want to get together to have a coffee or even watch a movie. No need to be a stranger!"

"Thank you," he said. "It's very much appreciated."

Her coffee done, Manijeh left him with the pile of texts and an ache in his pounding chest. She had at least opened a line of communication between them, and in the next while, he was definitely going to need her help to navigate through this pile so he and Rostam might find their own special project.

❧ • ☙

"So, am I right that the BSM Greeks are for European-style option pricing?" he asked, pointing to a page in the text he had littered with Post-It notes.

"Yes," she replied. "Because of the difference in the impact of expiration dates with American options."

"Have you read much of Heston? I've read that he accounts for volatility."

"Can't say I have," Manijeh replied.

"I wish I had better access," Brett moaned. "I noticed a paper of his that *just* came out in *The Review of Financial Studies*, but I can't get to it to read it."

"I can still get you papers as an alumnus if you can't find them. Just shoot me an email and I'll see what I can do."

"That would be awesome. Thanks!"

She handed him the marked-up pages she had been writing on and said, "I circled your mistakes."

"There are no mistakes," Brett replied. "There are *proposed solutions*. Some less stochastic than others."

Quinn Tyler Jackson

Vancouver, December 1998

Touched by Fortune's Shadow: a triptych

41

About half-an-hour into his Wednesday lesson, Brett wiped the keys of Taraneh's piano clean, closed the cover, wiped it as well, and then turned around on the bench. "Let's go for a long walk," he suggested.

"Certainly!" Taraneh agreed.

Soon, they were walking briskly beside one another on the quiet backstreets of the Kitsilano neighborhood where she lived. They had already discussed the finer logistic details of her renting the penthouse and agreed that she would move in on the sixteenth of January, using professional movers he had already vetted about being able to move her piano by the service elevator. This walk was to discuss other matters.

"Brett, did Manijeh talk to you at all about what she and I discussed on our Seawall walk?" she finally broached the subject he knew had been on her mind their entire afternoon together.

"She did," he answered. "But only *very* briefly. She deferred the matter to you, since it is about how *you* feel."

"Manijeh really is *so* kind," Taraneh said. "I have become fond of you *both*. It's all been quite unreal for me at times."

When they reached the corner curb, they turned right and continued down that sidewalk, very slowly. A lady with tight, gray curls, walked her Yorkshire Terrier on its leash, and they both took time to greet the lady and her dog, petting the dog, offering it one of the treats the lady had on her for guest treats, and then they moved on to continue their discussion as they walked together through the neighborhood.

"I've fallen *deeply* in love with you," Taraneh finally said aloud. "Soundly. I've *no* doubt of it from my side, so I'm not going to wrap it in ribbons and bows for you."

"I'm flattered," Brett said. "If it wasn't so chilly out, you'd realize my cheeks and ears are red from shy embarrassment, not from the cold."

He smiled and reached over to hold her hand. It was cold from the day's weather, but warm from the life and joy that burned just beneath the surface of what simple weather could alter.

"You *should* be flattered. I know my value. To be honest, I don't know how *any* of this works," she added. "Well, I know how *some* of it works, that's a moot point by now, with all we've shared this last while, but I'm not sure about the human heart."

After spotting a bench in Delamont Park, he pointed to it, and they went to sit down. "Who is?" he asked. "Sure about the human heart, I mean," he explained.

His pager buzzed, he checked the number, and saw that it was from the office. Although Wednesday afternoons were sacrosanct due to his lessons with Taraneh, with the business at hand with Klein *et al.*, he had asked to be paged if anything with that came up and nobody knew how to deal with it. He made a note to pass a payphone they had earlier walked by during their walk when they were on the way back.

"Is that important?" Taraneh asked. "We can…"

"It's not as important as this," Brett replied, pointing first at her heart, and then at his.

"I wasn't expecting *any* of this in my life," she said with a sigh after a long silence.

"Any of what?"

"I always had this vague notion that one day I would meet my soulmate. My *bashert*,[46] my *one*."

"We saw where chasing the *one* led our dear Rostam," Brett replied. "It had him building staircases like Farhad for Shirin and look where that got him."

"Ah, you've finally read of Khosro and Shirin," she noted. "Yes," she returned in an almost sad voice. "We saw that. I was very much like Rostam in that respect; I just didn't find that the-*one*-ness in *him* the way he says he found it in me. It was simply a waiting game for me. This, I felt, was the reason I didn't feel jealousy in any of my relationships; I simply wasn't *invested* enough in them."

---

[46] *Bashert* (lit. "destined" or "fated"), a Yiddish term used in this context to mean one's predestined soulmate.

"In the sense that you didn't care if they up and left, if that was what they wanted, you mean?"

Taraneh smiled brightly as she spoke. "I knew I was worthy of love, and also knew that if someone did not want to be with me, they had the option to move on, it was not for me to keep them like a gemstone in a horde. I know my value."

Brett held her hand more tightly. "You're *magnificent*," he assured her.

She smiled even more brightly. "Thank you. I deeply *wanted* to feel invested enough to become jealous, hoping that would tell me everything I needed to know. This did not turn out to be a good long-term strategy, it seems. And so, I was secretly hoping that the Magic Key would turn and that would rush into me and set the matter right."

"Please don't get me wrong, I'm actually not cynical about Rostam's romantic aspirations as pertains to his idea of finding the *one*," Brett insisted. "He may still yet find his *actual* one. His construct, his life, his path." He then moved around. "But that is him, not *you*."

"I worry how he would react if he found out about *any* of this," she said. "But—and I'm not going to feel like a villain for what's in my heart, so I'm going to come out and say it—I care far less about how *he* feels about this than I care about how *you* feel. I know how I feel, and I think Manijeh made it clear to me that she's *more* than happy to have me in both your lives as this unrolls."

"I'm just stretching my back; no need to get up," he said as he stood, moved his stiff shoulders about, and then sat down again. "I've known Rostam since I was all of twelve-years-old. Manijeh just as long…." He crossed his fingers and held up his hand. "We're tight. Always have been. The Three Musketeers."

"Three…."

"Actually, there were *four*. D'Artagnan, Athos, Porthos, and Aramis. So that leaves wiggle room." He winked. "And since we're on it, let's not forget the 1974 sequel, *The Four Musketeers*. It's good enough to be canon."

"Ah, I see," she said, winking back.

"What I'm saying is that Rostam knows the very crux of me," he said. "He knows my views on love, open relationships, my distaste for notions of ownership, and such. He's been along that journey with me, as I went through the changes of becoming a young man, and he as well."

Touched by Fortune's Shadow: a triptych

"Let's walk about some more," Taraneh suggested. "I need to move around to get rid of the electricity in my system."

Brett stood, offered his hand, and they walked hand-in-hand toward Arbutus Street. A few minutes later, he continued to speak. "So, as I was saying, Rostam and I grew up through a lot, side-by-side, shoulder-to-shoulder. I was his wingman, he mine, through our failed dates in the early days. He and I had conversations about many things, not the least of which of course crossed into *this* territory we find ourselves in now. What happens if either of us stops dating someone?

"He'd broken up with women I wanted to date. And *vice versa*. Though not often, it did happen. It might have been quite difficult to remain so close if we hadn't figured out such things. So we have always had an understanding."

"What understanding is that?" she asked.

"It is for the *woman* to decided. Not *us*."

"The woman? You mean if one of you broke up, it was for the *woman* to decide if she wished to date the other? Sorry for being slow. I'm trying to understand," Taraneh explained.

"Indeed. Who are *we* blokes to decide who a woman wants to spend her time with or be intimate with? Out of respect, we would not act on anything while we were actively *in* a relationship, but afterwards, it was up to the woman, not us two fools honoring some anachronistic notion founded in oppressive patriarchal ownership politics."

"So you're saying he wouldn't mind what we've been to one another since he and I broke it off?" she asked.

"I'm saying that it's not for *him* to decide or mind. We live in the real world, so others who knew you and he were an item, like his parents and yours, well, that's another story for another day. The world still seems to enjoy walking uphill both ways when it comes to matters of other people's hearts. One ought to be discrete in such situations.

"But otherwise, it's between the parties actually involved. And that, now," he emphasized, "is you and me. Not Rostam. We should be considerate, but we don't demonstrate consideration by honoring oppressive property contracts on human beings."

"I see that you have given these issues deep consideration," Taraneh commented. "Very much of what you have said about autonomy resonates with my own views, even though in some cases, your wording and mine may differ slightly but actually seem the same perspective at core."

"My perspective on this may be slightly more mathematical and algorithmic behind the fancy wallpaper," he suggested. "I am willing to compromise and adjust many things. But to show *mauvaise foi* to one's *own* beating heart is akin to self-annihilation for no common good."

"Ah! Here we are!" They were coming toward a payphone. "Just a moment," he said as he went to it, found some change in his pocket, and dialed the office.

"You paged? What's up?" he asked Katja.

"Charles Holdum wants to do lunch with you tomorrow at the Hotel Vancouver."

"Alone?"

"Yes. Just the two of you."

"Please confirm. And thanks for the interrupt."

"I figured this was going to be important," Katja replied. "Sorry to bother you, though. One does need time to pursue one's loves in life."

"Thanks. And yes, indeed, one needs time to pursue one's loves," he replied as he hung up the receiver.

"I'm sorry about that, Taraneh," he said. They would soon be approaching her house near Arbutus and Third. "Business."

"No problem at all!" she replied, holding out her hand for him to take in his again.

"There's been some very complex business lately," he said. "Where were we, then?" he asked.

Taraneh smiled and teased, "You were about to tell me that you love me, too, and we were about to trip the light fantastic and…."

Rostam smiled back. "Oh, goodness, was I, then?"

"Well, Brett, in *my* dreamy, fluttering heart, you were," she replied. "You've said a lot of things and you've also asked a lot of your own questions, but what's in your *heart*, Brett? How do you *feel* about all of this? About me? I have no desire to pressure you, but some questions can't be answered by guessing."

Her black eyes were aflame with the "*Appassionata*" at full fury, her lips perfectly asking to be kissed, and he leaned in fully and let his lips linger on hers, feeling their pulse beating together as they did. His heart wanted to hide on the right side of his body so desperately that it pounded unreservedly, but Brett Lloyd-Ronan found himself at a loss for words despite the torrent inside. By the middle of January, Taraneh Khoshrangi would be living down the hallway from him and Manijeh.

Touched by Fortune's Shadow: a triptych

By putting what he was feeling into words for her, he feared that he would be pouring molten metal into a mold, its fate to be decided by how fast it cooled into its final shape, and he knew that hearts and souls and minds did not work like high-grade carbon steel alloy, making swords and batons and gears. Finally, after some time, their kiss ended.

"To tell you about what my heart feels," he said as they then continued their walk up her stairs to her front door, "I would first tell you about what happened when I was seven." They entered her house, took of their coats, and went to her kitchen.

"Tea?" she asked.

"I'm good with just some juice or something for now, thank you," he replied. The sound of pounding surf in his eardrums he knew to be the blood in every vein and artery screaming to escape and be free of its carnal chains. A simple compliment could make him blush, but a blade passing before his face no longer drew such a reaction from him. He knew now, having gone through with Manijeh this delicious gymkhana of fondness and fright that he was beyond deep affection alone. Knowing what passionate *love* felt like and finally able to sit still in its water, he did not doubt his constricting chest and his trembling abdomen under his shirt.

She went directly to her refrigerator, found some apple juice, and poured two glasses. "So tell me," she said. "*Befarma'id*," she said as she handed him his glass.

"When I was a child, I was with a friend, and to make an ugly long story short, he threw an ice ball at a girl's head, and this triggered events. Her brother and his friends found us in the streets that night and were going to throw ice balls at us but ended up attacking us with switchblades."

Her face crumped into sour disbelief. "*Che nâgahân!*"[47]

"Now, what I don't tell people, but what I'm telling you, is what happened in the final seconds of that encounter. At first, the boys *were* just going to pelt us something awful with ice balls." He anxiously drew tiny circles on the table in front of him with his right index finger.

"The story that most hear is that he was stabbed to death, and I was stabbed in the heart and left for dead," he said. "Clearly I was rescued. He was not so lucky. What they hear is that it escalated, and that I don't remember *why* it did."

---

[47] "*Che nâgahân!*" (lit. "How unexpected!")

Her eyes shot open, her tears formed quickly, and she put both her hands over his so he stopped drawing circles. "That's *awful*!"

"The part I don't tell people, and I only tell very few as much as I've already said, is *why* they pulled those switchblades on us. We were children, and they were teens. There *should* have been no reason for escalation of that kind. No reason whatever."

Taraneh was transfixed.

"The girl's brother called out a standard slur on us. 'Are you two *gay* or something' I think were his exact words. Think about that for a minute. Think about how that sounds."

Taraneh nodded.

"'Well?' her brother called out. 'Are you *gay* or what? Tell us!'" He sipped his apple juice. "So, there I am, seven years old, risking an ice ball pelting at worst, and I called back, 'I am whatever *you* say I am!' You know, I'm thinking, appease these assholes and let's get out of here with some bruises and get it over with. Who cares what they *call* me or *think* about me? I most certainly did not, and just wanted to be out of there as quickly as it could be managed."

She nodded once again, this time adding, "Might makes right. Sticks and stones. They had all the power and you had none. So, yes, I understand."

"Yes, might certainly makes right when you're all of seven-years-old. But Richard, my friend, he let out a stream of hate and garbage and nastiness against this crew like none you've heard in your life, I am pretty sure." Brett lowered his hand. "Being called gay completely triggered something ugly and hateful in him, and all of that came straight out his mouth, directed at this group of teens. *That exact moment* is when the knives came out and flashed in the streetlamps and the rest is history. I almost never tell people about what Richard did or said. You and a *very* few others."

"Why not?"

"Some people might be idiots and think Richard's so-called 'standing up for himself' was justified in some nonsensical universe," Brett explained. "That *surely* I should not have been willing to be so-called 'insulted' by this attack on my… what the hell… *masculinity*? What even is that at the age we're talking about anyway? At any age? Who defines that? Some idiots with knives? Is that what people would think was being so-called 'threatened' by all this? *Masculinity*?"

"Such a *sick* world that it taints the young so," she hissed.

Touched by Fortune's Shadow: a triptych

"Richard certainly seemed to believe that *masculinity* was at threat, whatever that means, and to no good end. I don't want to add to that kind of thinking. So on those rare occasions when I do tell what happened, I make it all about the snowball thrown at this guy's sister, and *not* the ugly nastiness that followed.

"And on top of all that, I don't want him to be remembered for what came out of his mouth when he was a child and the product of his world without enough time to figure that out and walk away from it all in one piece."

"And why have you told *me*?" she asked.

"You've seen my scar? Where my heart is?"

"I've seen it and touched it, yes," she said. "I didn't know the story until now, and tried not to speculate, but I was there that evening when you were using real swords at the ceremony, and I just assumed it was an old accident while doing something like what you did that night with swords."

"You asked me about how I feel about you. Where my passion comes from." He lifted his shirt and turned slightly so the scar was clear. "That's my tattoo to remind me that we are literally half-an-inch from *death*. Life might only want to beat us up, and instead of just taking the beating it had in mind for us, we let ourselves *lose control*, and it kills us or stabs us in the heart instead, leaving us for dead without a second thought.

"It only takes one moment for Fate to sort us between the Quick and the Dead. *One* bad decision. One *indecision*. One foul-mouthed tirade from a ten-year-old. *My* passion comes from that half-an-inch of margin I know I'm dancing on. Every day is new. Yesterday is gone. I am here today from yesterday because of that half-an-inch some twenty years ago. Right near my heart. I honor it by *living* it—mindfully, for sure, if possible—by truly *living* it. A tight-rope walk on half-an-inch margin for error."

"You might have been Omar Khayyam in a past life," she said. "Yes. I see your point about being cautious. So many things about you hide behind that intrinsic caution of yours."

"There's also a bright side of the coin used in this flip," he said as he put his shirt back in order. "On the shiny side, when a wonderful person like you enters your life and tells you that she loves you and you are given such trust by another person to cross the very threshold of the door to *their* heart, you remember just how precious the human heart is, and what a *gift* is being offered to you."

"I have offered you my love, Brett," Taraneh said. Her eyes were clear as she spoke, and she looked serene.

"And such words must *never* be taken for granted, or pushed away, or hastily considered, because they come from a heart that is just as fragile and exposed. That is a vulnerable moment of human stewardship, and we form connections by boldly stepping *toward* such expressions rather than away from them."

Taraneh started to smile, and sipped her apple juice until the glass was empty.

"Life's too short and too fragile to push love away when it declares itself, is what I'm saying." He stood, walked over to her side of the table, and hugged her from behind. "We'll figure out the rest as we seem to have managed so far to now. We three make a formidable team, and that's a pretty optimal place to begin."

Taraneh's hand touched his forearm. "You're complicated."

"Pretty soon, I'll be getting *much* simpler," he said. He kissed the top of her head. "Are we on for gin or *Pasur* this Saturday?" he asked. "I haven't been keeping track."

"Of course! Tell Manijeh that I'm planning on showing you a new recipe for dinner."

"Which?"

"For me to know, and you two to find out!" she said. "Just make sure you have good red wine to go with it." She smiled and then added, "And just what is going to happen 'pretty soon' to make you much simpler? As if that can even *be* a thing with you."

He thought of lunch at the Hotel Vancouver that he would be having with Charles Holdum the next day, and because he could not say what he knew to answer her question, he instead returned, "For me to know, and you two to find out!"

"Complicated *and* enigmatic!"

Touched by Fortune's Shadow: a triptych

42

They'd ordered their drinks and their lunch, and now Charles Holdum and Brett Lloyd-Ronan were seated across the small table at the Hotel Vancouver restaurant, with Brett more than ready to hear what Holdum had called upon him over lunch to say. He unfolded his napkin in anticipation of placing it on his lap when the food arrived.

"We've been over *everything* you gave us," Holdum finally spoke. "Before I go on, I have a question for you."

"As far as the regulatory guidelines on such discussions and Margaret Kaur will allow, I shall answer," Brett returned. "I may use a few euphemisms along the way."

"Always good policy," Charles replied with a nod. "I'll also mind my tongue. Thanks for the reminder. So, my biggest question is, why *now*?"

"Do you have any hobbies you've done your whole life?" Brett asked Charles.

"Do you mean like building model trains in the basement?" Charles replied. "That and my obsessively collecting antiquarian books on esoteric and occult subjects; I have a large home library full of these."

"My life, since the age of seven, has martial arts," Brett said. "I hold a black belt in judo, I'm a competition level fencer and I've a *Menkyo Kaiden* in *kenjutsu*. I am teaching a class of that tonight, actually."

"*Menkyo*…? I'm afraid to say that my only Japanese comes from some business I did there back in the early eighties."

"Just think black belt," Brett explained. "But with *samurai* swords." The food arrived and was placed on the table, at which time Brett put his napkin on his lap. "Anyway, in your and my world, we see how things fall into place by accident, more or less.

"And we learn that sometimes things fall into place so well that one must seize the day, right then, in that exact moment. Now is one of those moments. The iron is hot, and I am striking. Just as with swords, one does not wait until *after* being cut in two to decide whether or not to move out of the way or defend oneself with one's blade. One *acts*."

Charles put down his salad fork and said, "There certainly does seem to be some serendipity in what we're doing at our firm and what you've been doing over at VAI with Proteus. Especially given what Manijeh will be doing once the year rolls over, with the European Union adopting the euro, and so on. I think I read all the writing you put on the wall, Brett. Hell, you pretty much spray-painted it in neon green and pink."

Brett leaned back. "Exactly. All of that *happened*, and all of the serendipity is why *now*. And you have the contractual right to first refusal, so I was in a position to put out an offer to you without it being seen as unduly preferential, as that clause has been there since Adam."

"Thanks for getting that straight in my head. I had concerns that there might have been something behind the scenes going on, what with the change at the helm at VAI since Rostam's fluctuations recently. I had a colleague up there in the Revolving Restaurant on Canada Day, and word on the vine was that Rostam was having one tipple too many, leading to some amount of commotion. Naturally, I was concerned, given how his stepping down as CEO might be taken in light of that bit of local gossip."

"It's not a fire sale, if that's what you're getting at," Brett said. "We're in a solid position now without changing a comma in how we're working with you. That's why I had Katja include those projections both with and without this. If you push it away, you'll be partaking in less of that Proteus goodness and we'll maintain or better our *status quo*."

"I got that message straight away. Those projections really helped and were in keeping with our independent comparatives. So, you'll be teaching martial arts, I take it?" he changed tack.

"Partly," Brett replied.

"That's really nice! Good for you! Do you plan on making yourself available for consultation?"

"In what capacity?"

"Whatever you are willing to say," Charles returned. He took a bite and motioned to Brett to continue.

"I'd entertain advisory consulting and will likely be doing the symposium and conference circuit at a more economic theoretical, less practitioner level, because I enjoy presenting, but I'm not terribly interested in chasing any more dragons to slay in finance in terms of new innovation specifically tied to the markets." He bit into a crouton, finished it, and sipped some of his chardonnay. "I've got most of my commercial Holy Grails in the display case at home for the time being. I like to keep my mind busy: offer me things that fit *that*, and I'm good to go and send you a bill at month end."

"I was surprised to find that you *personally* own twenty-five percent of the three VAI patents," he then said. "That's just plain *atypical*. As rare as hen's teeth, that kind of thing."

"Give me a lever and a place to stand, and I shall move the world," Brett replied. "That patent assignee percentage is my lever *and* my place to stand."

"I'd have loved to have been a fly on the wall during the meetings where *that* was negotiated," Charles said with a big grin.

"Actually, Chuck," Brett said, "it was like this: My father is a master machinist, and he holds five patents over the years, so I grew up around the idea of personal ownership of one's own inventions. Rostam and I were filing our first patent and I said, 'I want to be twenty-five percent assignee of this patent, and any in future where I am listed as sole inventor,' and do you know what he said to me, Chuck?"

Charles shrugged as he placed the salmon from his fork into his mouth.

"You have seen the results of that conversation, so of course you know what he said," Brett replied. "He just said 'yes.' There was no *drama*. Friends for life with that guy. I'm marrying his sister next year, after all."

Charles Holdum then sat straight, wiped his mouth with his napkin, positioned his cutlery on his plate, and pushed the plate forward. "I have always felt very good doing business with you kids," he said. "You'll pardon me for calling you that, but my face betrays my age. Manijeh has that same quality you two always struck me as having. An insatiable ferocity for living."

After cleaning up his own place and making sure his face was wiped, Brett replied, "It's been a good run."

"Our relationship with VAI has netted us a tidy sum over the years," Holdum agreed.

"It certainly hasn't landed anyone in the Poor House."

"I apologize for my questions. I've been around this block before with a few others over the years. All good people with good intentions, I'm certain, but we still ended up with a few orphans after acquisition. Orphans that came with enough sad backstory, provisos, and had the smoke of fire sale still wafting from them, I'm afraid. And thus the unfortunate tooth drilling."

"We all must do our full and due diligence," Brett said with as understanding a tone as he could muster. "Early on at VAI we got taken for a trip on a few deals. *Small* deals, thankfully."

"So listen... and this subject to regulatory approval, of course, which will be noted in the header, I am going to ask Conrad Dunlevy, my assistant, to have in your hands by the close of business tomorrow—*latest*—a signed Memo of Understanding, accepting your offer as-is.

"I have talked to those concerned and accept your proposal that you personally retain your ownership percentage on each of the patents and the residuals to you that this will entail, in lieu of the option you presented to buy your personal interest in the same outright. I'm going to add, Brett, that this isn't because we *cannot* buy you out of your patent interests, but since you're stepping out of our world after having made us all some good coin since you started working with us all, I think some passive income wouldn't hurt your future as you start your marital journey with Manijeh.

"Less up front, but over the remaining life of those patents I think you'll net considerably more than you would otherwise. Life is not a zero-sum game. My wedding gift to you both is to pick the best of the two options you have given me to pick as I see it. You with this all so far?"

Brett nodded.

"I'm sorry to mess up a perfectly good business lunch with actual business talk. Now, the moment I sign this thing, I've been advised that Manijeh can be told, as there would be no negotiation that could be influenced, given this is an as-is acceptance. I needed to talk to you one-to-one, face-to-face and figure out what was going on in that mysterious head of yours, and I'm satisfied that we've no need to play at negotiating, as your mind has likely already gone down the list of counterarguments ten thousand times over before even presenting this to us, and thus such dancing is a monumental waste of time.

"Or, as you put it, I'm just saying 'yes' to your ask. Second time in my life I just said yes. First time is when my wife Linda proposed to me."

"*You* tell Manijeh," Brett said.

"You don't want to give her the good news?"

"She works for you, and this is about your work and how this will help you penetrate the EU market if played right. That's pretty soon not going to even be *my* world anymore. Just let her know that I wanted her to know one thing from me, and that's that I already talked about it with Rostam; he was *completely* behind it. She might wonder on that."

"As you wish," he said as he stood, offering his hand.

Brett reached across and shook Holdum's hand hard.

"You ever do demonstrations with that sword stuff you do?" Charles asked.

"Could be arranged. I know the boss."

"I think I'd like to come by with Linda and watch that. I used to box, back when I could carry heavy rocks around on my back. Fascinating way to stay fit, swords."

"Carry rocks… When did you do that?" Brett asked.

"When I was a kid," he replied. "We did that for *fun*."

"Uphill, both ways?" Brett teased.

"Are you kidding? When we got to the top, it fell off our back and rolled down the hill, proper Sisyphus-style. Uphill both ways we left for getting to and from school. On those day the snow wasn't nine feet deep if it was an inch and we *could* get to school."

When they reached the outside sidewalk in front of the hotel, Holdum took Brett aside. "Brett, there's something else I want to let you know."

"Yes?"

"Let's walk and keep our voices down," he said. "I noticed a few people in there I didn't want to hear what I have to say next, even in code. *Audere, scire, tacere.* To dare, to know, be *silent.*"

Brett immediately went on alert and looked over each shoulder to see who was about. "Shoot."

"*Toronto,*" Charles said simply.

"Pardon?"

"I'm not going to play lawn darts with you, Brett," he said. "You can neither confirm nor deny. I get it. But we did *our* due diligence. Straight out of Harvard, up to Toronto. Quite a career trajectory. Just one thing didn't fit: *Toronto.*"

"A former trader from our firm and I keep in regular touch. Small talk. Industry chatter. She now works at that same place," he said solemnly.

Touched by Fortune's Shadow: a triptych

Brett understood the direction the conversation was going but held his tongue firmly still and just listened.

"Let's say that her former boss no longer does," he said.

"No longer works at the same place?" Brett asked.

"If what you mean by 'same *place*' is 'same *industry*,' then, that's what I mean. His welcome wore out."

Brett nodded. "I appreciate the heads up."

Charles put his arm around Brett in an almost fatherly way and said, "I told you that I really like you kids."

"I would love to see your trains, and every last one of your books," Brett changed the subject.

"Anytime you want!" Charles returned as each went their own way at the next intersection. "Just say the word."

43

In the sharp bite of mid-December, the harbor below stirred beneath a fading shroud of frosty haze, its surface reflecting the dawning eight-forty-five sky. Atop a modern tower, nestled like a fortress on the northwest edge, Brett Lloyd-Ronan and Manijeh Yazdpour's penthouse dominated the dual views of the North Shore's mosaic of winter greenery and Stanley Park's managed wildness. This refuge offered not only elevation but clear insight, blending the urban rhythm with the living tranquility of nature, positioning the dwelling at the ideal balance point.

As he sat there in his slowly fading meditation, he put aside yesterday's concerns and brought his current instant into the center of his focus. He could feel one warm hand in his left and another in his right. When he felt those hands stir, he slowly opened his eyes and saw their faces, Taraneh to his left and Manijeh to his right, and the three smiled as they arose from their personal centers of bliss.

"I've always loved roasted chestnuts," Taraneh said. "Let's walk down to Robson Street today instead of going around the Park and see if we might find a vendor. I've seen a few down there lately. What do you two say?"

"It's that time of year," Manijeh said.

The three of them formed an equilateral triangle as they sat, hand-in-hand.

"A great way to celebrate," Brett said.

Brett could still see the joy on her face as he'd opened the apartment door on returning home from work on Friday. She rushed inside, held him tightly, and did not ask for a word of explanation, as if she had seen the weight he had been carrying for so many years, for so many other people, suddenly lifted from him. It had been all he could do to let Charles be the first to tell her.

Touched by Fortune's Shadow: a triptych

Taraneh's turn to find out fully what had happened would likely come a few months later, due to restrictions on what could be said and to whom, but when she arrived on Saturday, ready to cook dinner and play cards, she was easily convinced to go to the Sitar and celebrate in style that Brett had just had a significant business success. She did not seem to mind that he was not allowed to give details yet, since this was not uncommon to her anymore.

They emptied the full dishwasher, prepared breakfast, and watched music videos for a while before it was likely that they'd find roasted chestnuts down near Robson Street. Eventually, near the Museum, they found a vendor, and soon they were all on a bench with their paper bags of scalding hot Vancouver winter delight. As Brett carefully peeled the shell with his teeth, Manijeh said something that caught him off guard and he burned his lip.

"So did you two figure out your overly complicated subtexts yet, or to what city's that train headed anytime soon?" she asked.

Taraneh started to laugh at this. "We talked on Wednesday," she said. "So, I just assumed you already discussed it between the two of you."

"This matter seems to be between the two of *you*," Manijeh explained, pointing at them both. "I'm looking for the Sunday comics tagline, not the whole Elle Loughlan-Kent exposé." She kissed each one on the cheek, as she was sitting between the two. "Believe it or not, we all have boundaries. They're just in different places sometimes, is all.

"Mine are pretty simple. If it happens with me, to me, in front of me, or impacts me, that's one thing. I'm on it. If it doesn't meet these basic guidelines, tell me if you *want* to, and I *may* have something to say about it, because if it means enough to you to share, I'll do whatever I can to support you through it, and I hope you'd do the same for me, any day of the week. But beyond that, I can't micromanage *people* like I can *portfolios*, is what I am saying here. Portfolios are specifically *designed* to be constantly shuffled about and reconsidered. The parties directly involved typically have a better chance at arriving at an understanding than if I get *my* foot stuck in *their* door trying to barge in on *them*."

Brett finally finished the nut he had been eating and was able to say, "I *think* we got most of it on Wednesday. That's coming from *my* side, of course."

"Although, I will admit to still being confused on where you stand in your heart about me, Brett," Taraneh said.

"Confused?" Manijeh asked. "How did you go and *confuse* her, Brett? He *can* be confusing, I agree. Most of the time, it's almost actually quite endearing."

"We've figured out that we can all go to bed together. The bodies being out of the equation, next comes the heart. I wanted to plain and simple hear him say if he loves me," Taraneh said with a sparkling mile.

"Of course," Manijeh agreed. "I mean, who wouldn't? Did he tell you that I call him the *Huma*? I don't think he's fully put his mind around what that *means* that yet."

"The *Huma*? What's that all about?"

"Yes, the *Huma*," Manijeh insisted.

"Nobody mentioned this to me," Taraneh said. "Go on!"

The two spoke in Persian for a few minutes before switching back to English. "Sometimes you tend to dance around what you're being asked when it's about feelings," Manijeh told him after she and Taraneh had discussed matters between themselves. "I've known you long enough to agree with Taraneh on this one. The ask here is: *cut to the chase*."

"I think that what I said was that when love is offered, one doesn't push it away," Brett said.

"Such a *quant*. Seriously. How sweetly your sweet nothings roll off that iconically Canadian tongue you've tuned to the common ear. And it probably took you all of five minutes, plus or minus, to say even *that* little, Mr. Quant." Manijeh was clearly amused at what was nonetheless a serious conversation. "And if I know you the way I *think* I know you, you tacked this fine gem of a declaration onto the very *end*, when you finally did get around to saying it."

"The way we three have… well, this is all *new* to me," Brett confessed. "I try to be careful. I understand that I can come across as… cautiously verbose."

"There's *precision* and there's *passion*," Taraneh said. "Play your piece to the metronome that is your heart and decide which of these you're going to hear most loudly: metronome or heart? Precision and carefulness cloaked in your ultimately ephemeral euphemism, or unmistakable passion in your phrasing, adorned in fire? There's a time to talk and feel your pulse speed up and your hands sweat as you get overwhelmed in the phrasing that *only* that other has made ring through you."

"I find it difficult to find words sometimes for the swirling sea of what goes on inside me at this level" Brett confessed.

"You kissed me this Wednesday with such *starlight* to send me to an ecstatic abandon as never has shaken me before—it was *truly* something, beyond every other even passionate kiss we've shared!—and then you *immediately* proceeded to talk about the *macabre* tragedies of youth. Try not to *muddle* your precision and your passion."

Manijeh said, nodding solemnly, "Keep it simple. Read the room. Avoid switching gears."

"What do you *feel* about me, knowing full well that I *love* you? I have closed my eyes in front of you *both* and have allowed myself to fall backward while I confessed this love and would confess it again *and* again—not to be obsessive or obstinate, but to be certain I've not been misheard—and please play your answer in a *moment* as quick as sixty-fourth notes in pure *staccato*; we'll hear the whole story some *other* day, though, please, as our treat cools as we speak."

Brett had *never* imagined such a situation. When Manijeh had asked him how long he had loved her at Prospect Point, he could conveniently hand her an unsent letter he had labored over carefully years before. Now, he was downtown, in the cold, eating chestnuts, as shelled and open as one of them.

"I love you, Taraneh," he said.

She shifted in her place on the bench, turning to face him more directly, her eyes bright with attention as he spoke.

"At first, it grew from admiration of your intellect and grace, as well as your authentic glow, and this became a deep fondness over time. *Vali alân man mitavanam begoyam ke man to râ kheili dust daram, âshaqetam.*"[48]

There was simultaneously a loud sigh of relief from all three of them seated there. Taraneh stood, walked over to his left, and sat beside him and held him firmly, saying nothing. Manijeh held his hand tightly in hers.

"Wow, you really *have* been upping your Persian language game," Manijeh finally broke the silence. "I fell in love with you *all over again* after hearing your almost-Tehrani accent." She then added, "I don't know about the two of you, but I'm all for keeping this *right* where it is and not messing up a good thing by being *greedy* about life. I love and adore you *both*, but I think we've converged." She turned to Brett and added, "What do you say to that, Mr. Open?"

---

[48] "But now I can say that I really love you; I am in love with you."

"I second the motion," Brett agreed. "My heart and body are sealed between us and I've no desire to throw pebbles into this pond and upset the balance we've found."

"Three votes and we have an accord," Taraneh concluded their pact. "This is complicated enough for me to figure out as is."

"As above, so below. Now, let's find a theatre and watch a movie," Brett suggested. "How about *Shakespeare in Love*? It just came out and I heard it's great."

"Seriously?" Manijeh sighed. "I'm *saturated*."

"It's either that or the remake of *Psycho*. Besides, it can't be anywhere near as convoluted as Real Life."

"Well, there's always *Playing by Heart* with Angelina Jolie," Manijeh proposed.

"'Talking about love is like dancing about architecture,' Jolie says at some point," Taraneh said. "And that's pretty much the whole thing in a nutshell."

"*Shakespeare in Love* it is, then," Manijeh conceded. "I'm done with nutshells for a while."

"Yes, I heard that the *Psycho* remake is really not that good," Taraneh added. "Don't get me wrong, I'm all about Vince Vaughn, but I'm also perfectly willing to sit and watch Joseph Fiennes as the Bard."

Touched by Fortune's Shadow: a triptych

Coda

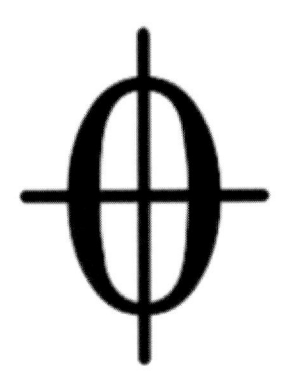

> "Music is enough for a lifetime but a lifetime is not enough for music."

—Sergei Rachmaninoff

Touched by Fortune's Shadow: a triptych

Quinn Tyler Jackson

Epilog: Paris, late April 1999

After a day's shopping on the *Avenue des Champs-Élysées*, having already done the same at the *Faubourg Saint-Honoré* the day before, Brett, Manijeh, and Taraneh sipped *café au lait* in the Spring air outside. Rostam was due to meet them for coffee, and they approached being a quarter hour late, he finally arrived.

"*Mazarat mikha'am*," he forgave himself. "I lost track of time. That's what you get for waiting to the last minute to call me to set this up."

"You're so *fit*!" Manijeh immediately noted.

"I owe it all to good living!" he said with cheer as he hugged his sister. "And coffee and baguettes!" He leaned to give Taraneh a quick kiss on the cheek, and then pulled Brett out of his chair with the same strength Brett had once pulled him out of the muddy creek as a child, the day they met. "It's great that we could meet up. I really wasn't expecting this at all. So you two... do Mom and Dad know yet? I should have asked earlier."

"Mom suspected when I said without any advanced notice that we were flying to Paris, and it wasn't on business. So I told her, and she was *fine* with it. Dad, too."

"Just fine? Like that?" he asked.

"I think your father and mother have been waiting for some time on this one," Brett commented. "Longer than they let on, probably. They may have already factored in the accelerated pace of things since last year this time and just ran with it when we told them about it."

"I can see that," Rostam agreed.

Brett proudly displayed his Rolex saying, "I *finally* get to use the GMT to its fullest extent now that I'm not in the Pacific time zone."

"Tell me about the ceremony," Rostam pressed.

Touched by Fortune's Shadow: a triptych

"Just the three of us to in front of a marriage officiant and a pond full of *koi*," Manijeh said. "Well, the officiant's assistant was also there and took *many* photos for us. We'll be sure to get printed copies those to you."

"The three of …?" Rostam asked.

"Taraneh was our witness," Brett explained.

Taraneh smiled and said, "It was near the New Westminster Quai. It was totally dreamy."

"We had nice, matching floral de la Renta tea-length dresses," Manijeh added. She pulled a single photo of the three of them from her clutch. "Here we go. Sorry I've only this *one*. As I said, more will follow! by email once we're back. I have some scanning to do."

Rostam took the photo of the three of them in front of the *koi* pond, with the April sun reflecting from it, and smiled before pushing it back to his sister. "You all look absolutely *smashing* and I expected no less. Simply *stunning*! Now I can show you off too all my new friends here in Europe."

"No, you keep that," she said, returning the photo to him. He carefully placed it in his inner jacket pocket.

"My sister eloped with my best friend," Rostam laughed, tapping the pocket he'd place the photo into. "My best friend sold the company we built from scratch together, right from under me," he then added with a gigantic wink and smile. "Such a life you've lived, Brett."

"Haven't we all, though?" Brett said. "As for selling VAI right from under you, remember Cincinnatus."

"Pardon?" Rostam replied. "Cincinnati? You've lost me."

"Cincinnatus was a Roman, but he wasn't just any Roman. Back in 458 BC, well before we *usually* think of Rome, he was out there, plowing his fields, minding his own business, when the Senate and Populus of Rome came calling. They were in a *tight* spot—army besieged by the Aequi at Mount Algidus and all that. The Senate needed a leader who could handle the crisis without a second thought for personal power."

Straightening up, Brett continued with, "So they appointed Cincinnatus as *dictator* for six months. Just like that, he leaves his plow, organizes an army, and not only breaks the siege but defeats the Aequi decisively. And here's the kicker—after his quick victory, he doesn't cling to power. No. Just sixteen days later, he resigns and goes back to his farming. He could have stayed on for a full six-month term as dictator."

"But Rome has been served and there is no longer need for him to have any—let alone *absolute*—authority, for even another day. He did something very similar about twenty years later, same results. Needless to say, Cincinnati was named after him.

"Selling VAI wasn't about cutting you out or pulling the rug out; it was about doing what *needed* to be done, when it *could* be done. We built it up, it served its purpose, and when the time was right, it was time to let it go. Not for personal gain, but because it was the best move for everyone involved at that point and in the future. *Carpe diem sed finem respice.*"

"I was heading into a tunnel that might not have had another end to it," Rostam admitted, putting his hands on the table, face down, as if in defeat, but then turning them over and clenching them. "But I'm well along now. I'm no worse for wear financially after the sale, for certain."

"All the stars told us that *this* was *our* season, and we returned to the fields and brought in the harvest," Brett said. After a pause, he concluded, "Ours was a campaign to maximize our collective joy at a moment that afforded this in the form of freeing up our time *and* our longer-term fiscal concerns. Such opportunity is *fleeting* and… the many paths to the mountaintop are completely littered with gravestones marked …"

"… Hamlet," Manijeh finished Brett's sentence for him.

"The sale of VAI to Klein, Holdum, and French caught me off guard," Taraneh added, "but I understand why nobody could say anything to me for so long. Life certainly has been turned upside down a few times this last while."

At this, Rostam turned to her, smiled, and said, "I heard about your move to Brett's rental unit. How have you been, Taraneh?" he asked. "Has the new location been good for your teaching practice? Are you recovering from being 'turned upside down?'"

"*Hâl-am kheili khub*-e, *merci*.[49] Yes, I thought I would lose a few students when I moved, and I did one or two, but I gained three times that when I was actually there in Coal Harbor," she said. "I guess it had more curb appeal for the kinds of students I was looking for, I really don't know. So I now have as many as I can handle and have had to put together a waiting list for the first time since starting teaching."

The waiter came to see what Rostam wanted, and he ordered a *café au lait*.

---

[49] "I'm doing very well, thank you."

"I've decided to stay in Europe," Rostam said.
"Oh, really? Like long-term?" Taraneh asked.
"Yes. Based out of Paris," he said.
"I meant to mention this, Taraneh" Manijeh said. "But really I wanted Rostam to tell you."
"Klein *et al.* offered me a position if I was willing to set up their European Union office, so it looks like I'll be working closely with Manijeh, actually, to coordinate with her on EU hedging. *Officially*, I report to Chuck Holdum, but Manijeh is my for-real boss in the day-to-day."

Manijeh grinned with clear satisfaction. "Charles Holdum is practically semiretired now, in his huge basement playing with trainsets with Brett. You won't be hearing much from *him*."

"Unless it comes in HO scale!" Brett added. "And we don't *just* play with trains! I *also* borrow and read some of his esoteric book collection."

"Can I show my industry ignorance and ask why Paris? Why not London or even Frankfurt?" Taraneh asked.

"The UK is not in the Eurozone, for one," Rostam began to explain. "British pound volatility versus a single currency for multiple countries was a big one. It's so much easier to apply monetary and regulatory policy by not focusing just on London, despite its size. Second, I somehow ended up, after years of Canadian schooling, speaking passable French, so that puts it ahead of Frankfort for me. I was able to find my own around in Luxembourg quite nicely in French, for instance, and they're in the Eurozone. It's about an hour flight to Luxembourg City from Paris, and London and Brussels are just a Eurostar train way. Just as examples.

"Then we have the fact that Paris is centrally located, as well, making the logistics of getting around when I need to much simpler. And just look around. It's *the* place to be." He turned in his seat to do a panoramic sweep of the bustling life around them. "Finally, France is technology friendly when it comes to the markets."

"All that sounds reasonable," Taraneh agreed. "Clearly, you put a great deal of thought into this location, that's for sure. I should have expected no less." She smiled, held up her cup, and gestured her appreciation for his thorough answer.

"We'll know more as time moves forward how it ultimately pans out, but honestly, if one fails in *Paris* of all places, then *what* a place to fail," Rostam said.

Rostam then said, "Now on to the big question in all your heads, and the answer is no, not a *drop*." He made a small bow. Taraneh gave Rostam a warm hug, her happy tears saying what she wanted to say about Rostam's good news.

"Rostam, the three of us all have a little bit of news…"

Rostam put up his hand. "Brett, buddy. I already know what you're going to say. How long have I known you?"

"Years and years."

"And years," Manijeh added.

"I've held your hair clear as you puked at the party, man," Rostam said. "And you returned the courtesy with me many a time. Back when *those* kinds of things were news."

He looked at each in turn. "I know you to your *code*, Brett. And you, Manijeh. And Taraneh, although we never had *that* level of connection—and that's not spite speaking, that's my admitting a truth to myself out loud—I can see that you *three* lovebirds are here in Paris to celebrate as *only* Paris in the Springtime permits."

Rostam lit a cigarette and asked, "Anyone want one? And do Mom and Dad know about this?"

"All sets of them," Taraneh replied.

"We figured it would be better to find out from us than *az zebân beh zabân*,"[50] added Manijeh. "And to answer your question, they all said what amounts to *khoshbakhti-ye shomâ, khoshbakhti-ye mâst*.[51] They accepted long ago that our futures are ahead of us, not behind us in the ashes."

"God bless secular humanism," Taraneh interjected.

"And all that it represents!" Brett added enthusiastically.

"That's family solidarity for you," Rostam said. "Indeed, *khoshbakhti-ye shomâ, khoshbakhti-ye man ast*."[52]

Brett then reached over for a cigarette, and when he did that, Manijeh and then Taraneh joined in. Rostam set the lighter afire with a flick of his thumb and Brett leaned over to take the flame and start his smoke. The others followed suit.

"To the *four* of us!" Rostam toasted with his *café au lait*.

The others lifted their glasses. After a few minutes of small talk, Rostam asked Brett what he planned to do now that he was a free agent in the career sphere again.

---

[50] *az zebân beh zebân* (lit. "from tongue to tongue"), "from the grapevine."

[51] "Your happiness is our happiness."

[52] "Your happiness is my happiness."

"And on *my* career front," Brett offered, "*Soke* Hashimoto's daughter-in-law is doing well, but still has a rough road ahead of her with the chemotherapy and surgery. He offered to sell me his *dojo* and he moved to Ottawa to help his son run his *dojo* there as the central *dojo* of the *Ryu*. This will also allow him to eventually pass on the *Soke*-ship to his son, in keeping with tradition. I accepted the offer, and I'll be putting my time into developing the *dojo* into a fully active local branch." He took a drag from his cigarette before putting it out in the ashtray. "The place currently breaks even."

"I imagine you quietly meditating in a Zen rock garden by a creek," Rostam said wistfully. "Dicing onions with Japanese chef knives.."

"So, you heard about the knives, eh?" Brett asked.

"Yeah, Dad told me about that. Sounds good."

"I agreed to help out with some of the business there, as well. They're making use of Katja's skills now that she works with me."

"Oh! Katja followed you after the sale! I heard about that!" Rostam exclaimed. "You sold the company *and* poached her!"

"Everyone is always so *dramatic*. I just went with the talent," Brett replied. "Anyway, getting the alloy into kitchenware is another step towards the *katanas*, which may never happen at worst and could take *years* at best. But I think we're definitely heading in the right direction for all these little things to come together and keep us busy for a long time yet.

"That's two markets they have now, so the metallurgists will be busy and learning what this alloy is good for. They take their kitchen knives almost as seriously as their *katana*, so this feels like no small push forward. In any case, they're now fully solvent, and Katja's set it up so they have every likelihood of staying that way. Enough to justify keeping at it for the time being."

"I suggest we stroll to the *Place de la Concorde* and look at the Eiffel Tower all at once in the same place," Taraneh said.

"Excellent plan!" Rostam agreed, standing up and pushing his chair in.

"Oh, I forgot to ask you two," Rostam said as they began their march to the Tower. "The matter of the Marital Surname. How did you decide to go about that?"

"I'm keeping Yazdpour," Manijeh replied.

"Socially? Legally?"

"Legally and socially. I would have been completely *fine* with Lloyd-Ronan," she insisted, "but Brett convinced me to stay with Yazdpour. He had a very convincing and heartwarming argument as to why."

"Oh?" Rostam replied. "Something I may be familiar with? I know a few of the heartwarming arguments, don't I?"

"Not so much of an *argument* really. A *story*. First off, you know my views about people not owning other people. Marriage doesn't change that. The custom of adopting the groom's name has origins that do not sit well with me. Do you remember the day we met?" Brett asked.

"Pretty well!" Rostam replied.

"I explained that I had three nationalities. Four now, with the EU passport," he said.

"Yes. Something about how your parents hyphenated their surnames when they married one another. I'm a wellspring of such information now that I'm sober."

"Well, there's a little story behind it."

"Do tell," Rostam insisted.

"Dad was living in Cardiff, finishing up his apprenticeship as a machinist. Mom, from Cork, was apprenticing as a seamstress, also in Cardiff.

"So Dad, being Welsh, and thus a lover of things musical and poetic, especially if a piano and a crowd were involved, attended a get together where she happened to be playing piano. Long story short, they met, fell in love, and decided to get married. I'm skipping large chunks of time here, of course."

"A clear case of love at first re*ci*tal," Taraneh said, taking Brett's other hand in hers.

"Wait a second. Irish and British. Catholic, I'm assuming, and Anglican. *That* must have flown with the families like a lead canary," Rostam observed. "I *still* heard some of that during my trips through the UK and Ireland this last little while. Europe has a memory longer than an Iranian grandmother."

"They were willing to get beyond that," Brett explained. "But the Ronans of Cork, Mom's family, having had only a single child, did not sit well with grandchildren taking on the non-Irish Lloyd name, as this would end their line. They refused to give their blessing. Flat refused to have the Ronan name be smitten to ashes by some 'fecking Brit,' true love or not, Welsh, in fact, or not. Obstinance. It almost put an end to their whole relationship."

"The death knell of so many relationships," Taraneh said. "In our community, cultural resistance to some relationships is more complicated than playing *Transcendental Études* at times."

"Yeah," Rostam said. "Not Mom and Dad, but I've certainly seen it happen. It can be hit and miss; I think. Some parts of life just haven't caught up with others in the present day, and here we are, about to enter the next millennium and we still bicker about the placement of commas and semicolons, telling us what our hearts should feel."

"So anyway, Dad came up with a solution. He suggested they would hyphenate *both* their names and promised to use this hyphenated surname with any child. Thus, the Lloyd-Ronan line was formed. A family alliance was thus cemented, and here were are today."

"We could not rightly come upon a similar compromise, as this would've produced the unwieldly Lloyd-Ronan-Yazdpour," Manijeh said. "Imagine signing *that* to pay the bill."

"The longest Iranian last name I have *ever* the joy to come across is Esqâhinajafabâdi," Rostam said, pronouncing it very carefully. "How's that for a ten-foot pole?" He then added, "And keeping Yazdpour is fitting, really, isn't it? Since you're all equal partners in this, and there's only so much name real estate to go around. When destiny knocks on your door at the end of the day, it asks to see your heart, not your surname."

"You're becoming a poet, Rostam," Taraneh observed.

"I'm certainly no Rumi or Khayyam, but I can rhyme once in a while, by accident," he conceded with a brief, exaggerated bow. "Kind of like a stopped watch."

The four of them continued to drift down the street, three with bags, one without, and Brett felt incredibly fortunate to be with the three people who mattered most to him in all Creation, and he knew how good it was to be alive..

And he hoped deeply inside himself that they, too felt some of this absolute joy, and when they laughed together as they made their way to an iconic view, he could tell by the birds in their laughter that they, also, had found this bliss, coveted by rich and poor across time.

When they at last reached the Eiffel Tower and were all staring at it, hand-in-hand and huddled together as they were, Taraneh quoted Antoine de Saint-Exupéry: "Love is not about looking at one another, but about looking together in the same direction."

An Unsent Declaration of Love

Brett Liam Lloyd-Ronan,
[Port Coquitlam, BC]

Saturday, 29 September 1990

Ms. Manijeh Yazdpour,
[UBC Student Residences]

Dear Manijeh:

If I were the kind of young man who could look you in the eyes, reach over to you, hold your hand in mine, and still somehow find the courage to speak, you would not be reading this letter, since I would simply be speaking my mind stood before you. Instead, I must act as my own de Bergerac. Indeed, it may yet turn out that I am not even the kind of young man who will find the courage to send this letter once it is written. Even so, I will push forward and write it with great hope that it will find its way to your eyes, and through your beautiful eyes, it will travel on to your even more beautiful heart, where I hope with all optimism that it will find reciprocity there.

Some have pestered me for being roundabout with my words when they touch upon the personal, but I will not do that here, and instead will simply come out and declare that I love you, Manijeh. The sound of your laugh, your voice, even a teasing (sometimes scolding) chastisement, your breathing. I'm lost in you when we are together and lost in the memory of you when we are apart.

I have callused hands and, were it not for my teaching myself manners over the years from books and observation of those around me, there would be far rougher aspects to me than just my hands. You have been part of helping me become who I have as I have had to face life's challenges. How many dark pathways might I have looked down, were I not instead looking at them through your radiant optimism? I do know that I've avoided so many such disappointments altogether because I've known you.

Touched by Fortune's Shadow: a triptych

I know from experience of passing through others' lives that someone with such power over the heart is rare: and this is where I find myself with you. "I can no longer live by thinking," said Orlando in *As You Like It*. I must form my words with hope that they will be faithful to my intent.

Your eyes have the fire of your intelligence, and you are generous with your cheer. Do you know how that can light up a room the moment you walk in? Now that I find myself so far from you, with such a trip on transit to get to watch even a movie together, that I feel I must stand back even as I struggle in this letter to stand bravely forward. My ambitions have been upended by my poverty.

I cannot afford anything even near the life you've always had. Even so, I still love you despite my impecunity, and so I must not stop myself from declaring it. I considered asking if you wanted to date, to give you and me a fair try, but no matter what I pretend to myself, it doesn't feel as if such would, in fact, be *fair* at all.

Maybe I am hoping that by standing on the mountain and singing it for all (or at least you) to hear, some magic will fall down and make it all *just work out*. As if by some ancient magic, fate beholden to *a wish*. That sounds quite optimistic, and not even cautiously so, and *this* is the optimism you instill in me. But such magic is for those who have not yet seen life's ropes and pulleys as they push broom backstage as *others* play their anointed parts as Rosalind and Orlando. Having mopped such places, I've seen that it is but expensive, complex rigging that keeps angels' feet aloft. Souls hoisted by sandbags full of cash.

You're in general studies now, but it will come to you what you truly want to pursue for yourself as a career. I'm mopping floors and mucking toilets, not the most romantic chores, but they somehow get me through, and I do know that there's no disgrace in eating an honest day's meal. You know that I have no shame of my blue-collar origins, though I am honest about the social limitations being seen as working class can entail, and I know that you'd love me—if you *were* to love me, that is, I am not trying to presume—no matter what my social class happens to be.

As much as I am okay with all of that, I want more. I want to win. I want to hold your hand in my own and dance boldly down the *Champs-Élysées* in Paris. I want to qualify for the Barcelona team in 1992. My fencing coach says they are real possibilities given my official performance to date.

In short, I want to be so much *more* than I currently *can* be. It doesn't matter what I would have wanted to be if you and I had never met. We *have* met, and I want to slay dragons in your name. And I want you to take your own spear and slay them *with* me.

Realistically, the most I actually can do is put my soul to paper and hope that you may one day return my feelings.

I want what only a declaration of love such as I feel for you can bring. The rest I put to the universe, and to you, assuring you that any reply at all would be far better than silence; I can bear a sad truth, but not the echo chamber of my own soul, which I have been listening to alone now for far too long.

Most affectionately,
And with love,

Brett

Touched by Fortune's Shadow: a triptych

Quinn Tyler Jackson

Manijeh's Reply to Brett's Love Letter

Manijeh Yazdpour, BCom MBA CFA CSC
Director of European Portfolio Diversification
Klein, Holdum, and French, Inc.
[Vancouver, BC]

Saturday, December 26, 1998

Brett Liam Lloyd-Ronan, CFA CSC
Chief Executive Officer & Chief Analyst,
Vector Affinity Insights, Inc.
[Vancouver, BC]

Delivered by hand. PERSONAL AND CONFIDENTIAL.

Dearest Brett:

When you gave me your letter from 1990 this past May, I told myself that every such letter delivered deserves a reply, and though eight years delayed, my reply is thankfully less delayed than that. I took some time to *really* observe our life, so that any answer to you would respect the patience and hesitation you had when composing yours, as these were considerable for you, I'm certain.

I will begin by saying that had you sent that letter when you first meant to, your words would have been as warmly received by my heart as they were when I finally did read it. Would the *extravagance* of our gifts differ given the different budget? Of *course*, but that doesn't matter to me. *Eshq pul nist*—money is not love, not now, not then. Yes, I like good things, but I prefer good *people*.

I had no notion of your financial circumstances except in so far as they constantly tormented you and limited you to a place in the world that had been *exceedingly* stingy toward you. Three years after you wrote that letter, even though I never knew your feelings, having earned by BCom, I asked Rostam to make sure you knew you could borrow all my used textbooks, and I would even tutor you if you needed.

Touched by Fortune's Shadow: a triptych

He had told me that you'd already burned through all of his engineering and calculus texts and were a man on fire—as you are so very often. I encouraged him to pull himself out of his rut and talk to you about putting *both* your heads together.

What I'm trying to say is that I wanted you to find a way, your own way, to the top of that ravine, and thought that maybe your computer programming brain would find inspiration in the safety and potential profitability of mathematical economics. And you *did* find a way out. We *all* did. Just like back in the day. We lifted one another up. There were no bags of cash to make *these* angels soar! We jumped and hoped for the best. Even when the best was *not* what was in store for us. And we swept up our mess. Mostly.

Yes, my love, we were all broken. I didn't know some things that I know now about your pain, just as you didn't know some of the Yazdpour family pain. That is not what is important. We understood that to get to the top of the mountain, there are many paths. You had your way of saying it when we were bratty kids, but we all resonated with that because it felt like the kind of thing one should consider rather than disregard.

Willard and his two goons came down that mountain looking to cause hurt. They were going to beat us to a pulp. They didn't care that I was a girl, I was on the list, too. I'd seen them before that day. I knew what they were capable of doing, and of saying: they had called me *foul* names before then. I knew what human beings are capable of doing to other human beings; we are no strangers to the ugliness that came hulking down that hillside that day. But this time, I was with *you*. And before his mouth could utter another hateful word, you had him under your command, and you did not hesitate to act.

You stood between Rostam and me, and you refused to let *anything* happen to us. I could think of a hundred moments far more mundane than this to light a crush on fire than *that*. It provided a good basis for how my feelings for your grew over the years that followed. It served as my North Star to knowing who you were on the inside: because as *honest and forthright* as your mouth sometimes (always!) is, it does not often speak of that *deepest* you as much as I (or others) might wish to hear shared.

And then there was Boston. No place better than Harvard to teach a person who they are and are not, and when I was there, I *constantly* felt the pull to return. I missed family and friends.

Sure, I *loved* that I would have a Harvard MBA, but I did *not* love being away.

I missed *you*. I didn't doubt myself about this. I knew it outright. I delighted in the dream that you and I might one day… even just kiss. As pedestrian as that may sound, but honestly, who keeps track of such matters?

The stretch in Toronto sure did not turn out to be what the Brochure promised, but once I hit that final wall: I knew it. I knew I wanted to flee and be free of it. *Nothing* else would be enough. To be home. To be in Vancouver. I needed to fly.

And specifically, I flew to *you*.

I told you then and I will repeat it in writing: I returned to *you*. I didn't want to waste one more instant of my life trying to find a North Star in some other human being, as I had *already* found you. Here we are, nearing 1999 and the next phase of us, and I'm *still* walking on sunshine.

Ah, to that career stuff, though, which burdens us all so and messes with what would otherwise be pleasant self-accord. You unfairly beat yourself up back then about being a rough working-class bloke: but you *always* wore it well and with dignity.

And here is what I would say to the forces that made you struggle so much to achieve what others have been handed on gold gilt platters for having done far less than you, from Hafiz himself:

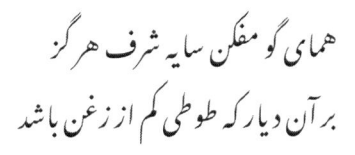

همای گو مفکن سایه شرف هرگز
بر آن دیار که طوطی کم از زغن باشد

"O *Huma*, never cast your shadow of honor on that land where the parrot is valued less than the starling."

I have addressed this reply to your letter with all of our career flourishes, my love. All of them. Yours, too. You're allowed to feel proud of earning your way out of toil; never apologize for success if you were kind, and you were as kind as anyone I've known to be.

You can stop playing the rigging hand swinging from the ropes behind the Globe Theater, lifting angels with bags of coins. We *made* it. We made it to the top of the mountain, again. We brushed ourselves off, pulled out the twigs from our sweaters, and pushed beyond what fate *really* wanted for us all. And best of all, because we didn't make it to the top alone, now that we're here, we don't have to *be* alone.

Touched by Fortune's Shadow: a triptych

That is where the *Huma* too often go, my love, into the lonely acme: never able to alight, just passing by, lifting others to their higher calling, but *always* on the wing.

But you are not swabbing deck for the Bard's players now, Captain! You are the CEO and CA of a major going concern, interviewed in the glossies, poised, and properly presented, tall, and proud, in the CEO uniform we bought together and had your mother hem. Atop this tower, with me. With all who love you and who feel your love for them.

And if for only one single day: what a *glorious* day!

With equal love and affection, always,

Manijeh

از کفر و دین برون صحرائی هست
من و تو را در آنجا قراری هست

> Beyond heresy and belief, there is a desert wilderness;
> You and I have an appointment there.
> —Rumi

Back-matter

> "The *explanation* of a work is always sought in the [one] who produced it, as if it were always in the end, through the more or less transparent allegory of the fiction, the voice of a single person, the *author* 'confiding' in us."

—Roland Barthes, "The Death of the Author"

Touched by Fortune's Shadow: a triptych

Quinn Tyler Jackson

On Writing Brett as Autistic

I intentionally depicted the protagonist Brett Lloyd-Ronan as autistic, drawing from my personal experience as an autistic,[53,54] without explicitly having him diagnosed as such within the story. I do not want my intentional portrayal of Brett as autistic to be interpreted as my having "coded him" as such by the clever application of an agreed-upon industry-standard checklist of traits, as sometimes happens in the popular media.

I could have portrayed him as having been diagnosed, were it not for the fact that, in a 1998 setting, Brett might well have been diagnosed as an adult with Asperger's syndrome, a term I have deliberately avoided due to Hans Asperger's association with and facilitation of the Nazi regime.[55,56]

This is in no way whatsoever a comment about the *person* being thus diagnosed but is about the unsatisfactory taxonomies available to diagnosticians of that era. Absent any satisfactory alternative to an offensive and exclusionary label, Brett very well may not have been diagnosed with anything at all, per DSM-IV criteria.[57] Given this landscape, Brett remains free of any such diagnosis herein.

---

[53] Quinn Jackson, "Reflective Practice: On Diversity & Inclusion in Science & Technology," *The Tech Magazine of the IST*, Vol. 2 No. 1, March 2021.

[54] Quinn Tyler Jackson, "Dismantling Lionization in STEM," in *Midnight at the Arcanum*, Knight Terra Press, November 2023.

[55] Herwig Czech, "Hans Asperger, National Socialism, and 'race hygiene' in Nazi-era Vienna," *Molecular Autism*, April 2018.

[56] Cohen *et al.*, "Did Hans Asperger actively assist the Nazi euthanasia program?" *Molecular Autism*, April 2018.

[57] American Psychiatric Association, *Diagnostic and Statistical Manual of Mental Disorders, Fourth Edition* (DSM-IV), American Psychiatric Publishing, 1994.

Touched by Fortune's Shadow: a triptych

Moreover, my literary aim was to explore Brett's character in relation to his warm circle of friends and associates, not through marginalization and medicalization, given the term's ableist implications and history. This portrayal seeks to offer insight into the multifaceted experiences of an autistic individual, fostering understanding without confining Brett's identity to an ablest, medicalized, disorder-oriented diagnosis.

Why depict Brett as autistic at all? To answer that I ask: should I have entirely excluded an entire subset of human identities from representation over my own ideological disgust with the DSM-IV *status quo*? Of course not! Many autistics, me included, consider autism to be an *identity* that is lived, rather than a disorder to be suffered or given a standardized label. We are autistic; we do not *have* autism. To remove Brett's autistic identity because I did not wish to indirectly endorse DSM-IV thinking would serve only those who might be uncomfortable without the familiar-but-flawed imprimatur of *status quo*. Modern fiction need not answer to such gatekeeping and can admit to the existence of the autistic identity as it *actually self-presented* in 1998, not which classes the hegemony imposed.

This self-validating, non-gatekept approach to an entire identity such as autism is the *point* of the introductory essay, "Reclaiming the Narrative Pedagogy," found in *Midnight at the Arcanum*, the first book of the Epiphanies trilogy, captured here in its final three paragraphs:

> Moreover, such oeuvres foster Socratic dialogic problem-posing education by inviting readers and authors to engage in conversations about the complexities of personal stories and the many perspectives one must fully consider as one interprets one's life events. It encourages the active questioning of the dominant cultural ethos and invites readers to become active participants in their own meaning-making process. Next, it can empower individuals to find or reclaim their authentic truth and voice, allowing the previously marginalized to be heard clearly. Through its self-representation, meta-autobiography becomes a platform for empowerment and constructive resistance.

This literary form embodies the integration of theory and practice, encouraging individuals to not only reflect on their own experiences but also to act upon their newfound awareness. By using story-telling strategies to disrupt traditional structures and challenge the entrenched power dynamics, meta-autobiography becomes an avenue to fuller transformative praxis. Finally, meta-autobiography effectively aligns with emancipatory education as it empowers individuals to tell their own stories on their terms and according to their own lived experience.

Through the process of writing and sharing their stories, individuals can gain a sense of agency and empowerment that may have been denied to them in other contexts. They can also contribute to a broader process of collective meaning-making and thus open up new possibilities for understanding the world, thereby more actively contributing to a broader project of social equity and liberation.[58]

"Coding" Brett autistic would be a level of indirection and source of speculation, and as near as I can tell, society has been speculating about autism quite long enough that we autistics are due to take our own seats at the Caucus and start talking about ourselves. Diagnosing Brett with an offensive (by his and my own reckoning) label would be to bend the knee to a hegemony that already found the good manners and sense to vanish with the DSM-IV, and I prefer to push forward with the slightly improved canon we now have and keep my uneasy hindsight for my personal meditations.

The present note is intended to clarify my approach to ensure transparency and prevent any speculation about whether this depiction was intentional in the sense of E.D. Hirsh. To Barthes we grant free roam of the novel's other aspects, and with that, to the limitless imagination of the Reader.

—Burnaby, April (Autism Acceptance Month) 2024

---

[58] *Midnight at the Arcanum*, Knight Terra Press, November 2023, p. 14.

Touched by Fortune's Shadow: a triptych

Quinn Tyler Jackson

On Writing a Novel *Tabula Rasa*

A Multiverse of Self

I had a momentary fragment of a polished facet of a thought about what I may have done or could have, should have, didn't, and like a shooting star, a wish made by indecision, or by decision that was in fact the only choice I could have taken and that momentary nucleation point of a hint of sweet regret made a Moiré pattern shift in the drop of a single bead upon the pond and this was just me, yesterday, deciding to wake up, and as my eyes wide-opened, I jumped into this multiverse of self.

In March of 2024, there was a void, and into this void was projected a protagonist, a young man from the working class of British Columbia, who had somehow managed, by the age of twenty-eight, to be living in a fully-owned loft apartment in Vancouver's Gastown. In the way fictional constructions of the artist's early imaginings sometimes (or often) do, the loft apartment transformed into a well-situated, well-appointed two-bedroom Coal Harbor penthouse suite overlooking both North Vancouver and Stanley Park. My own (albeit rented) panoramic view of the North Shore from further east up Burrard Inlet in Burnaby, was set out before me from the window of my home office, and before the month was out, the first draft of this novel poured out of my head with Athenian audacity.

My head, being nothing like that of Zeus, did not yield a fully battle-ready character, and so what is seen in this revision has been through the process of editorial review and subsequent revision. This closing note is written on my fifty-fifth birthday, and I consider the novel done, excepting only the final polish every work sees nearing actual day of press.

Taken together with my other two novels, the present work completes the Epiphanies trilogy. I most certainly did not set out to do this almost absurd thing. A year back, after a thirteen-year complete hiatus with my creative writing, I began chipping away at my previously published novel, *Janus Incubus*, and from this impetus, between March and November of 2023, with exceptional editorial support, I turned what had been a novel into my literary monograph, *Midnight at the Arcanum*.

Touched by Fortune's Shadow: a triptych

Having had what I considered good success with this first update, it felt time yet again to bring a past work into my present esthetic, and so, the novel previously published as *The Succubus Sea* became *The Ancestral Sea*. Extending *The Ancestral Sea* involved some conflation with applicable material taken from the ending chapters of the original *Janus Incubus* that were dropped in the monograph, but which had crossover in the characters of Cohen Benjamin, Cyrus Drake, and Salomeh Arashpour that provided insight into the relationship fate of Cyrus and Salomeh that was not in *The Succubus Sea*. Both works were better off for the revision and additional narrative, which in each resulted in about twenty-five percent completely new prose.

Though I consider the two resulting works *new*, since they were extensively reworked and revised and conflated and new narrative was constructed to bring them cohesively together more fluidly than their prior incarnations could achieve, they were not produced from clean slates: they were palimpsests that came with their specific histories, thematic tone, and esthetic choices, which had in some cases been irreversibly made some decades ago.

Revising an already published novel to the extent that I revised in order to be able to produce *Midnight at the Arcanum* and *The Ancestral Sea* gave me a appreciation for how difficult it is to imbue contemporary understanding and insight into a work first set in ink two decades past. It can be done, but to negotiate between the ethics and mores of then and now is a subtle (and also brutal) sociolinguistic exercise. Indeed, the exercise is sometimes so arduous from the first assessment that entire novels might better be left as-is or taken out of print, rather than attempt to hammer them into a modern ethos.

This is what I did with three other of my most adventurous works, since they did not, in the final analysis, warrant the full effort: *Abadoun*, *The Lament of an Architect of Babel*, and *Anders' Contrition*. These novellas were permanently retired as part of the same career process that brought the two novels that did survive the cut into new light. There are those amongst my past reviewers who considered *Abadoun* my best work. It was the first novella published (in digital format only) in 1995 by Knight Terra Press and was the first work ever published by the press. But all these years later, it did not make the cut, and this only after having sought a professional second opinion.

Writing something *completely* from nothing is a chore I have typically reserved for short stories. Across my career since 1990, I have had fifty-eight original short stories and nine flash fiction published across seventeen publication venues, from print to online. During that same period, three of my novels (*Abadoun*, *The Succubus Sea*, and *Janus Incubus*) were written and published, along with two novellas that evolved from published short stories (*Anders' Contrition* and *The Lament of an Architect of Babel*).[59] Each of these books, as already mentioned, was developed from earlier, shorter publications. As mentioned, various portions of *Janus Incubus* were developed into *Midnight at the Arcanum* and other portions were, with published version of *The Succubus Sea*, the basis of what became *The Ancestral Sea*.

Both revised editions were works I considered myself most artistically proud for having produced, but each was the product of many *years* of writing, rewriting, revision, publishing, and reworking. As mentioned, this was how I wrote novella and novel length works: one short-story-chapter at a time. Publish a short. Get feedback from readers. Revise. Publish another. Conflate to two, with narrative putty to hold them together as a new whole, if they could be conflated, or keep working until something that could be adjoined arrived.[60]

To produce more than my longest ever work of narrative prose cut from whole cloth, in so brief a span, implies to me, as the creator of the work, that what things the human brain occupies itself in its off cycles is baffling to consider! Though also written completely from a clean slate, at least *Abadoun* had been architected and fully laid-out before being written. *Touched by Fortune's Shadow*, however, had no such napkin sketch to serve as a scaffold to hold the architecture in place as I called in the narrative team to put in the plumbing, wiring, and drywall. Not even a vague story board to use as a makeshift compass. Before it began, it did not exist in concept, implementation, or hazy flicker of inner vision.

---

[59] Some of these works had other titles during their lifetimes, but these are the titles by which they will be referenced here.
[60] This same methodology had brought other works, such as *The Lament of an Architect of Babel* and *Ander's Contrition* into their final forms. Before *Touched by Fortune's Shadow*, the last work I had written completely from a *tabula rasa* was the novella *Abadoun*, in the mid-nineties, which at forty thousand words, was quite short.

Touched by Fortune's Shadow: a triptych

And then, suddenly, on 29 February 2024, a Leap Day, in the morning, I sent an email to Dania Sheldon, the editor of my other two recent novels, who had contributed so much to their recent contemporary reconstruction, declaring that "the idea of writing a novel from whole cloth [had] seriously been turning in my head," although I had not written a completely new work for over a dozen or so years.

We now sit before this final work in the trilogy consisting of *Midnight at the Arcanum*, *The Ancestral Sea*, and *Touched by Fortune's Shadow*. All in the short span from that extra day we sometimes get in February, to my birthday. I had budgeted myself at least a year-and-a-half when I first started this venture, but apparently miscalculated the impact of the creative epiphany that was awaiting me.

As I had no roadmap to navigate from… oh, but then I actually did. One principle I set out to uphold from the first word: those in the close circle of family and friends would show *absolute* loyalty to the group and there would be no betrayal from within this circle. *That* was the map. An ethical unit of friends and family, from 1981 to 1998 Vancouver. From *there* flowed the narrative, written start-to-finish in first draft, completed by the end of March, and given finer articulation and phrasing (one hopes!) in subsequent passes, which occupied the rest of the time to completion.

This might seem to be an overly simple guiding principle, but there were moments during the composition of the work that I felt the need to consult this basic moral compass to assist with deciding how an ambiguous situation the characters had been written into would turn: and having them *never* turn on one another as the one inviolable rule brought fidelity to my vision for their collective narrative. It also strongly resonated with the overarching theme of all three novels in the trilogy: relationship loyalty and fidelity (and by extension disloyalty and infidelity).

This novel had a very rapid conception-to-implementation period, but I do not claim Kerouac's single-roll of typewriter paper any more than I claim Hemingway's infamous ability to hammer out five billion words a day while living on a diet of ground glass on pumpernickel. I've hopefully already dispelled the notion that I did this by myself: I have had *strong* editorial support throughout. But there are perhaps some points to note about this *almost* stream-of-consciousness.

As already hinted at by use of the word *trilogy*, when taken alongside *Midnight at the Arcanum* and *The Ancestral Sea*, the current novel sits in a trilogy of epiphanies as the third, final work that holds relationship loyalty and fidelity at the core of its themes and topics.[61]

In *Midnight at the Arcanum*, Conrad Kirk, having become infatuated with the married Anne-Jolie, a dead ringer for his ex-lover, declares to her that he does not *care* that she is married: he wants her anyway.

> When she passed again, three days later, I quickly walked to the front of the shop. Monsieur Guillaume and the others were out. I opened the door and called out to her. She turned, saw me, and walked up to me. Without thinking, without reasoning whether it was the right thing to say or not, I looked directly at her and said,
> —I don't care.
> She seemed startled at the exact words I'd chosen to use: "*Ça ne me fait rien.*" It was true. It meant nothing to me that she was married. I wanted to continue to see her, married or not, whether she looked like anyone I used to know or not. I wanted her absolutely.[62]

While the two spend a short, passionately raucous while in his Park Avenue suite together, her husband is transferred to Paris, and she follows her marriage, not her affair with Conrad, leaving him alone, dejected, and deeply unhinged. We are left to assume that Conrad's many years in his unhappy marriage following his affair with Anne-Jolie, skipped in the novel but definitely alluded to in the closing chapters, were his self-inflicted penance for having been careless.[63]

---

[61] *Anders' Contrition* and *The Lament of an Architect of Babel* also have this as central to their outcomes, but these novellas are not further discussed here, as they are no longer in print and are very short, compared to the three novels of the trilogy here introduced.

[62] *Midnight at the Arcanum*, Knight Terra Press, November 2023, p. 181.

[63] This is never stated explicitly either in the narrative, or in the monograph surrounding the novel, but his subsequent entry into an identity-crushing marriage of penance was intentional, stated here by the author.

Touched by Fortune's Shadow: a triptych

The only interaction between Conrad and Roxana, his wife, as seen in the chapter "Wake Up!" is one of *nightmarish levels of misunderstanding*. Conrad makes it quite clear to Phoebe, his lover after leaving his failed marriage, that he lived his entire married life locked in a state of Sartrean *mauvaise foi*, and the entirety of his failed first marriage becomes the story "When a Stranger Wandered in," an allegory about a soldier returning from the most desperate fighting seen by American forces in Europe during their participation in the Second World War. He had chosen to be whom *others* wanted to see, to not be alone.

As penances go, his seems to have been a scalding on his psyche, but even so he finds peace with Phoebe, even if just for that moment that their paths cross in New Westminster in early 2007 as Conrad gets his collapsed life back in some order. The freedom, peace, deep human connection, and personal ecstasy Conrad is *capable* of feeling when he is truthfully able to live authentically comes out allegorically in the short-story-chapter "Barefoot Sonata" and later (timeline wise) directly in the first chapter, "Midnight."

Whereas relationship infidelity thematically plays a central part of *Midnight at the Arcanum*, it pours torrentially from storm clouds and saturates the pages of *The Ancestral Sea*, as the pivotal obstacle of Cyrus Drake, the protagonist's entire existence sits squarely on the creative block he is suffering as a result, it turns out, of his inability to reconcile his own role in uncovering his mother's adultery, which he witnessed as a boy, committed with a close friend of Cyrus Drake's father. In short, the novel centers thematically upon human fidelity across its various social strata.

The unspoken taboos, the spoken ones, the consequences of family "shame" when its so-called "honor" is at threat, press on a child in ways they do not press on that same person decades later as an adult, as he tries to paint, to live, but cannot. Rather than free himself from the guilt of his own role in his mother's dire fate, he learns what his true role was, and in doing so, eventually comes to finally forgive himself for what he *actually* did to make matters worse, rather than for what he simply *thought* he did. Notably, he does not come to these insights alone, how he has lived to his early fifties. He is only able to move forward with support.

Having partly faced the past, Cyrus faces more relationship infidelity when his love, Salomeh, angry and hurt that he has been focusing *entirely* on his art now that he has been freed of his creative block, sleeps with his friend Cohen Benjamin.

In *The Ancestral Sea*, as in *Touched by Fortune's Shadow*, the male protagonists have enough martial prowess to *seriously* injure someone else. Both novels have controlled close-quarters combat scenes, by design. Aggression is portrayed as something that the protagonist deals with in a controlled and neutralizing way without causing loss of face in others and without stoking an even bigger fire. Rushes of adrenalin in both are seen as needing self-control to attenuate. Diplomacy arises from equity, not from aggression. Violent dispute settlement is seen as immature. This is an intertextual juxtaposition to Robert Cohn's aggression toward those he considers to be in competition for Brett Ashley's attention and affection in Hemingway's *The Sun Also Rises*.

The *Ancestral Sea* explicitly and methodically sets out to deconstruct Hemingway's toxic masculinity. At the party that Cyrus Drake is struck so hard that he ultimately loses a tooth, his host, Copernicus Roth, brags that back in Spain in 1938, he and Hemingway once set to fists, leaving Roth with his own trophy tooth hanging around his neck.[64] Cyrus has had enough violence in his life, and so we see this later passage, which soundly puts aside any notion that violence is admirable:

> A month passed and Drake's Maryland bridge, fully paid for by Copernicus Roth, still felt a bit foreign in his mouth. Unlike his benefactor, Drake did not opt to hang the spent upper right premolar around his neck; he'd worn dog tags for four long years back in his twenties, and that was enough for him to have had his day with such overt martial displays.[65]

In Cyrus Drake's case, it is shown early in the novel during the fight at the Roth home that he knew how to fight and *could have* chosen to *hurt* Cohen later. Instead of fighting, however, Cyrus chose to be Cohen's friend by trying to work through Cohen's betrayal with him directly. Cyrus is not even *angry* at his friend, and the story is not cast in a way that might diminish how the reader understands his love for Salomeh.

---

[64] This would have made the *fictionalized* Hemingway about forty-years-old at the time. By the time of his own fight, Cyrus Drake was in his early fifties.

[65] *The Ancestral Sea*, Knight Terra Press, February 2024, p. 107.

Touched by Fortune's Shadow: a triptych

It is not indifference toward her; he is not angry because he has accepted that the human heart of others is not for him to know or control. He does not own Salomeh in *any* way. She is free to be who she is. Jealous anger has no place in what has happened, and so, he simply ignores Cohen when he begs and almost taunts him to hit him in the head to "make it all clear again." For Cyrus, it is a matter to be *discussed* like adults. It is an act to be forgiven, or not forgiven, and if forgiven and turned into a *kintsugi* bowl, put on the shelf to be admired from a distance as we move on to the next day's broken pieces.

Upon hearing this from his friend, Cohen pushed his chin into Drake's finger so that it hurt. "Come on, damn it, hit me hard. […]

"Why?" Drake asked. He seemed amused with the whole situation. "What would that amend? That path ends badly."

Not knowing what else to say, Cohen leaned over the terrace railing again and took two deep breaths in quick succession. […] "Well, I guess, if you hit me, then I'll know you're willing to fight like hell for her, and I won't do anything stupid."

Drake put his arm around his friend again and said, "You've already gone and done something extremely stupid, Benny." He lit another smoke and handed it to Cohen. "And there's nothing I can do about that, now, is there?"

[…]

"No sabers at dawn? […]" He shrugged. "A nice whack in the head would make it all clear again, Drake."

[…]

"I truly wish you hadn't done it, Benny, but I'll surely learn to live with this. It's all part of the ebb and flow of real life."

"What am I, charmed?" Cohen smiled at his friend.

"Must be," Drake replied, blowing circles out into the cold New York wind. "But let me tell you something else in case you think I've tickled your ears when I should, in fact, be boxing them. Something I've noticed about you. I think I can tell you?"

> "Please do," Cohen said. "I'm due a mental wallop at least."
>
> [...]
>
> Drake pressed his finger on Cohen's chest, hard, until it felt he would almost pierce the skin, and said, "Something deep and dark and ugly is in there, Benny. Something that makes you go around, not quite being who you are. Something that takes you out of your head ten feet, twelve feet, a mile—whatever it takes to mess with my woman after I've been a friend to you.
>
> "Getting back to your question," Drake continued after he took another deep drag, "I honestly cannot figure out if you are charmed or cursed. Oh, I reckon I could easily hit you square into tomorrow, and it wouldn't do any damned good. Instead, I decided to have this little talk with you. I'll fix things with Salomeh if they can be fixed; that's on us to figure out. You fix things with yourself, sit in your discomfort, and reflect deeply on what that discomfort is telling you, or I can guarantee that you will most certainly crash."[66]

As for the present novel, I think Brett Lloyd-Ronan has danced his delicate verbal way around his view of relationships and what any of this means in this poststructuralist novel. To add any more to this would be putting words in his mouth, and once the epilog was done, I signed off that clock.

Given that the first novel I ever submitted for consideration for publication, *The Succubus Sea*, which later became *The Ancestral Sea*, had the protagonist's mother endure the same fate due to her confession of adultery to her parents as seen in its later embodiment, and since it was 1990 when I sent that version of the novel to Goose Lane Editions, one can see that I began narratives within these themes from age nineteen onward. Oddly, it took me years to notice the leitmotifs, but once I did, the likely source came clearly to mind.

Early into my dating life, a girlfriend stepped outside of our relationship, more than once, and I found myself confronted with the realization that I did not care that she had done this.

---

[66] *The Ancestral Sea*, Knight Terra Press, February 2024, pp. 182-185.

Touched by Fortune's Shadow: a triptych

I certainly cared about my girlfriend, and enjoyed our time together, and my discovering what happened did not impact her and my relationship. Our relationship ended due to other complex issues that had nothing whatever to do with such matters of fidelity; life is complicated and comes with many different kinds of logistics that must be navigated if one is going to make much of the time one has.

I had not seen this reaction coming. Every societal message from youth on was that I should have been aghast. By this point, I had read *The Scarlet Letter*. In a blue-collar world, I had seen my share of these matters ignite into fistfights in backyards during previously friendly barbecues. I had overheard conversations my mother had with other mothers over coffee in our kitchen where these things sometimes ended up going, and from my secondhand experience, it was almost always very messy and painful and it typically involved a pile of clothing being tossed out a window (either metaphorically or literally). Real human lives fell asunder under the specter of adultery. They also did so on daytime soap operas and evening shows like *Dallas* and *Knotts Landing*. Everything had wanted me to learn that it typically all ends badly.

But when it happened *to* me, after all was said and done, I asked myself why I *should* have cared? Ah, those were different times; anyone of my age who wasn't horrified by the notion of getting HIV/AIDS wasn't watching or reading the news. That's not what I mean about not caring. What imaginary offense had been committed against *me*? None whatever. It seemed I would either have to invent a *new* reason or borrow an *outdated* one if I was going to find an imaginary reason to be upset. What I knew was that I didn't (and shouldn't) have property rights over *anyone*, so why would I feel any claim to time that wasn't mine to monitor or be the crux of some constructed transgression?

Jealous attachment felt *grotesque* to me. If someone *wanted* to be with me, they would find time for me. Knowing when they were with me that they *wanted* to be was enough. Space and time. Gifts to and from others. Coins of our souls' realms. Time together in the present is what matters the most. The opportunity to share more time together can vanish with one's last offered heartbeat.

Memento mori.

Any paragraph that begins with *let's just say that* is suspect when discussing a topic such as this, but let's just say that the span of time from when this revelation was fraught with its own painful difficulties and drama.

I did not date exclusively, and never pretended I did, and such agreed-upon relationship overlap is complex when multiple drivers and perspectives are considered. It's all good and well in theory until you three cross one another's path while on a movie date at Lougheed Mall. Prompt the *canned* laughter, as nobody's *actually* laughing.

Sartre makes it clear that the price of freedom is going to be a big mess for everyone concerned. Rather, what Sartre said about individual freedom is that it comes with an inherent responsibility that can often result in complex, even chaotic, interpersonal dynamics. To be truly free is not merely to act according to one's desires (*carpe diem*), but to correspondingly acknowledge and accept the net consequences of those actions (*finem respice*), understanding that our freedom intersects with the freedom of others. This can lead to conflict, misunderstandings, and the big *mess* as sovereign individuals navigate their own twisting paths while intersecting the equally twisted paths of others.

The existentialist viewpoint emphasizes that freedom is not the liberation from all constraints but the conscious choice to act, with the onus of those actions borne by the individual. In the context of relationships, this philosophy underlines the idea that while we are free to form human connections as we see fit, the overlapping freedoms of individuals can create intricate and often difficult situations, demanding a continual process of negotiation of boundaries, desires, and mutual respect. We can, in *mauvaise foi*, wear the masks and veils of society and hope that we *pass* as authentic, but this comes at the cost of actual *authenticity*. How this impacts the human soul is beyond my ambitions to describe.

Love, passion, the need to belong, and the need to be safe. These do not always—not even often, let alone always!—fall upon us, and yet sometimes we chase them, and in doing so, we might care too little about just how little we care. And in that vacuum between the real and the ideal, between the intention and the instantiation, is the liminal space whence literary fiction has its spontaneous emergence from chaos. And being authors, these rivers of pleasure and pain both pour into our cup, and we drink it up, before our incense, chanting our rendition of whatever gets us through the beckoning day.

Some of us, through the personalized creative process, turn these intricate architectures we built of our entangled lives, into our version of piano pieces: Fictionalized autobiographies Essays.. Autobiographical metafictions. Meta-autobiographical fiction.

Touched by Fortune's Shadow: a triptych

Plays. Short stories. Flashes. Novellas. Novels. Monographs. Or, absent the written word, perhaps just bullshit we sometimes tell ourselves for comfort, relief, or even human spite.

Stories, all.

We wait a while, think some more, consider again, and write another one. We find the passion in the phrasing when our work resonates with something we wanted to say the very first time we read a work that inspired us to want to do to a reader's mind what this particular author did to our *own* way of thinking.

Books can go on forever, but trilogies end at three. Having been *kintsugi* bowl restored, *Midnight at the Arcanum* and *The Ancestral Sea*, and having both taken decades to complete, find in the third installment, *Touched by Fortune's Shadow*, their sudden capstone. However it came about, this is the Epiphanies trilogy, and these are its stories, forged from both quiet and eye-catching mistakes and triumphs.

These three novels are unified not only thematically, but by being explicitly placed in the same narrative universe, with at least some part of the lives central to all three narratives being also on the same timeline, including the seventies, and nineties, in the intersection at the least. Because they inhabit the same fictional universe, each of the key figures in all three of these works could've been invited to the party at Copernicus Roth's New York mansion in August of 1994.

And had they gone to such a party, they all would have been at the respective primes of their lives. I, the author of these works, could also have attended same. Because, after all, this was *my* multiverse of self.

But as instantiated in the trilogy, *they* do not attend the same party, and instead their lives intersect more subtly through my overarching authorial *littera manet*; sufficiently interwoven to establish their coexistence on the same narrative fabric but decorating different rooms at the caravanserai. I took the old maxim to write about "what I know" to its furthest conclusion but wrote about what I knew in different ways than one might have expected me to, given the hegemonies to which I must answer to practically, through different kaleidoscopic lenses, as far as this form permits.

For instance, when Brett buys a gift watch for Manijeh on his way to pick her up at Vancouver International Airport, he buys it from a (completely fictional) downtown Vancouver jewelry store, *La Preziosità*.

This store is placed near where I, the author, and Conrad, a complete fictionalization, in 1987 once bought a knockoff Gucci from a street vendor. This is where Conrad Kirk and his love interest Vanessa worked back in 1987, in *Midnight at the Arcanum*, the window with which he is tasked with cleaning in the winter cold and wet, pushing him into pneumonia.

Because of this cruelty, this event does not occur at a store with an actual correlation in reality. Named public places in this fanciful trilogy universe answer to the author's reality and so controversy happens on *fictional* sites. (It's the only way Margaret Kaur and Gerald Cheung would approve.) My personal bout of debilitating pneumonia came from another window washing cycle in Hell in another part of the city, but around the same time.

Meta-autobiography does this intentionally.

It is notable that Brett purchases a watch there specifically, since when Conrad collapses with pneumonia in *Midnight*, he is given a watch by his employer at *La Preziosità*, by way of implied apology for being assigned the task of cleaning the window, a gift that he in turn gives away to the patient in the bed next to his.

When I was struck with pneumonia that same season, I had no real Gucci to give my hospital roommate, and instead wrote him a note on nurse-supplied paper wishing him well. Who knows, Conrad may have been in the adjacent room?

In a later chapter, as Manijeh begins to settle in to living with Brett, she purchases a Reuben Hurst painting, and Brett purchases a Cyrus Drake painting to pair with it. Cyrus Drake is the central character of *The Ancestral Sea*, and Reuben Hurst is his long-time friend, both having served in Vietnam in the mid-sixties, and both having decided to become painters at the same period of their friendship, with different results.

By 1996, Hurst's career in New York was picking up, thanks in part to a dual-agency agreement with Cyrus' agent in San Francisco and Hurst's in Manhattan. So for a West Coast trader to have bought a Hurst painting in 1998 when Manijeh did, implies that Hurst's ascent in the art world continues in good health beyond the timeline covered by *The Ancestral Sea*. Hurst's painting is also notable because it replaces Brett's *own* silkscreen; both Conrad Kirk and I began our art careers as silk screeners' assistants.

That Brett also dabbled in screening is not surprising. Even though I've styled *some* narrativized aspects of these characters *after* me, principles, they are *not* me, or even who I was. Or anyone else, for that matter.

Touched by Fortune's Shadow: a triptych

As instruments of application of poststructuralist narrative author-reader co-creation, they are all calculatedly *simulacra*.[67]

The authorial me who is writing at *this* very instant, is who I *actually* am. In meta-autobiographical contexts we must not lose sight of this important *caveat*, lest we blur lines as readers. The rest, as written, whether read on screen or in print, are negotiated encodings in *littera manet* intended to be interpreted and completed by the *lector oraculum*.

Tiny scripts that are briefly instantiated upon reading. They are who they *become* to the reader. Because one cannot step into the same river twice, it is improbable that any reader, having read this, can go on to read the entirety of this novel (or, indeed, any in the Epiphanies trilogy) in the same way they might have otherwise. Every reader reads a multitude of Bretts.

Narrative as high-order dimension reduction.

The multiverse of self is a network of could-have-been and if-only-I-had alike. An exercise in liberated self-expression if we elect to free the fictional protagonist from some millstone we perceived ourselves as having had to unfairly carry under the crushing weight of whatever hegemony Bob Dylan's iconic song says we've got to serve. Is this to provide some wish fulfillment—perhaps it does temporarily feel nice to disarm some sock-puppet bully who pushed us or our friends around as a child—or perhaps to provide instead (or as well) a model for how people might *consider* alternative paths up life's many mountain ascents?

Other progress in this universe of novels has been made as well. The novels' timelines are synchronized, even when they don't overlap. We find Brett reading Cohen Benjamin's latest novella, *No Hero over New York*, in keeping with Cohen's promise to Cyrus while in New York to not write himself as a hero in his next work.

This novel-in-a-novel can only exist if a promise in yet *another* novel was kept. Specifically, in July of 1996, Midtown Manhattan, on the balcony overlooking Central Park, the novel seen being read in 1998 by Brett has not been written yet, but we see this promise made between friends.

---

[67] In the literary context, simulacra, introduced by Jean Baudrillard in *Simulacra and Simulations*, can be understood as characters, settings, or narratives that no longer reflect a genuine reality but are constructs with no original reference point. These literary simulacra challenge the distinction between the real and the artificial, often creating a hyperreal experience where the simulated version of events becomes more influential or meaningful than any factual counterpart.

[…] "Now listen, Cohen, I *know* you write what you live. I get that. Dress it all up and turn it into archetypes. And I know how much you *hate* to be told what to do," he set up for his closing remarks to his friend. "But—on your honor—if you *ever* turn tonight into a template and write it up, please do *not* go writing your part as a *hero*. I expect *better* from you."
"Villain it is, then…."
"No. *Neither one*. Haven't you been listening? […] No binaries here, my friend. No coin flips. And certainly *no* hero's cape and cowl for you, Cohen."
Cohen started dialing for a taxi but paused before entering the last number. He brushed himself off and stood up straight […] He put his hand out after spitting into it and then added, as they clasped palms on his oath, "I swear on the friendship you've continued to extend to me after my egregious sin against you: *no* hero."[68]

Since this occurs at the *end* of *The Ancestral Sea* in 1996, having Brett read that novel in 1998 connects the timelines in continuous flow in this accidental universe. The jewelry store, the paintings, the novella by Cohen Benjamin, in each of these cases anchors from one novel have found their way into *Touched by Fortune's Shadow*. These are concrete things. Cohen Benjamin's novella has pages.

The paintings smell of oil paint, put there by Hurst and Drake's hands. The watch can be worn on the wrist. Fictional promises can be honored inter-novel. These little things connect entire narrative realities, in a context where intentional intersection implies by induction universal unity.

Other symbols, such as the phrase "The Syncopated Cup," echo between the ponds of the decades between the novels. These represent shared thematic elements that don't necessarily tie to a single physical item. If one considers a saxophone to be a grail, the syncopated cup for me is the saxophone, and in *The Ancestral Sea*, it is also the name of the rathskeller where my friend and mentor Fred Candelaria recites the poem that altered my artistic vision as a young novelist. Amongst Cyrus' three Friday bar friends is Jules Hatchet, a professional saxophonist.

---

[68] *The Ancestral Sea*, Knight Terra Press, February 2024, pp. 187-188.

Touched by Fortune's Shadow: a triptych

The *truth* is that I first heard Fred read his poetry live at his book publisher's event in Vancouver in the early nineties when I was a freelance editor and literary agent, out to record authors and poets read their works of poetry and fiction live for use on *Airwords: Literary Radio Magazine*, my weekly program on SFU's CJIV 93.9 Cable FM. Friend had named the show when I asked him for help. Sixteen episodes of complete fun. It was during that publisher's reading event that the pianist played Peterson's take of "C Jam Blues" upon my request.

It's possible, based on how Conrad Kirk plays saxophone for Phoebe on a New Westminster bench on or around Valentine's Day, 2007, in the very first chapter of *Midnight at the Arcanum*, that he has already performed live down in San Francisco at the very same Syncopated Cup that Fred read his poetry from *Chinese Chamber Music*, reawakening the painter Cyrus Drake to the suppressed images from childhood. The very phrase "The Syncopated Cup" itself occurs in each of the two novels' opening chapters. Fred agreed to be transported to San Francisco for a reading, why not put Conrad Kirk there as well?

As portrayed in *Janus Incubus*, Cohen Benjamin, originally created in short stories in the early 2000s, actually was the post-Anne-Jolie Conrad Kirk (with a name and passport change). Cohen *is* Conrad in that version of the novel, and it is *this* Cohen who originally betrays Cyrus by sleeping with Salomeh.

When *Midnight at the Arcanum* was later reworked, this identity-shift aspect of the original novel was reimagined, later in *The Ancestral Sea*, introducing Cohen to Cyrus in the same way (they met when they were both editors in San Francisco), but on a different timeline that did not involve his actually *being* Conrad Kirk taking on his deceased friend's identity, Cohen Benjamin. (This also explains the title *Janus Incubus*.) From this perspective, we become aware of even more activity in the narrative cusps between these three works.

There are other intertextual conceits in *The Succubus Sea* and what it later became. Chapter 14 of *The Ancestral Sea* has Cyrus Drake discussing Cohen Benjamin's most recent novella, *Passing Through*, which is a *very* thinly veiled fictionalization of my own novella, *Abadoun*.

The novella *Passing Through* becomes important later in the narrative, since Cyrus has had Cohen inscribe the copy of the book with a plea for Salomeh to move in with Cyrus. This in turn interests Salomeh in the book, which she reads.

The novella gives her questions about the protagonist's being nameless and ambiguous in terms of whether or not he is a hero or a villain, driving Salomeh's intellectual engagement with Cohen in the crucial post-Iran epilog chapters.

The final chapters are new to *The Ancestral Sea* and extend the original novel at both the level of character progression and overall narrative theme. During a conversation near the end of the novel, Cohen tells Salomeh of one of his failed attempts to write a novel early in his career, which he relates to her as follows:

> "Has [Cyrus] *always* been so... aloof? So *distant*?"
> [...]
> "More or less," he ... replied. "He's someone I always had difficulty getting a handle on. That's why I didn't ever really *attempt* to base any character on him in any of my work. He's too complex, but in a minimalist way, if that makes any sense at all. Starts like a grocery list, ends like a poem."
> Salomeh's gaze did not leave his. "I have done my utmost to bring him out of that," she said. "For a while, after we returned from our trip to Iran, he seemed almost out of his secret place. But then...."
> "Actually, before you go on, which I certainly want to hear, I'll correct what I said. I *did* try to write him, back in my editor days, when I was working on my aspirational first novel. I had a novella with his fictional counterpart, Morgan. Tried to get it published as *Returning*—to no avail. Revised it. Fought tooth and *nail* to get to the essence of what it needed to be to... and all these years later that thing has been in a closed box in a closet, forgotten because I still don't know how to get a bead on him." After a sip of water, Cohen said, "Enough from *me*. You go on."[69]

This is a metafictional nod to the length of time it took to *finally* be able to write *Morgan* Drake (*Succubus*' original protagonist) as *Cyrus* Drake as he finally ends up appearing in *The Ancestral Sea*.

---

[69] *The Ancestral Sea*, Knight Terra Press, February 2024, p. 178.

Touched by Fortune's Shadow: a triptych

Three meta-autobiographical artistic interpretations, three interconnected but distinct novels, finally tied off with a Celtic knot. All this multiverse of self: each novel an instantiation of three possible exploratory outcomes of a young Canadian man whose high school graduation photo note reads that his favorite classes were Painting, English Literature, and French, and that he hoped to become one day a "literate painter in France." This trilogy somehow by happenstance also stands as a *single* work that I certainly had no notion I would ever compose, nor would I have actively pursued had I known it was ahead, for had I planned to write such a thing, I would still be only halfway done composing the first installment..

Before concluding, I wish to note that it strikes me, over the decades-spanning history of this trilogy, that all three novels are love stories with happy endings. The relationships are messy or driven by absurd forces in the Sartrean sense, but they are portrayed as mutually meaningful bonds that merit effort to maintain. Sartre expressed that individuals must create their own meaning and identity through actions and choices, despite the inherent absurdity of intrinsic meaninglessness, and in all the three novels of this trilogy, authentic, open, and constructive communication points to a reason to have hope in love in its many manifestations.

While it is true that soulmates *are* deconstructed across this trilogy, they are also then ultimately reintroduced as articulated *humans*. To have encoded that core optimism across an artistic career feels existentially satisfying. This final novel officially made it a trend, since a trend requires three or it stands the off chance of being just a coincidence.

Yesterday catches in a flame and vanishes in a mist, as we reach down, take our cup of coffee, carefully place it at our lip and…
… open our eyes to now: *Tabula rasa*.

—Burnaby, 15 April 2024

Quinn Tyler Jackson

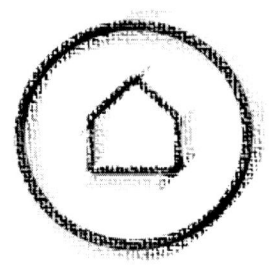

The Epiphanies

We are.
Audere, scire, tacere.
    To dare, to know, to be silent.
Carpe diem sed respice finem.
    Seize the day but consider the end.
Pendâr-e nik, goftâr-e nik, kerdâr-e nik.
    Good thoughts; good words; good deeds.
The past is gone. The future is not yet. There is only now.
Every morning is a new creation.
Be brave. Be kind.

تمام شد [70]

---

[70] *Tamâm shod* (lit. "It is finished").

Manufactured by Amazon.ca
Acheson, AB